TH ⌐⌐ DRAGONS

The life story of a 17th century Sussex farmer and his family

Clemens Lucke

Cover designed by Sarah Jane Bennison from a painting by Robert Nicholls

First published in the United Kingdom in 2014

by Completely Novel.com

Copyright © Joan Angus 2014

ISBN: 9781849145756

To Tony Lucke

"*And this shall be for a bond between us: that we are of one blood you and I; that we have cried peace to all and claimed fellowship with every living thing; that we hate war and sloth and greed, and love fellowship....and that we shall go singing to the fashioning of a new world.*"

William Morris

Descendants of John Lucke of Durgates

will proved 29 April 1560   m. Agnes

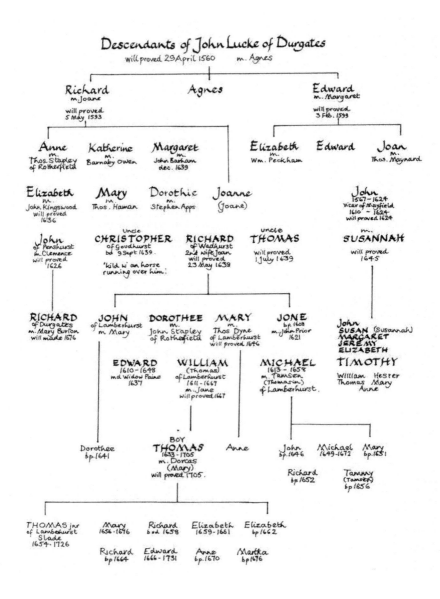

Richard
m. Joane
will proved
5 May 1593

Agnes

Edward
m. Margaret
will proved
3 Feb. 1599

Anne
m.
Thos. Stapley
of Rotherfield

Katherine
m.
Barnaby Owen

Margaret
m.
John Barham
dec. 1639

Elizabeth
m.
Wm. Peckham

Edward

Joan
m.
Thos. Maynard

Elizabeth
m.
John Kingswood
will proved
1636

Mary
m.
Thos. Haman

Dorothie
m.
Stephen Apps

Joanne
(Joane)

John
1567 - 1624
Vicar of Mayfield
1610 - 1624
will proved 1624

John
of Penshurst
m. Clemence
will proved
1626

Uncle
CHRISTOPHER
of Goudhurst
bd 9 Sept 1639.
'kild w' an horse
running over him'

RICHARD
of Wadhurst
2nd wife Joan
will proved
23 May 1638

Uncle
THOMAS
will proved
1 July 1639

m.
SUSANNAH
will proved
1645

RICHARD
of Durgates
m. Mary Burton
will made 1676

JOHN
of Lamberhurst
m Mary

DOROTHEE
m.
John Stapley
of Rotherfield

MARY
m.
Thos Dyne
of Lamberhurst
will proved 1646

JONE
bp 1608
m. John Prior
1621

John
SUSAN (Susannah)
MARGARET
JEREMY
ELIZABETH

EDWARD
1610 - 1648
md Widow Paine
1637

WILLIAM
(Thomas)
of Lamberhurst
1611 - 1667
m. Jane
will proved 1667

MICHAEL
1613 - 1658
m. Tamsen
(Thomasin)
of Lamberhurst.

TIMOTHY
William   Hester
Thomas   Mary
         Anne

Dorothee
bp. 1641

BOY
THOMAS
1633 - 1705
m. Dorcas
(Mary)
will proved 1705.

Anne

John
bp. 1646
Richard
bp 1652

Michael
1649 - 1672

Mary
bp. 1651
Tammy
(Tomsen)
bp 1656

THOMAS jnr
of Lamberhurst
Slade
1654 - 1726

Mary
1656 - 1676
Richard
bp 1664

Richard
b od 1658
Edward
1666 - 1731

Elizabeth
1659 - 1661
Anne
bp. 1670

Elizabeth
bp 1662
Martha
bp 1676

Historical notes and Glossary on pages 435 and 437

4

Part 1

The Family

Chapter 1 1619
Sixteenth year in the reign of King James 1

William kicked a stone onto the grassy verge of the road, punched the air and shouted, "I be minded to be a farmer when I'm a man!"

His brother Edward, ahead of him, was slashing the grasses with a stick. "I be going to hunt and kill dragons."

William laughed, and ran to catch up. "There be no dragons," he sneered.

"Yus there be!" shouted Ed. His eyes were bright as he looked at William. "I've seen 'em."

They walked on together shuffling their boots in the dust. "Whereabouts did ye see dragons?" asked William, still doubtful.

"Flying in the night. They had long snouts and tails and breathed fire."

William stopped for a moment to consider what his brother had said.

Ed swivelled round to face William and walked backwards. "Muvver told me a story of a brave knight in shining armour, called Saint George. A dragon took his princess, and Saint George killed the dragon and saved the princess." He turned and ran on ahead.

William lagged behind. Their mother was no longer around to confirm the story. It was a mistake to question his elder brother, who was always right. Edward was in charge today. It was the first time they had travelled on this road unaccompanied by adults. They had just delivered their father's letter to Uncle Thomas in Lamberhurst, and were walking home to Wadhurst.

There was little on the road except the occasional gentleman riding past them on a horse.

William caught up, and they continued on their way, leaping over the ruts and jumping in the puddles, splashing each other.

"Uncle Christopher tells us stories, and lets us ride in front on his horse, when he comes to visit," he said.

"Saint George had a horse," remarked Edward, still in the world of dragons.

"I'll have horses when I'm a farmer." William galloped ahead, thwacking the flank of his imaginary steed.

An unfamiliar sound in the valley caught his attention. He stopped, and listened, but couldn't make out what it was. After a moment, he could not resist the temptation and he ran, whooping and hollering, across the meadow towards the source of the noise. Ed followed. A strange scene met Will's eyes, and he lay down on the grass to keep out of sight. Ed flopped down beside him. On the bottom, between the embankment and the river, were hundreds of men running around and shouting to each other. In the centre there stood a tall round brick funnel, shooting flames and sparks into the air. Orange liquid gushed out near the base of the funnel and was being collected in receptacles by burly ironworkers, who poured it into trenches in the ground. A stream from a pond cascaded down the gully, driving a water wheel, which was connected to giant bellows, fanning the fire. Every time the bellows blew, the flames leapt higher with a roar.

Ed gasped. Some distance away William saw the origin of the noise they had heard: clang, clang, clang. A blacksmith was holding a red hot metal rod with tongs on an anvil, as a great hammer beat it into shape. This hammer was driven by a water wheel. There were men unloading charcoal for the fires and loading ox carts with lumps of iron. All had bare arms and their skin was shiny and red from the heat. William could feel it from where he crouched. He was breathing acrid fumes, which stuck in the back of his throat.

"There be dragons," he whispered. He knew they shouldn't be there. He'd heard of these places and the cruel foremen who were in charge. He looked at Ed, who was absorbed in the scene before them, his eyes sparkling.

He nudged William. "Look! Look at the chimney breathing fire!"

"We'd best be bodging," said Will to his brother.

Ed wasn't listening. "Let's go down there and see what they're making."

One of the carts, loaded with iron and pulled by six black oxen, started towards the track which led up to the road.

Will was afraid. "Come away," he said, grabbing Edward by the arm.

They scrambled to their feet, and ran back to the safety of the road. Edward lingered on the verge, waiting for the approaching cart. William tugged at his brother's sleeve. They watched the great lumbering beasts snort and slaver as they pulled the laden cart up the slope. They thundered onto the road. The cart jolted and creaked over the ruts. The driver shouted and lashed the oxen with his long whip. He didn't notice the two small boys standing nearby. In a cloud of dust the cart and its load trundled away. The boys looked at each other, mouths ajar. Ed laughed and broke Will's tension. After brushing the mud and grass off their frocks and breeches, they scampered home along the footpaths and byways, jumping over streams and running through meadows playing tag.

The boys arrived home hot and dusty from their journey. A smell of fresh bread wafted towards them at the door. The house was all hustle and bustle. Their two older sisters had been baking and cooking, and there were pots and pans and freshly baked bread all over the parlour. Some hens had found their way indoors and were picking up the crumbs.

Dorothee shooed them out in a flurry of feathers and cackling. "Edward, go feed those hens for us, and shut the door after thee. Will, Farder wants to speak with thee."

William ran out with his brother, went and swilled his face from the well bucket in the close, and had a quick gulp of the cool water. He was wondering what his father wanted to speak to him about. He and Ed had taken a long time coming home, and their father would want to know what they'd been doing. Since their mother died, father had become stricter and would not tolerate disobedience. Ed had been in charge today, but it was William who had been summoned. He went indoors to find his father.

It was dark and cool in the hall. After the bright sunshine outside, William could only just make out the bulk of his father on the settle by the empty hearth.

"Did ye wish to speak to us, Farder?" he asked.

Richard Lucke looked up and beckoned to his son. "Come here, William," he said. "Did ye deliver the letter to thy Uncle? What took thee so long?"

William walked across the hall. "We gave the letter to Uncle Thomas, Sir. Uncle Christopher were there, and they gave us coger. Uncle Thomas told us about the trees he's going to plant to make a copse." Will could see his father clearly now. He looked serious, with his piercing blue eyes and stern countenance. The sun threw a shaft of light through the window onto the stone flagged floor between them. William saw sadness in his father's eyes. He didn't look angry. At last he spoke.

"Come and sit by me, Son."

William went and sat on the settle next to his father.

"Thy Uncle and I have been discussing thy education, William. 'Tis time ye were larned to read and write, and to rackon with figures. Thomas is willing to larn thee these things. Ye will go and work for him as a farm boy, and he will teach thee some husbandry. You'll be going to bide with him come May Day."

William sat by his father, taking in the enormity of what his father had said. He'd be leaving his brothers and sisters and going to live with strangers. His heart missed a beat.

He looked up and said, "Will Edward be coming?"

"Nay. He don't show so much promise as thee. He'll start lessons with Mr Hatley 'forelong, as would you if ye were not going to my brudder."

William's mind was in a whirl. His ambition was to be fulfilled! He said, "Thank ye, Sir. I'll be glad to go and work for Uncle Thomas."

Richard's face relaxed, and he smiled. "I be pleased that's agreeable to thee, Son. Thy Uncle Thomas is a kind man and will larn thee well. Mind all that he says, and ye'll grow into a fine man."

The boy sat feeling safe and comfortable next to his father, and a little afraid of the wide world waiting for him out there. He remembered the scene at the ironworks that afternoon. He was full of questions.

There was a risk that his father would realise where he and Edward had been on their way home, and of a larruping that may follow. His curiosity got the better of him.

"Farder, there's summat I wanted to ask thee," he said.

"What's that, Son?"

"The ironworks in the valley, what be they making?"

His father's sharp eyes peered at him under hooded brows. William quailed.

"So that's what delayed thee on the way home," he said. "Edward were in charge, I'll speak to 'im later." He drew a deep breath and paused before he said, "They be melting down a strong metal called iron that's found in the earth. They make all manner of tools for the farmers, making their work easier; metal coulters for the ploughs, fagging hooks and scythes. When ye work with thy Uncle Thomas you'll be using some of these tools. They also make horseshoes and the backs of fireplaces."

William recalled, "There was a cart full of lumps of metal, being pulled by six great oxen along the road."

"They would be going to the iron foundry to be made into big guns called canon, and other weapons for the military," said his father.

"Uncle Thomas said that all the trees are being cut down for charcoal for the ironworks."

"That's right. The trees also needed to make ships to go to war, and grand houses for the ironmasters. On account of that we need to plant more trees, to replace those that have been cut down."

William nodded. He would be proud to take part in this process; to help the nation to defend itself and to provide food for the people. After a few moments he looked up at his father and smiled, slid off the settle, bowed and walked through the hall into the close. Here, the chestnut mare was tethered. William put his hand up to her nose, and she lowered it to touch his cheek with her soft muzzle. They stayed there a while, then he gave her a pat, and walked towards the house and his brothers and sisters.

Ed came round the corner into the close, waving a wooden sword.

"You be the dragon and I'll fight thee," he commanded.

William thought for a moment. He wasn't sure he was ready for this sort of challenge.

"This dragon needs to find a cave to lay-up. Give us time afore ye starts a-hunting." He ran off across the yard and into the orchard. Here he found his sister Jone, her fair straight hair hiding her face as she bent to gather spring flowers. He took hold of her hand and pulled her towards a stack of wood.

"Come Jone, you can be the damsel. I be the dragon. Ed shall come and rescue thee. Be quick."

Jone, who was slow, protested at being dragged away from her peaceful occupation. They hid behind the wood pile.

Saint George found them easily, led by the damsel's screams, and challenged the dragon to a fight. His sword gave him an advantage, and he overcame the dragon, throwing him to the ground and pinning him down with one foot on his chest, his sword raised in triumph. The damsel ran off to find her older sisters for protection.

Edward dropped down onto the grass beside his brother. "What did Farder want?"

William turned over onto his front. He plucked a tuft of grass, and tore it up into tiny pieces.

"He says I must go and bide with Uncle Thomas. He be going to larn us to be a farmer, and to read and write."

"I don't want to go and bide there," replied Ed, his eyes on the ground.

"Nay, Farder says you'll stay here with the fambly at Marlinge and go to Mr Hatley for lessons."

Edward became silent. William knew the impact the news would be having. They'd always been together. People thought they were twins they were so alike. Since the loss of their mother two years ago, Edward had looked after his younger brother and helped him to be strong. William had learnt to understand Ed's moods of anger and frustration, and how to deal with them.

"Will ye come and visit us at the Slade in Lamb'rst now and again, Ed?"

Ed sighed heavily. "Yus, I'll come," he said, rolling over onto his back to lie flat.

Jone came out of the house. "Dinner's ready."

The boys jumped up to go indoors. The gap between them widened as they walked across the grass.

William didn't feel like joining in with the conversation at dinner. He understood that things were not right with Ed, and was unable to make it better. He had only a few more days before going with Uncle Thomas to the Slade. Soon they had finished the meal. Jone took little Michael to settle him into bed. Then, after helping with clearing away, the others retired to their chambers.

The three young boys were in one room. William shared a cot with Edward. He undressed and slipped quietly under the woollen blanket, lying on his side, facing his brother, ready to talk if need be. Ed was facing the other way. It took William a long time to get to sleep.

He thought of the ironworks, and how Edward was attracted by the fire and heat; the power behind the great bellows and the blacksmith's hammer. The gap between them had cracked open before William had broken the news of his future as a farmer. He thought of his other brothers and sisters and the safe surroundings of home. Excitement welled up as he imagined what his new life would be like. Ed stirred. The familiar noises of other members of the family as they came to bed were comforting to William as he drifted off to sleep.

Chapter 2

It was Mayday, and the last day William had in Wadhurst with the family before he went to Lamberhurst with his uncle. There was to be a fair in town. The girls had already been out in the early morning a-flowering; picking the May blossom from the hedges and decorating the house. They made garlands, each with two twiggy hoops bound together to make a ball, covered with flowers. William loved this day best of all the days in the year. Everyone would be there, to celebrate the coming of spring when the planting season began after the long winter. There would be music and dancing, trinkets and coloured ribbons to buy, and friends to meet.

Dressed in his best frock and breeches, William sat in the hall and watched the three girls getting ready for the fair, with new straw bonnets trimmed with blue and yellow ribbons. Dorothee, her dark curly hair bouncing round her face, broke into a little song, to quell her excitement. Jone was having difficulty with her ribbons, and needed some help tying them up. Mary came to the rescue. Father was waiting to accompany them into town. John, the eldest, asked if the boys could go on ahead. William and Edward, unusually subdued today, walked out with their elder brother. Michael, the nipper of the family, ran on ahead of them.

There were crowds of people all going in the same direction, some of whom they knew. They waved and shouted to each other.

"Good day to you."

"Fine day for the fair."

"How are you today?"

"Bravely thank 'e."

The town bustled. Street vendors of cakes and delicacies were calling. Flower-mongers in their white linen bonnets curtsied as gentlemen bought bouquets for the ladies. Children ran round playing tag, weaving in and out of the groups of people who stood gossiping. There were foreigners speaking strange languages: skilled ironworkers who had come from France and Holland, as well as Huguenot refugees. The boys passed the alehouses where these men had gathered. Some were arguing and brawling. Michael stopped to watch.

"Michael, keep away. We're going down here," called John. The boys slipped down a narrow street where Thomas Upton had his shop. People called him the Archimedes of Wadhurst, as he was something of an inventor. The boys had each been given a groat to spend today, and they were eager to see if they could buy something from Mr Upton. A bell tinkled as they opened the door and crept in reverently. There he was, sitting on a stool behind his counter, a small, stooping man, with twinkling eyes, a bald shiny head, and spectacles perched on the end of his nose. He was tinkering with the workings of a watch. As the boys came in, he looked up and put his tools down. He clasped his hands and smiled.

"What can I do for the young gentlemen today?"

"Good day, Mus Upton. We've come to see thy wares," said John.

William stared wide-eyed around him. The shop was full of curious instruments, clocks, pieces of stoves and tools, as well as wooden boxes and small toys, bowls and spoons, and leather gloves. All at once they were surrounded by the chiming of many clocks, some tinkling, others booming. John picked up a bottle with a ship in full sail inside, but it would cost more than a groat to buy, and he put it down again. William found a tiny wooden model of a horse pulling a cart loaded with little sticks, representing a cord of wood. He asked how much it would be.

Master Upton considered a moment before saying, "I believe that small object'll cost exactly a groat." He went to search in his back room for a box to hold William's treasure. Edward found a miniature anvil with its little hammer, and Michael chose a brightly coloured top with a whip. They spent some time drinking in the wonders before them. There were measuring tools, watches, scales, working models of windmills, tiny furniture and metal bells of all sizes that played tunes.

John finally chose a brass hair comb for himself. "I'll have this comb if you please, Mus Upton."

"D'ye wish it wrapped, young Sir?" asked the shopkeeper.

"Nay, thank thee kindly." John slipped the comb into the pocket of his jacket, and handed over his groat. They took their leave of Thomas Upton, thanking him for his help.

When the boys reached the field where the fair was being held, the dancing was already under way. On a flowery throne was the young girl who had been chosen as Queen of the May. She was dressed in a white shift with a crown of May blossom. John lingered for a while, gazing at her. William saw his friend Nick Longley and his parents and little sister Jane walking towards him. They stopped to greet him. Jane hid behind her mother's skirts.

"Come and see the archery, Nick," said William. They went over to the far corner, where they found John, Michael and Edward, watching the competition. William admired the skill each man used to shoot his arrow, and the speed with which he drew another from the sheath over his shoulder. He imagined them in battle; rows and rows of archers shooting their arrows, the whooshing noise they made as they flew through the air and the screams of the injured as they fell.

"I be going to bide with Uncle Thomas in Lamb'rst today, Nick," said Will.

Nick wrinkled his brow. "Why?"

"I be going to larn to be a farmer," Will said proudly.

Nick said, "My Uncle John bides in Lamb'rst. We go en see 'im now and again. Mebbe I shall see thee there."

"I surely hope so," said Will.

A man in black clothes and a tall hat came towards them. It was Mr Hatley, the vicar. "Good day to you, Masters Lucke. What a pleasant day for the May Fair." Then to Edward, "So you're the young man who'll be coming to me for lessons next week. I'm very pleased to meet thee." He held out his hand, and Edward shook it.

"Yus Sir," he replied. "Will ye larn us how to write, so's I can send letters to my brudder in Lamb'rst?"

"I most certainly will, and I'll teach thee to read the letters he sends back to you. And you, William, you'll be going to become a farmer one day, I hear."

"Behopes so, Sir," said William. They smiled and thanked him, and he went on his way.

There was a shout behind them. The girls came skipping across the grass, and suggested that they all join in the dancing. Jone took Michael's hand, and John led Dorothee to join the circle of people dancing round a pole decorated with ribbons and flowers. Not keen on dancing, Will, Nick and Ed went off to find the tug-of-war. They ran to join the Wadhurst team who were struggling to pull the Ticehurst team over. With a few more hands to the rope, they succeeded. Ticehurst let go as they reached the line midway, and everyone in the Wadhurst team fell to the ground in a heap, cheering and roaring with laughter. The boys untangled themselves from the mass of arms and legs. William saw his father on the sidelines, with other family members.

He and Nick ran over to them shouting, "We won!"

Two of his aunts were there with their husbands, Margaret and John Barham, and Elizabeth and John Kingswood. Short, round and middle-aged, Margaret doted on her husband, a wealthy ironmaster. Tall and slim, Elizabeth considered herself as the head of the family. She kept firm control of her equally tall, slim husband and two plump teenage daughters, who stood demurely by her side. They were talking about the recent tragic accident in Rotherfield in which the son of their oldest sister, Anne Stapley, had been killed by a wain. William was ignored.

Nick nudged Will and said, "I'll go en find Muvver and Farder, Will. Behopes I'll see thee somewhen." He ran off.

William felt lonely and sad. He tried to listen to the conversation, knowing he had to be brave.

"The wheels was caught in a rut, and the wain canted, throwing John to the ground. It rolled over and crushed him," John Kingswood was saying. "He were killed dracly-minute."

"I've seen sister Stapley since the accident. Both she and her husband Thomas be in terrible order, particularly as John were the eldest son," Margaret added. "His fambly must be finding it lamentable hard. Thomas be managing John's farm along of his own, I believe, though 'e be getting in years. I rackons he be all of sixty-five. It were so sudden. John's mistus has her muvver biding with 'er, to help with the liddle ones."

"'Tis a test from the Lord. They must keep their faith and be strong," pronounced Elizabeth, the lace on her headdress trembling.

"How be our sister Haman getting on in Teec'rst? I ain't seen her since dunnow the time when." Margaret looked at Richard as the most likely source of this information.

"She be with child again," answered Richard. I saw Thomas Haman in town t'other day. He were main chuffed."

"How many be there now?" asked Margaret, "Four, or five?"

"More than enough," pronounced Elizabeth. The tendons round her neck appeared like tight ropes.

Richard turned to John Barham. "I believe you've been and bought Shoesmiths, John."

Margaret fluffed up her feathers and smiled, her eyes on her husband.

He said, "Oh yus, I plan to build a fine mansion there, with a deer park, as befits the Barham fambly."

William knew that John Barham and his brothers all owned ironworks in the surrounding area, and were leading figures in Wadhurst. Passing gentry raised their hats in recognition of these pillars of the community.

Uncle Thomas came and joined them with Michael and Edward.

Elizabeth greeted her favourite brother. "Thomas, how be ye today?"

He came to kiss her hand. "I be bravely thank ye, Sister." Then to Richard, "Young John has an eye for the maids, surely. He be middling handsome. They be like bees round a honeypot!"

Richard laughed. "He's likely a dozzle cranky with the mead. He's usually main shy!"

Elizabeth turned to Richard. "You needs to keep that young man in order, Brudder. 'Tis time you was looking for a good mistus for 'im, and turning his attention to managing his inheritance. Things seem to have got out of hand since Joane died. And you, boys, mind thy duty to thy farder. Young William, you be a fortunate young man. See to it that ye works well for thy Uncle."

The three boys bowed, and said in unison, "Yus, Aunt Kingswood." William added, "I will."

"Best we was bodging, I rackon," said Richard, ignoring his sister's admonishments. William noticed his father's right eye was half closed, a sign that he was getting impatient. "Edward, go and fetch the girls. We'll leave John to make his own way, as he be enjoying himself. Will ye dine with us, Thomas?" Uncle Thomas accepted. They bid the others goodbye and walked back to Marlinge, where there was a meal awaiting them, of cold meat, bread and pickles, and home brewed ale.

With his sister Mary's help, William packed his clothes and a few treasures into a small wooden chest before dinner. He had some new round frocks and breeches, and the last thing he put in was the box containing the little horse and cart.

In the parlour, he sat quietly on the bench by the wall, taking in the scene, knowing that he wouldn't be living here again for a long time. Everyone else was standing or sitting around the table. His father and Uncle Thomas were standing by the fire, which gave out a warm red glow. Their faces were flushed and animated. His uncle, having a slight stoop, was a good deal shorter than Father.

"Elizabeth were on her high horse again today, Brudder," Thomas said, laughing.

"Yus, she can't keep 'erself to 'erself. She do rackon I don't manage the fambly as well as I should, now Joane's gone. Mind thee, it's been hard, I don't deny."

Uncle Thomas said, "I believe you be doing the right thing by William. I rackon he's got it in him to shape up on the farm grandly like. And I shall enjoy his company."

William looked at his Uncle and saw kindness behind his eyes. He felt less nervous about going to live with him. He went to get more food from the table, where Mary was standing. She was a slender, plain girl, not at all like her older sister Dorothee.

"You'll be fine, our Will. Uncle Thomas be a knowledgeable man, and he'll answer all them questions ye keeps on asking! Mind ye comes to see us now and again." She put her arm round his shoulder and gave him a hug.

"Ed be broody about us going away," said William.

"I'll see that he has plenty to do. 'E'll soon scratch along."

William went and sat down again, with a full plate. He watched them all as he ate. There was young Michael, with his curly black hair, tickling Jone's neck with a feather. She was squealing, and trying to grab the feather, but he was quicker than she was and pulled it away. Dorothee was bringing more food out of the dairy to replenish the table, her eyes bright and her face a rosy pink. He believed she enjoyed being a housewife and a hostess. His eyes wandered over to John, who was talking to Ed in a fatherly fashion. Ed looked a bit testy, and William knew he wasn't really listening to his big brother.

After dinner they bid the family farewell. It was getting dark. William climbed up into Thomas' cart with his chest of belongings, feeling apprehensive. They rolled away. William waved until the family and Marlinge disappeared into the gloom, then crouched down and held on tight, as the cart was thrown from side to side along the rutted road. Suddenly he felt excited. He was going to learn to be a farmer!

Part 2

The Copse

Chapter 3

Uncle Thomas, William, Robert Longley and the two farm labourers, Adam and Ned went to the field opposite the house, carrying picks, spades and the trees that Thomas had bought. They started by planting apple, pear and plum trees. The pigs had been left to graze and forage there all winter, manuring as they went, ready for the new orchard. Adam was a big strong man with a kindly face. He went round the field pushing stakes into the ground, marking the places where the trees would go. His red hair shone in the sun. Ned was older, thin and wiry, with a permanently solemn look. The men sliced into the clay soil with their spades as easily as cutting butter. William and Robert fetched the trees one by one: apple and plum, cherry and pear. They held them straight in the holes as the men filled them with earth. This took them a whole day.

The next day they took the tools and the remaining trees up the whapple way where Uncle had set aside a piece of land. This was the site of an old copse. There were a few hazel totts left over, but all the trees had been felled, leaving waste ground. It took another day to plant the oak and beech trees. William admired Robert's strength. He was Nick's cousin. He'd been helping his father on the farm over the road ever since he was a nipper. He raced Will to collect the next sapling when it was needed, making it into a game. Then they played tag in and out of the trees they had planted. William tripped and fell over on the soft leaf-mould, gasping with laughter. He caught the musty, earthy smell as he got to his feet. Uncle Thomas shouted at them to stop fooling around, and to get on with their work.

The next two days were spent planting new hazel whips between the young trees. This was a lighter job. When all the whips had been planted they stood and surveyed the scene.

"That's a good job well done," said Uncle Thomas. "Thank ye for thy help, Robert."

Robert grinned and raised his hand before turning to walk home.

Uncle Thomas said to William, "This copse be yours, young man. As the oak and beech grow up they'll provide a canopy to encourage the hazel rods to grow tall and straight. After about seven year, they'll have grown enough and we'll cut them, to make them grow new rods from the base. We'll use the cut rods for hurdles and other things needed on the farm. I'll larn thee how to care for the copse, and you'll be rewarded for many years."

They walked back to the house together. William felt he was growing closer to his uncle. They both had the same dreams for the farm, and it was good to work together. He thought of his uncle as a beech tree; a canopy over William while he was growing tall and straight, like the hazel rods.

The afternoon sun was beginning to sink towards the horizon, throwing William's long shadow behind him, as he walked to the pasture along the whapple way from the house. He was going to fetch the five cows for milking. This task was his daily duty. William liked this time of day, though he was sometimes very tired after working on the farm.

He opened the gate into the pasture, and the cows came to his call, "Cows, come on."

They followed him down the whapple way, through the close and into the cow stalls next to the house, where he'd left hay for them to munch. Each cow entered a stall. Then William sat on his little stool, rested his head on the flank of the beast, and pulled milk from her warm, soft udder. It squirted powerfully as the thin white stream hit and frothed the milk in the pail. Martha, Uncle Thomas' housekeeper, was there to carry the full pails into the milk-house, some for the churns to make butter, and the rest to be used for drinking and baking. When all the cows were milked, William led them back to the pasture before returning to the house.

He pushed the parlour door open, and a deep voice shouted, "Who goes there?" He recognised the voice of Uncle Christopher. He braced himself for whatever happened next, and replied, "William Lucke Esquire."

In front of him stood a tall bearded figure dressed in a black cloak wearing a large cooking pot on his head, the long handle of which pointed out in front like a snout. He was waving a massive sword in his hand, which landed on William's shoulder, nearly knocking him over.

"I now dub thee, Sir William Lucke," said the figure, and transferred the pot from his own head to William's, who immediately found himself in pitch darkness, staggering under the weight of his headgear.

He heard Uncle Christopher bawling in the distance. "Now catch us if ye can."

William stumbled forward, giggling at the buffoonery, knocking into furniture and groping with his hands held out in front, occasionally feeling soft fabric brushing past him.

He heard a woman scream, "Massy- 'pan-me!" and gales of laughter.

He tripped on a stool, and plunged straight into the softness of Martha's ample bosom. The pot was lifted from his head, and they all rolled around hilariously. Uncle Thomas came into the parlour from the hall, disturbed by the hullabaloo. He declared that he thought witches had invaded the house, at which they all burst into more laughter.

Martha had a good mutton stew ready for them with plenty of fresh bread and butter. After Uncle Thomas had said grace, they talked about the time that he took over the farm. He'd spent years restoring it.

"The barns and cow stalls was in terrible order," said Thomas.

"Were ye here when Thomas took over the farm, Martha?" asked Christopher.

"Yus. I'd been looking after my gaffer until he passed away. He'd been renting the farm ever since I were a babe."

"Was ye born here?" asked William.

"Nay, I were born in Lamb'rst. My sister lives in the house we was all born in."

"My farder let this farm to Martha's gaffer, Jeoffrey Beale, Will," said Thomas. "When father died, he left the property to me. I weren't old enough to manage the farm alone, so I left Mas Beale here until he passed away."

"Your uncle were good enough to keep me on as his housekeeper," said Martha.

"You be part of the fambly now, I rackon, Martha," said Christopher.

"Mus Lucke's been unaccountable kind to us. I would have had to go to the poor house if he hadn't kept me on." She got up to fetch the pot of stew, to offer for second helpings.

William asked, "Who'll take on this farm after thee, Uncle? Will ye get wed and have children?"

"I believe 'tis a liddle late for that, Will. But maybe ye'll be able to be my farm manager one day. You be larning well, but ye've a long way to go yet."

"'Tis hard for one so young," said Martha.

"I rackon Will needs a holiday now and again," agreed Christopher. "We should take him hawking tomorrow, brudder."

"That we shall," agreed Thomas.

After the meal, William settled himself on Christopher's knee in the parlour, and asked him if he'd tell one of his adventure stories. He was never sure whether his uncle had made them up, but they were always different and full of scary creatures and brave knights.

"One dark night, as I were a-riding through the forest..." Christopher began. But William never heard the end of it. He fell asleep in his uncle's arms.

Martha picked him up and carried him off to bed.

The time passed quickly for them, with baby animals being born and needing attention. Chicks, lambs, calves, piglets kept William and his uncle busy every day and some nights. They checked the young trees they had planted, and when William had the chance he'd go to the copse and sit among the saplings. He imagined them growing into tall trees, and marvelled at the delicacy of the bright green leaves unfurling before his eyes.

One day, Dorothee and Edward walked over to the Slade, to see William. He delighted in showing them what he was doing in his new life. They went into the close to see the pigs and horses and the young animals. Then they went through into the orchard and found the hens with their baby chicks. They walked up the whapple way, past the growing corn, and the cows in their pasture, and he showed them the young copse, in full leaf now. He heard news of the family; how Aunt Mary Haman had had another baby girl, and what was happening in the town. But he'd no desire to return at present.

"I be going to bide with Aunt Stapley in Ratherfild, 'forelong, Will," said Dorothee. "I'll be muvvering her, and helping in the house. She be dearly grieving for her son who were killed a year ago. And she's ailing now."

William looked at his eldest sister. "Be there cousins in Ratherfild? I've heard Farder speaking about them."

"Yus, they be Aunt Stapley's gran'children. They be nigh my age."

Edward followed them round, looking at the ground and kicking at the occasional stone. He didn't take any part in the conversation, and he didn't seem interested in the baby animals or the copse. They went back to the house through the close, into the milk-house and buttery and through to the parlour, where Martha was baking, and gave them some titbits. Then they went up the back stairs to William's little chamber.

"How be ye fairing with lessons with Mr Hatley, Ed?" asked William.

"Oh, he says I be doing bravely. Reading and writing be easy." But he couldn't remember what books he was reading, or what he'd learnt.

William was going to bed that evening, thinking about his brother Edward, and wondering why he'd been so quiet that day. Before blowing his candle out, he looked over to his treasures on the table, and saw that his horse and cart was missing. He jumped out of bed and searched around on the floor, thinking he may have brushed it off when he got undressed. It was nowhere to be seen. He decided to leave it until the morning, when it would be lighter.

Next day the horse and cart was still missing. There was no time to look now, and he went out to feed the piglets.

Later on in the day, he was going into the village on an errand for Martha, and he caught sight of a familiar little wheel, lying in the dusty entrance yard. Then he saw the rest of his treasure, lying in pieces, having been crushed by a heavy object. His heart sank. Gathering the pieces together, he realised that it was ruined, and threw it back onto the road. He walked down to the village wondering if Edward had dropped it by accident, or did he stamp on it on purpose? William felt hurt and sad that Edward should do this to him. William's life in Wadhurst was over. His family was becoming remote, though he still wanted to see them now and again. Then he thought of the baby animals and how they would have to be separated from their mothers one day soon, and taken to market to find new homes. He was learning that life is a journey, and that one can never go backwards.

Chapter 4 1622

The months rolled by on the cycle of the seasons. The years passed and it was spring again. William had been writing letters to Edward, as he had promised, to tell him the latest news, that Uncle Christopher was teaching him to ride, and that soon he would be allowed to have his own pony. Ed wrote back sometimes, but William noticed that he wasn't much good at writing.

On one of their trips into Wadhurst to see the family, Uncle Thomas bought William some new round frocks and breeches, and a cap and jacket for Sundays when they went to church. Today the boys went into the town together, to meet some of Ed's friends. They were playing creckett on the green, and invited the brothers to join them. Ed had been teasing William about his new cap. William was irritated, and relieved when they had the chance to do something different. But he wasn't as good at creckett as the other lads, who had plenty of practice. When it came to his turn to take the bat, Edward was bowling, and William felt sure the ball was being aimed at him, rather than the wicket. Once or twice he was hit on the leg. He swiped at the ball without success, feeling increasingly frustrated and embarrassed. Then the ball hit him square in the chest, knocking him over. Edward laughed, but the other lads came to help William up. Winded, he couldn't carry on playing, so he gave the bat to another boy, and went to sit down at the side.

"Liddle William don't want to play no more," mocked Edward, and carried on bowling. When his turn was over, he ignored William and walked away to field the ball. William, feeling better by now, went over to him and asked his brother what was wrong.

"Why d'ye twit us? I believed we was bre'ncheese friends."

"Not no more," said Edward.

"Why d'ye say that?"

"They all favours thee. Ye gets to do all manner of things with the uncles, and I just bides here and do's lessons all-on," said Edward, and pushed William away.

"D'ye want to fight about it? Would that make thee feel better?" said William, and pushed his brother back. The pushing continued, and soon they were having a fiery wrestling match. William was stronger than Ed, although Ed was heavier. The other boys gathered round, cheering and egging them on. Before long William found himself on top of Edward on the ground, sitting on his back. He was tempted to rub his nose in the dirt but refrained. He still loved his brother. He held his arm up in the air as the winner.

Then he got up, helped Ed from the ground, and said, "Come on, let's be bodging." They shouted goodbye and raced each other up the hill to Marlinge.

When William and his uncle reached home that night, William took the parcel with his new jacket into the house to show Martha. But he couldn't find the cap anywhere. Uncle Thomas said it must have been left behind by mistake, but William was sure he'd put it on the cart.

"We'll fetch it next time we go to Wad'rst," said Uncle.

One dark, rainy day in November, Uncle Thomas led the household in morning prayers and read a lesson out of the Bible as usual. Then he went away for the day, to do business and attend Court as one of the Hundred jurors. William cleaned out the stables and fed the pigs, then settled down to practise his writing and numbers in the parlour. After he'd had coger with Martha, he went into the hall, and found a paper to read about new farming methods. There were pictures of implements which he'd never seen, machines for casting the seed evenly, and a plough with multiple coulters drawn by oxen, instead of one man guiding a single coulter. He was so absorbed that when Martha came to find him it was already nearly dark.

Martha scolded him. "Ye'd best be fetching them cows in dracly, Will, afore Mus Thomas be a-coming home."

He ran out and across to the pasture, calling as he went. But the cows were nowhere to be seen. His eyes were adjusting to the failing light, and after looking round the field he started to skirt along the hedge by the whapple way. The cows often found fresh green leaves to munch there. He stumbled along, peering into the gloom and came to a place where the hedge was thin. Branches had been broken, and he clawed his way through the gap, where he guessed the animals had breached into the whapple way. The hawthorn scratched him as he went. He turned towards the copse, groping his way along the muddy track. He was shouting now. "Cows, come on." A clap of thunder ripped the sky open, and a flash lit up the scene. He caught sight of hoof prints in the mud. Near to tears, he plunged on.

He could hear one of the cows bellowing in the copse, and turned towards the noise. Then he recognised a white rump and fought his way through the undergrowth, trying to find a path in the darkness.

Brambles slashed across his face and neck. They clung to his clothes. He stopped and disentangled himself. Another rumble of thunder, and big drops of rain splashed onto his head and face, stinging the scratches. The next flash was dazzling, and he was afraid it would catch a tree, or even himself. Was this a punishment from God? He circled the edge of the copse, pushing away the undergrowth until he'd gathered all the cows together. He picked up a hazel rod, and roared and screamed at them, whacking their rumps, until all were making their way down the lane towards the house.

The rain was pouring down now, dripping down his neck, soaking through his clothes, which stuck to his legs and arms as he walked, his feet squelching in the soft ground. He was cold, and shivering. Streams of water ran down his face, mingling with the tears. He thought he saw some lights coming towards him. As he drove the beasts into the yard, Martha, and Uncle Thomas having just arrived home, were setting off to search for him with lanterns.

"Where've ye been, boy? I can't turn my back for a minute..." His uncle looked and sounded angry.

"The cows breeched the hedge, Uncle. I've been seeking 'em."

Martha said, "Fetch 'em in anon. I'll help thee with the milking." Then she said to Thomas, "Sir, ye'll catch thy death out here. Go in and take off those wet clothes. I'll hot up thy dinner 'forelong." She drove the cows into their stalls with William.

The milking done, William, shivering, went into the house to change his clothes while Martha heated up the meal. He was afraid his uncle would be angry with him, but by the time they'd warmed themselves by the fire and eaten a hot dinner, there seemed to be no more to be said. Dozy with fatigue, they all retired to their beds.

The next morning William rose early. He hadn't mentioned that he'd found the cows in the copse, and he was worried about the damage they may have caused. Adam was working on some repairs to the roof of the barn. William went and told him what had happened the night before, and asked him to bring a hurdle for the gap in the hedge. They carried the hurdle to the pasture, and pushed it firmly into the hedge to make it secure. In the coppice they could see a trail of broken branches and trampled saplings where the cows had been. Adam managed to save one or two saplings, but William was devastated. How would he tell his uncle? It was his own fault.

Adam calmed him down, "Don't be so put out, Will. We can replace the trees what's broken, and I rackon the others'll recover."

The boy went back to the house with his heart in his mouth, he dreaded telling the news to Uncle Thomas. But Martha came out to meet him. She couldn't rouse her master, and, not wanting to invade his privacy, needed William to go and see what was wrong.

He ran up the stairs and into Uncle's chamber, to find the bed thrown all over, and Uncle Thomas tossing and turning, his face and hair wet, his nightgown soaked. He seemed unaware of William as he approached, and was shouting and groaning in his delirium.

William had never seen anything like this, and ran out of the room crying, "Uncle be took bad, come and see!"

Martha came running up the stairs, took one look, and said, "Go to the doctor. Fetch him anon, Will, thy uncle's catched hot," and she rushed away to find cold compresses and towels. William ran to the stable, leapt onto his pony, and rode bareback down to the far end of the village where the doctor lived. He knocked and hollered until a woman wearing a nightcap leaned out of the window.

"Please send the doctor to Mus Thomas Lucke at the Slade, dracly-minute," he pleaded. The window slammed shut. William hung around, not wanting to leave until he was sure the doctor was on his way. Presently the doctor appeared at the door.

"Mus Thomas Lucke is taken bad with the ague, 'e be dying," shouted William.

"Alright, alright, I be a-coming," grumbled the old man. He looked hardly capable of mounting his horse, let alone riding it, thought William, but he decided he must trust the doctor to come at once, and, anxious to get back to his uncle, he cantered away.

Chapter 5

Thomas Lucke was feverish for several days, despite the potions supplied by the doctor, and Martha's patient caring. But at last he was still, and his colour restored. Very feeble, and with a bad cough, he wasn't allowed out of his chamber for another week.

William said to him one day, as he sat by the bed, "Uncle, what would I have done without thee, if ye'd died?"

"You've larned well, boy. I rackon you'll be a good farmer. But I'm not minded to die yet, and will soon be fit to carry on larning thee."

"But there be so many things to remember. I couldn't manage the farm without thee."

"You can read, can't ye? And Ned and Adam be trusty men who'll help thee. There's much I don't know, and times be changing. Come the time I be gone there'll be new ways of doing things that I can't larn thee. Stop worritting and read our favourite story from the book of Dan'l."

William sat on the edge of his seat and straightened his back. "First, there be something I must tell thee, Sir, that's been troubling me."

Thomas looked at him, "What be that, lad?"

"The night of the storm, the cattle breeched the hedge, and I found them in the new copse." His face puckered.

"Go on, go on," said Thomas, his brow wrinkled with concern.

"They trampled and broke some of the young trees and hazel rods." William looked up at his uncle, waiting for a reaction.

Thomas' face relaxed. "But they didn't destroy the entire copse, did they?" William shook his head. "We should have been watching the hedge, so's not to let it become so thin," said Uncle.

"But it were all my fault. I were late calling 'em in for milking. I forgot the time because I were reading."

"Well that'll larn thee not to get so buried in books. We'll buy more saplings if need be when I'm well enough. Let no more be said. Now, find the story in the book of Dan'l. I'll mind thee when 'tis time to fetch the cows." He settled himself back on the pillows.

William picked up the Bible, and, finding the place, he began reading. They had reached the part where Shadrack, Meshach and Abed-Nego had been thrown into the fiery furnace, and had survived the fire:

"Daniel, chapter 3, verse 24-28

Then King Nebuchadnezzar was astonished, and rose up in haste and spake and said unto his counsellors, 'Did not we cast three men bound into the midst of the fire?' They answered and said unto the king, 'True, O king.'

'Lo.' He answered and said, 'I see four men loose, walking in the midst of the fire, and they have no hurt; and the form of the fourth is like the Son of God.'

Then Nebuchadnezzar came near to the mouth of the burning feiry furnace, and spake, and said, 'Shadrach, Meshach and Abed-Nego, ye servants of the Most High God, come forth, and come hither.' Then Shadrach, Meshach and Abed-Nego came forth of the midst of the fire.

And the princes, governors and captains, and the king's counsellors, being gathered together, saw these men upon whose bodies the fire had no power, nor was an hair of their head singed, neither were their coats changed, nor the smell of the fire had passed on them.

Then Nebuchadnezzar spake, and said, 'Blessed be the God of Shadrach, Meshach and Abed-Nego, who hath sent his angel, and delivered his servants that trusted in him, and have changed the king's word, and yielded their bodies, that they might not serve nor worship any god except their own God!'"

A door banged and someone stumbled through the hall and up the stairs.

"What's this I hear? Is me liddle brudder dying?" bellowed Christopher, as he entered the room. He was ageing noticeably. His tall figure was beginning to stoop, and he needed a stick to steady him while walking. He was hard of hearing, and shouted when he spoke, as if he expected not to be able to hear his own voice. He staggered into the room looking tipsy.

"They said ye was ailing. Whatever'll I do without thee to muvver me, Thomas?"

"Sit ye down brudder, while we finish the passage. Continue, William," demanded Thomas.

Christopher slumped down in a chair that was too small for him and started to grumble. It was impossible for William to read any more, so looking for a nod from Uncle Thomas he closed the Book and put it down.

"How be ye, Christopher? You be moithered, seemingly," said Thomas. "Come, sit closer, so that ye can hear us," and he indicated a nearer chair.

The old man struggled out of the chair he was in, and came over to the bed saying, "I be getting in years, and can't do no more than just doddle about. When I heard you had the ague I were mortaceous put out, I can tell thee. Behopes ye're better now."

Thomas said, crossly, "There's no call to create so. We all be getting in years, but I'm not buried yet. Though it be time we put our houses in order."

"Oh, I cannot be doing with all that!" exclaimed Christopher. "I've no heirs, and there'll be nothing left betimes I be gone." He chuckled.

William stood up, and said loudly, "I'll leave thee to talk, Uncle Christopher. 'Tis time I fetched the cows for milking."

"What? What's that, boy? Don't go abroad, I can tell thee a story."

But William bowed to his uncles before leaving the room quietly.

A week later, Thomas could be restrained no longer, and came to take the reins once more. William was relieved to have his uncle back, and took him round the farm, showing him all the work that had been done since the storm. He felt more like a partner to Thomas, having been left to do the work without supervision.

One day just before Christmas William's father, Richard Lucke, and his eldest son John rode into the yard.

William ran to meet them. "Farder, John, I be main glad to see thee."

"My, what a stocky young man! Be this justly my liddle boy, William?" said his father as he dismounted. William ushered them into the hall, where Uncle Thomas was warming himself by the fire.

"Brudder, thanks be to see thee looking alright," said Richard. "We be going to Pens'rst to see Brudder John. I've some business with him."

Thomas got up from his chair and greeted them warmly. "Will ye stay and have coger with us afore ye rides on? I too have call to discuss business with John. Maybe you could take a letter to him, as I be put by from travelling far."

William and his elder brother went back into the yard. They tethered the horses and gave them a bag of hay to munch.

"Come and see my new pony," William said, and took John over to the stables.

"That's a cushti liddle fellow. Does he ride well?" said John.

"Oh, 'e do run like the wind. I calls him Excalibur. I goes over to Gowd'rst, to see Uncle Christopher now and again. He be getting in years, and forgets sometimes. But 'e can still tell a wonderful story. He's agreed to take me to the races come spring, over agin Frant. I rackon he'll need me there to muvver 'im!"

"You'll be riding over to Wad'rst to see us," said John. "There be but four of us along of Farder now. Dorothee bides with Aunt Stapley, and be getting on bravely with her cousins."

"What about Jone?" asked William, puzzled.

"She be wed, and bides in Teec'rst."

William gasped. "How can that be? She be too young."

"She went with John Prior at the May Fair. He got her with child, and Farder forced 'im to ringle 'er," John said. "'Tis true she be no'but a child 'erself. The babe's due next month. She ain't hem strong."

"Poor Jone. Behopes she'll be alright." William had his doubts, and was afraid for Jone.

"How be Edward?" he asked. "We had a disagreement last time I were there. He were main put out."

"Nay," said John. "He be lapsy at his lessons, and would rather be with 'is friends, I'll warrant. Farder be worried that he be going with pesky people. Some of them be refugees who work in the ironworks."

William bent down and picked up a length of straw, pulling it through his fingers as he said, "'E don't want to call cousins with me no more."

"Michael's growed, and has begun lessons with Mr Hatley," continued John. "He be a mischievous nipper, and partial to checking his sister." They laughed.

"Mary'll keep him in order," said William.

The brothers went into the house to spend some time with their elders over a mug of ale and some bread and cheese. William told his father how much he had learnt at the Slade, and how kind Uncle Thomas and Martha were. They said they were looking forward to seeing each other at Christmas. William watched the visitors ride away. He found himself wanting to be home in Wadhurst with the family as it used to be. Uncle's voice was calling him to come into the hall for his lessons, and the feeling was gone.

Chapter 6

A few weeks after Christmas, the snow came. It had been icy cold since early January, freezing the water in the troughs and the well bucket. William's hands became swollen and sore, which made working outside difficult. One morning he woke to an eerie silence, and looked out to see everything covered in a white blanket. Big fat snowflakes fell softly and persistently, covering everything. Martha tried to open the door into the close, but it wouldn't move. The snow was piled high against it. There was a way under cover through the milk-house, and from there to the cow stall. William found shovels and spades propped against the wall, and the morning was spent cutting paths to the animals, indoors and out. The farm workers were late getting there that day, having had to negotiate deep snowdrifts. Martha and William were grateful for the extra manpower as Thomas was not fit enough to shovel snow.

Robert Longley and his elder brother and father came and helped them clear the snow along the routes between houses and village. John Longley and Uncle Thomas had been friends for a long time. They shared their salted meat, hay for the animals and wood for the fire, exchanging one for the other as stocks ran low. Martha found an old quern, and ground the flour by hand, as they couldn't get the corn to the mill. The farmers were self-sufficient in their daily needs. They used horses to pull sleds round the village, making sure that the poor and elderly were not left without food and warmth.

When they were not clearing snow, Robert and William had snowball fights and rode on Robert's sledge down the hill into the village, shouting with delight. William went home each evening with cold fingers and toes, and mats of snow clinging to his clothes like fur.

The snow hung on, and no sooner had the paths been cleared than it snowed again. Then it iced over, making the footpaths slippery. They worried about Christopher in Goudhurst, but there was no way of reaching him, and they hoped that his stable lads were able to see to his needs. Nothing could be done on the farm. No one could remember this happening before, and some people thought it was a punishment from God. Many elderly people died of cold and hunger, and some babies didn't survive their first few weeks. Wood stores were running low.

Towards the end of March the weather warmed up, and the snow started melting. By the beginning of April they were able to proceed with ploughing and sowing.

One morning after prayers, Uncle Thomas said to William, "'Tis time we took a look at the copse and the hedge that was breeched." They went together up the whapple way, and found that cows are not the only ones to damage trees. The weight of the snow had proved too much for some of the branches, which had snapped off. William thought that his copse was ruined.

Uncle re-assured him, "Ye must larn patience, Will," he said. "Husbandry be hard, and these setbacks happen now and again. We must let the seasons come and go, and work along of the weather. We'll use the broken branches for stakes when we mends the hedge. The trees'll restore themselves."

And of course, young green leaves were emerging from the buds already, and yellow cats' tails danced on the branches. William sighed, and was glad that Uncle had survived his illness, but resolved to have more faith that all would be well, remembering Shadrach, Meshack and Abed-Nego. They went to look at the hedge where the cows broke through. William couldn't imagine how it could be restored.

Uncle Thomas said, "The whole hedge needs relaying. We'll larn ye how to do that 'forelong." He looked down at William and added, "But today I want thee to ride over to Gowd'rst and take some vittels for Uncle Christopher."

William left his uncle to make his rounds on the farm, and went to ask Martha for supplies for Christopher. They filled a satchel, which he slung over his shoulder, and went to saddle up Excalibur. Through the village, big heaps of cleared away snow lingered along the verges. Streams of water coursed down the roads, making deep channels. When he came to the bridge, he saw the river was in spate. Snow huddled in the corners of the fields on Goudhurst hill, where it had drifted up to the height of the hedges.

He found Uncle Christopher in excellent health, if a little thin. "'Twill take more than a liddle snow to lay us low," he said. But his larder was nearly empty, and his uncle was glad of the food William had brought with him.

"When all this snow's gone, we'll go to the races, Will," said Christopher.

"I'll surely look forward to that." William would enjoy a day out with his uncle. He rode home in good spirits.

A few days later Uncle Thomas and William went to fetch bill-hooks and cleavers from the skillon where the tackle was kept. Robert came to learn how to lay a hedge and to help them. When they got to the field Adam and Ned were already driving strong stakes into the ground.

Adam called William and Robert over. "These stakes must go in at equal intervals all along the portion of hedge to be repaired, to create a binder which will stabilise the new hedge. You go and help Mus Lucke to do the trimming. He'll show thee."

Robert, William and his uncle trimmed the thin lower branches from the thickest tall stems of the old hedge, leaving bare trunks. Then Ned came with his bill-hook and cut almost through the base of these trunks until they were hanging by a thin piece of bark, and bent them over. William was afraid they would be too frail to survive.

Uncle Thomas said, "They're not cut right through. That little skin will keep the branches alive. Now we can bend them over and weave them through the stakes, like a basket." He showed them how to do this. William and Robert set to. It was hard work, and William soon tired. He was scratched by the hawthorns, and his hands grew sore. He was glad when, at the end of the morning, Thomas said he and Robert should go and get some coger.

The two boys walked back to the house together.

Robert said, "Ye be friendly with my cousin Nick, ain't ye?"

"Yus. I ain't seen 'im since I dunno the time when," said William.

"'Is muvver passed away in that cold weather. Nick's liddle sister, Jane, she be a-coming to bide with us. Me muvver'll take care of 'er."

William felt sad for Nick and Jane. He knew how they must be feeling. "Will Nick be going with 'er?"

"Yus, 'e'll bring Jane over with their farder. Then 'e'll go back. 'Is farder needs 'im and his brudder on the farm.

"I'd like to see Nick when 'e comes over," William said.

The next day the men had layered more of the hedge. Adam showed William and Robert how to take the thin branches, which they'd trimmed off the lower stems, and weave them into the top end of the stakes, to secure the weaving. They stood back to admire their work. No cow would find a way through that. Will felt like one of the men as they clapped each other on the back. A month later the young leaves were appearing on the woven branches. It was a miracle!

The day of the races dawned, and Christopher arrived at the Slade in gaily coloured doublet and loose breeches over his hose, tied at the knee. A dark green velvet cloak was draped over all, and a neat black hat crowned his bushy greying hair. He wore black leather boots with wide tops turned over at the knee. Will led Excalibur out into the yard, already saddled and bridled. He tightened the girth and mounted.

Uncle Thomas was there to wave them off, calling, "Mind ye bides close with your uncle, Will."

"Yus Uncle," William called back, and they trotted away.

The field was a mass of horses and their riders mingling with the spectators. There were ladies and gentlemen in their best clothes, hats with feathers and elegant legs in long boots. The grooms and the racing riders wore brightly coloured jerkins. They ran around to register in the races, groomed and calmed their steeds and loosened up around the course. There were booths for placing wagers, others selling bait and ale. Christopher led William over to where they could tether their horses and leave them with some hay. Then they joined the crowd. There were shouts from friends who came to greet them, and a great deal of gossiping ensued. Christopher raised his hat to the gentlemen, and bowed deeply to the ladies. William wanted to go and see the horses that would be racing, particularly the two being entered by Christopher. They wound their way through the crowds to the jockeys' enclosure. Dan'l and Tim, the stable boys, were jockeys for the day. They were there with the horses, Felix and Hercules, brushing them down. On the way back to the course, Christopher went to place his wagers, and the races started. Because he was so tall, he could see over the crowd. He urged William, "Go thee forrard, boy, agin the finish, where you'll see them a-coming in."

William pushed his way through the crowd to the front, where he sat on the ground with some other boys. He had a good view from here, and was confident that he would easily find Uncle again because of his height. He'd remembered that Uncle Christopher's jockeys were wear-ing yellow and blue, and cheered loudly as they came in. The atmosphere was exhilarating: the cheering and shouting; the thundering of hooves on the turf; and the jostling of the crowds. One of Uncles' horses, Hercules, came third in his race, but Felix stumbled and fell. William was horrified to watch this, but rider and horse recovered themselves unhurt, and walked off the course as if nothing had happened.

After three or four races, William was feeling hungry, and went to look for his uncle among the crowds. He'd vanished, nowhere to be seen. William made his way to the booths and to the jockeys' enclosure, asking people if they'd seen a tall elderly man with grey hair and a beard, wearing green and black. The jockeys hadn't seen him. William went to where their horses were tethered to refresh their hay. Christopher wasn't there either. It was quiet round here, and William rested awhile, talking to Excalibur, who was munching away, unaware of the panic building in William's chest. He wandered round the field again, a small lump forming in the back of his throat. He felt stifled in among the crowds, who pushed and shoved each other to find their way through. He looked for the people who Christopher met when they first arrived, and found some. None of them had seen the old man. Uncle Christopher couldn't get home without his horse, but what if he was collapsed somewhere? At last William returned to the booths. Uncle would go to collect his winnings.

Asking again, "Has Mus Christopher Lucke been to get 'is winnings?"

The bookie replied, "Yus lad, I saw him a while back. Then he were away dracly to buy ale."

So William went to the next booth. "Did ye see my Uncle Christopher Lucke hereabouts?"

"He were 'ere. Went yonder," was the reply, as the vendor pointed towards the jockeys' pound. So back went William. But Dan'l and Tim hadn't seen Christopher. It was nearly the end of the day. They would not be racing again and they offered to accompany William in his search.

"We'll look round the back of the booths. You go that way, Will," said Dan'l, pointing in the direction of the racecourse. The crowds were beginning to disperse, and it was easier to move around. When he was sure Uncle Christopher wasn't in this area, he went to find the others. He saw Tim and Dan'l by the tethered horses, having found nothing. They continued searching together; under hedges, in and under waggons, and among the trees in a small copse.

At last, behind a hay wain, they found Uncle Christopher lying on the ground, apparently unconscious, his best clothes soiled, his hat and cloak discarded some distance away. They assumed he'd had too much ale at first, but then Tim noticed blood coming from a gash on the back of his head, and examined it more closely. William thought Uncle Christopher was dead. He felt sick, his heart pounded, his eyes smarted with approaching tears.

Christopher stirred. William breathed again as he watched the old man come round.

"Jigger me, ye did give us a fright, surely, Mus Lucke," said Dan'l. "Where be thy winnings? Be they all spent?"

Christopher moaned as they sat him up. "I were having a quiet sup, away from the crowds. There come two reskels, set upon us. I put up a fight, but they hit us with a bat." Then, fumbling among his clothes, he said, "Dang! They've had my money purse!"

Dan'l helped him to his feet and took him to the horses. He was confused and unsteady.

Dan'l said, "We'll ride home with thee, Will." They went to fetch Felix and Hercules and helped their master onto his horse. The four walked slowly back to Lamberhurst. The excitement of the day had worn off. William was shocked. He did not want to go to the races with Uncle Christopher again.

When they reached the Slade, Uncle Thomas came out to meet them and they explained what had

56

happened. Martha appeared, wiping her hands on her apron, looking worried.

"He'd best stay with us here until he's recovered," said Thomas. William thanked the lads, and they rode on to Goudhurst. Thomas and Martha helped Christopher from his horse and led him indoors.

William took the horses to the stable, removed their saddles and bridles and gave them hay. He couldn't get out of his head the sight of Christopher sprawled on the ground, bleeding. He stayed in the stable, wiping the horses down and drawing comfort from their strong warm bodies. He gave Excalibur a hug before going indoors.

Chapter 7 1625
First year in the reign of Charles 1

It was becoming lighter in the mornings. A grey dawn showed itself at the small square window of William's chamber. He climbed out of his cot and slipped his nightshirt over his head, revealing a strong, healthy torso on the verge of manhood. He stretched his arms above his head, and looked down as had become his habit. He saw that his body was indeed different. His member had changed shape, and he'd noticed recently that it had developed a life of its own. He'd noticed too, that his voice kept disappearing when he spoke. He pulled on his breeches and they only reached his ankles. He scratched his scalp under his tousled brown hair to wake himself up, went down the narrow wooden stairs and out through the milk-house to the well in the close. He swilled the cold water over his body, gasping and spluttering, then took a drink and went over to the stable.

He fondled Excalibur's muzzle and ears, and gave him a new bag of hay to munch until it was time to take him out. Then he went over to the cow stalls, where he counted the notches he'd carved in the middle post. One for every May Day he'd spent at the Slade, except the first, the day he arrived. "On, two, free, fower, five, six."

Having dressed himself in his working frock, he went into the parlour for breakfast. Uncle Thomas was already sitting at the table.

"Uncle, d'ye know how old I were when I first come here?"

Thomas looked up. "I believe you were about seven or eight, Will. Why d'ye ask?"

"That makes me, er..." and he counted on his fingers, "thirteen or fowerteen, don't it? I be taller of a sudden. I hit me head on the stable doorway this morning!" He smiled as he sat down at the table.

"You're surely growing into a fine young man. You'll be starting to look after the maids, I'll warrant," said Martha, who was serving out their bowls of porridge. "And I'll be having ter get ye some new breeches 'forelong, or they'll be laughing at thee!"

William blushed. He cleared his throat and started eating.

"Shall we go over to Gowd'rst today, Will?" asked Uncle Thomas. "Christopher hasn't been over here for a while and I'm worried. Last time I visited, he were forgetful and confused. I tried to get him to sell some of the horses, but he weren't having none of it."

"I'll come with thee, Uncle. Uncle Christopher is surely getting himself in a boffle."

They fed and watered the animals before they went. Martha said she'd milk the cows and take them to pasture.

On the way to Goudhurst, William dismounted at the foot of the steep hill. He was too heavy for Excalibur. As they trudged up together, he said, "'Twill soon be time to say goodbye to thee, my liddle bren'cheese friend. I'll miss thee sorely."

They found Christopher in a mild state of inebriation. His house was untidy and smelled stale, and his clothes were grubby. But he was pleased to see them, and took them out to see his horses. He petted and talked to them over the stable doors.

Thomas said, "D'ye need all these horses, Christopher? Thy money's all going on fother and wages for the stable lads. The horses aren't ridden. Ye'd best be letting 'em go to good homes, and make some money afore they're worthless."

"There be a young mare for Will here." Christopher led them across the yard to another stable, where a grey face with a creamy white mane looked over the door. "Bring her out, Dan'l," he called. "This be Damsel."

Dan'l put a leading reign on the mare, and brought her out into the yard. She was shy of the strangers, but William succeeded in putting his hand up to her cheek, and patted her neck before she pulled away. He was delighted.

"Thank thee, Uncle. She be a fine mare." They arranged for Dan'l to bring her to the Slade, and went indoors to discuss what was to be done with the other horses.

"I believe you be right, brudder," said Christopher as he sat down heavily. "I can't ride with these latchety legs and I keeps forgetting things. Will ye help me with the arrangements? I'd like to keep the old nags, and Dan'l can stay and muvver them. Come to think on it, he can muvver me too!" He chuckled.

"I'll manage thy affairs for thee, brudder. I suggest that you sell the property to me, so ye won't have the pervension, and ye'll have more money to live on." Christopher agreed. William and his Uncle came away relieved.

"I be surely worritted to see Uncle Christopher so doddlish," said William, as they rode back slowly. "He were so spry when I first come to the Slade."

"'E always were a contrary man to deal with," said Uncle Thomas. "I'm surprised he agreed so willingly to my suggestions. But 'tis dearly ernful that he's so mucked-up."

A few days later, Dan'l brought Damsel to the Slade. William spent time in the evenings getting to know his new steed. She'd not been ridden much, and needed some patient handling to give her the confidence she needed. She responded well to his care, and began to recognise his voice when he called her, coming to him for a caress and a carrot.

It was the end of March. The wind was cold, but the ground was drying out, and William was looking forward to sowing the corn in the field he'd ploughed a few weeks ago. He was on the way back from taking the cows to the pasture. Adam and Ned were repairing hedges and clearing out ditches after the winter, and he went to have a word with them as he passed.

"Will that be done soon?" he asked. "Mus Lucke noticed the stable roof needs patching up."

Adam paused in his work. "T'will be another two-three days, Will. We'll get onto the roofing 'forelong," he said.

As he walked back towards the house, a horseman galloped into the yard. The horse was all of a lather, and William ran to hold it while the man dismounted.

"Message for Mus Thomas Lucke," he said, and handed a letter to William. He took it into the parlour where his uncle was coming in from the close. After giving the letter to Thomas, William went and drew a tankard of ale, and took it out to the messenger.

"Have ye come far?" he asked.

"From Pens'rst. 'Tis urgent that Mus Lucke comes to his brudder dracly," The man gulped the ale down. "Thank thee for the drink." He handed the tankard back, wiped the froth from his mouth with his sleeve, mounted his horse, and rode away.

William watched him go, and went back into the house to find his uncle putting on clean boots. He gathered up his cloak.

"Me brudder John's been taken ill," he said. "It seems he be took mortal bad. He's sent for us to attend to his will. I'd best be quick," and he hurried out to the stables.

William was left in charge of the lambing. There were three more sheep due to produce, and the newly-borns to keep an eye on. Soon he could put them all in the pasture to skip around in the sunshine.

The next day he was coming in from the pasture when Uncle Thomas rode into the yard, looking weary. William took his horse and, after tethering him in the close with a bag of hay, he went into the parlour to hear the news of Uncle John.

"I came to my brudder's house in time, to help him settle his affairs. I was there with his fambly at his passing. I'll return when they put him in, and I rackon thy farder will accompany us."

"I be sorry to hear of Uncle John's death. Were he taken ill sudden?" asked William.

"Unaccountable sudden. One day he were labouring on the farm. Next day he took to his bed. I only just got there in time," said Thomas, shaking his head.

There was a pause, then he looked up and said, "Will, I be minded to talk to thee about my plans. I've been hankering after returning to Wad'rst to bide there afore I die. John agreed a while back that I should rent his house at Bedifields Hill when I be ready. He's left the property along of Durgates to his son Richard. After me brudder's laid to rest, I'll talk to Richard, and propose that I buy Bedifields Hill."

"Will that mean ye'll be leaving us at the Slade?" William was concerned.

"Not yet awhile, but I be failing sometimes, Will. I've built this farm up from nothing. Now I believe ye'll be able to manage it on thy own, and I'll feel happy to leave thee in charge. Would ye be agreeable if I handed over the farm to thee prensley, while I bides here, so as ye'll have my support?"

William smiled. "I'd be main glad of that. Thank thee." The time had come. William had become a farmer, with all the responsibility of keeping things running smoothly, of keeping the books balanced, and planning for the future. He went and poured himself a tankard of ale and sat down opposite his uncle. His heart welled over with love for the man who had brought him here and taught him so much. They smiled at each other and knocked their tankards together.

"To the Slade!" they said in unison.

Chapter 8

Later that year news came that there was to be a wedding in Wadhurst. Margaret Lucke, eldest daughter of the deceased vicar of Mayfield, was to marry her father's successor, John Maynard. Mr Hatley, a friend of both families, would perform the ceremony in Wadhurst. There was great excitement among the Lucke family there, as this would give them a chance to meet their cousins from Mayfield, whom they barely knew.

Uncle Thomas and William arrived to find the church packed, with many relatives from Mayfield. Thomas pointed them out, nodding and waving to them as he passed. There were Luckes, Peckhams and Maynards, of which there were several branches. The Luckes of Wadhurst squeezed in. After the congregation was seated, Susannah, mother of the bride, led her family up the aisle, nodding to each side as she caught sight of familiar faces turned towards her. She was a handsome woman, dressed in widow's weeds, which accentuated her stately figure. She was swollen with child. Her modest hat crowned a head of bright copper curls, surrounding a face of rare beauty. Three girls followed their mother. A teenager held the hands of her two younger sisters, one a toddler. They were all dressed in black hooded cloaks over simple dark green velvet dresses with tight bodices. Three sons followed, their ages ranging from six to sixteen. They wore black cloaks over dark green velvet hose and doublets. The eldest sported their mother's copper hair, the others' hair was raven black. They all filed into the front two rows of seats and settled themselves. William saw that the boys' cloaks were off one shoulder, in the new Cavalier style.

John Maynard, the groom, dressed in his clergyman's attire came and stood at the chancel steps, and waited.

There was a hush as the bride entered, led by her elder brother and accompanied by her elder sister. Margaret was dressed in pale blue satin, with a lacy white collar covering her shoulders, and long sleeves with lace cuffs. John Hatley appeared from the vestry, and the ceremony began. William heard people sobbing, as the family and their friends remembered the bride's recently deceased father.

Margaret's face was all smiles and tears as she was led back down the aisle on the arm of her new husband.

The teenage members of the families from Mayfield raced ahead of the bride and groom, as they made their way up the village street to Durgates. At the front door, they formed an archway with their hands, so that the newly-weds must bend their heads to pass through the tunnel before entering the house, amid much laughter. Joane Lucke, widow of the deceased Richard Lucke of Durgates, and Great Aunt of the Mayfield Luckes, had offered the use of the Durgates mansion for the wedding celebrations and family gathering. She was the grandmother of William and his brothers and sisters, and a very old lady. She hadn't ventured out to the church, as it was February, and the weather was cold. But she presided over the party with relish. She was a true matriarch, wearing black silk and a lace cap on her white hair. She sat on a high-backed chair by the fire at the end of the hall. Her black eyes peered out of a deeply wrinkled face as she welcomed her guests. Each one came to her and curtsied or bowed, some kissing her hand. She smiled and said a few words to them all.

Uncle Thomas knew Susannah and her family well, and went to greet Margaret's new husband, leaving William to his own devices. He watched them all for a while. Uncle quickly found his cousins and went over to talk to them. William saw Dorothee talking to Mary, and went to join them.

"Will, I hoped you was here," cried Dorothee, and hugged him warmly.

"D'ye know the fambly well?" asked William.

"Oh, yus. I visits them at Mayfild with Aunt Stapley. She's a friend of Susannah, the mother. Margaret and me have become bre'ncheese friends.

"There be some good looking boys in that fambly, Dorothee," said Mary. Don't ye have thy eye on any of them?"

Dorothee coloured slightly, and said, "Nay, there be other handsome young men in the Stapley fambly. But I can introduce thee to Margaret's brothers," and she led Mary towards a group of young men, who were all stunningly handsome. John, the eldest, was dark haired and already growing a substantial beard, which was trimmed to a point. His manner was gracious and flattering, and Mary looked impressed. They spent some time talking and flirting gently with each other.

William's brother John was standing by their grandmother, pointing out who was who, and surreptitiously eyeing up some of the girls. He went and handed plates of food to those who were not eating, gleaning snippets of information from conversations he overheard, to take back to the old lady. She loved a good gossip, and liked to know everything about everybody. Then William caught sight of his Aunt

Kingswood and her family, talking animatedly to a large florid faced man, who must be Hugh Lucke. He decided to steer clear of them, and went to join Edward and Michael who had sought out a group of boys and girls of their own ages. Edward was boasting outrageously about his possessions and achievements. William felt acutely embarrassed and walked away, looking for someone else to talk to.

Susannah beckoned him over to where she was sitting, and he went and introduced himself with a bow. He had never seen such a beautiful lady. He wanted to touch her hair to make sure it was real. Her face appeared to him to be made of the finest porcelain. As she spoke to him in the voice of an angel, he was transported to another world.

"You are Thomas Lucke's nephew aren't you? I've heard what a promising young farmer you are. Are you not lonely at the Slade with no other young people around you?" It had never occurred to William that he might be lonely.

"Nay, there be all manner of work to be done, Ma'am. I don't have no time to be lonesome. Besides, there be the beasts, and the birds in the trees. They talks to us all-on like."

"It sounds to me as if you love your work, William. Do you have time to play, too?"

"Uncle Thomas takes us hawking now and again, and I goes up to Gowd'rst to ride with Uncle Christopher regular like. We went to the races by Frant. I liked that well enough."

"I've never been to the races. Was it good sport?"

"'Twere that, surely, Ma'am. But ye would need an escort. 'Tis middling rough for the likes of thee,

Ma'am." William smiled shyly, hoping he hadn't said anything offensive.

"You're a fine young man. Perhaps one day you can be my escort to the races. I don't think any of my sons would be interested." They continued to talk about the family and their ambitions. William promised to visit her in Mayfield one day.

Soon it was time to make their way homeward, and newly made friendships must part, with promises that might or might not be kept.

In the days that followed, the image of Susannah invaded William's mind during his work and in his sleep. He wondered if he would ever see her again, and what he would say to her if he did. But as time went on, the image faded, and eventually it all seemed to be a dream.

Chapter 9

It was time they had some more corn ground at the mill. Martha was getting short of flour. Uncle Thomas was out, and Adam and Ned were repairing the roof of the stables and didn't need his help, so William prepared to take a cartload of corn into Lamberhurst. The men helped him load up. He liked to watch the corn sliding into the sacks like a great river of gold: last year's harvest. He dipped his hand in, and let the grains of sunshine run through his fingers. They loaded the sacks onto the cart. William put the harness on old Bess, the carthorse, and climbed up, taking the reins.

Bess led the cart down the hill into the village. As they passed the water pump there was a group of women standing around gossiping. One or two of them looked round when he passed and stared at him, but he thought nothing of it. He left the loaded cart at the mill, as Joshua, the miller, wasn't quite ready to take the corn. Then he led Bess up the road to the blacksmith for a new shoe.

The blacksmith was busy with another horse. The roaring of the furnace and the clang of the anvil reminded William of the scene at the ironworks. He waited until Harry had completed the shoe he was making, and had plunged it into the water to cool. There was a hiss. The acrid smoke irritated his nostrils. He indicated which of Bess's shoes needed replacing. While that was being done, he went to call on his friend Gregory Dyne, the builder's son, to arrange to meet him at the tavern that evening.

When he came out of the house, the group at the water pump had grown and they all had their heads together. He felt uneasy. He went to collect Bess, paid Harry, and proceeded down the road towards the mill.

Having delivered his corn, he hitched Bess up to the cart and started driving home. As he was passing the pump, he felt something hit his shoulder, and a shout rang out. He chose to ignore it.

"Gee up, Bess," he said as he drove her up the hill, puzzling over what had happened.

Arriving home, he found Martha and Adam in the close, bending over a figure lying on the ground. He ran over. It was Ned, who appeared to be unconscious.

"What happened?"

Adam looked up at William. "'E fell off the ladder and hit his head. He still be alive… I think." He looked down at Ned.

Ned stirred, and they all breathed a sigh of relief.

"Stay there," said Martha, "while we check if ye've broken any bones," and she carefully lifted each limb. "Tell us if it pains thee anywhere."

Ned moved and adjusted his position. "'Tis me head," he said, and raised his arms to hold his forehead, where there was a lump appearing. "Oh, and me shoulder." He winced as he moved. They sat him up gently.

"Can ye walk?" Adam asked, holding Ned under the uninjured arm.

"I'll try," and he slowly and painfully raised himself with Adam's help. Then his face became deathly white, and he slumped against Adam's body.

"Let's get him indoors," said Martha. Adam wrapped Ned's good arm around his own neck, holding him round the waist. William went ahead to open doors, and Martha scurried after him to stoke up the fire and place Uncle Thomas' chair where they could get

Ned into it easily. Adam and Ned limped through the milk-house, and finally Ned was helped into the chair. His colour slowly returned, but the lump on his head was growing.

"I'd best take him home in the cart," said William.

"Wait," said Martha. She went into the hall and came back with a glass of brandy.

Ned sipped the liquor slowly, and began to look better. "Me Mistus'll take care of us," he said. "Could ye take us home, Mus William?"

They took Ned out and lifted him onto the cart, which was still hitched up to Bess, waiting patiently. William climbed up and took the reins once more. Ned was relieved to be home. William helped him into the house, and his wife, after recovering from the shock of seeing her husband in this state, took care of him.

On his return William found Adam up on the stable roof, finishing the job. He climbed the ladder and spent the rest of the day learning how to mend a roof.

He had forgotten the incident in the village.

Uncle Thomas brought some news on his return, "I went to Mayfild today, Will, and saw Susannah Lucke. She was birthed of a darter last year. They christened her Anne."

William was taken aback. He couldn't imagine the lady of his dreams being reduced to the messiness of the birthing process.

"Oh," he said, "another child," then paused in thought. "I'd be partial to visit them sometime, Uncle." Uncle Thomas agreed that they would go together, when work allowed.

William walked down the road that evening, and found Gregory Dyne waiting for him outside The Vyne.

They went into the crowded tavern and bought their mugs of ale. The atmosphere was stifling. People were shouting across the room to each other, among raucous laughter. The lads took their mugs outside and sat on the bench against the wall. The air was cool and clean. They could hear each other more clearly out here.

"How be ye fairing with the house ye're building for Mas' Darrell?" asked William.

"Grandly like," his friend replied. "Me farder's taken on two more labourers to speed it up. Mas' Darrell be an impatient man. Me brudder Thomas is on another job over in Wad'rst." He took a gulp of ale. "Be ye riding out with Damsel yet?"

"'Twill not be long. She be a liddle gantsey just now, but come Lady Day I'll be riding her out. My uncle's going to take us to Mayfild to see our cousins there."

"Be ye still a-dreaming about that lady cousin of yours?"

"I can't get her out of me thoughts," said William. "She's given birth since I've seen 'er."

Greg said, "She'll be a sight more wonderful to behold now." They laughed.

At that moment, a man came out of the door of the alehouse, turned to look at them, spat at William's feet, and staggered away.

Gregory sprang up and shouted, "Hey! ye filthy gummut!" He ran after the fellow, and laid a heavy blow to the side of his head. The drunk fell over, and lay sprawled on the floor.

William called to his friend, "Greg, lay off, there'll be a proper start-up. Let's be bodging." He went over to take Greg's arm and dragged him away. The two went to Greg's house for the rest of the evening. Both were shaken by what had happened, and William told Greg about his experience that morning. He couldn't understand why he was being picked on in this way.

Chapter 10

After prayers one morning, Uncle Thomas was in the parlour preparing to go out and he asked William if he'd like to join him. "Ned's back at work now. We can spare the time for visiting. I've business to attend to in Mayfild, and I'm minded to visit Susannah and her fambly."

William's heart jumped. "Oh, yus, I'd like that. I'll go and tell Adam." He went to catch up with Adam on his way to the meadow. It would be Damsel's first time out on the road. His fingers were shaking as he put the harness on. His heart was beating and his face was flushed. He caught sight of Uncle Thomas looking at him in amusement as they set off down the road.

William had never been to Mayfield before, and Uncle Thomas showed him round the village, pointing out the houses of the Lucke family. Then he called at another house to do his business. William could hardly contain his anticipation as he and Damsel waited for him. At last Thomas came out, said goodbye to his host, and they continued through the village.

As they entered the courtyard, William gazed in wonder at the great mansion, with many tall windows, and a grand entrance. They dismounted and a boy came to take their horses and led them away. The front door opened. Susannah appeared and showed them into her home. William's heart leapt, and a lump came to his throat. She was as beautiful as he'd imagined.

"Welcome! Come and meet the family. John and Susan are away, and Jeremy and Elizabeth have taken Timothy riding. They should be back soon."

She led them into a large hall. They removed their wide-brimmed hats and gave them to a waiting servant. William's breath was taken away at the size of the room and the height of the ceiling. A great table stood in the middle, and chairs with tall backs placed around it. They were led into the parlour, where there was a carpet on the floor. Glass filled the windows and it was very warm in this room. The chairs were soft with cushions on them, and brightly coloured tapestries of country scenes covered the walls. William's attention was drawn to four young children who were playing with some toys on the floor.

Susannah said, "This is Hester, who is eight years old, and Thomas, who is six. Come and meet your cousin William and Uncle Thomas." The two children came and shook William by the hand.

Hester took William to where her little sisters were playing. "This is Mary, she's three," she said, "and Anne, our little treasure, born last year. She can almost walk already. Show William how well you walk, Anne." She grasped the baby's hands and pulled her up, steadying her while she staggered across the room to her mother, then flopped onto the floor. Everyone cheered and clapped their hands. Anne clapped her hands too, and laughed, her red curls bouncing on her shoulders.

The door opened, and three young people burst into the room.

"Uncle Thomas!" two of them cried. "How lovely to see you!" They went to stand round Thomas, talking and laughing. William watched the youngest of the three go over to his mother and kiss her. Then he looked at William. Their eyes met, and William felt a shiver down his back. The boy was about the same age as himself. He had dark rings around unfriendly eyes. He seemed to glide away, leaving the room through another door.

William stood by Susannah, who was now sitting on an elegant padded seat large enough for two. She patted the space next to her and William saw how smooth and beautiful her hands were. His own felt rough and dirty in comparison, and he hid them under his jacket as he sat down. He looked at her face and the waves of auburn hair which lay around her shoulders. She had swept some of it up into a knot on top of her head, and covered it with a little lace cap.

"That was Timothy," she said. "He has difficulty meeting new people." She turned to face William. "Tell me what you've been doing. 'Tis a long time since I saw thee. Have you been to the races again?"

"Nay, Mistus Lucke, my Uncle Christopher be getting in years, and can't go far abroad. I goes to see him now and again, now I haves my own horse."

"Do you know the family of Rumney? They live in Lamberhurst. They have an eligible son who we hope will make a good husband for Susan."

"Nay, I can't say as I do, Ma'am. We don't have much cause to get to know Quality, like." He cleared his throat and looked at the floor. Her gaze was too intense for him.

"How are your brothers and sister in Wadhurst?"

He looked up at her again. "Bravely thank thee, Ma'am. Michael comes and helps on the farm sometimes. Have ye seen Dorothee lately?"

"We see her when she comes to call on Margaret, who is expecting her first child."

At that moment more people came into the house. Margaret appeared with Dorothee, both looking radiant.

"We saw your horses!" said Margaret. "Dorothee, here's your brother!" William stood up and embraced Dorothee. Margaret came to greet her mother. Everyone was talking at once and the children were arguing. Susannah remained calm and serene.

Dorothee introduced Jeremy and Elizabeth to William, who stood up to meet them.

"These be my favourite cousins, Will," she said, her face flushed after the walk from Rotherwick.

"You're Dorothee's brother from Lamberhurst, aren't ye?" said Jeremy. He had his mother's red hair and a pale complexion.

"Yus, I be helping my Uncle Thomas on his farm." replied William.

"Oh, we adore Uncle Thomas," said Elizabeth. "We have known him since we were little children." She wasn't as tall as her brother, and had straight yellow hair. They both looked delicate. They were friendly and made William feel at ease, asking him about the work that he did on the farm, which was completely outside their experience.

"What be *thee* at all day, if ye've no labouring to do?" he asked.

"We have lessons with our tutor, and we play the clavicord and sing. There are games to play, and we go out riding." They showed him the board games they played, backgammon, chess and draughts. Then they led him into the hall where there was a piece of furniture he didn't recognise. Elizabeth opened the lid to reveal the keys of a clavicord. She sat down on a stool, and started to play. William was amazed to hear beautiful music coming from the instrument, as her fingers fluttered over the keyboard like butterflies.

The front door opened, and John Maynard, Margaret's husband came in, a permanent look of surprise and harassment on his round, bespectled face.

"Have you seen my wife?" he asked.

"Yes, John," said Elizabeth, "she's in the parlour with Mama." He went through to the parlour, and the music continued. Jeremy began to sing. William went to sit on the settle by the wall, and became oblivious to anything except the music. Then came a tune he recognised from church, one of his favourite hymns: *Be Still My Soul.* He joined in huskily.

Dorothee came into the hall, "I'd best be bodging afore it gets dark, as I'll be footing it. 'Twas hem good to see thee, Will." She waved as she went out of the door. John and Margaret Maynard followed close after.

"Sermon to write," John called, as he ushered Margaret out.

William followed Elizabeth and Jeremy into the parlour. Uncle Thomas was bidding Susannah goodbye. William was disappointed that they had to leave so soon. He bent his head to kiss Susannah's hand. She held onto his own briefly before getting up to show them out.

They retrieved their hats, went into the courtyard and mounted their horses.

The family stood at the door. "Do come and see us again," they called, as Thomas and William started back to Lamberhurst.

William's head was reeling with new experiences. He was gently nudged out of his reverie when he heard his uncle saying, "Ye be quiet, Will. 'Tis not like thee."

William looked up and sighed. "Yus Uncle, I be thinking of Susannah and her fambly. They be so different. I can't think what it must be like, living there."

"'Tis a different life, surely, and one which you'll never understand, if ye want to be a farmer. They're kind people, and we can meet them sometimes in friendship, but that's all." They trotted along companionably. The evening was mild and calm, and the birds were singing their last songs, accompanied by the rhythm of the horses hooves.

Thomas said, "I be minded to do the coppicing 'forelong. 'Tis dry enough. Can ye get Michael to come and help?" William was jerked away from his thoughts.

"Yus," he said. "I'll do that." His mind was now back in the world of the Slade, and he felt more at ease.

After they'd gone to bed that night, there was a hammering on the door, and William heard Uncle Thomas hurrying downstairs to answer it. There were men's voices shouting and his Uncle protesting. William got out of bed and went to see if he could be of assistance. Uncle Thomas was standing in the dark hall by the open door in his nightshirt and cap.

A group of men barged in, carrying flaming torches. "We've orders to search this dwelling. Stand aside, Sir." There were five of them, wearing hooded cloaks, their faces lit up by the torches. They searched in the corners of the hall and parlour, while two proceeded upstairs to Thomas' chamber.

"There be no Papists in this house, I tell thee," protested Thomas, as the intruders turned chairs over and removed books from the shelves, throwing them down after glancing at the titles. The flickering flames flung their shape-shifting shadows across the walls as the men moved from room to room.

William was about to intervene when another man appeared at the door. William recognised him as the curate from the church. He shouted at the men, "Desist, hold off, this man be no Papist." The intruders stopped their search and came to speak to the curate. They stood in a huddle like hooded crows. The flames wavered over their heads as they talked among themselves.

The curate came over to Thomas. "I be mortaceous sorry that you've been disturbed, Sir. There's been a misunderstanding." With that he signalled to the men to leave, and they all followed him out of the door, banging it shut.

Stunned and baffled by what he had just witnessed, William said, "What were all that about?"

Thomas poured them each a mug of ale and put them by the still glowing embers of the fire. He lit a candle. William picked the chairs up, and replaced the books on their shelves. They sat down with their warm toddies.

"There's some folks that follow a different faith to us, called Popery. Us Protestants, and some of them what's in Parlyment don't like these Papists. They attempted to blow up the Parlyment building a few year ago, but they was stopped just in time. 'Tis on account of that the church bells ring on November the fifth, in celebration."

"So why did those men think there was Papists 'ere?" William held his hands round the warm mug and shivered.

Thomas explained that the Darrell family who lived in Scotney Castle were known to be Roman Catholics, and there had been rumours in the village that they were sheltering a Jesuit priest, which was against the law. This had led to a series of raids, aimed at flushing out any Papists living in the village.

He said, "I've been visiting Mas' Darrell with some business we was doing, and somebody must've seen us and come to the wrong conclusion."

William was gazing into the fire. He remembered his recent experience. "That's why they was staring at us in the village the other day," he said.

"You didn't tell me about that. Who were they?"

"I didn't take much notice. But Greg Dyne nearly started a fight when one of them spat at me. His farder be building at the Darrell's place. He'll likely be the next one to be raided." He took a sip of ale.

Thomas said, "'Tis difficult to know who these Papists be. They attend services at church to cover up their recusancy and also go to the Roman Catholic services held in secret by the Jesuit priests. The Darrells are powerful people, and hide their bad practices well, so nobody can prove that's what they be up to."

After drinking up they wished each other goodnight. It took William a long time to go to sleep. He had never imagined that anyone should think ill of Uncle Thomas.

Chapter 11

The copse resounded with the chopping of wood. The herby aroma of trampled vegetation and newly cut hazel rods hung in the air. William and his copse had reached maturity. The coppicing was under way. He'd gone there beforehand with Uncle Thomas and divided the woods into cants of three acres, so that each could be coppiced in a yearly rotation, giving them a continuous supply of rods.

William was cutting the hazel rods from the old totts. The new ones for the next coppice would grow from these stumps. He passed the rods over to Ned, who trimmed them of their branches and twiggy ends. The stout ones were cut into even lengths and stacked in cords, ready for the charcoal burner. Thinner pieces would be used for weaving into hurdles, and for pea and bean sticks and stakes in hedge laying. Each of the team was busy with his task, and little was said, except the occasional call "Look out!" when a body was in danger of something being thrown his way.

William stood up straight and rubbed his back. He looked around him, filling his nostrils with the damp, earthy smell, and enjoying the scene. What had been a thick wood of undergrowth this morning was becoming a spacious clearing, with only the young oak and beech trees rising above. He looked over to where Uncle Thomas was bent over collecting the twiggy brash and bound them into faggots for the bread oven. Martha would use some for making new besoms. Michael brought Bess and the cart up the whapple way. They loaded up all but the cords, and Michael took it to the wood store by the house. Adam was cutting more hazel rods nearby. Ned went to trim back the new frith they'd planted when William came to the Slade, to encourage them to develop totts. These would produce rods next time round.

William stuck his bill-hook into the ground where it could be seen and not tripped over, and went over to his uncle, who was grateful to stand up straight. He smiled. William said, "'Tis a wunnerful proud day for me today, Uncle. This copse marks my time at the Slade. I rackons us should celebrate when the work be done. What d'ye say?"

"'Tis a proud day for me too, Will, and fitting that we should celebrate. Tell Michael to bring us a barrel of ale next time he goes to the house with the cart." They started clearing up the brash and odd pieces of wood left around, and made a pile for the small animals to find shelter. Adam and Ned went round collecting the fagging hooks and bill-hooks.

Michael arrived with the barrel and Martha on the cart. She'd brought mugs and coger cake. The workers gathered round beneath one of the young oak trees. Thomas and Martha sat on a fallen tree trunk, left over from the old copse. They toasted the copse. Then they toasted William, then Thomas, then Martha, by which time the ale had loosened their tongues and diluted their weariness. Ned found his wooden whistle and soon they were capering round to his tunes, and singing songs until the sun began to slip away. Michael drove Bess, pulling a cartload of contentment and a half empty barrel back to the house. The workers dispersed for home.

After dinner, sitting by the fire enjoying a last tankard of ale, Uncle Thomas said, "I rackon ye'll make a fine Master here 'forelong, Will."

William looked at his uncle, who was smiling at him. Did he really mean that he was going to leave the Slade to him in his will; that he would be the owner of this farm?

Part 3

There Be Dragons

Chapter 12   1626
Second year in the reign of Charles 1

Strong gusts of wind blew across the rolling downs, bringing periods of heavy rain to the sodden earth. William held onto his hat as he rode towards Mayfield, the image of Susannah before him. He was tired of working in the fields in this weather, and had taken a day off, hoping to see the owner of the face that continued to haunt his dreams.

Having arrived at the house, he left Damsel in the hands of the groom, and the maid took his hat and cloak as he entered the hall. He was ushered into the parlour. Elizabeth put down the book she was reading and rose from the couch by the fire. She came to greet him, her fresh face flushed with pleasure.

"William, what a nice surprise – and you're soaked – come by the fire and dry yourself. Mother is in her chamber today. She has a headache. The children are in the nursery, but Jeremy is around somewhere. I expect he'll come to see who the visitor is! How are you?" William's heart had sunk with disappointment.

"Fair to middling thank thee, Elizabeth. I be sorry to hear about thy muvver. Behopes 'tis naught serious. Be ye alright?"

"Yes, but I'm aching to go out riding with my brothers. The weather is so unpleasant. Mother won't let us out in the rain and wind." She sat down again, and William stood with his back to the fire, his hands clasped behind him. He was afraid to sit on the soft furnishings in his wet clothes.

"'Tis unaccountable coarse for April. The crops be failing this year. The seed's lamentable slow to come up, 'tis so cold, though the grass be growing well."

"That must be a worry for you. My brother John is gone to Ingerstone to take over our father's estate there. He'll have to learn about farming, though I expect there'll be a bailiff to manage it for him." She paused, looking thoughtful.

"Will he be biding there?" asked William.

"Oh yes. There's nothing for John to do here. Susan will also be leaving us soon. She's to marry Simon Rumney, who lives in Lamberhurst."

"Thy muvver told us last time I was here. Will the wedding be in Mayfild?"

She became animated again. "Yes, in one month from now. Our brother-in-law John Maynard will marry them. And did you know that Margaret's expecting her second child, due in August?"

William smiled. "Nay, that is good news."

Jeremy entered the room and his face lit up. "William, you've come all this way on such a wet day. Are you well?" He came to the fire and, warmed himself.

"Bravely thank thee, I be main glad to see thee." William shook Jeremy by the hand.

"I've been playing chess with Timothy. I cannot beat him, try as I might!"

William ventured to say, "Timothy seems quiet. Be he alright?"

Elizabeth and Jeremy's faces closed up, and Elizabeth said hastily, "He's very clever, and stays in his room most of the time, studying."

"He's not very sociable, and has difficulty meeting people," said Jeremy. "Elizabeth, have you told William that our sister Margaret's expecting another child? She and John are very excited. John dotes on Margaret and fusses over her like a mother hen!"

Elizabeth laughed. "Margaret's becoming a little impatient, and he is so distracted she has to remind him to prepare his sermons. One day he was late going to church, and kept the congregation waiting!"

"Come, William, we'll teach thee to play backgammon, and we'll have some refreshment before you leave us." Jeremy led William over to some seats round a small table, on which there was a backgammon board. "Are you quite dry now?"

"I be hem comfortable thank thee." William was a little nervous about playing a game. He wasn't sure whether he could master such a competitive activity. But his two hosts were patient, and he began to relax and enjoy himself, realising that it was no more difficult than planning a day's work on the farm.

After they'd partaken of a light drink and some small sweet biscuits, William felt it was time to go. The rain had eased and the wind had dropped. His cloak and hat were quite dry when he put them on, and warm from the heat of the fire over which they'd been hanging.

"Please to give my compliments to Mistus Lucke. I be ernful that I didn't see 'er," he said as he bid them goodbye. They weren't to know how disappointed he was, and he rode away thinking of her, having spent time so close, yet so far.

Deep in his reverie, he was startled when a hooded rider stepped out onto the road in front of him, apparently from nowhere. Damsel shied nervously, and grunted.

The voice was as a snake sliding from a cold cave. "Hello farmer's boy, did I frighten thee?" William shivered, and recognised the dark eyes as belonging to Timothy, who went on, "Should you not be labouring in your fields? What d'ye want with my family?" he said sharply.

"I – I..." William couldn't answer.

"Do you know that my brother and sister laugh and joke about thee? They mock thy rude farmer's speech and thy rough way of dressing," sneered Timothy.

"I did believe they liked me. They be upstanding people. They wouldn't be so unkind," said William.

"That's because they know how to behave in company. It's all pretence." A sly smile stretched Timothy's tight cheeks, disappearing as suddenly. His voice rose in anger, "We don't want you in our house. I'll thank thee not to come again. Go back to your fields and your beasts where you belong." He galloped away, laughing.

William sat on Damsel, looking after Timothy in disbelief. He'd felt that Elizabeth and Jeremy were his friends. The thought of never seeing Susannah again was devastating. He rode home swiftly, his cloak flying out behind him, in a whirl of pain and anger at himself for having been drawn into this sinister family. How could he have made such a fool of himself? They'd given him the impression that Timothy was a frail, timid person. They had deceived him!

Uncle Thomas was home after a day in the Courts. He came to the dinner table looking concerned. He'd been talking to the Justices of the Peace, who were country squires, some of whom were also Members of Parliament.

After giving thanks for their food he sat down and said, "There be bad news of Lunnon. The King and Parlyment be disagreeing. There be plague and poverty. People be dying in the streets. There's seemingly no end to it."

William felt remote from politics and all that was happening in the capital. But this must be important if Uncle Thomas was so worried.

"What do the King and Parlyment disagree over, Uncle?"

"Parlyment wants to change the tax laws, to help the poor. But King Charles wants to charge more taxes, so that he has more money for his wars with Spain. Parlyment refuse to pay the King's bills."

Martha added, "I've heard tell as the King and his friend Lord Buckingham spend all the money on fancy rigging and jewels, and ornaments for their grand abodes. They have grand parties all-on. I be well avised they all be Papists."

William was reminded of the last time he went into Wadhurst. "I heard a preacher in the market place shouting out about the bad omens that's abroad. There've been rocks falling from the sky, signifying the wrath of God. He said they were on account of the sins of the rich and powerful, and that the only escape from damnation is repentance."

"'Tis said the Papist Queen's barren," rejoined Martha. "No good will come of that marriage."

Thomas went on, "Parlyment has accused Lord Buckingham of the ruination of the Navy, and of stealing from the King, among other things. They want an enquiry, but the King has imprisoned the complainants in the Tower, and threatened to dissolve

Parlyment and rule hisself. That would make things worse for the poor people."

William asked, "What's to be done, Uncle?"

"We must keep our faith, Will," answered Thomas. "Thanks be we're far away from Lunnon. Though we'll have to pay the King's taxes, and be worse for it."

Chapter 13

The weather continued cold and wet. The haymaking was disastrous, with much of the hay lying out in the fields going mouldy. The corn didn't ripen, and people feared there would be a poor harvest, and a danger of famine. This was another bad omen. The church authorities declared that there should be a day of public fast, with prayers for sunshine, and the ripening of the corn. On the appointed day, August the second, they all went to their churches and prayed, asking for forgiveness for their sins. They ate nothing all day.

In the afternoon, Uncle Thomas and Martha were sitting quietly with their own thoughts in the gloomy hall. Thomas was reading the Bible and Martha was sewing. William got up and walked up and down restlessly, not able to settle himself to anything. Life was all doom and gloom at present. Even the light of his life had been denied him. He remembered Susannah's face and touch, her voice and the way she listened to all he had to say. He felt deeply sad, and prayed silently for help to bear this burden.

A shaft of sunshine lit up the room. Tiny motes of dust twinkled and danced around them. Martha and Thomas got up excitedly and rushed outside, where the sun was shining brightly, and steam rose from the buildings and the roofs. William joined them. They shouted and danced in the warmth, and hugged each other. Thomas said they should go back to church, and give thanks. On their way they met many people in the street going in the same direction, laughing and rejoicing.

It stayed fine all that month, and though the harvest was late, the yield was good.

The sun shone brightly on the yellow corn, which fell in swathes under the swishing scythes. The men, in round frocks and wide brimmed hats, sang the ballad of John Barleycorn to the rhythm of their sweeping scythes through the standing corn, which fell in tidy lines as they walked forward, legs astride:

...Then they let him lie for a very long time
'Till the rain from heaven did fall,
Then little Sir John sprung up his head,
And soon amazed them all.
They let him stand till midsummer
Til he looked both pale and wan,
And little Sir John he growed a long beard
And so became a man...

There was laughter and shouting as the young people gathered the cut corn into sheaves, tied them tightly to form a waist, and propped them together into stooks. Children chased the mice and rabbits, which made a dash for it when their hiding places in the corn were revealed. The women brought napkins wrapped around the baits of cheese, bread and apples for the hungry workers.

William was in a line of men, doing his best to handle the scythe. He also had half an eye on Jane Longley, who was carrying the sheaves to be stooked. He'd met her many times since he came to Lamberhurst, when she stayed with her Uncle John Longley. But he'd never noticed how bonny she was; fresh-faced, with sparkling blue eyes and fair hair, tied back today with a gaily coloured scarf. At last he stopped cutting and handed the scythe to his friend Gregory Dyne, who had just arrived. He strode over to where Martha was binding the sheaves, and asked where she'd laid the bait, as he was thirsty.

"Me bundle be yanger," she said, pointing to the edge of the field. "There's a costrel of ale there, and I'll warrant Mary and Michael will want some." William turned to go, but Martha called after him, "There be news from Mayfild." He turned back, and felt himself go cold. Martha continued, "The day the sun came back, Mr Maynard announced in his thanksgiving service in church that his wife, Margaret, was delivered of a baby boy that day. They're calling him John. I thought ye'd like to know that, seeing as ye're friendly with the fambly." She turned back to her sheaf binding and gossiping, and appeared not to notice William's distress.

He quickly pushed the resurfaced pain to the back of his mind. He'd been trying to forget Susannah and her family. He found the bundle of food, and carried it to where his brother and sister were making stooks. Then he called to Jane and her cousin Robert to come and join them. They sat down on the prickly stubble and tucked into bread and cheese, and apples and plums from the orchard. Jane caught William looking at her and she blushed. He felt a stirring in his chest, which was not at all unpleasant.

"Will ye be coming to harvest supper tomorrow, Jane?" he asked, handing her the costrel of ale.

She took it, had a drink and said, "Surely. I be biding with Uncle a few days. Where will it be this year?"

"In our close at the Slade," said William. "Behopes the rain'll keep off."

Jane turned to Mary, handing her the ale, "Will ye be there, Mary?"

"We surely will. We wouldn't miss it, would we, Michael?" she said.

"Nay," said Michael with his mouth full. "We'll be there."

During the next two days, work continued in the fields, going from one farm to the other, until all the corn was gathered. They finished at John Longley's farm late in the afternoon. William stopped work before the others. The sun was beginning to lose its heat, and their shadows lengthened as he walked with Martha and Mary back to the Slade to prepare for the feast. Ned was already there, having collected steddles and benches from other farms and was setting them up in the close. Martha and Mary went in to prepare the pies and puddings, bread, soup and cakes. The men trundled barrels of ale from the buttery, and musicians came and struck up with their fiddles, drums and whistles. The workers arrived, hot and tired after another day in the fields. The first mug of ale revived them, and the music raised their spirits.

William filled three mugs and settled himself on a bench alongside Jane, with Mary on his other side. They tucked into the food.

"'Tis a pity Edward weren't interested in coming," he said to Mary.

Mary sighed, "Edward's out of favour with Farder. He and 'is friends stole a barrel of ale from the buttery and took it abroad. They was all night supping it."

William was shocked. "How did Farder take it? I'll wager he were justabout mad."

"Ed laid up for two days, I rackon to sober up afore coming home. By then Farder had discovered the missing barrel. He worked out who took it, and he questioned Ed. Ed confessed and was given a gurt larruping. Then Farder brought him to face the fambly and told us what he'd done, and that if any child of his behaved in such a way he would be given the lowly tasks he deserved. He's forbid to leave the house for a week, and has to work on the farm, cleaning out the beasts."

William didn't recognise this picture of his brother. He now felt completely alienated, and wondered what would become of Ed.

They brought themselves back to the merrymaking and food. They jostled with their friends, storytelling, teasing and joking. Faces grew red as the apples, and when they got up to dance some found themselves on the floor. Young men and women paired up, and William enticed Jane to join in the dancing. He felt a great tenderness towards her as their hands and bodies touched, weaving through the sets and prancing down the avenues of people. When it was time for Jane to go, he walked her to the garden gate. They squeezed each other's hands as they said "Good night", and William lingered there, watching her as she walked down the road in the moonlight.

Chapter 14

As he came back up the garden path to the house, William thought he could smell smoke, and went through the yard to make sure all was in order. He turned the corner towards the haystacks, and saw a flickering light reflected on the brick wall of the house. The yard was lit up and one stack was ablaze. He watched for a moment in horror. The flames licked high, sending sparks into the night sky. There was a tremendous crackling and roaring as the hot air rose and spread, carrying pieces of dry hay, which floated up as they burnt red.

"There be dragons," William breathed, as he thought of the precious hay they'd cut and gathered for winter fodder, now being destroyed. He recovered his senses, and ran round to the well, shouting for help, "The hay be afire! Fetch pails dracly-minute."

There were still a few people around the table in the close. They roused themselves from their semi-consciousness and stumbled over to the milk-house to collect pails. They were too slow. William saw Robert Longley follow him to the milk-house, and handed him a pail of water, then Greg Dyne and Michael tripped over each other in their haste. Ned and Adam organised a chain of men from the well to the haystacks, passing buckets along the line. William, at the well, hung each bucket on the hook and let it down into the water. Bringing it back up was heavier work. He unhooked each one and handed it to Ned, who handed it to the next in line, while William filled the next bucket. The air was filled with smoke being blown by the wind into the close.

Someone shouted, "The horses! They be screeling!"

William handed the next bucket to Ned, and asked him to take over at the well. He ran towards the house to find Uncle Thomas who had retired early. He'd been roused by Martha, and was already running over to the stable. The horses were rearing up and bucking against the door, screaming. William went to the corn store and brought a couple of sacks. They caught hold of the horses and covered their heads. This calmed them down enough to bring them out of the stable and lead them out into the croft, away from the smoke.

They came back to see figures passing the buckets along the line, silhouetted against the brightness of the burning stack.

Thomas said, "Will, take the hay knife and cut away the good part to save so much as ye can."

William found Adam and together they went to fetch the heavy knife from the skillon. It needed two of them to carry it. They took it to the burning stack. The heat by this time was unbearable, and they couldn't get near enough to use the hay knife.

The small amount of water coming out of each bucket was having little effect on the roaring flames. William had an idea. Not being able to make himself heard above the noise, he took a bucket of water from Robert Longley, who was about to throw it onto the fire. He grabbed hold of Robert's arm, and pulled him round to the good side of the stack, nearest its neighbour. At least they could stop the fire from spreading. The others followed and William took bucket after bucket, wetting the unburnt hay, hoping that the fire would reach no further. They developed a trancelike rhythm. Each man handed a full bucket to the next, and took an empty bucket going the other way. They became numb with fatigue, but carried on automatically, until eventually the fire sizzled and spat, meeting the soaked part of the stack. A heap of wet hay collapsed onto the hot embers. Acrid steam blew towards them. They carried on, coughing and shielding their stinging eyes with their sleeves.

At last there was only a pile of wet hay between William and the embers of the fire. He pushed this onto the glowing red remains of his haystack with his foot, jumping back to avoid the steam and smoke. The fire hissed and died. The others continued throwing water onto the embers until they were sure their job was done. They turned wearily back to the house, and to their homes, leaving William and Uncle Thomas watching the last of the smoke disappear into the night air.

After a long silence, Thomas said, "This didn't happen by chance, Will. Who would do this?"

There was a cold tightening in William's throat as he remembered the anger which simmered in his brother Edward's eyes the last time they met.

"I be afeared to say," he replied. He walked away into the darkness, needing some time to gather his thoughts and feelings, and to attempt to think logically about the events of the evening. He wandered down the whapple way into his copse, and sat among the cool trees, listening to the small animals scuffling in the undergrowth, and the occasional hoot of an owl. At last he went back to the house, but couldn't sleep, for his mind turned the thoughts over and over. What should he do about his relationship with Edward? He was hoping against hope that his suspicions would be proved mistaken.

William rose early and went to look at the damage. Ned and Adam were already there, kicking at the still warm black ashes.

"There be naught we can do about this prensley," said Ned, "Only one of the stacks were burnt, thanks be."

Adam spoke up, "Mus Will, I saw two men loping off towards Wad'rst on me ways home last night."

"Could ye tell who they was?" William took a deep breath.

"Nay, but they was young uns, no'but sixteen, seventeen. They was cheering and laughing as they went."

William considered for a moment. Then he said, "I be going to Wad'rst dracly. May be all day. Ye knows what's to be done here." He walked quickly to the stable, saddled up his mare and cantered off up the road, anger welling up from his stomach.

He called at Marlinge to begin his search, and found his father coming out to meet him.

"Farder, I've bad news. Whereabouts be Edward?"

"He be gone since yesterday. What's happened?" asked Richard.

"After harvest supper last night one of my haystacks were fired to the ground. I rackons Edward were there."

"He were housebound for stealing a barrel of ale," said Richard, "but he crept out after dark. We've not seen him since."

"Where do 'e go? Who do 'e keep company with? I must speak with him."

"I'll go along of thee," said Richard. "Leave thy mare in the close. We'll go afoot."

They made their way through the town, keeping their eyes open as they went. William was relieved that he wasn't alone. He didn't want to get involved in a drunken brawl. They looked in a couple of alehouses, with no success. There was a hullabaloo coming from The Queen's Head, which was overflowing with tipsy men. As they drew closer they realised there was a fight going on. The noise stopped. The men at the door moved to one side, and two came tumbling out, followed by the landlord who used his foot to help them on their way. One of them struggled to his feet, the other lay still and was subjected to a final kick from his opponent who then stumbled off down the street. William recognised Edward, and he and his father ran towards the recumbent body to examine the damage. Ed didn't stir. William checked his breathing, which was feeble but regular. He gasped at the fumes coming from his brother's mouth. They were certainly not going to get any sense out of him for some time.

"I'll go and fetch my mare," he said, and his father stayed by Edward to prevent any further violence. They carried Ed back to Marlinge on Damsel, and laid him on his cot in his chamber. The family gathered in the hall to discuss the events of the last three days. Mary went to bathe her brother's wounds and to make sure there were no serious injuries.

It wasn't until the afternoon that they heard Edward stirring, and William went upstairs to talk to him. As he entered the room, his brother raised himself painfully onto his elbow and looked alarmed on seeing William.

"Ye've come to give us a larruping I rackon." he said.

"Somebody did the job for us by the look of thee," William replied. "I must talk with thee, man to man, Ed. Get thee up, and look at us straight."

Edward, surprised at this approach, sat up on the edge of the bed and ran his fingers through his hair. William sat on a nearby stool and regarded the wreck of his childhood companion. His anger and hurt slid away.

"D'ye recall the day we saw the ironworks on the road back from Lamb'rst?" he asked. Ed nodded and looked down at the floor.

"I believe I heard thee say then, ye would be hunting and killing dragons." Ed nodded again, pain contorting his face.

"Ye was a sight more of a man then, than ye be now," continued William. "I trusted thee and believed in thee. You was in charge." Tears began to trickle down Ed's face.

William raised his voice, angry again to see his brother so broken. "I rackons ye've swallowed the dragon, en *he* be in charge of *thee*." He couldn't bear to watch, and left the room to allow Edward to consider what William had said.

Downstairs, he said to the family, "I'd best be bodging," not wanting to discuss the matter further. He looked at his father, whose face was still burning with anger. Hoping he wouldn't be too hard on Edward, as he knew that wouldn't be the solution, he said, "Let be how 'twill," and left the house.

It took several weeks for the anger smouldering in William's breast to die down. There was nothing anyone could do about Edward. How could he have become a drunken lout and a disgrace to the family? William felt that he could never trust his brother again.

Chapter 15   1628

In a clearing in the copse there was a mound, with a blanket of turves covering the cordwood beneath. This was the charcoal burner's pet, or clamp, which was cooking steadily. William found Earl mothering it with loving care. The old man was bending over, closing up some of the smoking holes, and opening more in different places. William stood and watched for a while, knowing that if this job wasn't carried out precisely, the fire within would burn too hot, and the coles would be wasted. Sensing his presence, Earl looked up, revealing a brown and wrinkled face resembling a rotten apple. But the eyes twinkled, and one of the wrinkles split into a smile showing that this old apple was anything but rotten, though the teeth that remained in his mouth had seen better days.

"Good day to thee, Mus William. She be going bravely now."

"I see there be some cords left over," observed William. "One pet of coles will be plenty for us. I rackon I'll take the rest to sell to the ironworks, Earl."

"As ye wish. I'll be finished up here in a day or two then," and he turned back to his pet.

William went to get the cart and loaded it with cordwood. Adam came with him to the ironworks as a witness to the business deal. They rolled down the steep rough track that led to the furnace, and William was reminded of the day long ago when he and Edward had their first view of the place. It wasn't so frightening now. He found the foreman and brought him over to look at his load, hoping to get enough for it to pay the charcoal burner and have some profit.

Soon the deal was done and they took the cart to the wood store to be unloaded, with the help of one of the ironworkers. William was astonished to find himself face-to-face with his brother Edward. His clothing was in tatters, he was dirty and greasy, but standing upright and looking strong and healthy. He had not been seen in Wadhurst since the aftermath of the fire, almost two years ago.

Edward smiled. "I be fighting the dragons," he said, offering his hand to William. William took it and held it for a moment, while he slowly recovered from the shock.

He swallowed. "Whereabouts be ye biding, Ed?" he asked.

"Ye don't want to know," replied Ed. He turned away and started unloading the cordwood. William and Adam gave him a hand. When the cart was empty, Ed gave them a wave and went back to work by the furnace. William watched him go, feeling the old loyalty and affection bubbling up. It certainly looked as if Edward had reformed. But could he be trusted? Adam brought the cart round. They climbed in and pointed Bess in the direction of home.

It was a dark winter evening and William and his Uncle were sitting at the table in the hall. William had brought some books and pamphlets, the contents of which he wanted to discuss with his uncle. He'd strewn them on the table and was ready to start. Martha fastened the window shutters and bid them goodnight. The candles guttered in the draught as the door closed. Thomas put another log on the fire and sat back in his chair.

He said, "William, I be minded to talk to thee about me will. As you know, I've no descendants. But you've been like a son to me, and I wish thee to have the Slade when I be gone." He paused, and looked at William.

William's heart missed a beat. He allowed the words to sink in. "Uncle, I never thought… That be a wonderful gift. Thank thee."

Thomas continued, "We've worked hard on the farm together, and I believe you'll manage it as I would wish. Hopefully in time ye'll have a fambly to pass it on to."

William's mind was in a whirl. He was overwhelmed with excitement and gratitude.

Thomas was speaking again. "As my heir, you'll also be my executor. This means that after my death you'll see to it that my wishes regarding my other property in Gowd'rst and Wad'rst be carried out according to this will. Your farder and brudder John will be overseers, and will help thee to do thy duty. We'll all meet to sign it when ye've read it."

William nodded as Uncle Thomas handed him the document. He sighed deeply. Before reading the will he said, "I'll do my best to carry out your wishes, Uncle, come the time. Hopefully 'twill not be for a long while." Thomas sat quietly, watching the burning logs glowing in the fire. As he read through the document, William pondered on his future as the owner of his own farm, and the family he would pass it to. His plans had taken on a different meaning now. He turned back to the table, where the books and pamphlets about the latest in farming practises were lying.

"Now, what d'ye think of this, Uncle?" he said eagerly, taking one of the pamphlets and showing it to Thomas. "This new plant, clover. He can be grown in the summer, and harvested for winter fother for the beasts. That'll mean we can keep more beasts and don't have to slaughter them afore winter."

Thomas stroked his neatly cropped beard, turning the pages. "Mm, there be turmuts too. Ye can grow them for winter fother. Ye wouldn't have to depend on hay."

"Yus, and the clover, it says here, 'twill feed the land for more crops," said William pushing another booklet towards his uncle. He sat back in his chair, with his hands clasped behind his head. "More beasts over winter'll make more manner to dig in." He thought for a while. The population was increasing and towns were growing, with a need for more produce from the farms. He said, "More beasts gives us more meat and milk, butter and cheese." He scratched his head. "'Twill make more work, and we'll need a bigger cowstall."

"Don't rush into it lad," advised Thomas. "Consider these things for a while, and plan what to do first, plant fother crops, build cow stalls or keep beasts over winter?" They shuffled through the other pamphlets on the table reading them again.

William said at last, "'Twould make sense to grow crops first, to be ready for winter, and see how much yield we gets. Then we can work out how many beasts to keep, and how many we needs for meat over winter."

Thomas nodded. "I knows John Longley and John Kingswood be making plans to increase their yields. Ye should talk to them and find out what they be minded to be at. They both have many years' experience."

The next day they walked over the land around the farm, considering which fields were suitable for the first crops of turnips and clover, and planning a site for the new buildings they would need.

Going through the close, past the pigs, William said to his uncle, "Pigs and chickens be already grattening in the corn stubble for the grain left over after harvest. They be feeding the land with their droppings ready for the next crop. If we grow turmuts on that field, and follow this with pasture for the cattle and sheep the next year, the manner they leave can feed the soil for clover."

"That makes good sense," said Thomas. Ye can carry on growing hay for winter fother, and I believe some farmers are growing corn over winter, to give greater yields."

The more William thought about them, the better he liked these ideas. The following spring he sowed his first field of clover.

It was a fine market day, and William went to Wadhurst with Martha in the cart, carrying eggs, butter, cheese, bread and a fat hen in a chicken ped. The men had slaughtered a pig, half of which William had kept for their own use, preserving it with salt. They'd cut up the remaining half and were carrying it to market to be sold.

Wadhurst was crowded with carts and their drivers, all looking for a place to set up their standings. Shouts and the clatter of horses' hooves on the cobbles surrounded them. William and Martha found a space. They erected the standing and arranged the produce. When Martha sold the first item, a crock of butter, she kissed the coin, the 'hansel', spat on it, and put it in a pocket by itself for luck, as was the custom. William left Martha in charge and went off to find his brother Michael.

"Hey, Will!" He heard a shout, turned round, and there was his sister Mary. He went and greeted her. Mary had baskets with her ready to buy the family provisions. She put them on the ground while she told William the latest news.

"Did ye know Grammer Joane be failing? She be nigh on eighty years, would ye believe?"

William was concerned. "I'd best tell Uncle Thomas," he said. "He'll want to visit his muvver afore she passes on. 'Tis a great age, surely."

"She don't see too well, and she don't walk no more," said Mary shaking her head. "But she be cheerful. 'Twill not be long now, I rackon."

William waved and raised his hat to a friend passing by. "What about our Dorothee?" he asked, "I believe she be walking out with Cousin John Stapley."

Mary laughed excitedly. "Yus, they'll be wed 'forelong. They've been shouted in church these last two Sundays. You'll be coming to the wedding, I'll be bound."

"For certain sure indeed! She's made a good match there," chuckled William. He thought of Dorothee and her gentle ways and home-building talent. "She'll make a good mistus and muvver," he said.

The church bells chimed ten o'clock. Mary bent down to pick up her baskets, anxious to get on with her purchases.

William said, "Be Michael at home this morning? I've a mind to speak with him."

"Yus, 'e be minding the farm. Farder's here in town."

William waved goodbye and walked up the hill to Marlinge to find Michael. John was in the parlour, looking pale and tired. He smiled as William came in.

"Sorry to hear about Grammer," said William. "You was close to her, wasn't ye?" He sat down by John.

"She muvvered me when Dorothee and Mary was born. We've always been good friends. She understands when I be unwell. I shall miss her." He took a sip from the mug of ale he had in his hand.

Michael came in, flushed, with his dark hair tumbling round his face. "Hello, Will," he said. "The piglings got loose. They're unaccountable pesky to catch. How be ye?" He sat down at the table.

William turned to his younger brother. "I'll be needing another pair of hands at the Slade come the fall," he said. "D'ye think Farder can spare thee? I be minded to take thee on full-time, if ye be agreeable."

Michael's face lit up. "I be ready when ye wants us," he said. "There be less to do round here now the cattle have gone. Farder's running the farm down, as there'll be nobody to take over when he be gone." William looked over at John, his eyebrows raised.

"I'll not be farming 'ere," said John. "I'm not fit enough. We'll rent the land out to a neighbour."

Michael continued, "I'd be partial to come and work for thee, Will."

"We must ask Farder first," said William. "I'll tell thee dracly I be ready." He stood up to go, then he remembered. "I saw Edward t'other day. He were working in the foundry by Lamb'rst." The others looked surprised, and he explained what had happened.

Michael said, "He'll be needing money for his ale." He pursed his lips and nodded.

"Time I was getting back to Martha," William said, and left the house. He walked back into town. The produce was selling nicely. He went to look at the other standings to see who else was selling, and to compare prices and produce. As he walked round, he noticed that more people were dressed in the simple Puritan manner. The women were wearing grey or black dresses with high necks, and plain wide white collars. There was no lace now. The men wore tall black hats, and had cut their hair shorter, some doing away with their beards. He and Uncle Thomas had also changed their dress style some time ago, when at church or in town. This left people in no doubt that they were not Papists. He reflected that the effect had been to modify their behaviour. They felt less able to relax, and more conscious of the way they moved and walked. There was no temptation to admire a woman's breasts, as they were well covered.

He went to see if Nick was at home. Perhaps they could go and have a drink in the tavern and catch up with their news. He knocked on the door, and heard a woman's step. The door opened and Jane was there, wearing a grey dress with a white apron and cap. Her sleeves were rolled up and her hands were red. She blushed when she saw him.

"Hello, William. My brudder and farder be in town at the cattle market. Nick would be pleased to see thee."

William felt awkward. He hadn't expected to see Jane on her own. She was evidently busy with housework and it would not be proper to go into the house to talk to her alone, much as he would like to.

"Oh. I er…" He gulped. Good to see thee, Jane. I'll go and find him." He backed away from the door, hat in hand, until she had gone indoors. He turned and walked down the path, wondering why his knees had turned to jelly.

He found Nick in the cattle market and they went to the tavern. They talked about their lives these days. William hadn't noticed before how alike Nick and Jane were.

"Thy sister's growing to be a purty young wench, Nick," he said.

"Yus, and I rackons you two be partial, my friend. She flushes when I mention thy name!" Nick replied.

They discussed Jane's best traits, which were many. After a while, it was time to go and help Martha pack up and take her home. William said goodbye to Nick and went on his way.

He drove the cart round the corner and clattered into the yard at the Slade. He saw his uncle coming out of the stables, having just arrived home after a day in Maidstone. William slowed Bess down to a standstill and helped Martha off the cart. She took her purse and some purchases into the house.

Thomas came over. "Will, ye're back, How did ye get on?"

"Bravely, Uncle. We've brought nothing home except the takings, thanks be!" he said as he unhitched Bess from the cart. "I saw Mary and she said Grammer be failing,"

"I believed she would be last time I called. I'll go tomorrow." Thomas walked into the house.

William led Bess to the croft and put the cart away in the barn, before going in to refresh himself and reckon up what they'd earned today. He found it surprisingly difficult to concentrate. The image of Jane kept getting in the way.

Chapter 16

Thomas went to Wadhurst and stayed with his mother at Durgates until she died, a few days later.

"The funeral's tomorrow," he announced to William at breakfast the following day. Will ye come with us?"

"Surely, I'll come and pay my last respects, Uncle. She were a chipper old lady." He wondered whether Edward would be there.

The old house at Durgates shook itself free of years of living in the past, having watched its children grow up and leave one by one, until only Joanne remained with her mother. The old lady had now taken her leave. The family returned after the funeral to bid her rest in peace.

The house was unaccustomed to the activity and hum of voices. The stairs creaked with the pressure of many feet. Dusty cobwebs hanging from the beams waved around in the disturbed air, and the stone floors echoed with the footsteps of adult versions of its long-absent children.

As he entered the hall, William was reminded of the last time he'd been in this room. He looked over to the place where Susannah sat after the wedding of her daughter Margaret. He fancied he saw a fleeting glimpse of her serene beauty, as he'd seen her that first time they met. He felt a surge of regret, and brought himself back to the present.

Everyone had news to tell, and gossip to share. It was not often they met together like this. Cousin Richard was now Master here, and he and his Aunt Joanne had provided a goodly table of food for the guests. William took an empty platter and chose little puddings, cakes and bread, along with the other guests. Aunt Joanne was standing by to assist if need be. She had an unusual twinkle in her eyes, looking tired, but relaxed, as if relieved of a heavy burden. Being the only unmarried aunt, she had looked after William and his brothers and sisters after their mother died. She had been kind, but strict and would stand no nonsense. They respected her for it. Now, she was enjoying being a hostess for a change.

"This be a fine table of vittels, Aunt Joanne," William said to her. She nodded and smiled, and leaned over to pick up some spilt food.

Cousin Richard was pouring small ale into glasses for the ladies and tankards for the men. William collected his drink, and moved away across the crowded hall to find a space, and somewhere to put his drink down. He turned towards the centre of the room. There were many people he didn't recognise mingled with the familiar faces. The old hall shuddered with the noise of laughter and loud voices, which reverberated into the rafters. He was surprised to see everyone so happy. He had imagined that a funeral would be a sad affair.

Someone approached from behind. He turned to see Aunt Elizabeth Kingswood at his side. She was dressed in deep mourning.

"William, why is Edward not here?"

William found himself flinching at the mention of his wayward brother. How was he to explain his absence? "I ain't seen Edward in a long time, Aunt Kingswood. 'E be his own master now."

"But he were in church." William was shocked. Elizabeth continued, "Several people saw him. I be avised that he be banished from the house for bad behaviour."

"Ye'd best talk to Farder about that," William said. There was no reason why Ed shouldn't attend his grandmother's funeral. But William felt unaccountably anxious. He searched the room for Edward, and was relieved to see that he'd stayed away.

Catching sight of John Kingswood, he went over to join him. This was a man whose opinion he respected. He was talking to Thomas Haman, another yeoman farmer. Haman was younger and well built, with a florid face and a receding hairline. The hair on the sides of his head was ginger and frothy, flowing down his jaws towards his chin. He looked uncomfortable in his best clothes.

Kingswood was saying, "Have ye heard talk of the new practise of growing a plant called hops? 'Tis added to the brewing of ale. They say it do improve the taste and the ale keeps longer."

Haman nodded, and said with his mouth full, "Yus, me neighbour planted it this year. It be growing well in our cledgy land. I believe 'twere brought from Holland."

William joined in, "Will ye be growing hops, Mas Kingswood?"

Kingswood took a sip of ale before replying. "I be considering it surely. 'Twould be another way of making money, but 'twould need a barn to dry the hops." Then he asked, "Did ye plant the clover and turmuts, William?"

"Yus, they be growing bravely. We'll see what the beasts make of their new fother come winter." They all smiled and nodded.

Kingswood added, "Be sure not to let thy sheep in a field with clover. They be main partial to it, and will gorge themselves till they fill with wind."

Haman confirmed this alarming information. "The shepherds have a pricking tool to let the air out. 'Tis the only way to save them from certain death."

William was considering this when he saw Michael making his way towards him. He looked concerned and took William to one side.

"Will, I've heard talk that Edward was in church. D'ye think he's up to something?"

William's nerves were set on edge again. "What d'ye suppose he could be planning? Hopefully he'll keep away." He had a vision of Edward making an entrance in a state of inebriation and behaving badly. "Where did he go after church?"

Michael shook his head and shrugged. "He slipped out afore we all turned round. No-one saw him go."

"We'll keep an eye open and catch hold of him afore he's seen," said William. Michael nodded and moved towards the door.

Distracted by Aunt Margaret Barham, standing behind him, talking to her sister Aunt Dorothy Apps, William looked round. Margaret was a good deal more elderly than when he'd last seen her. But she still wore the fashionable clothes befitting her position in society. Dorothy looked permanently unhappy and downtrodden. They were talking about the death of their sister, Anne Stapley. Seeing William, Margaret asked him about their brother, Christopher. He gave them the latest news, then Mary Haman, a small, plump, younger woman bustled over with another snippet of news, "I just heard young Richard say 'e be walking out with Mary Burton," she announced.

"Oh, that'll be another wedding in the offing," said Margaret, nodding knowingly. "She be a cushti woman, and she comes from an upstanding fambly."

"'Twill be middling fine to see this old house with a fambly again," said Dorothy.

William couldn't keep his mind on the conversation and went to refill his platter, glancing at the door on the way. It opened. His heart lurched into his throat. But it was only Mr Hatley, arriving late, having tidied up the church after the funeral service.

It seemed that everyone was talking about Edward. The hall whispered, "Edward, Edward, Edward," as William pushed past his relatives. He felt stifled, needing some fresh air, but duty told him he must stay.

He passed his cousin Richard who was speaking to Uncle Thomas, and overheard him saying, "Uncle Thomas, did I hear ye be coming back to bide in Wad'rst"

"Yus," answered Uncle Thomas. "Young William be managing at the Slade. I be going to bide at Bedifields Hill prensley. 'Twill give him space to make a go of it. And I'll warrant he'll be courting young Jane Longley 'forelong. She'll not want me cluttering up her house."

William marvelled at the way news travelled. It had apparently arrived before the event! He moved away, before it was noticed that he had heard. He came upon his father talking to John Barham and some other guests.

Barham, who mixed with nobility, keeping abreast of the political situation, said, "Did ye hear about the Duke of Buckingham, who were the King's Lord High Admiral and advisor?" They all looked expectantly at him. Stephen Apps came and listened, always ready for a slice of scandal.

Barham leaned towards them, lowering his voice. "He's been murdered."

"How?" "When?" "Who would dare?" they said in chorus.

"He were in Portsmouth, about to embark on another useless battle, and waste men's lives again, when this Naval Officer comes up and stabs 'im."

There was a stunned pause. William had little interest in the political scene. He couldn't understand the intrigue and immoral behaviour of those he'd been taught to love and respect. The King was supposed to be next to God in the hierarchy. His mind wandered again and he looked over to the door. No sign of his brother, except for the whispers of the hall, "Edward", "Edward."

William's brother, John, was sitting by the fireplace, alone. William joined him. It was the only corner of the room where their grandmother was being remembered in grief. Their sister Mary came and sat with them.

"'Twill pass, John," she said. "Time will heal thy grief."

"Did ye see Edward in church today, Mary?" asked William. Mary and John looked at William in surprise.

"Nay," said Mary. "Aunt Haman asked us why he weren't here. I just said I haven't seen him for a while. She were fishing for a morsel of gossip I'll be bound."

"He'll have some explaining to do if he comes in here," commented John. "Everybody wants to know where 'e be these days."

The day drew to a close. The house disgorged its guests and sank back to rest and muse upon the recent gossip, the air in the hall still echoed with their voices.

William rode home with Uncle Thomas. "Edward was seen in church, Uncle," he said.

"That be good. There's hope for him if his grammer's funeral was important to him," said Thomas. William felt a fool. He hadn't thought of it like that, and he was pleased, too.

They rode into the yard, and Martha came hurrying out of the house to meet them, her eyes wide with distress. She twisted her hands in her apron.

"Oh Mus Thomas, Oh, Will, thanks be ye're back. There's trouble in the clover field, and I've been that worried. I don't know what to be at," and she threw her hands into the air. "Oh my, Oh my!"

Chapter 17

"It's not the sheep, is it?" William dismounted with visions of bloated sheep lying dying in the clover. He tethered Damsel and ran with Thomas to the clover field to find not sheep, but plumes of smoke puffing into the evening air, a light wind blowing them diagonally across the field. They opened the gate and went to examine the source of the smoke. It appeared that someone had lit a series of little fires among the new clover. The weather had been dry recently and the flames had taken light on the undergrowth. The dragon was smouldering in the clover plants slowly and persistently, without flames. There was nothing they could do to save it. The field was too far away from a source of water.

They walked round the field in silence, stamping on any tiny flames they saw.

"We'd best leave it be, Will," said Thomas. "Behopes 'twill not spread to the hedges. I be going to me bed." He made his way back to the house.

William lingered by his clover, watching its slow death until darkness masked the tragedy. He sat at the edge of the field, hugging his knees, listening to the crackles and hisses, watching the grey smoke, barely visible but painfully present, wafting into the night, shielding the stars. He knew he wouldn't sleep. He felt he needed to be there with his dying clover. His mind wandered back to the events of the day. He thought of Edward, and wondered whether he had come to the funeral only to check that William and his uncle were away from the Slade, before coming here. How would he have lit all those fires? He'd need a tinder box and straw to start them. It must have taken a long time. Would Edward have the patience to do this? If not, who else? He would probably never find out.

The day had brought a series of bad news and omens: the deaths of Aunt Stapley; sheep in clover fields; the murder of the most powerful man in England. What had been an exciting adventure had turned into a constant struggle against the elements. People he had trusted were not as they'd seemed. And now this. Uncle Thomas was being unrealistic about Edward. He did not understand William's fears and trepidations. His head fell forward onto his knees and for a time he dozed.

He woke with a jump. His neck ached and his legs were stiff. He unfolded himself painfully. A pale light chased away the darkness. The dragon puffed its last smoky breaths, leaving a haze over the field. William struggled to his feet and limped back to the house and to his cot, where he lay fully clothed until dawn lit his chamber, and he prepared himself for another day.

The following Sunday, William came out of church after the service, to find Uncle Thomas in the porch, talking to two strangers. Beyond them, out in the litten, he was disturbed to see Timothy Lucke hovering.

Uncle Thomas said, "William, have you met Susan and Simon Rumney? Susan is Susannah Luck's elder daughter."

"Nay. 'Tis good to meet thee Mistus Rumney and Mas Rumney." He shook hands with them.

Susan smiled and said, "I believe you've made friends with my brother and sister in Mayfield, William. I'm pleased to meet thee at last. Now that I live in Lamberhurst we'll be seeing more of each other, I hope." William wasn't quite sure whether to believe what these people said. But she seemed to be genuine, which increased his doubt about what Timothy had said to him. Glancing over Susan's shoulder, he saw Timothy watching them. Then he started walking away, down the path to the gate.

Susan saw it too, and said, "Oh dear, my brother Timothy's staying with us for a while, to give him a change of scene. We have to keep an eye on him, you know. I'd better catch up with him." She hurried away. Her husband looked at Thomas, raised his eyebrows in exasperation and turned to follow her, giving them a wave of his hand.

As they were walking back to the Slade, William was increasingly puzzled about Timothy's behaviour, and said, "Uncle, d'ye know anything about Timothy? Why is he so unaccountable sidy?"

"Nay, lad, I knows very little. He's always been like that. I mind when he were a liddle boy, there were a younger brother who died. Since then, the fambly's been hem protective of Timothy, but they'll not talk about it. I've tried to talk to him, but he don't say much. They say he's wunnerful learned, and studies all-on."

William was silent. He didn't want to say anything about his meeting with Timothy, which continued to haunt him. Now that his sister was living in Lamberhurst, there was a possibility they would come across each other sometimes. Timothy had looked daggers at him outside the church. William still felt angry with him for the things he had said, and longed to see Susannah again.

Part 4

William and Jane

Chapter 18   1630
Fifth year in the reign of King Charles 1

William had been seeing Jane more frequently lately, and he needed her company. There were things that had been troubling him. It was a fine September day, and he knew she was in Lamberhurst. He would take some time off. Dressed in his best, he walked over to the Longley's farm and knocked on the door. John Longley answered.

"May I speak with thee, Mas Longley?"

"Surely, come in, Will." They went into the parlour.

"I be minded to walk out with Jane today. Be ye agreeable, Sir?"

John Longley beamed at William. "I've been waiting to hear thee ask. I be main pleased to say 'yus' and I give thee both my blessing." They shook hands, and John went to find his niece. William waited in anticipation.

Jane came into the room. Her cheeks were flushed and she had a dimple in her right cheek when she smiled. He took a few steps and was at her side. She was dressed in a simple blue frock with a laced bodice and plain white collar. Her fair hair was tied up under a white linen cap. Her uncle left them alone.

"Be ye agreeable to come walking out with us today, Jane?"

"I'd like that considerable, surely," smiled Jane, and she tucked her hand under the crook of his elbow as they left the house. "Shall us go to the Down to gather blackberries?" she asked.

"We'll pick up some bait from Martha on the way," said William, feeling comfortable in her company. They strode over the road to the Slade together.

Martha put some bread and cheese in a bag for them, with a couple of apples, and they set off hand-in-hand along the road. They talked about Jane's fondness for her uncle, who was like a father to her. William spoke of his concerns about Edward and how he was fearful of another attack from that quarter.

"I feel I can never trust him again, like" he said.

"I knows how ye must feel, Will. But have ye any proof that he's done anything to hurt thee?"

He agreed he hadn't. "But I can't think who else would have lit those fires," he answered.

He told her about his plans for the farm. She showed a great interest. She asked questions and made suggestions. She was pleased that Michael would be coming to help with the farm work.

They reached the Down where there were furze bushes and rabbits frolicking. The tangled blackberry bushes were laden with fruit.

"There be skits of 'em," Jane cried. She broke away from William and ran on ahead. "I'll race thee up the hill," she called. William ran after her and they both scrambled and stumbled up the steep hill, avoiding rabbit holes and the prickly furze seedlings and laughing till they ran out of breath. Jane had had a head start, and they reached the top together. They flung themselves down onto the soft grass, panting and laughing.

When William got his breath back, he sat up and said, "Ye do gladden me heart, Jane. I haven't felt like this for years."

She rolled over onto her back and looked up at him. "'Tis good to see a smile on thy face. Ye be so serious when ye be labouring," she said.

He leaned on the arm nearest to her, and turned towards her. He gazed into her sparkling eyes and said, "'Tis a serious business on the farm." He wanted to bend over and kiss her, but knew it would awaken forbidden desires. He turned away. "But I miss Uncle Christopher. He were always up to something."

"Michael will be good for thee. He be a chipper lad," she said.

They sat closely together on the Down with a clear view of the valley and the river below. William looked in the bag Martha had given them, and handed a chunk of bread with some cheese to Jane. They munched their way through their bait, listening to the sounds of the countryside. There were skylarks trilling above them and the chuckle of hens below.

"Look, there's a cart making its way along the road down there," Jane said, pointing. "'Tis so tiny. See the dust it's raising." They could just hear the sound of the driver shouting to the horses. William was reminded of the little horse and cart he'd bought from Mr Upton, years ago. They heard the clanging of the anvil at the ironworks in the far distance, like the tolling of a bell. He thought of Edward down there in the heat and noise.

Then, with his hand over Jane's, they lay back and looked up at the blue sky, hearing nothing now but the buzzing of the insects around their heads. He was aware of her vibrant body next to him. He wanted to hold her and to love her, and have her with him always. The desire became too great and he sat up suddenly and gazed into the far distance. He heard her voice behind him.

"Let's go and pick those berries," she said.

He got to his feet and took her outstretched hands to pull her up. They tumbled down the hill, and set about the blackberries to take their minds off each other. They ate as many as they put in the crock that Martha had provided.

William looked at Jane, and said, "Open thy mouth." He laughed at her black tongue and poked his own out to show her.

She said, "Show us thy hands." They compared stained fingers.

Soon it was time to go back to the Slade with their pickings. They took them into the parlour, where Martha was baking bread.

She looked at the blackberries, and said, "My, that be a fine day's work. If ye picks us a few apples from the fruit garden, I can make thee a pie for thy dinner."

They went out and rejoiced at the abundance of the fruit this year. They collected enough apples for Martha, and more. While she was making the pie they took the rest into the applety loft, to store them away. They sat on the dusty floor under the sloping beams of the roof. It was intimate in the enclosed space. Again, William was tempted to hold Jane in his arms, but he suspected that he wouldn't be able to control what happened next if he did. She seemed to sense the tension.

"When I were a nipper I slept in a room like this," she said, taking the apples from the basket one by one, carefully checking for bruises and insect inhabitants, then placing them on the floor with a space all round each of them. "There were no room for us all in the chambers below. Me two brudders had one cot, and me sister and me shared the other."

"I shared a cot with Edward until I left home to come here," William said, following her example and getting on with the task in hand. They talked about their childhoods, their hopes and dreams and their likes and dislikes. The job done, they stood up and looked at the red and orange apples sitting neatly spaced, exhuding their delicious aroma. Then the young couple carried the empty basket down the wooden ladder to join Uncle Thomas and Martha in the parlour.

They all enjoyed a hearty dinner of mutton hot pot, followed by apple and blackberry pie. William thought that food had never tasted so good. After the meal he accompanied Jane back to her uncle's house. He agreed to take another day off as soon as he could. In the meantime, Jane said she would come and help with tasks around the farm whenever she was in Lamberhurst. William took both her hands in his and kissed them gently before bidding her goodnight.

"It's been a fine day, Jane," he said. "Thank thee."

"Ye've been proper upstanding, and good company, Will." She smiled happily. The dimple appeared again.

His heart was glowing as he walked back to the Slade. He felt so happy, he wanted to shout and sing. How could he bear to wait to see her again?

Chapter 19

Dorothee's big day was approaching. She had been living at Marlinge since Aunt Stapley died, as she wished to be married in Wadhurst from the family home. William rode over to see her. He was in love, and wanted to share his feelings with the family. As he came into the yard, he met Dorothee at the door.

"My, ye looks justabout blooming, Will," Dorothee said when she saw him. "Ye be courting a fair young maid, I'll be bound."

"That I be, Dorothee. Young Jane Longley it be, and a purtier wench ye never did see." William dismounted. "And ye be looking woundrous purty thyself." He tethered his horse, and came towards her.

But Dorothee stopped him going inside, looking suddenly sad. "I've bad news for thee, Will. Margaret Maynard died. She were giving birth to a little daughter, who died too." Tears coursed down her face, and she rested her head on William's shoulder. He put his arm round her, but didn't know what to say for a while. He thought how precious life is, and how easily and suddenly it can be destroyed.

He wiped his sister's tears away. "I be main ernful to hear that, Dorothee. But don't spoil thy beautiful face with sadness. 'Tis thy wedding day tomorrow. It should be the happiest day of thy life. Margaret were a dear friend of thine and she'd want thee to be happy."

Dorothee recovered herself, wiping her face on her apron. She said, "I hoped Susannah would come to the wedding, but she be in mourning now."

William's heart turned over at the mention of Susannah. "'Tis surely an ernful time for her."

Dorothee looked up and smiled. "Aunt Joanne's here, helping us get ready. Come indoors a moment."

The house was humming with activity. Aunt Joanne was flushed and occupying herself with a dozen different tasks: giving orders to Mary and Dorothee; telling Michael to keep out of the way, making sure all the best clothes were clean and trimmed, checking that there was enough food prepared for a big feast and that Dorothee's dress was ready. William had thought he would be able to spread his happy news. But the girls were pre-occupied. He gave up the idea of a chat and took a walk into Wadhurst.

Everything looked different, more homely. He returned the greetings of old acquaintances with affection. He didn't feel the chill in the air and he knew that life was good. In the distance, he caught sight of two figures supporting a third between them, who looked like a woman. Hoping that the two men were not up to any mischief, he quickened his pace, ready to be of assistance. As he drew nearer he realised that the two men were his brother John and Nick Longley. He ran to help. The woman was barely conscious. Her clothes were in rags and her hair bedraggled. It wasn't until he came close that he recognised his sister Jone. He took over the support of Jone from his brother. She weighed very little. Her body was mostly bones, and very weak.

"She were lying in a dick. Likely she were footing it from Teec'rst," said John, relieved of his burden. "She don't seem to know whereabouts she be, or who we be."

"Don't let the girls see 'er like this," said William. "They'll have a fit."

Nick said, "Jane be at home. We'll take 'er there. She'll know what to do."

John said he'd go home and prepare the family for the news.

William's heart thrilled when Jane came to the door and let them in. The three of them brought Jone round with a hot toddy, and fed her a little gruel. Jane took the young girl to her chamber and fetched a bowl of water and some towels. William and Nick sat by the fire and waited.

"'Tis main good of thee to help us out, Nick," said William.

"I be sorry it's turned out like this for the poor girl and glad I could do something. She's had a rough time, by the look of things." Nick looked grey and tired. Worry lines rutted his forehead.

"I were sorry to learn of thy farder's death, Nick. Ye'll be all-in doing the farm work, I'll be bound."

"There be more than I can manage, that's certain sure. My brudder Charles has his own farm over Teec'rst way and he can't help us. I don't know what to be at with this farm." The furrows on his brow deepened and he looked down at the floor.

"Ye must find a labourer, Nick. If I can manage on me own, so can ye. Ye be grieving at present but it will pass. Can Jane help thee?"

"Yus. She looks after the garden and chickens en all, and comes to the fields with me sometimes." Nick looked at William. "But ye be courting 'er, Will. I can't stop 'er leaving me."

"We'll take our time, Nick. 'Twill be a while afore we be ready to wed…That's if she'll have me!"

There was a movement on the stairs. Jone appeared wearing one of Jane's dresses and looking refreshed but frail. Her eyes reflected the horrors she had been through. She sat down by the fire. William got up and took the bowl from Jane and followed her into the dairy. She turned to him and smiled her dimpled smile. "I've done what I could for 'er, Will. She be covered in bruises and needs a few good meals and a rest. She be mortal afeared."

"Thank thee for doing that, Jane. I'll help 'er home and the girls'll muvver 'er. 'Tis a great shock to hear of thy father's death. I believe Nick be worritted about the farm..."

"Yus. 'E'll have to find a labourer or two. I'll be biding here to help 'im for now, Will."

"So I won't be seeing thee in Lamb'rst?"

"Nay. I'll come when I can. But I'll miss thy company till then."

William took her hands and kissed them. "Behopes 'twill not be long," he said. Disappointment washed through him like a cold shower. They went back into the parlour together. Jane went upstairs to fetch Jone's discarded rags and put them on the fire.

Jone was ready to tell her story. For the first year or two after her marriage to John Prior they had been reasonably happy, except that their baby died soon after birth. John resented the fact that he'd married her for nothing. They had very little money. John went looking for other women. Then he started abusing Jone.

The news of Dorothee's wedding the next day frightened her. "I feels bad about coming home," she said. "I be afeared Farder'll have us back to Teec'rst dracly-minute." She sobbed pitifully.

"You're not in no fit state to go back," William declared fiercely. "You don't have to go to the wedding. I rackon ye should lay up for a while. I'll take thee home." He helped Jone up from the settle. He thanked Jane and Nick and said he'd see them the next day. Dorothee and Mary were waiting when they arrived at Marlinge. They took Jone in lovingly, asking no questions. William rode home with mixed feelings. He was disappointed that he wouldn't see Susannah tomorrow. But he was excited about Dorothee's wedding. His heart was full of love for Jane. But he was sad and angry that his sister had been treated badly.

On the way to Wadhurst the next day, Thomas slowed his horse and turned to William, to ride by his side.

"I be going to bide at Bedifields tomorrow, Will. All my housel be taken there already, and the housekeeper be expecting us."

William looked at his uncle. The time had come at last. He'd be on his own, Master of the Slade. He felt a mixture of excitement, trepidation and sadness. But he smiled as he slowed Damsel to his uncle's pace.

"'Twill not be the same without thee, Uncle. I wish thee well."

Thomas said with a twinkle in his eye, "Nay, ye be itching to take charge, I'll warrant." They laughed together and rode on, comfortable in their friendship and trust.

They reached Wadhurst. Thomas trotted up the road to Marlinge to collect Aunt Joanne, to accompany her to church. William turned the other way towards the Longley's house, eager to see Jane. She came to the door in her best dress and bonnet decorated with ribbons, and curtsied to William, then twirled around to show herself off.

"My, ye're a wonder to behold!" he exclaimed, and offered her his arm. They walking jauntily down the path, with Nick following, and met Michael and John in the street. They came to the church litten, where the strewers were waiting for the bride. The girls were chatting excitedly together. They were in their best colourful dresses, their hair released from their caps, as this was a special occasion.

The church was packed with family and friends, and William and Jane made their way to the front row to stand beside Mary. The brothers shuffled in beside them, just in time to hear a shout from the door.

"She be a-coming!" The congregation turned to watch. The strewers came first, spreading many-coloured autumn leaves, bracken, and berried and evergreen branches on the ground in front of Dorothee, as she came through the litten and up the aisle with her father. She glowed with happiness, wearing a pale green muslin dress with a wide white collar. A rosebud at her breast, her dark hair in ringlets around her face, she wore a crown of flowers and carried a tussy-muzzy of herbs; a token of long years of happiness and abundance with her man.

William was full of pride and joy for his sister. He was aware of Jane's presence at his side. He turned to look at her and reached for her hand. She smiled and blushed.

After the ceremony the newly-weds walked up the aisle. They stood in the porch as the congregation greeted them on the way out into a drizzly rain. They donned cloaks and hoods. Those who were able ran up the street to Marlinge for the celebratory feast. As William came out of the porch with Jane on his arm, he thought he caught sight of a figure slipping from behind a bush in the litten. Probably a villager. There were others in the street, regardless of the rain, waiting to see the bride and groom come out, to throw them nosegays of heather and herbs, and to give them horseshoes for luck.

William and Jane hurried up the hill to avoid getting wet. They came through the door of Marlinge's hall into a warmly lit room with a roaring fire, welcoming the guests. The table was piled high with food for the wedding feast. The younger generations had already arrived, having run up ahead of the adults. They were warming themselves by the fire. The children were chasing each other round the table, screeching with laughter in their excitement. They stopped when the adults arrived. Everyone tucked in to the food, and Dorothy and John circulated among the guests.

William watched his father, Richard, talking to Uncle Thomas. It seemed to him that Uncle was stooping more than when he first knew him. Richard was a good head and shoulders taller now. William was overwhelmed with a feeling of fondness for the man who had spent the last twelve years teaching him all he needed to know. Life at the Slade would be different without him. It would be up to William to make a success, using all the skills he had learnt. His childhood ambition had been fulfilled.

When the company had finished eating, the table was cleared and pushed to one side. Musicians came with their pipes, fiddles and drums. The music started. The guests moved to the edges of the room. Dorothee and John came to the centre accompanied by cheering and clapping. They danced round the room and William took Jane's hand to join them, followed by others when they had found partners. The occasion was celebrated in reels and gallops, stripping the willow and dosy does. William and Jane whooped with joy every time they came together. He held her hands tight as they whirled round and round, her hair and skirts flying, before ducking under the arches, laughing all the way.

They danced long into the night until the newly-weds went home to Rotherfield. The cousins followed close behind to watch over them and to make sure the marriage was consummated that night. Woe betide John if it was not.

William said goodbye to Jane, knowing he would not be seeing her for some time. Nick took her home. Uncle Thomas had left some time ago. William went to find Damsel and rode home on his own. The rain had eased now, and stars were appearing through the clouds. The cool air kept him awake, and his thoughts turned to Edward with regret. How he would have enjoyed such a happy family day. But maybe not. He was mixing with different company now, and would have felt uncomfortable among gossiping aunts and wealthy cousins.

Chapter 20

The family were all sitting down to dinner at the Slade one spring evening. Jane had been helping with the newborn animals that day and had stayed to dine with them. William gazed at her fresh face across the table. Sometimes their eyes met and his heart lifted.

Michael told them about the new friends he'd made, and about the disturbance in the village the previous evening. "There be a wild woman, Peggy Paine. She do drink more than is good for 'er, and starts picking a fight with 'er man. A crowd gathers round and eggs 'em on. There be a great start-up, surely!"

"Them Paines, they be a troublesome couple, always up to no good," remarked Martha. "I believe 'e works down at the foundry."

Michael continued, "The old Headborough, 'e were fetched, with the constables. They catches hold of Peggy and her man, haves 'em away and locks 'em up in the stocks for the night. The others was ordered to bodge off home en keep quiet." He laughed at the memory.

William said, "You be sure and keep clear of they varmints Michael, d'ye hear?"

"Yus, Mus William," said Michael, trying to keep a straight face. But William was remembering the brawl from which he and his father had dragged Edward, and dreaded Michael going the same way.

Michael took a gulp of ale and looked at William. "And there's another thing. I were talking to my friend Mart'n and he were telling us that he's gardener for a man called Rumney, who has a gurt house outside Lamb'rst. We saw his wife and her brudder riding past while we was supping our ale. She's the lady you sees outside the church of a Sunday, Will."

William's throat went dry. He swallowed his mouthful carefully, and took a sip of ale before replying. "Yus, she be the eldest darter of Susannah Lucke, who lives in Mayfild. D'ye mind the wedding of her darter Margaret to the vicar, John Maynard?"

"Oh, that be where I saw the brudder. Mart'n says he be a hem personable young man. He oftentimes goes to talk to him in the garden. 'E says he's a friend of yours, and asks how ye be getting along with the farm on thy own."

William hesitated. He'd never mentioned his sinister brushes with Timothy to anyone. He wasn't sure he wanted to in the presence of Jane. He'd considered that part of his life was over, and that it had no relevance for the future. But he saw the others looking at him expectantly, and cleared his throat.

"I visited them at Mayfild once or twice, but they be over wealthy for the likes of us. Uncle Thomas visits Susannah now-en-again." He handed the plate of bread to Jane. "More bread, Jane? When are we going to meet that girl of Nick's? They say she be a comely wench."

William worried about Timothy's enquiries of the gardener. What were his intentions? The news made William's flesh creep. It seemed that he would never be able to shake Timothy off.

The weather continued wet until midsummer. William was going round taking stock of the corn store and the small amount of hay they had managed to save. He met his sisters Mary and Jone as they came into the yard. Mary brought Jone to meet William, and she responded to his greeting with a shy smile and a curtsy. They had not seen each other for a few months, and she seemed to have forgotten who he was. She still had a haunted look about her. William showed his sisters into the house, and called for Martha, who took Jone into the parlour to help her with the apple turnovers she was making. William and Mary sat in the hall.

"She be unaccountable confused, surely," remarked William.

"Yus, she needs muvvering all the time," sighed Mary. "'Tis an ernful shame. She sits huddled in a corner sometimes, rocking herself and weeping. We don't know whatever'll become of her. How be ye fairing, Will?"

"Fair to middling thank thee, Mary. The weather's unaccountable coarse. The hay lay clung in the fields, and now the corn be slow to ripen. It looks like being a bad harvest."

"These be hard times for farmers, surely." Mary wrinkled her brow and sighed.

"'Tis good to see thee, Mary. What's going on in Wad'rst?"

"Naught but smoky weather. The road's in a sorry state. They wagons from the ironworks be spoiling it for footing." She indicated her muddy shoes. "En Michael, be he behaving himself?"

William smiled. "Here he be now. Ye can ask him thyself."

Michael came into the hall, looking healthy and cheerful. His clothes were wet, his breeches covered in mud and he had kicked his boots off at the door.

"I be hem glad to see thee, Mary. Be ye well?"

"Middling, Michael, thanks be. I brought Jone to get her out of the house. She be with Martha in the parlour."

"She be biding at Marlinge, then? I rackoned the overseers would have had her back to Teece'urst."

"Nay. Farder went to the Justice with her and reported John Prior for mistreating her. They took him to Court and sent him to the House of Correction. Jone's in no fit state to live by herself."

Michael looked concerned, then said, "I'll go en show her the young animals. She always were more at home with the beasts." He went into the parlour, and William heard Jone say, "Michael!" with pleasure in her voice. He looked at Mary and they both went to the door, to see Jone and Michael embracing fondly. They left the parlour together by the back door.

"She be a child yet," said Martha. "'Tis pitiful."

Mary looked at William and said, "I'd be partial to bringing her over here regular like. It may be just what she needs."

He agreed. Mary would have to keep an eye on Jone, though. None of them could afford the time to look after her.

Chapter 21

William and Michael were driving five young steers to market in Wadhurst. Adam was to follow with Martha on the cart, with as much produce as they could spare. The air was muggy and rain clouds were gathering again. The cattle were making slow progress along the rough, muddy road. William heard a shout behind them, and turned to see Adam driving the horse and cart. He was also having difficulty driving. The cart lurched around on the stony surface, sliding in and out of the ruts.

He drew alongside. "Martha had to go to her sister on account of she's had an accident," shouted Adam. "I'll go and set up and bide while ye get's there."

William waved and nodded. He said to Michael. "We'll call on Jane to ask her to help with the standing. Adam can give us a hand with the beasts." Michael nodded as they watched the cart rumble away.

William said, "Behopes the cart don't lose no wheels on this road."

Wadhurst was busy. William's heart sank as he realised that most of the local farmers had the same idea as himself, and had brought cattle and sheep to sell. That would push the prices down. He may not manage to sell his at all. He and Michael drove the beasts into an enclosure in the cattle market. Then Michael went to find Adam, while William went to call on Jane. The now familiar warm glow spread through his body when she opened the door to him.

"Jane, can ye come and help Michael with the standing? Martha's with her sister, who's catched hurt.

"Surely, Will," she said. "Ye be worried. What be the trouble?"

As they walked down the road together, William explained, "I were wanting to get a good price for the beasts today. There's no corn from the harvest to speak of. We needs to buy some for bread, but 'tis hem costly."

"All the farmers be wanting to sell stock so that they don't have to fother them over winter. Maybe the squires and gentry will be here, hoping to buy cattle at low prices," Jane said.

They saw Michael through the crowd, and pushed their way towards him. He was already selling produce, enjoying the bantering and bartering with his customers, many of whom he knew well. He was pleased to see Jane, who took her place behind the standing, and waved to William as he went to find Adam and the beasts.

The cattle pens were full. The beasts were lowing and bleating to find themselves in such crowded conditions. The smell of dung hovered over them. The farmers surrounded the market, adding to the noise with their chatter and shouts to friends across the sea of heads. The men looking to buy cattle were poking and prodding the beasts with their sticks, examining them critically, their hats at an angle, straws and pipes in their mouths. As Jane had hoped, William saw a few wealthy landowners among them. Adam knew some of them.

"That be Squire Campion. He be well known around these parts. He has a gurt estate. He'll be farming on part of it, I rackon."

"And over there be Mas Fowle. He be ironmaster of Shoesmiths and other forges," said William.

The auctioneer climbed up to his raised platform, above the crowds, and called for hush. The bidding started. William found it difficult to follow the rattle coming from the auctioneer's mouth. He watched the bidders wave or nod as the prices rose. Some of them he recognised. He took note of who was daring to bid higher, and the cautious ones, who wanted a bargain. The cattle were selling, but prices were low. William became more anxious as the lots were sold, some for next to nothing. But as lots went under the hammer, the number of buyers dwindled. There were only two lots left, his own and John Tapsell's. There were four farmers bidding, and they forced the price higher. William and Adam held their breath, knowing that their stock was of a higher quality than that of Tapsell's. It was their turn next. Two of the bidders quit as the price rose. The other two bid against each other until one of them gave in. The price William got for his steers was higher than any other lot that day. William and Adam looked at each other and whooped with glee, shaking hands in delight.

They pushed through the crowds to collect the money. William felt a wave of relief wash over him as he held the notes in his hand. He shouted to Adam above the noise.

"This'll buy us a few bags of corn to tide us over, come on." They ran to the corn merchants, weaving their way through the jostling streets.

The corn store was empty apart from a few sacks in a dark corner. William's elation sank to the soles of his boots. He went to the man in charge.

"D'ye have any more corn?"

"Nay, ye're too late. All sold. That in the corner be mine, in case ye're wondering, like." And he started shutting the doors of the corn store.

"D'ye know anyone else selling corn?" William asked, though he knew it was unlikely.

"Not unless ye care to fetch it from Teec'rst. I've got another store there. Had a delivery from Holland yusterday."

"Be ye going there prensley?" asked Adam.

"I be going to the tavern anon. I ain't had aught to drink all day," said the corn merchant. Then he looked at them both critically with narrowed eyes. "Mm, ye look like upstanding men. D'ye have aught to pay for it? How much corn d'ye want?"

"As much as this will buy," said William quickly, showing his bundle of notes.

"Gimme an hour or so, en come back here." The merchant touched the side of his nose and winked, then slammed the last door shut, locked it with a big padlock and ambled down the road to the alehouse.

When all William's produce was sold and the market was packing up, he said goodbye to Jane with a squeeze of her hand. Adam led Bess between the shafts of the cart, and Michael and William jumped in. Adam drove them down to the corn store. The corn merchant had miraculously whistled up enough bags of corn to fill the cart. William and Adam examined it carefully and were satisfied with its reasonable quality before loading it up. William bartered and brought the price down. He paid the merchant and found he had some money left over. He jumped up into the cart. Adam called 'stan'fast', as Bess pulled the cart forward with a jerk. They triumphantly made their way home.

It was damp in the copse in the misty twilight. Leaves of all colours were floating to the ground, covering their predecessors with a whisper. The ends of the branches held drips of water, reluctant to let go. William sat on a rotting tree trunk, fallen years ago. He breathed the cool air and listened to the rustles of movement in the undergrowth, feeling the peace. He took from his mouth the piece of grass he'd been chewing, and leaning his forearms on his knees, he absently twirled it between his finger and thumb.

He had loathed slaughtering his beasts. The noise, the mess and the smell was revolting to him. He felt he had let his animals down, pigs he had nurtured from birth, sheep he remembered as lambs, skipping about in the meadow, each with its own personality. But it had to be done. Otherwise they would all go hungry. But this year he had grown good crops of clover and turnips. And they were been able to buy more corn with the money he got from the sale of the meat. There was a supply of salted pork hanging in the brew house. He had kept his herd of cows for milk for the family, with some over to share out among the poor.

The most important thing in his life was the farm. But it belonged to the family. He was the custodian, and he was responsible for maintaining it in good order, ready to be passed on to future generations. He was the only one in the family who had any prospect of producing heirs at present. For this he needed a wife.

An image of Jane came into his mind; the way she held her head on one side when asking a question, the dimple in her cheek when she smiled. How he longed for her to be by his side as his wife. But this last year had been difficult, and the winter wasn't going to be easy, with only enough food for the three of them. He thought that to ask Jane to be wed at this time wouldn't be fair. Would it?

But he would be twenty-one next year. Time was passing. Maybe, come spring…?

Chapter 22

The road from Lamberhurst to Wadhurst was dangerous for riders, and walking almost impossible, owing to state of the road. The ironmasters had a duty to repair and maintain the roads they damaged with their heavy vehicles. When William neared Wadhurst, he was pleased to notice that work had started. He was relieved to dismount and step into the Longley's parlour.

Jane hotted up a mug of ale for him in front of the fire, then came and sat down beside him on the settle. She waited to hear the purpose of his visit.

"Jane, I be minded for us to be wed 'forelong, if ye'll have us. Things be difficult at the Slade prensley, with the bad weather and all. Hopefully come spring she'll be kinder. Ye would make us a good wife and I cares for thee for certain sure."

Jane put her hand in his, and came closer, her face glowing. "Will, I surely cares for thee. To be thy Mistus is all I wants in the world. We can make things better at the Slade together." She lifted her face up to his, and he gathered her in his arms and kissed her.

Their hearts pounding and full of joy, they went out and made their way up the hill to Marlinge. It was November the fifth, and the church bells were ringing to commemorate the foiling of the gunpowder plot twenty-six years ago.

"They're ringing for us!" They laughed at the coincidence.

Father, Mary, John and Jone were all at home, and they cheered when the happy couple entered the house, anticipating their news. Everyone hugged and kissed them and even Jone caught the excitement. Richard poured them all a flagon of cider, and they stood in the parlour talking about their plans. Then it was time for them to go and arrange the wedding with Mr Hatley.

He was delighted for them. They decided that they should be married in February. Mr Hatley assured them that the damage to the church caused by the storm would be repaired by then.

They ran down the hill hand-in-hand to Bedifields. Uncle Thomas' face twinkled with joy to hear the news. "Bless thee both," he said. "Ye'll be good for each other."

Then his face fell. "I've heard some bad news today, from John Hatley," he said. "Young Jeremy Lucke in Mayfild died last week. He were failing for a while. It seems that his sister Elizabeth has the same illness. She's not expected to live."

William sat down and put his face in his hands.

Jane was alarmed, and went to comfort him. "What is it Will? D'ye know these people?"

William looked up. "They're the son and daughter of Susannah Lucke. They was very kind to me." He sat grieving for a few moments, then he said, "I must go and visit Elizabeth, afore she passes."

He got up, and he and Jane said goodbye to Uncle Thomas. The shine had gone out of the day for William. He took Jane back to her home, and assured her that he'd be seeing her again soon. Then he rode on to Mayfield with a heavy heart, not knowing how he would find the family after all this time.

He rode Damsel into the spacious entrance yard. The groom was busy in the stables on the other side. William tethered Damsel by the jossing block. As he rang the bell he noticed that the ornamental trees each side of the front door had grown considerably. They were now taller than him. The door opened and he was shown into the hall and told to wait. He removed his hat and stood looking around him, feeling nervous. The clavicord remained as it had been, but firmly closed; a portent of the future. The house felt hushed and sad.

At last the parlour door opened, and the maid asked him to enter. He walked forward into the room which had been so welcoming before. Not even the fire had the power to lift the gloom that had descended here. Someone was sitting in a high-backed chair, screened from view except for a black linen cap. He came round to face his hostess and managed to contain his astonishment. Susannah's once lustrous face was lined and flaccid. Her hair had streaks of grey among the fading copper.

She looked at him with dark eyes. "Come and sit down, William. How long is it since we saw you?"

"Oh Mistus Lucke, I knows I'm not welcome here. But I heard the news and had to come," said William, sitting on the edge of the seat. "I would talk with Elizabeth if I may."

Susannah looked down at her hands, which were folded on her lap. She hesitated before saying, "I've heard that you and Thomas are Papists, and I wouldn't have agreed to see you. But we have some sweet memories of you, and little harm can be done now."

William was incensed. "So that old heresay be running around yet. How did ye hear it?"

"Timothy heard it in Lamberhurst. Is it not true then?"

"For certain sure it is not. We be good, honest Puritans like yourselves, Ma'am."

Susannah's face relaxed. She put her hand out to hold William's arm. "Oh! I am so sorry. What a terrible mistake we made." She shook her head sadly, then said, "Elizabeth's in her chamber. She's frail, but cheerful. I'll ask Molly to show you up." She rang a small bell from the table by her side. The maid came and led William upstairs to a long corridor on the first floor, then opened one of the doors. Elizabeth lay against the pillows wearing a white nightgown and bonnet, looking pale and weak.

She looked up when William entered, and indicated a chair. "William, I thought I would never see you again. Are we still friends?"

"Most surely we be, Elizabeth. I haven't visited because I thought ye didn't care for me."

"Why did you think that, William?"

"I met Timothy on the road and he said I weren't welcome here. It seems he told your muvver that we be Papists. That is not so." He blurted it all out and then remembered that his friend was failing. "I be sorry to talk like this, Elizabeth. I be ernful to hear that Jeremy passed away. I did enjoy your company last time we met, and ye've both been kind to me."

Elizabeth smiled, and took William's hand from where he'd placed it on the bed, and held it in both of her own. "I'm sorry that our friendship was so short. I don't have long. This will be the last time I see thee, William." She paused.

"You must be very wary of Timothy. He can be spiteful and jealous. Something dreadful happened when he was a little boy which I cannot tell you about. If he thought that you knew about it, you would be in grave danger. Our father was a very strict man, and, to protect Timothy, he has never been allowed out without one or two of the family to escort him. This has become more difficult since father died and Timothy has grown up. Now, Jeremy and I will no longer be around to look after him, and he'll become more independent. Mother has no control over him at all. He adores her in such a possessive way. I dread to think what will become of them." Her face was sad and worried. William sat quietly, taking his time to absorb what she had said.

"Thanks be I came to thee in time," he said gently, and added, "I'll be careful."

"And now, how about you, William? How is Uncle Thomas, and the farm?"

"I be managing the farm on my own. Uncle Thomas bides in Wad'rst." He brightened up, remembering that it had been only this morning that he and Jane had become betrothed. "I be getting wed in Feb'ry, to Jane Longley."

"Oh that's wonderful news! I wish you a happy and prosperous life together. And please give my love to Uncle Thomas when you see him."

She reached over to a table on the other side of the bed. "I'm glad you came, William. I wanted to give you this to remember me by. I've written inside it." She handed him a little leather-bound book. When he opened it, he found it was a collection of poetry by John Donne. He was overwhelmed. He took her hand and kissed it in appreciation. Her eyes glowed, though she was looking tired now.

"Jeremy and I made our wills when we became ill. It's a condition of the blood, which runs in the family. There's no cure. I don't have much to give, and my brothers and sisters want for nothing. But I thought it would be a comfort to our poor brother-in-law, John Maynard, who is suffering so. He is such a bad timekeeper. I've bequeathed £10 for him buy a watch. Do you think that was a good idea?" she asked, looking up with eyebrows raised.

"'Tis very fitting, Elizabeth." He laughed softly with her. They sat quietly for a while before he sadly took his leave. He watched her sink back onto the pillows and close her eyes before he left the room.

As he went down to the parlour, he struggled to control his emotions. His distress wouldn't come near to that which Susannah would be feeling. She remained in her chair by the fire, and he went to sit with her again. They talked about the farm, and William's betrothal to Jane, and how Dorothee was getting on as John Stapley's wife. Then she told him about her four younger children remaining at home and their progress. Hester and Thomas were now in their teens, and Anne was growing up to be a precocious child, always quarrelling with her older sister Mary.

"Our poor John Maynard's grieving for his Margaret sorely," Susannah said. "He's burying himself in his work more and more. His sermons are impressive, and he's becoming strictly Puritan in his preaching."

William held Susannah's hand between both of his for a moment or two and she returned the gesture. Then he got up to go.

She came to the door to see him off. "Please ask Thomas to come and visit me now he has time to spare," she said. He nodded and walked out of the house. He shut the door behind him and turned to walk towards Damsel.

He'd been expecting to meet Timothy before he left, and it was little surprise when two cold hands grappled him from behind, one over his mouth, the other around his throat.

A voice hissed in his ear, "I thought I warned you not to come here again. I'm Master of this house now."

William gathered all his strength and thrust his left elbow back into his assailant's chest, then swung round to catch him a blow on the chin with his right fist. Timothy was winded, and fell to the ground. At that moment, the groom came out from the stable. Timothy's tone changed, and he whined, "Get this lout away from me. He hit me!" and he shielded his face with his forearm. William didn't wait for the groom to challenge him. He walked swiftly to where Damsel was tethered, mounted her, and cantered out of the yard.

When he reached Wadhurst, he called on Uncle Thomas and recounted his adventures.

"Susannah's in a sorry state, surely. It would help her to see thee, Uncle. Just keep out of the way of Timothy if ye can."

Chapter 23

February seemed a long way off, but William went about his work with a lighter heart and stronger purpose. They didn't go short at the Slade during the winter, thanks to his careful planning. He dreamt of driving Jane home after the wedding in a smart trap pulled by a little black pony. He put a small amount of money aside every week towards it. By the beginning of February, he'd saved enough to fulfil his dream, and he walked into Wadhurst to make the purchase. He was relieved that the road was being improved and travelling was easier. And the work to repair the church steeple would soon be finished. He drove back to the Slade, the pony dashing along the road pulling him on the smart shiny black trap. Exhilarated by the unaccustomed speed, he imagined Jane sitting beside him with her hair flying out behind her. On reaching home, he stowed the trap carefully away in the barn until the day arrived.

William woke early. It was still dark, but he could stay in bed no longer. He dressed in his work clothes, and went out to check the animals. He wanted nothing to go wrong today. The air was cold and still. There were patches of frost on the ground, and a thin skin of ice on the water in the well bucket. He took a deep breath before swilling it over his head and upper body. The shock of it made his blood run hot. He threw his round frock over his head, and rubbed his chest and face with it.

Damsel was warm and snug in her stable.

"I won't be needing thee today. 'Tis me wedding day." He fondled her head and ears, and replenished her haybag.

His new pony stamped his foot as if to say, "This is my special day too." William brushed his black coat until it shone, and gave him an extra helping of hay and a turnip to munch. Then he went round checking the cows and the oxen, the pigs and the sheep. He opened the barn door. The straw was loose on the floor; there had been no-one sleeping there for some time. He brought the trap out into the close, found a handful of sheep's wool and gave the shiny black paint a last polish.

Back in the house, he joined Martha and Michael for breakfast. When Adam and Ned arrived, they all gathered for morning prayers. Afterwards the men shook his hand and wished him a happy day, before going to attend to their work. William was overcome with nervous excitement, as Martha and Michael fussed round him to make sure he was dressed correctly in his new jacket, and that he had the ring with him. At last it was time to go.

He drove Martha with him in the trap to Wadhurst, feeling like a lord. The people all looked his way as he drove through the town. They arrived at Marlinge where he left the trap behind a wall in the yard, and tethered the pony in the close with a bundle of hay. Michael had followed with Bess and the cart for his and Martha's return journey. They all walked down to the church together.

At the chancel steps William's heart was thumping so strong he thought it would be heard. When Jane came up the aisle with her Uncle John Longley, William turned to look at her as she approached. Her blue dress matched her eyes. They made their promises and his hands shook as he put the ring on her finger. It was with joy that he turned with her and walked down the aisle. They would be together now, for ever.

They greeted the family in the porch as they came out of the church, and William was reminded of Dorothee's day the year before. She was showing signs that her first child was on the way.

Aunt Joanne was one of the first to come out. "I have to be in the hall afore the guests. There's food to be put on the table," she said, all of a fluster.

"Thank thee for doing this for us," said Jane. "There's not enough room at home."

"'Tis no bother, my dear," said Joanne, as she hurried away.

Mary came winding her way through the crowd, to catch up with Joanne. She gave William and Jane a loving greeting as she passed.

Father and John appeared with Michael and Martha, all smiles. "I be main proud of thee, Son," said Richard, and "welcome to the fambly," as he kissed Jane on the cheek, holding her hand rather longer than he need.

Uncle Thomas followed soon after, and shook their hands enthusiastically. "Struth, this be a woundrous happy day!" They watched him walking a little more sprightly than usual, through the litten after his brother.

William and Jane turned towards the next people to be greeted and found Nick with a young lady on his arm. "This be Ann," he introduced her. "We be going to be wed sometime soon," he announced.

Jane hugged him and said, "I be pleased ye'll not be on your own for long." She turned to Ann. "Be sure to keep him in good order, mind."

Cousin Richard and his wife and growing family came through, with the Aunts not far behind, their spouses bringing up the rear. There followed other cousins and friends. William was amazed at how many there were. He helped Jane with her hooded cloak to keep out the cold, and, as they came out of the porch, he glanced around the litten. Again, he thought he caught sight of someone slipping away behind the bushes. He blinked his eyes; he couldn't be sure if it was a memory from Dorothee's wedding, or whether it had happened again. Was it his imagination, or had Edward really been there? There was a crowd of townspeople waiting at the gate to greet them and wish them health and happiness, with gifts of nuts and berries.

William and Jane followed the last of the guests up the hill to Marlinge, hands clasped tightly. The day wasn't over yet. They had more entertaining to do before they could be alone together. As they came into the yard, William felt uneasy. He told Jane to wait a moment, and went over to where he'd left the trap.

It was gone.

He ran round to the close. There was empty space where the pony had been. He felt as if his dream had never become a reality. Anger welled up inside him. The pony trap had been stolen. Would Edward do a thing like that? No matter who had driven them away, his plan to surprise Jane was dashed to the ground. Bess and the cart were still there. They would get home, but not in such style. He remembered that Jane was standing out in the cold, waiting for him, unaware that things had gone so wrong. He must remain calm, and not spoil the day for her too. He walked back to her, thinking he must tell someone so that the constable could be summoned.

Jane was waiting. "Is anything wrong, Will? Ye look put-out."

"Nay, my love. Naught that can't be fixed." He took her arm and they entered the hall, which was buzzing with noise. A cheer rose up, and they were absorbed into the warm room. William said to Jane, "I must talk to Michael. I'll join thee dracly-minute." He went off to find his brother, who was the only other person who knew about the pony trap, and could give a description to the constable. There he was, talking to Mary by the table.

"Michael, I don't want to spoil the gladding, but the pony and trap be gone."

Shock blanched Michael's face. "Nay, gone? How? Stolen?"

"They aren't where I left them, that's all I knows. Somebody's played a prank. Maybe we'd better search the place."

"No-one would be so unkind. You must stay here. I'll go and search."

"Will ye do that for us? And if ye can't find them, can ye go and report it to the constable?"

"If I do, he'll want to come and ask questions. The whole company will find out."

"I don't want to spoil the day for Jane. She don't know about it. 'Twere to be a surprise," said William with a worried frown. They stood and thought about the situation. Finally William said, "I can't imagine anyone here taking them. Whoever did it is long gone. That pony goes fast. We'll leave it until morning. Ye'll have to take us home in the cart." A blanket of disappointment descended on him, and he forced himself to concentrate on the matter in hand. He poured himself a tumbler of ale, and one of cider for his new wife, bracing himself to be host to his guests.

The family were good at celebrations, William thought, as he and Jane mingled, picking up conversations here and there, and enjoying the congratulations and admiration of his new Mistus. He heard Uncle Thomas call for attention, and there was a hush. All heads turned one way.

"William, Jane, come here, I've a gift for thee." A path opened up, and they came to where Thomas was standing by the table. "First, I have to tell thee a story." William thought of Uncle Christopher, and tears came to his eyes. He swallowed them back. Thomas continued, "When this young man were no more than nine or ten he were always forgetting the time, and were late fetching the kine for milking. One time it cost him dear. The cows breached the hedge, and he were caught in a storm seeking them." He turned round and indicated to William an object on the table, covered in a cloth. "I be giving them this, so that it never happens again." William cautiously took the cloth away, to reveal a beautiful clock, which proceeded to chime the hour. William and Jane gasped with pleasure as they listened to the chimes. They embraced Thomas, as the company resumed their conversations, nodding their approval of a generous gift.

There was feasting and dancing. William's mind kept wandering back to the missing pony trap, and the effort he'd made to save up to buy it. He would never see it again, he felt sure of that. At last it was time to take his wife home. The guests came out to wave them off, and Michael ushered them into the cart, carrying the clock. He'd laid sacking on the floor for them to sit on, and Martha climbed up next to him on the driver's seat. William and Jane huddled close together to keep warm, and William thought that this was the best way to bring his beloved home. He leapt off when they arrived, lifted Jane down and carried her over the threshold, kissing her as he put her down in the hall.

"Welcome home, Mistus Lucke," he said, and went to refresh the fire in the parlour. Michael and Martha took Bess and the cart round to the close, and disappeared up to their chambers to leave the young couple to themselves. William and Jane sat down together, and talked quietly about their day. Jane went upstairs to unpack the chest she'd brought with her containing all her belongings, and to prepare herself for bed. William put their new clock on the dresser, and sat in the peace and quiet, listening to the soft ticking, going over his memories of the day. Anger burnt like coles in the pit of his stomach. Could it have been Edward? If not, who else? The only other person who had a grudge against him was Timothy, who was at church last Sunday, when the banns were shouted for the last time. He would know that William was soon to be married. He could easily picture Timothy hitching up the pony and driving the smart vehicle down the road towards Mayfield, chuckling to himself. William resolved to find out first thing in the morning.

Then he remembered that Jane would be waiting for him in his bed, and strode upstairs.

Chapter 24

William rolled over, and opened his eyes to see Jane's head in the dim light, beside his own on the pillow. She was awake, smiling comfortably. Her arm came across his body. He stroked her face and kissed her on the nose.

"Good morning, Mistus Lucke," he murmured. They lay in each other's arms awhile. He thought of the evening before. The anger had subsided now, but he still needed to find out more.

"I have to go into Wad'rst this morning. I'll be back for coger. You settle yourself in like." He kissed her on the mouth, and rolled out of bed, stretched, then grabbed his breeches, and pulled them on over his already rising penis. He wondered if it was going to be like this all the time now. He picked up his clothes and a towel, and went downstairs to cool himself off at the well.

He found Michael there already, dripping wet.

"I be going to Mayfild. I've an idea that Timothy may have something to say about my pony trap."

Michael rubbed himself dry on his towel. "Go and report it to the Headborough in Wad'rst first," he said. "Ye may be mistaken."

William nodded. "Maybe ye're right. I don't want Jane to know about this. Tell Martha not to mention it." He couldn't wait for breakfast and went to saddle up Damsel.

On the way to Wadhurst he thought about Michael's advice. If he went to Mayfield, he would feel awkward knocking on the door and having to explain to Susannah. He couldn't sneak in and prowl around, looking for his pony trap. It would be better if the Headborough made enquiries.

The Headborough was annoyed at being disturbed so early. "Why did ye not report this dracly ye saw the trap were missing? "

"'Twas my wedding day," explained William. "I didn't want to spoil it for the Mistus."

"Ye be young William Lucke from Lamb'rst, aren't ye? What d'ye want with a pony and trap? They be for Quality folks."

William could feel the anger mounting again. "Well, I've reported the theft to thee. I rackon Timothy Lucke of Mayfild may know something. I'd be obliged if ye'd go and see if it's on his property."

"'Twould be more fitting if ye sorted thy fambly matters out thyself. Besides, he don't need to go round stealing things like that. He's likely got one already."

William was exasperated, and turned to go.

The Headborough called after him, "We haven't seen aught of thy brudder Edward in these parts lately. He be likely disturbing the peace somewhere else, I rackon." He went inside and slammed the door after him.

On the way home, William considered what had been said. So Edward's reputation was dragging down the family name. There must be gossip in the town. He wanted to call on Uncle Thomas, but was afraid that he'd say the same as the Headborough, that he had ideas above his status. What *did* he want a pony trap for? It had been a frivolous idea. Would Jane really want to be driven around in a trap? She was a working girl. He was a working man. They would never have time to go parading around in it. He sent a silent prayer to the Almighty for forgiveness for his grand ideas, and urged

Damsel into a trot, towards his new responsibilities. He would now be addressed as Mas Lucke, as were all married men who employed a team of workers.

Soon the weather was warm enough to be ploughing and sowing crops for the next year. Sometimes William worked with Jane at his side, hoeing, fetching fodder, and sowing seeds. They talked little, sometimes hummed a tune together, moving in rhythmic harmony. Spring sun shining through the trees threw dappled shadows over them like cloaks. The bluebells in the copse excelled themselves. He told her they had appeared out of nowhere a year or so ago. They both delighted in the wonderful rich perfume hanging over the sea of blue. He stopped her now and again to show her a bird's feather, a newly opened flower, a butterfly sunning itself on the nettles, or to listen to the birds singing lustily. They marvelled together at the beauty around them, their perception enhanced by their love for each other.

Jane's presence at the Slade had given William the confidence to make plans for the future. One evening after dinner, when they were sitting in the parlour on their own before going to bed, he said, "I've a mind to start growing hops, Jane. They say they do well on this cledgy land, and they'd be a good back-up when the harvest fails. They'd bring money in for us to buy corn if need be."

Jane looked at him and nodded. "Hops ye could sell to the brewery in Lamb'rst. Where would ye take them to be dried?"

"I was thinking maybe we can get Thomas Dyne to convert the barn to an oast. Then we wouldn't need to take them to another farmer."

"D'ye know how much it would cost? Have ye got that much saved?" asked Jane.

"I'll be going to talk to Thomas tomorrow. 'Twill be costly, surely."

"The beasts have had a good many young this year," said Jane. "There'll be plenty to take to market." They sat quietly and considered the idea.

Then William said, "Our Jone's looking better. She's taken to birthing the animals well."

Jane looked thoughtful. "'Tis surely uncanny, the way she talks to them."

William said gently, "There be no harm in it. 'Tis main welcome if she can tell us when they be ailing, and what to be at." He looked at his wife, knowing that she felt uncomfortable when Jone was there. She went to work out in the fields away from the house to avoid her.

"It be a sort of witchcraft," she said. "I don't know what to make of it."

"You get on together nicely with Mary, don't ye?"

"Oh yus, Mary be a good friend. Though, I wouldn't like to cross her. She be hem masterful."

"She can be stubborn, I'll allow," laughed William.

The following Sunday they all went to church as usual, and after the service William was talking to Susan Rumney.

"How be your muvver, Susan?" he asked.

"She took the deaths of Jeremy and Elizabeth very badly. After her other bereavements it was the last straw. She'll be grieving for a long time. We hope that the children will help her, though she seems to have lost interest even in them. Timothy tends to smother her with attention, which doesn't help. I've persuaded him to come and stay with us for a while." She looked round and said, "Ah! There he is, talking to your new wife." William looked over to where she indicated. There was Timothy, leaning with his arm outstretched, his hand supported him against the stone archway to the porch with his back towards them. He was talking animatedly to Jane, blocking her way out to join William. She looked awkward and embarrassed. William was about to go and challenge Timothy.

At that moment Michael came out of the church, and, seeing Jane's predicament, he took hold of her arm on the way past, and said, "Come Jane, we be going to see thy grammer. She'll be waiting for us." He tipped his hat to Timothy and led Jane away.

Susan and William looked at each other. William said, "Good day to thee, Ma'am. Give me best wishes to thy muvver when ye sees her." He joined Michael and Jane, who were walking down the path to the road.

Jane said, "Whoever were that? I thought I wouldn't get away. I be obliged to thee, Michael."

"That were Timothy Lucke from Mayfild. Keep away from him, Jane. He's up to no good," said William.

"He gave me a bad feeling. I don't want to talk to him again." They all walked home together, relieving the tension by laughing at Michael's ingenious rescue strategy.

Chapter 25

William and Adam selected a field for the hop garden, and Adam and Michael ploughed it before spreading marl and dung. William left them ploughing it for the second time, and went into Wadhurst to buy hop plants. He left Bess and the cart in town, and walked up the hill to Marlinge. Mary was in the parlour, stirring the contents of a pot over the fire.

"Be ye alright, Mary?" he asked. "We ain't seen thee en Jone at the Slade for a while."

"We be alright now. But Farder's been failing these last four days. I believe he caught something in town. Then John went down with the same sickness. I've been feeding them gruel, en they be middling now. Jone don't look too good today. What brings thee to Wad'rst?"

"I be going to buy hop plants. The land's just about ready. I were hoping you and Jone would help plant them. But ye must stay here until ye all be well. I'll be bodging." Then he remembered. "By the way, Michael saw Edward in Lamb'rst t'other day with some pesky people. It may be 'e's living with them." He left Mary looking surprised and walked towards the town.

On passing Durgates, he caught sight of a black pony and trap standing in the forecourt of Mr Hatley's house, opposite. He stopped and stared. Surely this was his pony trap. If it was Timothy who had stolen it, what was he doing visiting Mr Hatley? Bursting with curiosity, William slipped into Durgates' entrance and round the corner where he had a good view of the Hatley's front door from a hiding place behind some bushes.

He had no idea how long he waited there. He started fidgeting and having to change position. His legs were growing stiff and there were pins and needles in his feet. He wasn't used to standing still. Presently he heard footsteps coming his way from town. He moved further into the bushes to make sure he was out of sight.

Timothy walked round the corner and went to knock on Mr Hatley's door. A moment or two later, William saw the door open and a maid appeared. Timothy spoke a few words to her, and they went inside, leaving the door open. Then Susannah came into view with Mr Hatley. Her hair was quite grey now, and she stooped slightly, but she'd retained her stately beauty. Timothy took her hand and helped her over the threshold. The door closed.

They were both facing William and he heard Susannah say, "Shall we stop a little while in Wadhurst? I've not been here for some time."

"Only a little time, Mother. Susan will be expecting us," said Timothy. He helped her into the trap, then walked round to the other side and climbed in. They drove out into the road and the pony trotted off towards the town.

Anger bubbled up as William walked into Wadhurst. He was now sure that Timothy was intent on aggravation. He was blatantly flaunting his new acquisition, William's pony trap. What would be the next thing? And Susannah did not look happy. William's old infatuation had not entirely faded. He felt a great fondness for her. And he suspected that Timothy was not looking after her in a kindly way.

After selecting the hop plants and paying for them, William loaded them onto the cart, and drove Bess back in the direction of home. He had not gone far down the hill on the Lamberhurst road when the cart started lurching from side to side. He stopped Bess and jumped down. As he did so, the wheel nearest the ditch slowly leaned over and slipped off its axel. The cart toppled. William ran round to release Bess from the shafts. His fingers fumbled with the straps in his haste, but soon she was free. The hop plants were sliding from the back of the cart into the ditch. Then there was a great creaking and a tearing sound of splintering wood, as the old cart finally met its end.

At that moment, there was a sound of hooves. The pony trap went swiftly past him towards Lamberhurst. William caught sight of Timothy looking his way. He felt sure he saw him laughing.

It took a few moments for William to realise that he wouldn't be able to get the hops back to the Slade without help. He could ride Bess to Lamberhurst and fetch Michael or Adam to help, but that would be no good without a cart. He stood by Bess and scratched his head, looking down the now deserted road after the pony trap. It was eerily quiet. He felt helpless. Anger welled up. He wondered if Timothy had seen his cart in town and tampered with the wheel. Timothy seemed to know everything about William, even down to what he happened to being doing that day. Or was he imagining things again?

But this wouldn't solve his present dilemma. He thought of Nick Longley. His farm wasn't far away and he was sure to have a cart. The hop plants were beginning to wilt in the hot sun. He clambered up into the shattered cart, grabbed the empty sacks that were there and slid back to the ground. He covered the plants carefully, weighing the sacks down with stones. Then he climbed up onto Bess's broad back, took the reins, and gently urged her forward. She wasn't used to carrying a rider, but she was a patient old horse, who had a lifetime's experience of the antics humans got up to. She plodded along the road as if nothing had happened.

Nick was working in the fields when William arrived at the farm. There was a labourer in the yard, who gave directions. William found his brother–in–law spreading manure. He waved when he saw William, and came across the field to meet him.

"What brings thee here, Will. Is everything alright?"

"Nay, Nick." William gave an account of the morning's events. "I'd be obliged if ye could lend us thy cart, to get the hops to the Slade." But Nick's cart was full of dung.

"If ye can give us a hand shifting this lot, I'll help thee," Nick said.

When the manure had been spread, they took Nick's horse and cart and picked up the hops, with Bess walking behind. At last they came into Lamberhurst and rounded the corner into the yard at the Slade. Michael was there, with a stranger. William jumped down from the cart, and walked towards them.

"I found him wandering round the buildings in the close," said Michael. "He says he be seeking work." William's defences were up. Foreigners weren't welcome in country villages, for fear that they brought the plague from London. This one appeared to be reasonably presentable, albeit a little thin. There was then the question of how he came to be wandering the roads with no fixed abode. Perhaps he was a deserter from the militia or on the run after committing a crime, or maybe he'd lost his employment after a misdemeanour.

"There's no work hereabouts, and don't let us catch ye on me land again!" William shouted impatiently. Michael led the man back to the road, and watched as he trudged down the hill into the village. William told Michael of the day's events. Michael took Bess to her stable, and William and Nick climbed onto the cart to unload the plants into the shelter of the half-built oast house.

"Ye've been a real friend. I be much obliged to thee, Nick," said William when the job was done. "Will ye stay for dinner? Jane will be main pleased to see thee." Nick agreed, and they went indoors to warn Martha that there would be another mouth to feed.

It was later that week that William was woken one night by the sound of the hens squawking and cackling. He got out of bed quickly and crept downstairs to avoid waking Jane. After stepping into his boots at the door, he slid the bolt back and walked quietly through, hoping to catch the intruder before he left. He let himself into the chicken run. All was quiet. It was difficult to see in the dark if there were any hens missing. The intruder had escaped. Probably a fox, he thought, and resolved to shut the fowls in the roosting house in future, and bolt the door. When he checked in the morning, there was a hen missing, but no feathers left, and he knew that a fox would have run amok, killing several hens, leaving feathers, and only taking one or two.

A few nights later, the intruder had helped himself to a couple more hens, having drawn back the bolt of the roosting house, and shut it after himself.

Michael and Jane searched the woods and fields around the house, looking for feathers or footprints, and found nothing. William asked his neighbours if they'd had intruders. None of them had.

The next evening, Michael came back from the village. "I saw Edward with an ironworker called Rob Moon, in the tavern. They was huddled together talking and was too busy to see us. I kept quiet like. Then Jack Paine and his Mistus comes along and they all goes off together."

Chapter 26

It was William's first Christmas with Jane as his wife, and he wanted to make it an event to remember. On Christmas Eve morning they brought holly and ivy into the house, representing the promised return of the light and new life. William had cut a tree down the previous year to provide them with a yule log. He hitched it up behind Bess, and brought it to the door of the house. The four men carried it in. It filled the wide fireplace in the hall, where Martha had prepared a hot bed of coles. There it would burn for the twelve days of Christmas. Jane made a kissing bunch with two bisecting hoops of hazel. She decorated it with mistletoe, which they collected from the apple trees, and added holly, ivy, ribbons, nuts and apples. William hung the bunch from the ceiling in the middle of the room. The garlands would be left hanging in the hall until the 2nd February, the Christian festival of Candlemas.

William came through the parlour on his way to the buttery. Martha was busy cooking plum pottage and rolling out pastry for the mince pies. Michael was hanging round the parlour hoping for titbits.

"What be this ye're making, Martha?" he asked, poking a strange looking mixture of minced meat soaking in wine with dried fruit.

"That be the filling for the mince pies. They represent Christ's cradle, the manger," she said. "I makes the pastry case in the shape of the crib, so." Her plump floury hands picked up a small ball of dough. She made a cup of her left hand and pushed her right thumb into the middle, then deftly squeezing and moulding, the dough became a boat shape. She took a spoonful of the mince, placed it in the boat and placed a pastry lid on it.

"I've never seen they afore," Michael remarked. "We didn't do much at Christmas after muvver died."

William went and chose a pig's haunch, which was hanging in the buttery and took it to the Longleys to exchange for a fat goose. When he got the bird home, he wrung its neck and gave it to Martha, who plucked it and prepared it for roasting for the Christmas dinner.

On Christmas morning William, Jane, Michael and Martha all went to church dressed in their Puritan best, leaving the goose cooking in the oven. There was no sign of the Rumneys or Timothy. They walked back home through the village, wishing their friends and neighbours the season's greetings, tipping their tall hats and bowing to the ladies.

Adam and Ned had been invited with their families to the Slade for dinner. They fed the beasts, milked the cows and left water for them before going into the hall to join in the celebrations. William lit the candles, which flickered in the draught from the windows. Michael closed the shutters, to keep the warmth in. They brought mulled wine and cider to be served as well as ale. Adam's three children stared in amazement at the table spread with so much luxurious food, their eyes reflecting the candlelight. They ate hungrily, and asked for more. The games began, and Ned brought out his fiddle. William and Jane watched the children race round the room being chased by the 'blind man', shrieking and laughing with excitement. They danced, told stories and sang carols until it was time for the visitors to go home.

Before retiring to bed, William and Jane sat in their armchairs by the dying fire in the parlour. They gazed contentedly into the flames. William looked up at Jane, and was about to say what a good day it had been, when she turned her head towards him and smiled her dimpled smile.

"Will, I be with child," she said shyly.

When he realised the full implication of what she'd said, William was ecstatic. He jumped out of his chair and went over to her. Kneeling at her feet, he hugged her round her waist, and buried his face in her lap, saying, "Oh, Jane, I be so proud." She rubbed her fingers through his hair, then, lifting his chin, bent down to kiss him on the mouth, long and slow.

The 6th January, Twelfth Night, was a time for visiting and for entertaining their friends. William and Jane had kept their news a secret, even from Michael and Martha, but now it was time to tell everyone. They rode into Wadhurst, and called on the family at Marlinge, shared some festive pies and a mug of ale, then went to Nick at his house down the road. Anne was there visiting. Jane talked to her for a long time, getting to know her future sister-in-law. Then they went to see Uncle Thomas, who was entertaining some old friends, and enjoying his retirement in his snug house. As they went round, William invited all the family back to the Slade for the evening's entertainment. On their way home, they called in to see Jane's Uncle John and his son Robert in Lamberhurst. Robert announced the news that he, too, was courting a girl whom he hoped to marry soon.

William and Jane arrived back at the Slade and came through the door into the hall. They found Martha and Michael bustling round preparing food and drinks and laying out another great spread on the table. Martha was going to be with her sister for the day, so William summoned them both. They all stood round the fire in the parlour.

William said, "We be expecting a child."

Michael whooped with joy. Martha's eyes twinkled with tears. She laughed happily, mopping her eyes with her apron.

The visitors arrived in the afternoon. William's father and John came on their horses. They said that Mary and Jone were well on their way on foot. John Longley and Robert were the next to arrive, followed closely by Jane's brother Nick, and Anne. The company were beginning to relax with the best ale, when Mary and Jone came through the door, their cheeks rosy and their fingers cold. They came and warmed themselves by the yule log still burning there.

Michael said to Mary, "I'll take thee home in the cart after." She nodded gratefully.

Jane invited the guests to start eating. There was a lull in the conversation while they had food in their mouths, and William could contain himself no longer. He announced in a loud voice, "I have good news. We be expecting a child come summer."

Everyone clapped and cheered, and raised their glasses to their hosts. The atmosphere in the room became animated. Richard's rather sombre mood was raised, and he went over to talk to Jane and say how pleased he was at the prospect of becoming a grandfather again. William watched them all enjoying themselves. Jone was a little subdued, sitting in a corner on her own. Michael went over to her and led her to the table, tempting her with a plate of food.

The wassailers arrived, visiting the houses in turn, entertaining the occupants with their carols, and enjoying mugs of mulled wine and mince pies. Everyone was gathered round the fire toasting each other, when there was a banging on the door. It opened, and Uncle Thomas appeared. A cheer rose up. He came and warmed his hands by the fire, and was given a mug of mulled wine.

"I believe there be somebody eavesdropping by the front door," he said to William. "I caught sight of him when I rode into the yard. He'd gone betimes I'd dismounted and come round the corner."

William was in a mellow state of inebriation by this time. Whoever it was, he thought, would be cold and hungry. Uncle Thomas continued, "I went to see Christopher. He be in good spirits, but hem doddlish, and confused sometimes. His housekeeper muvvers him well."

William went into the parlour to make up a bundle of Christmas fare for the anonymous visitor. He found a kerchief and filled it full with food from the table, tied the four corners together and went out through the parlour to the barn. He put the bundle on a heap of straw, and left the door slightly ajar. Then he went to join the wassailers with their King and Queen as they led the company outside to the appleterre with kettles, pots, pans and drums.

They stood among the fruit trees in the still night air, with bright stars shining overhead, and sang the wassail song. Jane held William's hand tightly in her excitement. He thought of the child in her belly.

Wassail the trees, that they may bear
You many a plum and many a pear:
For more or less fruits they will bring,
As you do give them wassailing.

The Queen of the wassailers was lifted into the branches of a tree by the men, to place there a piece of toasted bread soaked in cider.

They all shouted, "Here's to thee, old apple tree! That blooms well, bears well. Hats full, caps full, three bushel bags full, and all under one tree. Hurrah, Hurrah!" A great noise followed; banging of drums, pots and pans, shouting and singing. A gun was fired.

All was quiet. The evil spirits had been dispersed. The ceremony was over. The wassailers moved on to the next farm.

As the family walked back to the house, huddled together for warmth, the moon cast their long shadows before them onto the yard. William noticed that there was one long shadow walking apart from the group. But he didn't look back. He knew that Edward had been as close as he could to the family Christmas, and William hoped he would find the bundle in the barn.

Their many feet scrunched on the cold ground. Michael said, "There'll be a sharp frost tonight, I rackons."

Chapter 27   1634

It was spring again. William was in the yard talking to Thomas and Greg Dyne. The barn was being converted into an oast house for the drying of hops. The building work would soon be done.

Greg asked, "Have ye had any more hens stolen, Will?"

"Nay, I rackon the foreigner moved on. Has he been seen in the village, d'ye know?"

"Not for a while."

Michael came running round the corner. "The sheep, Will. There be one missing!" William ran round to the meadow with his brother. Michael continued as they ran. "I were counting them. There be only eight."

William counted the sheep. "Ye're right, there be eight. One be stolen." They walked back to the house together. Martha was putting their coger on the table, and Jane was pouring out the ale.

"There be a sheep stolen," announced William.

Jane looked up, concerned. "Has anyone else had stock missing?"

"I'll go round today and find out." William sat down at the table and took a gulp of ale. "And I'll report it to the Headborough. The rascal must be caught afore he haves any more away."

This was worrying. He couldn't afford to lose sheep. Whoever was taking them was likely to be sent to the gallows. William made enquiries of the neighbouring farmers. He was apparently the only one who had had a sheep stolen. The other farmers were alarmed, and everyone was on the lookout for the culprits.

The next morning, Adam came to William and said, "I were talking to me brudder, and he told us how he saw Jack Paine and Rob Moon on the road to Medston yesterday. They was pulling a cart, what looked like cordwood covered over. He rackoned they be up to something."

That evening, Michael came home from the village. "I saw Edward and Rob Moon. They was arguing. Then Rob lashed out at Ed and laid him flat. Ed got up and bunted Rob. There was a crowd of men egging them on." He paused. Jane and Martha were listening, open-mouthed.

"Go on, go on," William said.

"There were no sign of the Paines. There was a gurt start-up! Rob laid Ed flat again, then Ed wrestled Rob to the ground and put his foot on Rob's chest. Rob pulled Ed down and they were rolling around on the floor when the Headborough showed up with a constable. They broke up the fight and searched Rob and Ed. They found a bag of money on Rob. He refused to say where he got it from. He were took away by the Headborough. The constable gave Ed a talking to, and Ed sloped off down the road."

On July 6th, early in the morning, William woke to feel Jane shaking him. "Will, Will, I believe my time's come. Fetch Martha, dracly-minute." She gave a gasp of pain, and lay back on the bed, breathing heavily. William was out of bed in a flash and called Martha, as he ran downstairs pulling on his breeches.

Martha came running and shouted, "Get the kettle on the fire and stoke up, Mas' William!" as she puffed up the stairs to the hall chamber.

William went out into the yard to tell Adam and Ned that there would be no prayers that day.

As he turned to go back into the house, he heard a horse's hooves galloping up the road from the village. Dan'l turned the corner, his horse in a lather. William went to meet him.

"Mus Christopher be in a terrible fit! He be lashing out and hollering! I can't hold him down noways. I be going to Mus Thomas in Wad'rst, but he'll surely not be fit to deal with him alone. Maybe ye could go on afore, Mas William, and see what can be done."

William was in a quandary.

Should he go and leave Jane giving birth?

He knew she was in good hands, and he could do nothing to help.

"I'll be going anon, surely Dan'l," he said.

"Mind ye the river in the village be in spate! I barely made it over the bridge!" shouted Dan'l as he turned and cantered out of the yard and up the road towards Wadhurst.

William went to tell Michael where he was going. His mind was in a whirl as he went to saddle up Damsel. He hurried down into the village, where he found water covering the road. The bridge could still be seen, and he started easing Damsel carefully through the torrent. She shied at first, but began to calm down. They walked on slowly, and came out safely. William wondered how he was going to get back if the bridge collapsed. He urged his steed on up the hill to Goudhurst.

Christopher had been shut in his chamber, this being the safest place for him to be. William found him lying curled up, crying and beating his fists on the floor. The old man was now nearly blind and very deaf. William touched him gently on the shoulder. His uncle cried out and cowered as if he'd been beaten. His hands were bleeding where he'd wounded himself on the furniture in his ravings. William asked Faithful, the housekeeper, for a cup of warm milk and a morsel of Christopher's favourite food. By the time she brought them, William had knelt down and managed to take hold of both of Christopher's hands. He was holding them firmly but gently and the old man was relatively calm. William held the milk to Christopher's lips, but after a small sip the cup was knocked from his hand and the old man shouted, "I ain't having none of that!"

The door opened and Uncle Thomas and Dan'l came into the room. Thomas went directly to his brother, picked up the ear trumpet from the table as he passed, and, with his hand on Christopher's forearm, shouted, "Brudder, I be come to take thee out for a visit to the horses."

Christopher recognised his brother's touch and voice and grabbed hold of him, nearly pulling him over. "Thomas, they be attempting to poison us! I won't eat none of their vittles. For certain sure I won't."

Together they pulled the old man up to standing. Dan'l brought a chair over and they sat him down. Thomas enquired of Faithful when his brother had last eaten or drunk anything besides his ale, which he would never refuse. She said there was no ale in the house; it had run out a few days ago. Thomas gave Dan'l some money to go and replenish the stock, and then tried to persuade Christopher to have some milk. This he now accepted, and a little food, fed to him by Thomas. William stood by, watching. He wondered how long this was going to take. Jane was giving birth. He wanted to be by her side.

When everything was calm, Thomas brought William over. He put his hand on Christopher's forearm. Shouting through the ear trumpet, Thomas conveyed that this was young William.

William took the trumpet and shouted, "I be come to see thee, Uncle. Will ye show us thy horses?"

Christopher exclaimed, "Struth, boy!" His hands came up to William's bearded face, exploring it. "Ye be a man of a sudden, and I hears ye be wed just now."

"Yus, I be, to a purty young lass called Jane."

Soon Christopher was calm enough to walk slowly out to the stables with Thomas and William steadying him, one on each side. The old man was pleased to stroke and pat his horses, going to them each in turn. He put his arms round their necks and his face to their cheeks, fondling their muzzles and feeding them titbits, and he murmured sweet nothings into their ears.

William said to Thomas, "Jane be about to birth, Uncle." His uncle looked shocked. "I must get back. Is the river still high in Lamb'rst?"

"Nay," said Thomas. "The bridge be quite clear now. Behopes all goes well, lad."

William mounted Damsel and galloped away to find out what was happening at the Slade, hoping he wouldn't have to seek an alternative, longer route.

The river was still high, but the bridge was visible. The water had washed away the road in places, but Damsel negotiated the potholes and carried William safely home.

He came into the parlour to hear Jane shouting with pain. Michael was there, looking concerned. "Thanks be ye're back, Will. Jane's had a hard time."

"Be she alright?" asked William.

"She's been shouting out this last hour on and off. Behopes 'twill not be long now."

An hour later, after much pacing up and down, with Michael trying to say the right things to William, the cry they were waiting for rang out healthily. Martha wouldn't allow William to enter the chamber until she'd tidied up. At last the door opened and she crept down the stairs, flushed, but quietly smiling.

William's feet hardly touched the stairs on the way up. He entered the chamber. Jane was sitting up in bed, looking tired but radiant. "Come and meet thy son, Will," she said. William was shaking with joy. He took his son in his arms, astonished at how small and light he was. He'd birthed baby animals every year for most of his life, but this was a completely different experience. This child came from his loins, as a result of his deep love for Jane, who had carried him for nine months, then given him back to William.

He kissed the baby on the nose and said, "Welcome, liddle man. We'll call thee Thomas." He sat on the bed, and gave the baby back to Jane. He put his arm round her and kissed her. They sat together awhile, watching their son squirm and wriggle. He yawned, and opened his eyes for a few seconds, before quickly closing them again.

"He'll need a crib," said William. He got up and went to the corner of the room. He picked up the little chest he'd brought with him to the Slade, containing his clothes, all those years ago. He carried it over and placed it on a chair by the bed. "This be good enough for now. I be minded to make a proper crib."

"That be perfect," said Jane, wrapping the baby tightly in his swaddling cloth and laying him down gently.

Chapter 28

When William had been a father for over a week, he stood in his hop garden in the still humidity. Dark clouds glowered above him. The air was heavy with imminent rain. Gaping cracks had opened up in the dry earth, which seemed to raise itself to receive the first heavenly drops. William watched the drooping leaves of the hop plants nodding with pleasure, as the drops fell on them. He lifted his face and hands, catching the cool water and giving thanks for the long awaited deluge that would follow. He walked to the house slowly, relishing the soaking rain.

He came into the parlour to fetch a jacket, and bent down to kiss Jane then his son on the way past. The baby was lying in his new crib after his latest feed. Michael had carved the head and footboards with animals and birds and Martha made a soft down mattress. Jane was rocking him gently and singing,

> Golden slumbers kiss your eyes.
> Smiles awake you when you rise.
> Sleep pretty darling, do not cry
> And I will sing a lullaby.

Michael came in from the hall with Mary and Jone. "See who's here," he said.

"We've come to see the baby," said Mary. "We'll start coming again to help, like. Next week, if that be alright." She came to Jane, and they embraced warmly, before she peered into the crib to see the child.

"He has the bly of his muvver," she said, and called Jone over to have a look.

Suddenly there was pandemonium.

Jone cried, "Me baby!" She reached into the crib and took the baby into her arms. She ran out of the house with him into the rain. Jane shrieked with alarm. They all followed Jone, who was hurrying towards the copse, the baby shouting lustily. She stumbled in her haste, but righted herself, and hurried on. Jane caught up with her. William watched her struggle to take the baby. Jone fought her off, and held onto the baby tightly. Jane was unable to take her son back.

Jone shouted, "He be mine! Nobody shall take him again," and broke away. She started running again. William caught up and held Jone firmly by her shoulders. Mary was close behind. She prised the baby out of Jone's arms, and gave him back to Jane, who carried him away, sobbing.

Mary said to Jone, "Whist, my dear. He ain't thine. Come away now." She followed Jane back to the house.

Jone sank to the ground, crying, "He be mine! Me own liddle baby."

William and Michael lifted Jone and tried to comfort her. They took her back to the house to find Jane sitting weeping and frightened, cradling little Thomas in her arms. Mary was doing her best to calm her down. William took the baby, who was quieter now. Michael stopped Jone at a safe distance. She was still sobbing.

Jane stood up and shouted at Mary, "Don't ye ever bring thy sister into this house again! D'ye hear? Now git, and take 'er with thee! Git!"

Mary stood speechless. She paled with shock and anger then grabbed Jone firmly by the hand. They turned and left the house,

William had misgivings about the way things had turned around, and when Jane had calmed down and there was harmony once more he tried to talk to her about the episode and to persuade her that there was nothing to fear. But she was adamant, and refused to talk about it again.

A few weeks later, William went with Michael down to the village one evening. He hadn't seen his friend Greg Dyne for some time, since the conversion of the barn was finished. He'd arranged to meet Greg at The Vyne, and Michael left him there to search out his friends in another tavern.

William and Greg had not been sitting in the tavern long, when Timothy walked in, with Edward.

"Struth!" exclaimed William. "I don't want them to see us, Greg. Come over here." They moved into a dark corner of the room, and watched Timothy as he bought Ed a large mug of ale, and himself a small glass of spirit. They went and sat down away from William and his friend, and started talking animatedly.

William couldn't hear any of their conversation, and tried to concentrate on resuming his own, with Greg. "Has thy Thomas been seeing anything of our Mary lately?" he asked.

"I believe they've met a couple of times," said Greg, shrugging his shoulders. "But why be ye so worried? That be your brudder, Edward, ain't it?"

"Yus," replied William, "and I don't trust that man who's with him. I believe he wishes me harm. Ed ain't in control of himself when he be tight." They continued to talk about the recent appearance of Edward in the village, and how he was mixing with unsavoury characters. Timothy and Edward were still talking when William and Greg got up to leave. Edward was looking flushed and excited, laughing loudly, and banging his fist on the table. Timothy was smiling coolly.

There was no sign of Edward or Timothy over the next few months, until the next spring. At breakfast one morning, Michael had hardly started eating when he said, "I were in the tavern last night. There were ironworkers telling of a terrible accident. A man were killed! Burnt to death! They couldn't say a name."

"Lord a mercy!" exclaimed Martha.

"Afore that I saw Rob Moon in the twitten, with Peggy Paine pressed up agin the wall. He were lifting 'er skirts. I were disgusted, and walked away."

"That Rob Moon be varmint," declared Martha.

"Did ye see Edward at all?" asked William anxiously. He was hoping it hadn't been his brother who was killed.

"Nay, nor Jack Paine. Everyone else were in the tavern, talking about the accident," said Michael.

Chapter 29

The hops were growing apace, and this year they needed poles to support them. William and Michael went to the coppice a few days later. They chose straight hazel rods, ten feet tall, and trimmed them to a point ready to be pushed into the ground beside every plant. While they were working, they heard a rustling in the undergrowth and Michael went to investigate. William looked up and caught sight of a man running through the trees.

"Michael!" he shouted. "Over here!" and ran to cut the man off. It took both of them to bring him down. He gave up struggling and sat among the beech mast and dried leaves, with his head in his hands. Then he looked up. It was Edward.

"I be in bad trouble," he said at last. "The hue and cry be after me, en I don't know what to do. I've been laying-up here, afeared they should catch us."

William and Michael stood over their brother, ready to stop him if he bolted. William asked, "Why be they seeking thee? What've ye done?"

Edward raised his voice. "Nothing! I ain't done aught. Me friend Jack Paine were killed in the founding t'other day." His face contorted in distress and he sobbed at the memory. "Bob Moon says he saw us bunt him, and that I murdered 'im." He broke down completely. William and Michael stood in silence for a while, taking in the gravity of the situation.

William said, "'Tis no good running. If ye ain't done nothing, surely ye've nothing to fear. Come on, get ye up and we'll go and talk to the Headborough."

Edward was weak with hunger and fright. Telling his story had somehow relieved some of the stress and the need to make decisions for himself. He submitted to William's advice and got up shakily. They left Michael to continue the work in the copse, and walked to the house, going through the close to avoid being seen. William didn't want Jane to meet them until he'd had time to explain. Martha produced food and a drink, while William fetched his horse. He helped Edward climb up behind him.

The Headborough was pleased to see them. He sent for the constables to call off the hue and cry and to bring Rob Moon to present his allegations. It took a long time for both sides to tell their stories, and it was eventually decided that much more evidence must be collected from witnesses before taking Rob Moon and Edward to the Justice of the Peace. It would be wise for Edward to leave Lamberhurst until then. William proposed to take him to Wadhurst, hoping that their father would keep him at Marlinge, rather than locking him up in the local House of Correction.

They rode to Wadhurst in silence, each with their own thoughts. When they dismounted in the yard at Marlinge, William said, "Don't ye go getting Farder's back up, Ed."

"Nay, Will. I knows. I be afeared he'll send us away."

Mary had seen them arrive, and came out of the door to meet them, looking concerned.

"Be Farder at home, Mary?" asked William.

"Yus, I'll fetch 'im." Mary disappeared into the parlour.

William and Edward went into the hall and waited. Richard came in a few minutes later. He stared at them both.

"Ed needs a safe house, Farder," said William. "He be in trouble, he'll have to go to the House of Correction if he can't bide 'ere." He explained the situation. Ed repeatedly pleaded his innocence. Richard at last agreed to shelter Edward until his trial.

"Mind thee, there'll be no visits to the tavern, Edward, until all is settled," he said.

"Nay, Farder. I be hem obliged to thee for taking us in." William left them standing in the hall, regarding each other for the first time for years.

The next Assizes in East Grinstead was at the end of the summer. Uncle Thomas, William and his father went to support Edward at his trial. The journey took them all day. The town was full of people with the same intention, and the inns were full. But Thomas knew of a place outside the town, which was quieter. They spent a sombre evening sitting in a corner of the dimly lit room, discussing Edward's predicament. They were served with a hot meal, and when they'd eaten, they called for more ale.

"D'ye rackon Ed be telling the truth, William?" asked Richard.

"Yus, Farder, he were considerable upset over the death of Jack Paine. I don't believe he'd kill 'is friend."

"Is there enough evidence to send him to the gallows?" Thomas had experience of the Courts and their proceedings.

"Behopes there ain't," said William. "We went round the village gathering information from his friends. They all said they couldn't believe Ed would do such a thing. And I rackon Rob Moon is not to be trusted."

The next day they went early to the Assizes, in order to get a good view of the courtroom. This was a formidable place to William, and he was afraid for his brother. They sat in the public gallery among a crowd of families and friends of the accused. Some of these people were already causing a disturbance, spitting, shouting and swearing. The gallery overlooked the floor of the courtroom, where the Magistrates, Judges and Justices of the Peace were walking around wearing wigs and flowing gowns, carrying bundles of rolled up parchment and books under their arms, bowing and conferring with each other like a flock of crows in the harvest stubble. Everyone found a place to be seated, and there was a call for silence. William saw Edward among the fifteen defendants who approached the Bar to stand face-to-face with the jurors. These were twenty men of the local area, some of whom William knew by sight. The constables from the local hundred and the foreman of the ironworks were among them.

The Clerk of the Court presented them, saying to the defendants, "These good men and true that were last called and have appeared are those that shall pass between our Sovereign Lord the King and you, upon your lives and oaths."

The jurors made their promise individually with a hand on the Bible, then stood either side of the Bar with the defendants between them. Every prisoner was then brought forward and told to raise his hand.

"Look upon the prisoner you that be sworn and harken to his cause," said the Clerk to the jurors. He then declared that each had pleaded innocent and had chosen to be tried by "God and the Country, which country are you."

When Edward's turn came he stood straight and still, listening to the evidence against him, submitted by the Justice of the Peace. Rob Moon, the complainant, had accused Edward of murdering Jack Paine. The coroner, John Luck of Mayfield, had reported that Jack died by falling into a pit of molten iron. His body was unrecognisable, but those present at the time had been certain that it was Jack Paine who died. The Justice of the Peace said that this could be an indictable offence, but that there was an element of doubt considering the character of Rob Moon, who had been suspected of sheep stealing. Rob Moon also alleged that Edward was living illegally in the Paines' house, and that he'd been fornicating with Jack's wife. He had seen Edward push Jack into the molten iron being poured into the moulds for making sows.

Edward denied the accusation, and defended himself by saying that he'd lent Rob money, and when Rob refused to repay him from the proceeds of selling the sheep, Edward had threatened to report him for sheep stealing. Peggy Paine supported Edward by saying that he and Jack had been true friends for several years, and that Edward was paying rent for living with them as a lodger. Others in the village supported this evidence, including the constable, who had arrested Rob Moon for having money on his person. He said that although they were all prone to drinking, he believed Edward to be an honest man. The foreman at the ironworks confirmed this, and no other person had seen Jack being pushed on that fateful day, though they had all been working together, including Rob Moon, at the time of the accident. It was reported by Michael that he had seen Rob Moon and Peggy in the twitten together. There was no evidence to prove that Rob Moon had stolen the sheep except the word of the defendant.

There was a long wait now, while the jury considered all the cases. The rabble around William, Richard and Thomas were again unruly, throwing rotten eggs into the courtroom, sometimes hitting the defendants. They farted and fought with each other. The atmosphere became heavy with unsavoury odours. The jostling of their neighbours threw the three closer together in their discomfort.

At last the Clerk of the Court called for attention. The jury had reached their verdicts on all of the prisoners. Both groups again came face-to-face.

The Clerk advised the jurors, "Look upon the prisoner," before the announcement of each verdict. When Edward's turn came, he was pale and trembling. The Foreman of the jury pronounced him "Guilty."

A gasp went up from the public gallery. Some people cheered. There was a pause while the Judges put their heads together to decide on the sentence. The crowd around William and his father and uncle once more became excited and rowdy. The clerk called for silence.

One of the Judges looked at Edward. "This is your first offence, young man. We consider that the evidence has not been conclusive. We will therefore reduce the usual death sentence to military service. You will be taken from here to join His Majesty's army in protecting our country from invaders." A sigh came from Edward's family and friends, and he walked forlornly away with the gaolers.

Richard and William pushed past the crowds in the gallery, ran down the stairs and round to the back entrance. Thomas followed more slowly. Edward was being loaded into a cart. He looked at them with tears running down his face, and they called, "God bless thee!" "Come home if ye can," and "Keep fighting they dragons," added William, as his brother was carted away. They turned sadly and went to find their horses and rode back to the inn. The next day they made the journey home.

Chapter 30

On William's return to the Slade, Jane came running out to meet him, and he fell into her arms, glad to be home again. Martha appeared carrying little Thomas, and they went indoors together. Michael was waiting in the parlour. They sat quietly, listening to William's account of the day's events. Then he suggested that Jane and the child should take a walk with him along the whapple way. He was exhausted, and needed to replenish his energy in the peace and tranquillity of his beloved copse with his precious family.

They walked hand-in-hand, Thomas between his parents, along the grassy pathway. They passed the new oast house, and the hop garden where the bines were climbing their poles. The cows came towards them, lowing softly as Michael drove them on their way to be milked. William led Jane and Thomas into the shady presence of the wood. The late afternoon sun slanted through the trees, a gentle breeze ruffled the leaves and a blackbird sang an evening song. After strolling among the trees the little family came out into the sunshine, warm on their faces.

"'T'will be harvesting time anon," said William, looking forward to the familiar routine, and happier occasions.

"Yus, and there another child on the way," announced Jane. She looked happily into William's eyes. His heart leapt for joy, and he caught her at the waist and twirled her round. Little Thomas laughed at his parents cavorting, and jumped up and down, asking to join in. They linked hands with him in a circle, and danced around, then lifted him high in the air between them. Jane broke free and ran on ahead. William hoisted his son onto his shoulders and followed her, galloping, to shrieks of laughter from the child.

The next few weeks were difficult for William. He remembered Ed's face when they said goodbye, and William wondered if he would ever see his brother again. He had heard of the rough life and poor pay in the military, and there seemed to be no hope of his ever escaping. Edward would be living among the dregs of society, criminals, vagabonds and ne'er-do-wells.

But there was work to be done, and little Thomas gave them an added dimension to their lives. Having got to his feet, he embraced his freedom with enthusiasm. He frequently went missing, and was discovered in the milk-house, the roosting house, barn, and vegetable garden. The family all took a turn in charge, whoever wasn't doing heavy work. He was taken to pick fruit and vegetables, collect eggs, bake cakes and joined in the milking and haymaking.

All was quiet in the village. Edward's friends were shocked at the punishment he had received. Peggy Paine stayed at home grieving, and Rob Moon and the foreigner had disappeared. Then word came that a sheep had been stolen from another farmer. Everyone suspected Rob Moon, and a hue and cry was set up. This time Michael joined in. He was angry about what had happened to his brother, and was glad to have the opportunity to bring Rob to justice. They caught him with the blood of the sheep on his hands. After a short enquiry, he was committed and sentenced to the gallows.

Martha was in her chamber spinning wool with little Thomas. William and Jane sat in the parlour together, quietly thoughtful after the funeral of Jane's Uncle John Longley, before going back to work. They listened to the ticking of the clock, the clickety-clack of the spinning wheel upstairs and the child's piping voice, chattering away.

"Uncle John were like a farder to me," said Jane. "I could see he were ailing at Christmas."

"It do seem he went sudden," said William. "He were a friend of Uncle Thomas since they were children. He'll be sorely missed. He were a kind, upstanding man."

"'Tis a comfort to know that he saw little Thomas afore he passed away," added Jane. They sat quietly, gazing into the fire for a while.

Presently, Jane said, "I be nearing me time now, Will. But it don't feel like it did the last time. The baby's not moving as it should."

William looked up at her, alarmed. "Have ye talked to Martha about it? I don't know nothing about these things."

"Nay, but there's naught to be at. I'll bide me time. But I wanted thee to know, like."

It was a fine April day, fresh and bright. William was by Jane's side all the time now. They were in the vegetable garden. William was preparing the seed beds, and Jane was dropping the seeds into the holes he had made with a dibber, one by one, along the rows. They stood up to look at their work so far.

"The next row will be here," said Jane, bending over to push a stick into the ground.

She cried out in pain. William came to her at once, and helped her straighten up. "Take us indoors, Will. I be afeared." Her face was white, and she fainted into his arms.

"Martha, come quick!" he shouted, as he carried Jane through the house and up the stairs. She came round as he laid her on the bed. Her brow was dripping with perspiration. The waters had broken and her dress was wet.

Martha came panting up the stairs and into the room. "I'll see to 'er now, Mas William. Go and put the kettle on. And keep an eye on young Thomas."

William didn't want to leave the room. His feet dragged as he walked slowly to the door. He looked back to see Jane lying on the bed. She was crying with pain. Martha turned and shooed him gently out. He stumbled down the stairs. Little Thomas was about to climb up. William picked him up, saying "Whist, boy. Mama be busy." He carried his son into the parlour, sat him on the floor and gave him some bricks to play with. He set the kettle over the fire, now moving in a semi-conscious haze. Everything slowed down. It became an effort to move. He sat on the edge of a chair and waited, listening. There was no sound from upstairs. The ticking of the clock echoed round the parlour. Even the child was quiet with his bricks.

Martha called for water. William jerked himself into action, picked up the kettle and carried it upstairs. He opened the door of the chamber. Jane was lying quietly now. Martha took the kettle and shook her head, gently pushing William out of the room. He made his way down the stairs again, trembling with fear. Little Thomas looked up at him as he entered the parlour. William couldn't speak. His throat was dry. He went back to the chair and waited, holding onto the arms tightly.

He started as the clock chimed, one, two, three, four, five, six, seven, eight, nine, ten, eleven… Then silence. After aeons of empty time, he heard the door of the chamber open, and the creaking of the stairs. Martha came into the room, wringing her hands in her apron, tears in her eyes. "She be taken bad, Mas' William. The child be dead. Go up en see 'er."

William came to life. He strode up two at a time, his heart in his mouth. He burst into the chamber.

Jane was lying there, pale and weak. She looked towards William. "I be hem sorry, my dear Will. Our child be lost. And I be mortal sick, love."

William went and knelt by the bed, taking her cold hand in his. "Nay, nay, don't leave us, Jane. I can't live without thee." He kissed her hand all over then lifted it up to his face.

"Take care of liddle Thomas, larn him well, as I be sure ye will." He could hardly hear what she was saying, and stood over her to get closer. "I loves thee, Will." She held tightly onto his hands and closed her eyes. Perspiration broke out on her brow. She coughed sharply then relaxed. A sigh escaped her lips.

All was quiet.

"Jane! Jane!" he shouted, "Nay! Nay!" and collapsed on the bed weeping bitterly.

Chapter 31

The screams of a child echoed through the house and broke through William's light sleep. It was still dark; as dark as his life was these days. He could hardly remember the funeral. Martha had taken little Thomas into her chamber at night, as William was unable to deal with the child's grief as well as his own. He lay in his bed wondering what he'd done to deserve this. It must be a judgement from God. He'd been so absorbed in his happiness and good fortune that he'd neglected to say daily prayers and read his Bible. There had been so many other things that got in the way. Now, every day, everyone in the household must attend daily prayers and Bible reading before work started, as they did when Uncle Thomas was Master.

William went about his work with his head down, seeing only what was in front of him, putting all his energy into the task in hand, trying to dispel the anger he felt over his abandonment. He worked alone, long hours, and could not rest. He was short-tempered and depressed, and had forgotten how to communicate with the family. Every time he looked at his son he saw Jane's face looking back at him. He couldn't show any love for the child, who became miserable and irritable, clinging to Martha's skirts, suddenly breaking into screams and sobs, shouting "Ma! Ma! Ma! Ma!" and struggling with rage when anyone tried to pick him up to comfort him.

William got out of bed and went down to the well. He swilled the sleep out of his eyes and towelled himself dry. The day was grey and threatened rain. He went back into the parlour, and sat down at the table to eat his porridge.

Martha was there giving little Thomas his breakfast. "Will ye be going to Wad'rst today, Mas William?" she asked.

"What would I want to do that for?" he replied, gruffly.

"'Tis market day, and we've butter and cheese to sell, and eggs."

"Michael can go. I'll be going to sow turmuts," said William. "'Tis time we was saying our prayers."

He got up and went into the hall to wait for the rest of the household, aware of his moodiness but unable to bring himself together. He prayed to God to help him out of this pit of despair.

After he had said prayers and read a passage from the Bible, the men all agreed on their tasks for the day. William went towards the door, but Michael stopped him.

"Will, Martha's all-in, looking after the nipper and doing all the other chores besides. We can't go on like this. We needs a body to fother the beasts and fowls, collect the eggs and milk the cows. Would ye be agreeable for us to fetch Mary and Jone sometimes to help out?"

William emerged from his daze. "Nay, not Jone. Maybe Mary will come." He stalked off to his day's work. Things were getting out of control, he knew. But there was a web around him. He was trapped in his own unhappiness.

He was in the barn, cleaning tools when Michael came back from Wadhurst. After putting Bess in her stable he brought the cart to the barn and William helped him pull it in.

"I went to see Mary," said Michael. "She were unwilling to come at first, after what happened last time she en Jone were here. But then she thought about it. She agreed to come, but she'll not come without Jone. And Mary says ye have to go and ask 'er thyself."

William spent the next day considering about what Michael had said, and knew that something had to be done. Thoughts went round in his head, repeating themselves. He felt incapable of resolving the situation. When he'd heard what Mary had said, he was even more concerned. Remembering what happened the last time Jone was at the Slade, he didn't want to go against Jane's wishes. He rode into Wadhurst to talk to Uncle Thomas.

The old man, now stooping badly, and walking with the aid of a stick, was at the door to meet William. He ushered the young man into his parlour, and they sat in silence for several minutes before William sighed and looked at his Uncle, not knowing where to begin.

Thomas said, "Is thy son well, Will?"

"Nay, and I don't know what to be at," replied William, looking down at his hands clasped in front of him. He suddenly felt angry at himself. He had always known what to do.

"What were the last words Jane said to thee afore she passed?" asked Thomas gently.

"That I should take care of liddle Thomas." Guilt seeped into his stomach.

"And be ye taking care of him, loving him as ye did afore? He needs thee to be a farder and a muvver to him now."

"Mary says she'll come and muvver him some days." Anger washed over him again. Jane should be here by his side. He shouldn't have to ask for help.

"That'll help surely, but she ain't his muvver. What else did Jane say on her death bed?" Thomas was insistent.

"That I should larn him to be a farmer, as ye did for me."

"Be ye doing that?"

William shook his head. He understood what Thomas was saying, and was aware how neglectful he'd been. He sat in his Uncle's parlour for a long time. Gradually the web that was holding him melted away. At last he was ready to go and talk to Mary.

Mary was adamant that she must bring Jone with her if she came, and it wouldn't be every day. She still had her father and brother to feed and the housework at Marlinge to do.

Everything was settled, and William returned home feeling drained. He went into the parlour where Martha was preparing the evening meal. Little Thomas was on the floor, playing with his toys. William flopped into a chair, and watched. The child got to his feet and walked over to his father, stood at his knee, and held out his arms to be picked up.

William held his son for the first time since Jane died. The boy sat on his knee and put his hand up to his father's wet cheek, then showed him the wooden doll he was holding in the other hand. Martha left the room, drying her eyes.

A few days later, after prayers had been said, Mary and Jone arrived ready to help. William saw that Jone made friends with little Thomas immediately. They all watched as he showed her his toys.

"Take them out to collect eggs," Martha suggested to Mary. "I believe they'll be good for each other."

"Thomas, show Jone where the fowls be. We'll take the basket along," said Mary. They all went out of the back door together.

William looked at Martha. "D'ye think they'll be alright?" he asked.

"They'll be fine surely, Mas William. Have no fear. I'll warrant Jone be a natural with the children, as with the animals." She went out to milk the cows, unhampered by a child clinging to her skirts.

It was time for coger. William came in to an empty parlour, and wondered where everyone was. Little Thomas often wandered off. They may be looking for him. Then he heard laughter and the child's voice calling, "Jo! Jo! Come quick!" Martha and Mary came in chatting together.

"I don't know who be muvvering who, between those two," Mary laughed. "I rackon Thomas'll show Jone what to do, surely." They looked up and saw William.

"The child's been content all morning," Martha told him. "Just like 'is old self."

They were all about to go their various ways to work a few weeks later, when little Thomas started running across the yard towards the road. Mary set off to follow him, calling, but Jone shouted, "Mary, wait!"

An emaciated brown and white hound turned the corner and stopped. Thomas stopped. They all stopped and waited to see what would happen next. The little boy and the dog approached each other. Thomas patted the dog on the head and turned round, leading him into the yard. The dog came and sat at William's feet, looking up at him. Martha went to find food and water for the dog, who ate greedily. He wagged his tail and licked his lips when the bowl was empty.

Little Thomas had never seen a dog at close quarters before. He pointed and said, "What dat?"

William said, "Dog," then pointed to Thomas and said, "Boy." His son repeated the words "dog" and "boy," pointing appropriately.

Jone came to say it was time to feed the chickens, and led 'Boy' away. 'Dog' followed, and didn't leave the child's side all day. He slept out in the close by the back door all night, and joined 'Boy' as soon as he appeared in the morning, again staying with him all day. In the following weeks the two went everywhere together. Michael laughed, and said that maybe they didn't need Mary and Jone. 'Boy' was frequently seen sitting on the ground talking his own language to 'Dog', who sat by his side and listened, or slept until 'Boy' moved off somewhere else. Martha showed the child what food to give the animal, and 'Boy' fed and watered his new-found friend before he went to bed every night. He had no more screaming fits.

Part 5

Boy and Dog

Chapter 32　　1637
Twelfth year in the reign of Charles I

The corn harvest was over, and the fruit and vegetables had been gathered. It was time to harvest the hops. The family and workers were gathered in the hall. William closed morning prayers by asking for blessings on the day.

Then he said to them all, "We'll be in the hop garden today. The quicker we pick, the fresher the hops'll be for drying." He addressed them each in turn. "Adam and Ned, when Michael comes with the pickers, you take them in teams to their stations. Michael will be in the oast house tending the kiln and spreading the hops as they come in. I'll find a suitable man to help him. Martha and Mary, bring bait and ale when needed. Jone, you must keep Boy close by thee, and help with picking when ye can. I'll take the hop bins and pokes to the teams, and choose the pole-pullers. The tallyman will be on his way."

They all dispersed to their various duties.

William was left alone in the hall. It was eighteen months since Jane's death. William's heart continued to ache. The future looked bleak without her, and he could only take each day at a time. She would have been so excited by this occasion; their first hop harvest. Little Thomas was his future now and his hope for the future of his farm. But the pain remained and he knew nothing of bringing up a child. He could not give his son the love he gave Jane, though he knew that he was part of her. He thanked God for the support of Martha and the family.

Jone and Boy came in. "Michael's coming with a cart-load of pickers!" said Jone excitedly.

William said to Boy, "You must stay close to Jone today, Son. There'll be a lot of people in the hop garden." Boy nodded, and took Jone's hand as they went out of the house.

The cart arrived and the hop-pickers jumped down. The yard was filled with people chattering, laughing and calling to friends they had not seen for a while. William chose the pole-pullers and led them to their starting stations. He provided each with a red necktie, to identify them to the pickers. The groups of pickers came into the garden, found their pole-pullers, and work was under way.

William came back into the yard and found the tallyman arriving with his measuring stick. They walked to the hop garden together. William picked up the hop bins and pokes from the oast house on his way.

"I'll go and get started." said the tallyman.

William stood and looked around him. A warm autumn sun was beaming down on the scene from a clear blue sky. There was a chill in the air, which whispered of the winter to come. The tall poles, covered in bines heavy with their cones, came out of the ground with the tug of the puller, who laid them on the ground within reach of the pickers. He saw backs bent over the bines, picking the flower cones. He heard laughter, singing and gossiping as the pickers worked. The tallyman was hard pressed to keep up with them as they filled the hop bins. He measured them with his stick to make sure they were full, and marked each one off with a nick in the wood. Adam and Ned were there to load the hops into the pokes, which they swung onto their backs and carried to the oast house.

William took a walk round the field to make sure all was going smoothly. He caught sight of Jone picking busily by the edge of the field. She stood up when she saw him coming, and smiled, pointing to a corner nearby. Out of the way of the pickers, Boy sat on the ground with Dog lying in the sun by his side. William went over to see what Boy was doing. He had the wooden horse and cart which Michael had carved for him, and was loading the cart with stones, pulling it along a track he had made in the mud. He looked up and saw William, and lifted his arms to be picked up. "Farder," he said.

"Nay, Son. Stay there and play, I be busy," said William, and walked away, anxious to get back to his hop-pickers, but feeling guilty for rejecting his son. Jone looked up and glanced over to Boy, who went back to his cart.

He came to the oast house, and watched the pokes being hoisted up into the loft, where Michael and his helper were receiving them. He went into the barn, and felt the heat hit him. He shut the door quickly to keep the temperature constant, and made his way up the stairs to find Michael spreading the hop flowers thinly over the horse hair mat on the drying floor.

"How goes it, Michael?" he asked.

Michael looked up and grinned. "This be just the start of it," he said, and indicated the pile of pokes full of flowers waiting to be dried. Then he went back to work, turning the drying hops. The heavy scent of pollen filled the air, which was thick with dust.

William felt stifled. "I don't know how ye can abide it up here," he said. "I be going below."

"'Twill take almost a week to get through this lot," called Michael. "I'll be here nights, tending the kiln. I'll be out to get a bite to eat when I can."

"Alright!" shouted William, already on his way down the stairs. He stumbled out into the fresh air, coughing.

Mary and Martha came from the house carrying bundles of bait for the workers. William fetched the steddle and took it to the centre of the hop garden. He summoned a couple of men to set it up, and took another to help him bring the barrel of ale out of the buttery. The pickers came, took their shares and hurried back to their places to eat. The picking continued, and Mary and Martha joined in.

Later in the afternoon, William stood up from doing some picking, and watched the hop garden being denuded of its hops. It looked as if a strong wind had laid it waste. Poles with their empty bines littered the ground, and the strong scent of the pollen hung around in the still evening air. He was pleased with the day's work. Then he saw Mary coming towards him, looking worried.

"Will, Boy and Dog be missing, and I can't find Jone either," she said. "I'll go and look around the farm buildings, and ask Martha to stay by the house in case they comes back." William was not too concerned. Boy and Dog often went missing. They wouldn't be far away. He went back to help with the last of the picking.

About half an hour later, William saw Mary returning, having found nothing. The picking was nearly done, and he went over to Adam.

"Boy and Dog have gone off somewhere. I be going to seek him with Mary. Will ye take over, pay the pickers, and take them home in the cart?" Adam agreed, and Ned said he would go to help Michael with the drying.

The day was nearly over, and it would soon be getting dark. William and his sister set off together to search further afield. They searched the copse. Mary found Jone, who was looking for Boy, and was in a state of panic. It took a while to calm her down and discover where she had been looking, and they set off again. They walked up the whapple way, searching in ditches and hedges, and scouring the fields. The orange sun sank softly over the horizon.

Mary and Jone were going back to the house to milk the cows, and lock up the animals for the night. "We'll catch Adam and Ned afore they be bodging and ask them to come and help thee," said Mary, as they set off.

It was quiet as a grave in the fields. William heard the occasional hoot of an owl, and the calls of the two men shouting for Boy. He was tired and worried, picturing his son caught in a ditch somewhere. It was dark now, and they wouldn't be able to see him. He could perish in the cold night. Or he might have wandered off Slade land, and be miles away, lost and afraid. William felt helpless.

He heard Mary and Jone come back, calling desperately. They came up to him and Mary said, "Why don't we get the Headborough to set up a search party, Will? Boy must be somewhere, and he may die of the cold if we don't find him soon."

Jone started crying again. "'Tis all my fault. I should 'ave been watching."

William said, "Yus, that's a good idea. But first, we'll kneel and pray to God to help us."

They knelt on the stubble of the newly cut cornfield.

William prayed, "Oh, God, keep me son safe and lead us to him." Tears came to the surface and he bent over, covering his face in his hands.

After a minute or two, something came and snuffled behind his ear. He opened his eyes. Dog was licking his neck and cheeks, pushing his nose into his chin. William sat up. The animal turned away, and barked. Mary and Jone cried with joy and they got to their feet and followed, anguish turning to hope.

Not more than a few feet away, curled up on a bed of forgotten straw, was a little figure. Boy was fast asleep. His father lifted him gently and cradled him in his arms. He kissed the child's cheek, tears lingering on his own face, and took him over to where Adam and Ned were still searching. They went back to the house, followed by Dog.

Martha was there waiting for news. She gave the sleepy child a bowl of gruel before tucking him up in his crib. Dog was rewarded with a hearty meal, and William took Mary and Jone home to Wadhurst in the cart. He had his first peaceful night since Jane died, falling straight to sleep. He woke refreshed in the morning. His anger and guilt had fallen away, to be replaced by a resolve to give all his attention to his son and his education. The morning prayers were a thanksgiving for his child's deliverance.

Chapter 33   1638

Evening was drawing in as William finished his work for the day. His heart was feeling lighter, and spring was in the air. He walked down the whapple way and through the meadow towards the house.

In the yard Michael was taking time out with Boy and Dog, kicking an inflated pig's bladder around. Dog sat to one side, watching the ball intently. His head followed its direction. The muscles in his shoulders twitched, ready to propel him towards the ball. William watched for a while, then ran to the ball and kicked it towards Dog, who leapt forward and pounced, stopping it in its tracks. But he couldn't hold onto it. It was too big and squashy, and it rolled away. Boy shouted with laughter, ran towards it, and kicked it back to Dog. But Dog ignored it this time, and it rolled towards William, who sent it past Boy to Michael. Boy protested. William and Michael repeated the move with more protests from Boy.

William became aware of a traveller who had limped into the yard and was watching them, leaning on a roughly made crutch. He looked exhausted. His clothes were dirty and tattered, and his matted beard and hair untrimmed. Boy ran to his father, stood by his side and held onto his sleeve. Dog went towards the stranger, barking.

The man stopped, and they all stared at him.

Then Michael shouted, "Edward?" and walked forward. "Be it truly thee, Ed?"

William's heart took a leap.

"Yus," said Edward, "I've been discharged on account of me leg. Not fit to serve in the militia no more."

William showed Edward into the hall, full of joy to see his brother home again, and shocked at the state of him. He gave him a chair and said to Michael, "Take Boy to Jone, and ask Martha for ale."

By the time Michael and Mary came in from the parlour, Edward was gratefully supping his ale. Froth caught in the hair round his mouth. They all listened while he slowly and painfully told his story. The military authorities had sent him to coastal guard duty, and he was billeted in a fisherman's cottage in Seaford. There were frequent skirmishes with pirates who came to raid the towns and villages. Sometimes it was the Hollanders, who were at war with the Spaniards, and hoped to replenish their supplies. It was in one of these skirmishes that Edward received a gunshot wound in his leg, which left him incapable of fighting. A doctor extracted the bullet and he was left to fend for himself. The militia hadn't been paid for some time, and the fisherman couldn't give him board rent free. Edward became a vagrant, begging and stealing his way back to his home ground, sleeping in barns when allowed, and ditches when there was nowhere else. Progress was slow, as his injury had lamed him.

"Did ye go and see Farder on thy way through Wad'rst?" asked William.

"Nay, I be ashamed of meself like this. Hopefully ye can help us clean up like. And I needs a place to lay me head down."

William hesitated. He didn't fully trust Edward, and certainly wouldn't have him in the house overnight. But he couldn't turn his brother away after what he'd been through. After considering, he said, "Ye can wash up at the well, and I'll give thee clean rigging. Then ye can have the lent of a horse to get thee to Wad'rst, so long as ye fetches it back."

Some time later, Michael and William helped a transformed Edward onto one of the horses, and he trotted off to see his father and plead forgiveness. William had no doubt he would be well received as the Prodigal Son.

Some weeks later, at the height of summer, William and Boy came towards the yard after a day's haymaking. The meadow buzzed with insects in the gloaming. Swallows swooped and dived to catch their evening meals.

"There be that man again," said Boy. William looked up to see Edward, respectably dressed in a long jacket and wide-awake hat. His hair and beard were neatly trimmed. He was talking to Michael. Two horses were tethered in the yard.

"That be thy Uncle Edward," replied William, as they approached his two brothers. "Edward, good to see thee. This be my son, Thomas."

"They calls me Boy."

"Hello, Boy. Pleased to meet thee," said Edward.

"Why d'ye carry a bat?" asked Boy.

Edward lifted his crutch and looked at it. "This be me third leg. It helps us doddle around."

William quickly intervened before Boy asked more awkward questions. "Come indoors, Ed. Will ye stay for dinner?"

"I'd be partial to that. Thank thee kindly," said Ed. They all went indoors, and Martha took Boy to clean him up. The three brothers sat by the fire with mugs of ale.

"How fares ye, Ed ?" said William. "Mary tells us ye be biding with Farder."

"Bravely, thanks be. Farder gave us a horse for meself. I brought yours back, Will. I'll be moving back into Lamb'rst 'forelong. Peggy and me be ringling next month. I come by to ask thee both if ye be agreeable to be witnesses." He grinned proudly.

"I'll be main pleased to do that, Ed." William looked at Michael.

"Me too," said Michael.

They both shook his hand warmly and wished him happiness and companionship.

"We'll be biding in Peggy's cottage," said Ed. "Farder helped us to get a pension from the military. That'll pay the rent. Peggy sells her eggs and honey, and I'll try my hand at growing beans and cabbages. We'll scratch along."

Martha and Boy came into the parlour, and they all went to sit at the table, while Martha dished up the pie and vegetables. William noticed the change in Edward. He had been weakened by his ordeals as a soldier, and was embarrassed by his disability. He had little confidence or self-esteem.

"Uncle Edward, I've got a dog," said Boy. "He bides in the close."

Edward was a little lost for words. He asked, "What be thy dog's name?"

"Dog," said Boy. His little face wrinkled with an infectious giggle, and the dimple appeared in his cheek. The room filled with laughter, and the tension relaxed.

After a few minutes, Mary announced, "Thomas Dyne and me'll be ringling come spring." The family all nodded their approval and gave her their good wishes.

"What's ringling?" asked Boy.

"'Tis when a man and a woman love each other so much they want to bide together and raise a fambly," explained Mary. "I'll be coming to bide in Lamb'rst," she said. "And Jone'll be biding with us, won't ye, Jone?"

"Yus. I'll be able to come and help most days," said Jone.

Edward came over on his horse one evening after dinner. William sat with him by the fire in the parlour while Martha put Boy to bed.

"Ye're not down the village with thy friends tonight, Ed," remarked William.

"Nay. Peggy and me be attempting to stay off the ale these days. Don't want to wake up they dragons." His eyes met William's and they both grinned.

"Michael saw thee with Cousin Timothy," said William.

"Yus, I don't know why he should befriend us," said Ed. "He be a strange man, and I don't trust him. I knows a thing or two about his past that I'll keep to meself for the present."

William felt the hairs rise on the back of his neck. He said, "I be avised he has a dark secret. His fambly won't say more'n he could be dangerous if he suspected anyone knows it."

"Mm, I rackon there be a cruel streak in him," remarked Ed.

William put another log on the fire, and said, "Farder were talking about writing his will. Did he say aught to thee while ye was there?"

"Nay, but he be hem doddlish. I believe he be ailing." Edward paused and looked down at his feet. "I've been a failure and a disappointment to 'im all these years. I don't expect him to leave me aught." He rubbed his face with his hands, as if to wipe away the past, then continued, "I've missed thy company, Will." He looked at his brother. "Thank thee for supporting us. Behopes we can be brencheese friends again."

"I'd be partial to that," replied William. "I hopes ye be happy with Peggy. Tell us if ye needs any help, brudder."

Edward chuckled, "At least I've a roof over my head and a wench in me bed."

On the 4th May, 1638, The family gathered for the funeral of their father, Richard Lucke senior, of Wadhurst. He was highly respected in the town, and the church was crowded. But there was a noticeable absence of the older generation. Most of Richard's brothers and sisters had passed on. Only Uncle Thomas and Uncle Christopher had survived them.

John, eldest son and now head of the family, presided over the closest family members who came back to Marlinge afterwards for coger. William asked him, "Will ye be alright in this gurt house on thy own?"

"We hired a housekeeper after Mary left. 'Tis hem lonesome, but Uncle Thomas visits now and again. I goes abroad when I'm able," said John.

"Come and visit us at the Slade, John. We'd be main pleased to see thee."

Mary came towards them, smiling. "I be with child," she said.

"That be grand news," said John.

"I be worried about Jone and the baby," said Mary. "Will, would ye be agreeable to have her bide at the Slade when the child be born like?"

"Surely," said William. "Take care of yourself, and tell us when ye want us to have Jone."

He left Mary and John talking, and glanced over to where Edward was standing on his own. It was Edward's first time meeting the whole family together. He looked uncomfortable. William went over to talk to him.

"I be hem awkward in among all these people, Will. I be minded to bodge off home."

"But they be fambly, Ed. Ye've seen them all since ye were home."

Uncle Thomas joined them and said, "Edward, welcome back! I believe ye be settled in Lamb'rst with thy new Mistus."

"Yus, Uncle, I be." There was an awkward silence.

Thomas turned to William. "I be minded to see Christopher afore long, Will. Would ye be agreeable to take us there sometime? 'Tis tedious troublesome for us riding these days, and I must see him afore one of us be buried. Ye can drive my pony trap."

A few weeks later, William took his Uncle Thomas to see Uncle Christopher. The old man was becoming more frail. William left the brothers together for the day, and promised to return to collect Thomas later and take him home. It wouldn't be long before he would have to say goodbye to his favourite uncles.

Michael was waiting for him at the Slade. Before William had had time to jump down from the trap, Michael said, "I've had word of Farder's will."

"Come inside and tell us," said William. They went into the hall.

"John came with a copy of the will," said Michael. "Farder left us the Ballats house and land."

"Did he leave aught to Edward?" William asked.

"Yus, he got Woodcroft."

William breathed a sigh of relief. Now his two brothers had property. They were more secure. "Shall ye go and live in Wad'urst?" he asked.

"Nay, I'll be biding in thy cottage if that be alright. There be tenants in Ballats, and I'll have their rent coming in. But my work be here, Will, ain't it?"

"Surely. I be main glad for thee, Michael. And it be good news for Edward."

"That it be," said Michael, nodding thoughtfully. William wondered whether his brother was courting. His mind seemed to be dwelling on nest-building and financial security lately. And there was something different about his demeanour.

Chapter 34

"See them swallocky clouds up there?" said Martha to William as they rode on the cart into Wadhurst, loaded up for the market. Boy was sitting among the chickens in their peds, a fat pig, and the crocks of eggs and cheese.

William's skin was prickly and he scratched the skin under his beard. "Yus, it says thunder, don't it, when the flies bite?" It had been sultry weather for days, with flies round the midden, and bad smells from rotting refuse. It would be worse in the town. A good heavy shower would refresh the air and settle the dust. They trundled along the road, sweltering in the heat. Dog trotted behind the cart.

"Bess be doddlish today, I rackons it be time she jacked up. I'll look for another cart horse while I'm in town. How be Jone, now she be biding with us?"

"She seems content," replied Martha. "She likes muvvering Boy. And she knows us well enough. I can't say she be missing Mary at all."

"Mary's baby be due prensley," said William. "I'll call on 'er tomorrow, and see how she be fairing."

They reached Wadhurst and William helped Martha to set up the standing. He left Boy with her and went to find the labourers who were looking for work. Several men wearing round frocks stood around the town square in a forlorn group, ignoring each other. Each held the tools of his trade. There were mostly agricultural labourers, a weaver and a tailor. Two women in grey dresses and white caps and aprons held their milking stools. William looked the men up and down, and spoke to some of them before he noticed one standing apart, who seemed to be a cut above the rest.

"Be ye for hire?" William asked. The man answered in the affirmative, and explained that he was skilled in hop drying, but would take any agricultural work. He spoke with a slightly foreign accent, and when William questioned him he explained that his father had come from Holland fifteen years ago, for work in the hop industry. Pieter had grown up in Sussex.

"I'd be partial to taking thee on, if ye be willing," William said. "Me brudder's in charge of the hops and the oast. But he could do with some help, and ye can give us a hand with the labouring othertimes."

They agreed a wage, shook hands on it and Pieter said, "I be much obliged, Mas Lucke. When d'ye want us to start?"

"We can take thee back along of us today, if ye can fetch thy rigging and all. Be ready here at the close of the market. Will ye be alright sleeping in the oast barn for now?" Pieter agreed that would be fine, and went to get his belongings together and to settle some business.

William looked around the market and bartered with other farmers. He offered his fat pig in exchange for fagging hooks for the coppicing and hedging, and barn shovels for the oast house. He heard a loud voice in proclamation; a preacher standing on a box delivered his sermon to a small group of men and women. He was dressed in a long black coat. The crown of his hat was round, with a narrow brim. There was a drip of water on the end of his nose. He took a grey rag out of his top pocket, and wiped his ruddy face. William stopped to listen.

"Labour to be more humble, and sensible of your own vileness!" the preacher shouted. The people round him murmured. William felt tired and despondent. How much more guilt and humility could he bear to carry on his shoulders? He turned away, and saw John Tapsell and Nick Longley coming over to talk to him.

"Fancy a drop to quench thy thirst, Will?" Nick asked. They went off to the tavern for a tankard of ale. The atmosphere in the small room was oppressive with the stench of body odour. They took their ale outside to join others who were discussing the effects of the heat wave.

"There be terrible sickness and infection in the town," said Tapsell. "Me mistus has been abed these last four days. Can't hardly lift 'er head off the pillow."

"My neighbour were laid to rest t'other day. 'E died of the fever," said another man.

"Yus, and I be avised of others, that's overcome with the vomiting."

William didn't need any of his family or farm workers to be laid off sick. Not wanting to hear more messages of doom, he bade his friends goodbye, and went to call on Uncle Thomas. He was relieved to find him well, but Thomas had more sad news. Thomas Upton, the 'Archimedes of Wadhurst' had died recently. Another treasure from William's childhood had passed on.

"He were a wonderful knowledgeable man," said William. "I recall the day we went to see his shop and all the marvellous things he made."

"The clock I gifted thee on thy wedding day. That came from his shop. He made the clock himself, for certain sure," declared Thomas. They mused on the passing of a remarkable man, until it was time for William to go back to the market.

He went to see how Martha and Boy were getting on. Boy was enjoying the banter with the customers and showing them his dog when William arrived.

He said, "Come, Boy, we'll go and find a new horse." He hitched his son onto his shoulders. In the beast market, Boy was quiet among the noise, heat and odorous atmosphere. William made his way to where the horses were tethered. Two young cart horses stood by a gate. The owner was hanging around nearby.

"Which one shall we buy?" William asked, as he lifted the child onto the ground. He looked the two geldings over and examined their teeth and their feet carefully. "He has to be strong enough to pull a loaded cart."

Boy walked over to the big horses. He appeared small next to them, but he wasn't afraid. He looked at them both critically then pointed, "The black one, Farder," he said.

"That be a good choice, Son," said William, and led Boy over to the owner. He asked a few questions of the man. A price was agreed, William paid for the horse and led him back to Martha and the stall. Boy and Dog followed.

Martha's face was flushed and her hair hung in wet strands from underneath her cap. Thunder rumbled in the distance.

William said, "We'd best pack up what's left and be bodging. I'll go and fetch the new labourer."

He brought Pieter along, and introduced him to Martha and Boy. It was as if the black sky formed a blanket over them. The air was stifling, and they hurried to load up. Pieter lifted Boy into the cart, and leapt up himself, just as the rain started. William tethered the new horse to the back of the cart, and asked Pieter to keep an eye on him for safety. Lightning flashed and thunder roared as they journeyed home. Boy and Pieter lifted their faces to catch the big drops of water in their mouths, laughing with glee. They were all soaked in the deluge, but it was a relief not to be sweltering in the heat.

It was still pouring with rain when they arrived back at the Slade.

"Go seek Jone, and get dry," William said to Boy as he lifted him from the cart. Boy ran indoors. William gave Martha a hand down, and Pieter helped to unload the cart and put it away in the barn. Michael came out and led the new horse away with Bess to the stable. They went into the house together, and into the parlour, where the fire was blazing cheerfully. William turned to Pieter, "Welcome to the Slade!" he said, and shook Pieter's hand warmly. "Michael, this be Pieter. He be come to give thee a hand with the hops."

William had a good feeling about Pieter. Their clothes steamed as they approached the fire, and they stood supping ale until the dinner was ready, talking about hops and the management of the oast.

At dinner that evening, William said to Boy, "What be the name of the new horse, Boy?" There was a silence while Boy thought about it.

Then he said, "Gaffer. I want to call him Gaffer, because he be big and strong like my Gaffer who's gone to live with God." The family all nodded agreement.

Chapter 35

The next evening William came into the parlour to find Martha checking the contents of the pot simmering over the fire. Her face was flushed and she was breathing heavily.

He said, "'Tis troublesome weather for standing over a hot fire, ain't it, Martha?"

Martha grunted and took a spoonful from the pot to taste. Jone and Boy came in from the close, followed by Michael and Pieter, who were discussing the condition of the hop plants. Pieter was saying, "If we get this weather all year, we could get two hop pickings, Michael."

They all sat round the table and waited for Martha to dish up. She ladled the food onto the first pewter dish and turned to bring it to the table. William saw her sway. She had to grab hold of the back of a chair to steady herself. She hesitated. The others stopped talking and stared. Martha took a few steps forward and dropped the dish with a clatter.

She looked up, shocked and shaking violently, then sank to the floor, saying, "Oh my! Oh my!" The three men jumped to their feet and hauled Martha into the nearest armchair. Jone fetched a ladle and scooped up the spilt food. Boy started to whimper. They found towels and bathed Martha's face in cold water, then helped her to her chamber, where she lay on her cot, shaking and moaning. Michael went off to find the doctor.

He came back soon after. "The doctor's main busy, and can't come yet. We've to keep Martha warm and give her plenty of liquids to drink but no food."

An hour later they sat down again to eat the dinner, which was still sitting over the fire, drying up. Jone had fed Boy and put him to bed. Then she tried to comfort Martha.

"She be sweating bravely," she said, as she dished up the food.

"Who's going to cook dinner?" asked Michael. "Can ye cook, Pieter?"

"Nay," said Pieter. "I can boil an egg." And he looked round, smiling with confidence.

"We can't live on eggs," complained Michael.

William was quiet with his own thoughts. How would they manage without Martha? She had always been there for him, since he came to the Slade. She had calmed him in crises, always knowing what to do. Mary was unable to help, as she would soon have a baby to nurse.

Jone's attempts at making porridge the following morning didn't come up to Martha's standard, and, after breakfast, the family offered sincere prayers for Martha's swift recovery. They all shared her tasks before joining Adam and Ned in the fields. Jone nursed Martha as best she could, and found bread, cheese and apples for their coger.

It was the end of the day. Jone and Boy had fetched the cows and were milking them. The men had come in from work early and were in the parlour finding something to cook for dinner.

They were distracted by the noise of a horse galloping into the yard, and William and Michael went to see who it was. A young woman leapt from her pony, her dark brown curly hair flying, her red skirts hitched up in a knot round her hips. She flounced up to Michael and set about him with her fists, beating his chest and shoulders. He was a good head taller than she, and enjoyed the attack, laughing and dodging out of the way with whoops and feigned fear. At last he caught her round the waist, and lifted her off the ground. She was still flailing her fists, and he wrapped his arms round her body, pulled her close and gave her a smacking kiss.

The girl was finally subdued, and Michael said to her, "Struth, I do like to see thee willocky mad, young Tamsen." She struggled to be free, unhitched her skirts, and smoothed them down impatiently.

"Don't ye leave us in the lurch like that again Michael Lucke! I waited for I dunnow how long, and ye never come," she said angrily.

Michael said, "Don't be so uppity. I couldn't come on account of Will needing help with Martha. She be sick with the fever, and we be hem mucked-up without her."

Tamsen's attitude changed. She looked concerned. "Let's see her. I may be able to help." Michael looked at William, who nodded his head. There was a chance this girl knew what she was talking about. William and Michael showed her to Martha's chamber. Martha was tossing around, her hair and nightgown were soaked, and she was gabbling in her delirium.

Tamsen looked closely at the invalid, feeling her hands and her face. She looked at Michael and said, "I knows a potion what'll help the fever, if ye'd be agreeable. William agreed that anything was better than nothing. They went down to the parlour where Tamsen set a kettle of water over the fire to boil. Then she went out into the garden. William looked at Michael, waiting for an explanation of this sudden turn of events.

Michael said, "That be Tamsen, my new girl. She be well versed in herb potions."

Tamsen came in with a handful of herbs. William, Michael and Pieter watched her as she searched in all Martha's pots and jars. Having found the spices she was looking for, she mixed the potion and took it up to Martha.

William remarked, "She be unaccountable feisty, that one. But I rackons ye can manage her well." They went back to helping Pieter to prepare the meal.

Michael grinned, and said, "We be rubbing along nicely, like. I ain't seen her so mad as that though!"

Tamsen reappeared and said that Martha was now sleeping peacefully. She looked at the men's attempts at cooking a meal, and they soon found that she had magically taken over, pushing them firmly out of the way.

Jone came into the house with Boy and stared in astonishment at this strange woman in the parlour, apparently in place of Martha.

Tamsen looked up and smiled. "I be Tamsen. I just happened along and sees ye was needing some help like." Turning to Boy, she said, "And who be this chipper lad?"

"I be Boy, this be Jone, and that be my Farder," Boy said, pointing to William.

"Obliged to meet thee all," said Tamsen, looking round with a radiant smile on her face. William approved of his brother's choice of a pretty girl.

Tamsen went back to her cooking, humming a tune. The others looked at each other and chuckled. William nudged Michael. "Ye've found a good one there!"

They were grateful to see a meal put in front of them that evening, and invited Tamsen to join them. She declined, saying that she must go and help her mother with her younger brothers and sisters, who would be getting hungry by this time. She went out, mounted her pony, and trotted away.

That wasn't the last they saw of her. She called every day until Martha was well enough to cook for them again, and she gradually became part of the family. Only Jone felt uncomfortable with Tamsen.

It was dinner time. William was passing the pond on his way back to the house. He found Boy and Dog there, splashing in the mud where the ducks dabbled.

"Come, Boy. 'Tis time for dinner," said William. They came to the back door where Tamsen was swilling the floor of the milk-house. William left Boy with her and went indoors.

"Let's get thee cleaned up, Boy," Tamsen said, taking the muddy child to the well.

William heard shouting, and turned back.

Jone had come in from feeding the animals. "What d'ye think ye're doing?" she shouted at Tamsen, who replied, "He be in a fair hike and needs a wash down. Don't take on so."

Jone's temper was up. "I'll do that. 'Tis not thy business, leave off!" She snatched Boy away. Boy's face screwed up and tears began to fall. Conflict always upset him.

"Don't ye speak to us like that!" shouted Tamsen. "That's the last time I helps thee out." She strutted away in a rage, barging past William, who saw that Jone was now attending to Boy.

Tamsen bumped into Michael on her way out. He'd heard the rumpus and could see she was upset. He stopped her and said, "What be going on here? Be ye upsetting our Jone?"

Tamsen shook herself free. "I ain't welcome round here. I be bodging," and she flounced out of the house. Michael didn't see her for some time, and thought it was all over between them.

"There'll be others. That one'll always be quick-tempered," said William, though he regretted Tamsen's absence. She was a good worker.

Chapter 36   1639

It was May Day, a balmy, blossomy day, echoing with birdsong and heavy with scents. Bees visited each flower to collect the nectar, buzzing around busily. William thought sadly that it would have been good to take Boy to the May fair, just like the old days. But fairs and public gatherings had been forbidden by the church authorities. Instead, he took Boy on a tour of the farm, showing him the green spears of corn piercing the brown earth, lambs frolicking in the meadow and the hops beginning to climb their poles. Pieter and Michael were hoeing between the rows with nidgets, their wide-brimmed hats shading their eyes from the bright sunshine. William took Boy to the copse. The bluebells were a wonderful sight, exuding their scent throughout the woodland and beyond. Hazy blue mingled with the fresh green of the new leaves above, stretching into the distance. Boy crouched down to examine a flower, putting it to his nose. William thought of Jane and the first day the bluebells appeared. He went to look at the hazel bushes, and chose which ones were to be coppiced this year. He showed Boy the spent hazel cat's tails, and the little green leaves popping out of their buds. They emerged from the copse into the hay meadow. The hay was in good condition and it should be possible to get a first mowing from it soon. He talked to his son all the time, explaining everything, and Boy listened intently, saying little.

The tranquillity was disturbed by Martha, hurrying up the whapple way. She puffed up to them and said, "Mas William, Mus Thomas be sick. They rackons 'e be failing. Ye must go to him prensley."

William's breath left him for a moment. He called for Boy, who was crouched among the tall grasses, watching a big black beetle crawl over his foot. They walked back with Martha. She took Boy by the hand and led him into the house. William went to fetch Damsel and saddle her up. He tried to grasp the fact that his uncle may be dying. Uncle Thomas was his closest friend and counsellor, his shelter in a storm. He dreaded his loss.

On his way to Wadhurst he prayed that he would keep calm, so as not to upset Thomas. When he arrived at Bedifields Hill, he dismounted and walked into the house, expecting to find his uncle in his cot. But he was sitting in a chair by the fire, in his nightgown and nightcap, wrapped in a woollen blanket. Aged fifty-five, Thomas was the youngest of the brothers, but he appeared an old man, frail, white as his nightgown. He was breathing with difficulty. He looked up. A twinkle returned to his eyes when he saw William.

"I be main glad ye've come, Will. I had to see thee while I still had the strength to talk to thee. Come and sit close." His breath was short and his voice was rasping. William pulled up a chair and sat by his uncle's side. Thomas held onto William's arm with a cold, bony hand. William took it and held it between his two strong warm ones.

"Don't beazle thyself, Uncle. Take it slow."

Thomas took as deep a breath as he could manage, and began to talk. "I've loved thee like a son, Will, ye knows that... I just wants ye to mind... don't let thy heart rule thy head... Listen to what the preachers say, then decide for thyself... and seek what's true for thee." He paused to get his breath back.

"Ye be a fine and capable husbandman... a good farder... God knows... and He'll guide thee...and comfort thee in thy grief... Look around thee and see how blessed ye be." Thomas rested again.

William said, "Thank thee for thy counsel, Uncle. I shall miss thy support, but I'll mind what ye've larned us for the rest of me days." He lifted the cold tired hand to his cheek, and kissed it, then added, "I'll come again tomorrow and sit with thee. Rest now." He tucked Thomas' hands under the blanket. But his Uncle hadn't finished, and beckoned to him to stay.

"Be sure and see to Christopher and his affairs when he goes... See that Martha be safe and secure for as long as she do live... and wants for nothing... She's been a faithful servant." Then he added, "Take the pony trap, it be yours."

"I'll do all those things, Uncle, be ye not fretting thyself." William sat close to Thomas until he fell asleep, then crept quietly away feeling sad and lonely. He took the pony out of the stable and hitched him up to the trap. He tethered Damsel behind, and took the road home. The image of the frail old man remained in his mind, and the sadness he felt stayed with him.

Next day William asked Martha if she'd like to see her old Master before he died. They went together in the trap. Martha sat by the cot, unable to speak. Thomas wasn't talking much, but he recognised his old friend, and held her hand affectionately. William spoke to the housekeeper and made sure his uncle had everything he needed. Then he went back into the parlour and read some passages from the Bible to Thomas, as he had in the old days.

It took a few more days for Thomas to slip slowly away, struggling to breathe, and barely conscious. William was there when he gurgled his final breath, and was able to gently close his Uncle's eyes as a last gesture of his love for him.

On the 13th of May, William and Michael took the pony trap to Bedifields Hill. They carried Thomas in his coffin on the journey to his last resting place among the family in Wadhurst.

After the burial, William looked towards the lych gate and saw another pony trap waiting outside the litten. It was the one Timothy had stolen from him. But Timothy had not been in the church. He felt a soft touch on his elbow, and turned to see Susannah, dressed all in black and holding a walking cane. She had aged considerably.

"Hello William," she said. "I'm sorry for your loss."

William was struggling with surprise. "Ma'am, I'd no idea ye were here. Thank thee for coming." He took her hand and held it for a while, gazing into her eyes. "'Tis a pleasure to see thee again."

"You've had much sorrow in your life since we last met. I hope you're recovering," she said.

"'Twas hard, but I scratched along. I be happy with my son, and proud of him," William said. "And the farm be doing bravely."

"I wish I could invite you to visit me. I would love to meet your son. But Timothy…" Her voice wavered as her gaze strayed anxiously over William's shoulder.

"Come, Mother," called a sharp voice. "You must come home now."

Susannah squeezed William's hand, and she hobbled away towards the gate. William turned to see

Timothy hustling his mother into the trap. He shot a spiteful glance back in William's direction as he climbed up and whipped the pony into action. The trap lurched forward. William caught sight of Susannah's face looking back, and her hand raised to wave.

Soon after the funeral, William sat in the hall, trying to work out, as executor, what he was going to do about Uncle Thomas' will. It was twelve years since it was written, and things had changed. Beneficiaries had died, and more children had been born. Other beneficiaries had acquired properties of their own. The main problem was the property at Bedifields Hill. This had been left to John Kingswood with the option of buying it. But both the Kingswoods had died. They had three daughters who were now married. If John Kingswood had declined to buy the property, it was to be passed to Thomas Haman on condition that he pay his brother and sisters and the Kingswood's granddaughter ten pounds each. The Hamans were not the easiest people to deal with, and William could see that there may be squabbles. He rode to Wadhurst and discussed the problem with John.

The next day, William took Uncle Thomas' pony to the blacksmith in Lamberhurst, to be shoed. He gave Boy his first ride. William walked beside them through the village. Dog followed. They arrived at the forge, and William lifted Boy down. He explained to the smith what was needed, and told Boy all about blacksmiths. Boy was intrigued, and stood watching the procedure with awe and wonder. He was holding a little treasure, a smooth pink pebble he'd found in the fields, and was fingering it while he watched.

William said, "Come, Boy. We'll go and see Uncle Edward, and return when the smith's put shoes on the pony."

"Nay, I want to stay here and watch, Farder. I won't go abroad." He looked pleadingly at William with his soft blue eyes.

"Don't ye get too close to the chafery, Son. Ye must stay exactly where ye be. I won't be long." Boy nodded.

William walked down the street to Peggy's cottage, and knocked at the door.

Peggy opened it. "He's out the back," she said. "Come in." She led William through the house and into the garden, where Ed was standing leaning on his crutch and picking caterpillars from the leaves of the cabbages. He looked up.

"These pesky critters do drive us mad," he said. But he seemed happy and relaxed.

William said, "I thought I'd happen along. I brought the pony to the forge."

Edward stood up straight, holding his back, and came towards William. "Good day, brudder. Have a seat," he said. They sat on chairs in the sun, and Peggy fetched a third from the house. She was a well-built woman, who rarely smiled, and said little. But William believed she was capable of looking after Edward, and keeping him on the straight and narrow. She brought three glasses of milk and handed them round.

"We don't have ale in the house," she said shortly.

William said, "I be obliged. I can't bide long, Boy be watching the blacksmith. He be a curious child. He's always studying something." They chatted for a while about the family and Uncle Thomas' funeral.

Edward said, "That Cousin Timothy's been seen with a pony trap round here the last few days."

William was surprised. "Were there anybody in the trap?" he said, thinking of Susannah.

"Not that I know of," said Edward.

A cold knot formed in the pit of William's stomach. He was anxious to get back to Boy. His pony should be ready by now. He took his leave and returned to the forge. The pony was waiting to be collected.

There was no sign of Boy, or Dog.

Chapter 37

"Where's my son?" William shouted to the blacksmith above the noise of the bellows.

The smith stopped his work to reply, "He were there one minute, gone the next. Not long ago. I rackoned he'd bodged off looking for thee." William turned to go. Where could they have gone?

"Be ye about to pay us today?" shouted the blacksmith. William stopped and searched in his money purse. His hands were shaking. He took the money from the purse and handed it to the blacksmith. As he went to take the pony away, he saw Greg Dyne coming down the road towards his house.

"Did ye see my son going up the road?"

"Nay, but there were a pony and trap travelling fast, and that dog of yours following."

"Which way?" asked William, beginning to panic.

"Up the hill. I believe he turned onto the road towards Frant," said Greg.

"Can I have the lent of thy horse? And you keep the pony for me?"

"Yus," said Greg. "Come, quick." They hurried to Greg's house to collect the horse. William galloped up the road towards Frant, his heart in his mouth. He knew that Timothy's pony had a head start, but they had to stop sometime.

The further he went, the emptier the road became. He saw a woman coming towards him driving geese, and stopped as she passed. The geese shrieked and squawked, and flapped all over the road.

"Did ye see a pony and trap going this way?" he asked.

The woman came closer, holding her hand to her ear, "I didn't catch that. I be thick of hearing."

William shouted, "Did ye see a pony and trap going this way?"

"Nay, I ain't met nobody," the woman said, as she drove the geese into the side of the road with her stick.

William galloped off. What would Timothy want with Boy? Where would he take him? He could be anywhere by now. Where should William start looking?

He arrived in Frant. The horse was lathering, and couldn't go much further. William asked several people if they'd seen a pony trap, with a dog following. None of them had.

William rode the weary horse back to Lamberhurst. He remembered that Timothy's sister Susan lived nearby somewhere. He wondered if Greg knew where. Greg was at home when William arrived.

"Will ye walk the pony back to the Slade?" he asked. "I'll ride up there and get Damsel. Then ye can have thy horse back."

Greg agreed.

"D'ye know where the Rumneys live?"

"I do," said Greg. "They live off the Frant road to the left, just outside the village." William cursed himself for not thinking of it sooner. Timothy could have taken Boy to Susan's house. He'd wasted a lot of time going all the way to Frant. He rode to the Slade, briefly told Michael what had happened, and went to saddle up Damsel. Greg walked into the yard with the pony just as he was leaving. William waved his thanks as he passed, knowing that Michael would look after Greg, and maybe give him a tankard of ale for his trouble.

William retraced his steps along the Frant road, looking out for a left turn. Night was falling when he reached the Rumney residence. As he rode up the long drive through an avenue of stately trees, a large manor house faced him. To the left was a courtyard of stables, barns and outbuildings. The place felt deserted. William knew there would be no-one at home. Nevertheless, he dismounted and approached the massive front door, which was studded with nails. He took the iron doorknocker in his hand. The house echoed to his knocking, and he waited for a few minutes. All was quiet. He was about to leave when the door opened a small gap and a young girl's face peered through anxiously.

"There be nobody 'ere," she said. "Master and Mistus be abroad visiting." The door closed with a resounding slam, and William heard the bolts shoot home. He led Damsel to the courtyard and tethered her. He searched every barn and stable, calling softly for Boy and Dog. The place was indeed deserted. No trap. No pony. No Boy. No Dog. He must go to Mayfield and question Susannah. It was his only hope.

On his way, he stopped at the Slade.

Pieter came to meet him. "Michael's ridden to Wad'rst, to spread the word and ask if anybody saw a pony and trap riding through."

"Thank thee, Pieter. I may see him. If not, tell him I be going to Mayfild." Pieter agreed.

Martha came out of the house. "Take this for bait, Mas William. You ain't eaten all day." She handed him a bundle, which he tucked into his pocket.

"Thank thee, Martha," he said, and proceeded to ride towards Wadhurst, through the dark of the night.

As he reached the outskirts of the town, he recognised Michael's white horse, coming his way.

"Be that thee, William?" Michael shouted.

William slowed to speak to his brother. "D'ye have any news?"

"Nick Longley saw a pony and trap going through town. But he were certain sure there weren't no passengers. He don't know which way it went."

"It mayn't be the same one," said William. "I be going to Mayfild prensley."

"I'll come along of thee. Two pair of eyes be better than one." Michael turned his horse and they galloped off together.

"I called on Cousin Richard, and Brudder John in Wad'rst," said Michael as they rode along the Mayfield road. "They'll call on anyone who knows Boy, and ask them to be on the lookout."

William and Michael galloped into the yard of Susannah's house and dismounted, tethering their horses by the jossing block. There was no sign of the pony trap, or the groom. Michael went to look in the stables and barns. William approached the front door and knocked. His heart was beating fast. The maid opened the door.

"Be your Master at home?" asked William. "I need to speak with him."

"Nay, he ain't been here all day," declared the maid. "But the Mistus be here. Come in." William removed his hat and went into the empty hall to wait. There was no light, except for one small candle on the table. The shutters were closed. What could he do if Susannah knew nothing, and Timothy had disappeared? He thought carefully about what he would say. The maid came out of the parlour and showed him in.

Susannah was standing by the dying embers of the fire. She wore a long white gown. Her nightcap covered her grey hair.

"William, what is the matter? Why are you here at this hour?" she asked.

"I beg pardon for disturbing thee, Ma'am. I be seeking my son. I believe Timothy took him this morning, and drove him away in the trap." Susannah's face paled, and a look of deep concern came over it. She put her hand to her mouth.

William continued, "I wondered if ye'd seen him, or if ye knows where he be."

Susannah regained her composure. "William, I am so sorry. Come and sit down." William remained standing, holding the back of the chair. Susannah sat by the fire, her face glowed in the flickering candlelight. "How did this happen?" she asked.

William related the events of the day, including his call on Susan.

"Oh dear, this is very worrying," said Susannah. Her face contorted with distress, and tears came into her eyes. "Timothy has always behaved strangely, but he's become worse, more aggressive and unreasonable. The groom left us this week because he wouldn't tolerate Timothy's treatment of him. The villagers think he's possessed of the devil. I'm afraid to go against him for fear he'll punish me with wicked threats, though he has never hurt me physically. He locks me in my room sometimes. I fear your child may be in mortal danger."

William's mounting anger burst out of him. He gripped the back of the chair and raised his voice. "The man should be locked up in the mad house!" Then he remembered who he was talking to. He said, "Ma'am, I'm sorry to say this to thee, but I must report to the Headborough tomorrow. There'll be a hue en cry out for your son."

Susannah was weeping now. "I understand," she said. She wrapped her arms around her body, as she let the tears course down her face.

"If ye have any news, I'd be obliged if ye would send word to the Slade in Lamb'rst. Good night Ma'am." He opened the door and walked into the hall, shutting the door behind him.

As William was putting his hat on, the front door opened. Timothy stood there dressed all in black, his breeches tied at the knees, and his beard and moustache neatly trimmed. A satisfied smile spread slowly across his face.

"Ha, I've caught you at it at last! I've told you to keep away from my mother. You'll regret this." He proceeded to take off his cloak and hat, and gave them to the maid.

William was completely taken aback for a moment. His anger returned and he approached Timothy shouting, "What have ye done with my boy?" He grasped Timothy's neck tie and pulled his face towards his own. There was a smell of foul breath. He shook Timothy vigorously. The parlour door opened behind William, and he was aware that Susannah was watching. He let go of Timothy.

"Where have ye taken him?" he shouted again.

Timothy recovered himself quickly, shaking his shoulders and adjusting his clothing. "I have no idea what you're talking about, farmer's boy," he said coolly.

"Ye were seen in Lamb'rst, in thy trap, going towards Frant," William said. "Where is he now?"

Timothy sneered. "How dare you attack me like that in front of my mother? Please leave my house immediately." He opened the door.

"You'll pay for this, ye willock," William said as he walked past Timothy out into the courtyard. The door slammed behind him.

Michael was waiting. "I looked in the trap after he went into the house. Boy's not there, but I found this." He put something in William's hand.

William's fingers closed round a small smooth pebble. It was almost certainly pink, though it was hard to see in the dark. He put it in his pocket carefully, with the bait he'd not yet eaten.

Chapter 38

William and Michael mounted their horses, and returned slowly and sadly to the Slade. They didn't speak much. There was nothing they could say. William thought of his little boy somewhere out there, maybe locked in a barn, or left in a ditch. He could even be dead. William hoped that Dog had managed to stay by Boy's side, and that they would both be found soon. But there was nothing anyone could do on so dark a night. As they arrived home, a light drizzle was falling. They took the horses into the stable and racked up. Martha and Jone were waiting for them in the parlour.

The family kept vigil all night, praying for the deliverance of Boy. The fire burned low. The candles guttered in the draught from the shutters. Michael fell asleep, sitting with his head on his arms resting on the table. Jone wept softly, and rocked herself to and fro in her chair, clutching one of Boy's vests. Martha was restless, and busied herself with little jobs, sewing a patch on one of Boy's round frocks, and polishing the copper kettle. William gazed into the fire, listening for any noise that would give them some hope, the return of Dog, or someone bringing news.

The crowing of the rooster heralded the dawn. William opened the shutters. The sky outside was duck egg blue. Martha stoked up the fire and put the porridge on to cook. Michael woke, and went out to the well for a wash.

He came back into the parlour almost immediately.

William looked up at Michael. His face was pale, his hair ruffled. He was staring at William.

Then he said quietly, "Dog be back. Just come in. He be beazled. And he's been horsewhipped."

William leapt from his seat. He dashed out into the close. Dog was panting, worn out and covered in mud. There were two open wheals across his back, caked with dried blood. He pawed at William, and turned to go out. Martha came with food and water. Dog drank the water, but refused the food, turning away again. He looked back at William and barked.

William went to the stable and saddled up Damsel.

Michael said, "I be a-coming along of thee," and went to get his horse.

"God speed!" called Martha, who stood at the door with Jone.

They followed Dog, who ran and walked towards Wadhurst. As they went through the town they saw Nick Longley

"We be going to seek Boy," called William as he passed.

Dog took the Mayfield road. He was limping badly, but soon picked up speed. William and Michael trotted behind. After a mile or so, Dog turned into Tapsells Farm entrance.

John Tapsell came to meet them, smiling.

William and Michael dismounted and led their horses as they followed John to the house. Dog lay panting on the doorstep.

"Boy's been sleeping in my barn all night," said John.

"Be he alright?" asked William, hardly able to believe that the search was over.

"He be fine!" said John's wife, appearing at the door. "Come in, come in!"

Boy came out of the parlour. "Farder!" he shouted, and ran to meet him. William picked him up and hugged him close, rocking him in his arms as if he were a baby again. They both laughed and cried with joy.

"He's had his porridge," said Dorcas Tapsell. "He don't seem to be hurt, just frightened."

"Where be Dog?" said Boy, as his father set him down.

"Out here! He came to tell us where ye was," Michael said. Boy went and crouched to make a fuss of Dog, who wagged his tail and licked Boy's hands and face. Michael examined Dog's feet.

"I be greatly obliged to thee for muvvering him," William said to the Tapsells as he shook their hands vigorously.

"Farder, a man took us away in his trap. I shouted to him to stop, but he just went faster." The memory of his ordeal crumpled Boy's face. "And he beat Dog."

William bent down and put his hands on Boy's shoulders. "Whist now, we've found thee, thanks be to God. Ye can tell us all about it when we've got thee home." He took his son's hand and led him to Damsel. Damsel snuffled as William lifted Boy up in front. He mounted and waved to the Tapsells. Michael lifted Dog and put him across his horse's shoulders, and followed William home.

Martha and Jone took Boy to be mothered. William and Michael were hungry now. They led their horses to the croft and came back to the house, where Martha gave them a meal of cold meat and pickle with whips of bread and butter. They didn't speak until they'd finished eating, and were supping their ale.

267

At last Michael looked at William. "Be ye going to the Headborough to report Timothy?"

"I don't see as it'll do much good, now," said William. "We've naught to prove it were him. And he'll deny it."

"But Boy will know him if he sees him again."

"Yus, but I don't care to put the child through that. He's been frightened enough." Now that Boy had been found and was back in the nest, nothing else mattered to William. Timothy had achieved what he wanted.

Boy entered the parlour and came to stand by his father. William searched in his pocket and brought something out. He took Boy's hand, and placed the pebble in his palm, then closed his fingers over it.

Boy smiled a dimpled smile. "I believed 'twas lost." Then he looked puzzled. "How did ye find it?"

"Michael found it. We knows the man what took thee away. We was seeking thee all day. We found the trap he took thee in."

Boy became thoughtful. His story came out in little bursts. There were tears in between, but he needed to rid himself of the whole horrible experience. Boy hadn't seen his captor's face, as he came from behind and lifted him into the trap. They travelled at speed at first, and when Boy looked out of the back he could see Dog running behind. They went up a long avenue of trees and came into a big courtyard, then into a huge dark barn. The man jumped down from the trap, and Boy heard him shouting, and the noise of a whip cracking. There was a yelp, and Boy knew that Dog was hurt. At this point he broke down in tears. William took him on his knee and soothed him.

After a while he said, "Did the man leave thee in the trap?"

"Nay, Farder. He got in beside me. He had a black hat and a cloak. I never saw his face, but his mouth smelt foul, like the midden. He said he'd chased Dog away, and he'd never come back, ever again. He said lots of wicked things about thee. Then he drove us out onto the road again."

Boy was taken he knew not where. He thought he'd be far away from home. He kept looking for Dog but he was nowhere to be seen. After a long time the trap stopped. It was dark. He was lifted down on the road. There were no buildings or people around. The pony trap drove away into the night.

Here Boy was upset again with the telling of it, and needed time to calm down. Martha brought him a drink of milk. William waited while Boy fingered his pebble, then he started talking again.

"I were lost and afeared, Farder. I footed it for a bit, but I couldn't see where the road were. I sat down and started to weep." He took a deep, sobbing sigh, then looked at his father and the dimple appeared in his cheek.

"Dog came to us." Boy laughed, remembering how happy he was to see his friend. Dog nudged him to his feet, and led him along the road. They walked and walked. Then Dog led him off the road into a barn with straw in it.

"We fell into the straw and made a bed. We was moithered. Dog came close, and we fell asleep. When I waked, Dog were gone, and I worritted again. Then a nice man found me and took me into his house."

Boy looked at William. "Dog was hurt considerable," he said. "Will 'e be alright?"

"Martha's muvvered Dog. 'Tis but a scratch. 'Twill soon heal," said William.

During the next few days, William spent time with Boy taking him around the farm and talking to him about ordinary things.

"Can I ride the pony again?" said Boy one day.

"Surely ye can. I'll larn thee how to ride him proper, like," said William. They went to fetch the pony, and William found a saddle for him. He lifted Boy up, and showed him how to hold the reins. He led Boy out onto the whapple way, and walked with him to the meadow. They looked at the cows, and gave Gaffer the cart horse an apple. Then they went to see the sheep and lambs. They counted the sheep to make sure there were none missing. On the way back, William let go of the reins and Boy walked the pony on by himself. William showed him how to guide the pony into the croft with the other horses and lifted him down. They removed the saddle and harness, and allowed the pony to run free.

"I shall call him Robin," said Boy. He went running into the house to tell Martha all about it.

Chapter 39

It was Sunday, and the family were gathered with the Lamberhurst residents in the church on the hill. After the service, on his way out into the summer sunshine, William saw Susan Rumney weaving her way through the crowds towards him. He waited.

Susan came up to him. She was out of breath. "Oh William," she said. "I'm so glad I've caught you. I want to tell you how upset my mother is after your last visit to her. I told her that you'd found your son." She smiled at Boy, standing close to his father. "But she's worried about the circumstances, and Timothy's possible involvement."

"Yus," said William. "I be sorry she's upset. Please tell her that Boy be safe. I've decided not to go to the Headborough. There ain't no proof that Timothy is guilty of taking him. Timothy will deny it. I hope thy muvver will be able to forget the whole thing." He tipped his hat to Susan and said goodbye, feeling upset and angry. He didn't like the situation Susannah was in, and wished he could talk to her.

He joined the rest of the family, who stood outside the church gossiping. Michael came over with Tamsen. They were beaming all over their faces.

"I won't be home for dinner today, Will," said Michael. "Tamsen's giving us dinner at her house."

"I be pleased to see you've made it up," said William. "I'll tell Martha."

On the way home, William's thoughts returned to Susannah. It occurred to him that he could write a letter to her, and Susan could deliver it. Timothy need never know.

Boy was walking by William's side as they walked up the hill. "I'll be writing a letter this afternoon, Boy. Will ye tag along with Jone?"

"S'pose so," said Boy, looking at the ground. William knew that his son was tired of Jone's fussing over him. It would soon be time to allow him more freedom.

In the hall, William was labouring over his letter to Susannah. He didn't find it easy.

Madam, Susan telld us that you be upset about what happened wen I called. I be main ernful that I spoke to thee with anger, en I wish to apolgise. We found me son the next dee at a fren's bidance. He weren't harmed. I knows it were Timothy wot took him away, but I am so happy to have un back, I won't report him like I sed I wud. I hopes you dount mind...

There was a knock on the door. He got up to see who the visitor was, and found his brother John standing there.

"Come in, John," he said. "Go into the parlour and wait while I finish this. I won't be long."

"I've been to see Mary," said John, as he walked through the hall. He was more relaxed these days. "I thought I'd happen along here, like."

William continued writing:

...us ritting ter thee loike this. I do not want ye ter be distressd on our accont. Behopes Timothy dunt find this letter. He may punish thee for it. I send thee me bes regards.
William Lucke.

He shook sand over the ink and blotted it carefully, then folded it and sealed it with wax heated in the candle. He put it away in the drawer with the account book. He would give it to Susan next Sunday.

He went through to the parlour. John was sitting at the table with a mug of ale. Martha was preparing the dinner. William had forgotten to tell Martha that Michael wouldn't be home for dinner. It was too late.

"How be Mary?" he said to John.

"She be grandly," said John. "That liddle baby be growing fast. She has the bly of Mary, for certain sure."

"They called here t'other day. Boy took to baby Anne, it seems. How was Jone when she saw them, Martha?"

"She were non-plush at first, but pleased to see Mary. Then she came round to playing with the baby, real natural, like."

Jone and Boy came in from the yard. Jone started laying the table for dinner.

John said, "Robert Haman came knocking at my door. It seems that his brudder Thomas hasn't paid his dues to his brudder and sisters. Justabout mad, 'e were. I said he should speak to thee about it."

William's heart sank. He'd had enough of the Hamans. They were fighting among themselves over their inheritance from Uncle Thomas. "That ain't good news, surely," he said. "Be ye dining with us, John? Michael's eating at Tamsen's house. You can have his dinner."

Jone put the spoons on the table with a clatter, and grimaced at William. "I thought we'd seen the last of that one," she said.

"I believe he be unaccountable fond of 'er," said William, understanding Jone's jealousy. Michael had always been Jone's favourite brother. "We must get accustomed to her ways."

"She'd best keep out of my way," said Jone.

Pieter came in, and they all sat round the table, ready to eat. Martha served the dinner and Jone carried the plates to the table.

When she put his plate in front of Pieter, he said, "You look hem purty today, Jone." William watched as she looked at Pieter in surprise then went to sit down opposite him. Pieter smiled and winked at her. She blushed.

John was saying, "I saw Cousin Richard in town. His wife's expecting a third child."

"'Tis a long time since I saw Richard," said William. "I don't believe I knew about the second one."

"That one were born soon after Aunt Joanne died," said John. "Richard told us he were offered a knighthood by King Charles."

William was impressed. "That be a great honour for the fambly, surely."

"'Tis not all as it seems," said John. "The King's trying to raise money for his army. Richard would have to pay a regular fee for the privilege, and would be expected to be present at Court on gurt occasions, and wear grand rigging."

They were all listening, fascinated by this glimpse into the way other people lived.

"That sounds a costly business," said William. "Will Richard be able to do that?"

"Nay, he's declined. He'll have to pay a fine of £10. He says there be others of his friends who have turned knighthoods down."

"That be unaccountable devious of the King," said William.

The conversation turned to Edward and his change of behaviour.

"He seems hem upstanding these days," remarked John.

"Peggy keeps 'im in order," said William. She won't have ale or any drink except milk in the house!"

"Poor Ed!" said John "That must be hard."

There was a silence while they all ate their dinner.

William enjoyed having his brothers and sisters dropping in on him. He was missing Uncle Thomas, and it gave him comfort to have his family around him. They had all migrated to Lamberhurst. He felt that they were beginning to regard him as head of the family, rather than John, who never really fitted into the role.

Chapter 40

It was a warm day in late summer when William mounted his horse and trotted to Goudhurst to visit Uncle Christopher. He arrived to find Dan'l with Christopher in the yard. He dismounted and took Damsel to the far end to tether her, then went to join them.

Christopher stood in the middle of the yard, with his arms round the neck of a chestnut mare who was nuzzling his thick beard. Not wanting to confuse the old man by trying to communicate with him, he went over to Dan'l.

"How be the old man, Dan'l?"

"Fair-to-middlin', Mas William. He don't get any better. I dunnow what we'll do betimes he can't get out to talk to 'is horses."

Christopher patted his horse on the neck and said, "Get back in your stable now, Dolly. I have to go and see to the others."

William heard the sound of a horse galloping up the road.

"Somebody be in a hurry," remarked Dan'l.

The horse slowed to turn the corner into the yard. Hooves clattered and slithered on the cobbles.

Christopher was giving his horse a final pat. He turned away as Dan'l led Dolly towards the open door of her stable.

William made a futile move to stop Christopher. It was too late. He watched, paralysed with horror as Christopher, oblivious of the danger, staggered into the path of the oncoming horse.

The rider strained on the reins. He gave a shout as his horse reared up, snorting and shaking its head. Lather flew from its mouth. Eyes bulged with fear as it towered over the old man, hitting his temple with a hoof.

Behind William, the chestnut mare shied and panicked. Dan'l struggled to control her. The other horses were stamping around in their stalls in distress.

With a cry of shock and pain the old man flung his arms up to protect himself. For a ghastly moment, he appeared to hang in the air with the horse, sparring. Then he fell to the ground, like a discarded rag doll. The hooves came down on Christopher's body and trampled on him before the horse backed away.

William ran over to Christopher who lay motionless in a pool of blood, which was seeping from a gash in his head. Dan'l managed to lead the chestnut into her stable. As he joined William, the intruder leapt to the ground and roughly tied up his steed. He came over to where William and Dan'l were bending over Christopher.

"What d'ye think you're doing letting the auld gaffer stotter around like that?" shouted the intruder.

William scrambled to his feet. "I'll thank thee to be more civil. This be private property. Ye've killed him, charging in here. And who may you be?"

The stranger was calming down, but ignored what he had just been told.

"I've come to find William Lucke. I went to the Slade and they said he were here."

"I be William Lucke."

"Me brudder Thomas Haman ..."

William shouted, "You've no call to be so impatient. This old man's dead on account of thee. The constables will know about this. When I've dealt with my Uncle's death and buried him, I'll see about your complaint and not afore. Now, git."

William and Dan'l turned back to the crumpled heap of Uncle Christopher. William wept. He knelt down and took his uncle's limp body in his arms. He rocked it, sobbing. Dan'l stood back in respect. The servant Faithful came out of the house, wringing her hands and wailing.

"I'd best go and fetch the Headborough, Mas William. We'll need him to be a witness of how Mus Lucke were killed." Dan'l went to saddle up his horse.

William sat on the ground by his childhood friend, stroking his hair and the laughter lines round his eyes. He held the limp hand to his face. "I be hem sorry, Uncle. I be hem sorry."

In the weeks that followed, the coroner was called and an inquest held. Robert Haman was admonished, but the verdict was accidental death, due to Christopher's state of mind. He was buried on September the 9th at Wadhurst Parish Church, next to his brothers. William became an executor again, seeing to it that Uncle Thomas' property in Goudhurst was passed to Stephen Apps. He took the issue of Bedifields Hill to the courts. It was finally decided that the property should be sold. William bought it. Thomas Haman became his tenant, and the other beneficiaries were paid their dues. The matter was closed. William could once more return to being a farmer, though the manner of Christopher's death continued to haunt him.

Chapter 41   1640

William and Boy returned from a visit to Mary and Anne. There was a letter waiting. It lay on the table in the hall. He sent Boy through to the parlour and picked it up. He held it in his hand for some time. Then he sat down, and gently eased the seal open. He unfolded the paper, and looked at the writing, imagining Susannah sitting at a table with her goose feather and ink pot before her, writing to him.

My dear William,

How kind of you to write to me. I was so grateful to read your words after what had passed between us last time we met. It has comforted me to know that your son was delivered to you unharmed. Thanks be to God.

I am sure you are right, that Timothy was the culprit. He's so possessively jealous of any man who comes near me. It annoyed him that I came to your dear Uncle's funeral and spoke to you. That is why we should never meet again.

The only people who are allowed to visit me are dear John Hatley and my son-in-law, John Maynard. But he's always in London. I never even met his second wife, now deceased, poor dear.

I would like you to write again, telling me all your news. It would brighten my days considerably. Susan will bring the letters to me. I will make sure that Timothy does not discover them, and I'll burn them when I've read them.

I hope we can continue our friendship in this way, William. I am very isolated here, and it will do me good to have news of the outside world.

May God be with you always, my dear. Susannah Lucke.

William read the letter through three times. His heart was full of tenderness, and he would find Susannah invading his thoughts and dreams as she did in the old days. He determined it shouldn't distract him from his duties. He put the letter in a drawer, and went to find out what was happening on the farm.

The wind died down and the land slowly released the water it had been holding all winter. William and his team were hard pressed to catch up with ploughing, manuring and sowing of seeds before young animals demanded their attention. There was a quickening in the earth, which flowed through all living things. Romance was in the air. Michael and Tamsen were courting again, and John had married Maria Porter from Court Lodge in Lamberhurst. He now lived with her and her family, and Marlinge was let, bringing him an income.

One morning William came through the parlour where Martha and Jone were standing at the table, up to their elbows in flour.

"Nay, not like that, Jone, make it so," and Martha demonstrated again, how to knead the dough and form it into balls to make dumplings.

"I can't do it," said Jone, throwing the lump of dough down onto the table. "'Tis no use us trying." She stomped out of the room.

Martha said to William, "She be main aggy these days. There's something troubling her."

"It be Michael and Tamsen," said William. "I believe she be jealous."

"She could be hankering after a man for 'erself," suggested Martha. "She be growed into a woman since she's been here. En she be left on the shelf."

"Boy be growing too, and he don't need Jone so much. He goes off on his own sometimes. Jone be missing having him to muvver," added William.

In the copse, the charcoal burner had built his makeshift shelter out of discarded hazel rods, and stayed there tending the charcoal pet day and night. Boy and Dog were sitting on a log, watching old Earl whittling some wood.

Jone came and found them. "Come thee here now, Boy. What d'ye mean by wandering off like this, where I can't watch thee?"

"Mas Earl be making a whistle for me. I want to see it finished," Boy complained. He was tired of being interrupted by Jone.

"'Tis ready prensley, young man," said Earl, and blew into the whistle, making three notes.

Boy leapt up from his seat and went to take the whistle. "Thank thee kindly, Mas' Earl." He followed Jone, blowing the whistle all the way back to the house.

"We must gather the eggs anon," she said, taking hold of Boy's arm, "and feed the fowls."

"I beant going to gather eggs. You can do it. Ye don't need me to help," retorted Boy. He broke away and marched off towards the orchard, leaving Jone cursing with frustration.

Boy went and sat by the duck pond and put his arm round his friend Dog, who lay down and rested his head on his master's knee with a big sigh. They watched the ducks dabbling until they all went skidding and flapping for food in answer to Jone's call. Boy found some pebbles to throw into the water, and watched the ripples spreading out to the edge of the pond. After a while he heard Martha calling him to coger, and, the quarrel forgotten, he and Dog went scampering towards the house, Boy blowing his whistle.

The next morning after prayers, during the usual family conference to pick up the day's duties, Jone spoke up. "Mus William, I wish you'd tell Boy to do as he's told. He do make us lash and swear. Soon as ever I'm backturned he's off after some game or other."

Before William could answer, Boy said, "But Farder, I be growed prensley. I don't need muvvering no more."

"That's as maybe, but you must always do as you're bid by your elders, whether ye be agreeable or not. I believe 'tis time you begun your lessons in reading en writing, and to do some work on the farm, seeing as how you're growed."

Boy fell silent.

Jone spoke again. "Ain't I in charge of him no more, then?"

William told the rest of the family and the labourers to go and start the day's work, keeping Boy and Jone back. To Jone he said, "Martha's getting in years, and needs more help around the house. I'd be obliged if you could take on the work in the milk-house, and help with the laundering. Go and ask her what she wants thee to do." Jone stomped out of the room. William knew she would much rather be outside with the animals and Boy, than inside doing housework.

Boy stood looking at the ground, shuffling his feet, and waited for his father to give him his tasks.

William said, "Thy work will be to help with fetching the cows in and milking them. Then you can feed the fowls and gather the eggs by thyself. You must look after thy pony. Do all that needs to be done. Clean out his stall, fother 'im and ride him every day around the farm. Every day I'll spend some time larning thee to read and write, and I'll give ye practice to do. Now off you go and help with the milking. I'll give thee a lesson after coger."

Boy left the room looking bemused at the turn of events. William smiled to himself. That should give the lad something to think about, and he himself would have to be careful to keep his side of the bargain. He looked at the clock on the mantle shelf and remembered his Uncle Thomas.

Chapter 42

Boy was now able to organise his own day, and could wander further than before. He soon completed his work on the farm, and he had time on his hands. One day after his work was done, and he'd struggled through his lessons with his father, he ventured onto the highway with Dog, in the direction of Mary's house. He felt the need to confide in someone, and Mary had been one of the few most stable and dependable people in his life since his mother died.

Mary was surprised to see Boy alone.

"I be come to see Anne," he said.

"She be here in the parlour. She'll be considerable pleased to see thee," said Mary. Boy followed her into the parlour, and a squeal of delight came from Anne, who was sitting on the floor with her toys. Boy went straight over to her and picked up a doll, making it dance, and sitting it on his head. Anne giggled and shrieked, and crawled around the floor after the runaway doll. Boy showed Anne his whistle, and blew on it. The shrill noise startled Anne, and they both laughed.

Boy turned to Mary and said, "Farder's been larning us to read and write, and to rackon with figures."

"Oh, and how be ye getting along with that?" asked Mary.

"I ain't hem clever at larning, and Farder gets short with us. I've been considering. Maybe I could do it if ye helped us, like. If you'd be agreeable, Aunt Mary?"

"Surely I could help thee. Fetch thy reading books and slate next time ye come."

Boy stayed and played with Anne and her wooden doll, while Mary got on with knocking back the bread she'd left to rise near the fire.

There was a tap on the door, and Uncle John came in looking very pleased. "I've good news," he said. "Maria be with child."

"That be good news indeed," said Mary. "I be hem pleased for thee, Brudder." She came and gave him a floury hug, and invited him to sit down.

"Boy, you can get the mugs and pour us all a drop of cider, while I cleans meself up." Mary put the bread onto its baking tray and placed it in the oven before going out to wash her hands. They all sat round the table and Mary and Boy raised their mugs to wish the expectant father well.

"Be Maria alright?" asked Mary.

"Fair to middling," said John. "She be unwell in the mornings."

Boy listened for a few minutes, and decided that the conversation didn't really interest him. He went back to the Slade with a lighter heart, leaving his Aunt and Uncle to talk.

He came into the parlour. "Where's Farder?" he asked Martha.

"In the hall. He be busy prensley," she answered. "Talk to him at dinner."

Boy went out to Dog again. They ran to the meadow to see Robin. By the time he came back for dinner, Boy had forgotten all about Uncle John's good news.

William was ready to write another letter to Susannah. He sat down before dinner and put pen to paper once more.

Madam,

I thank thee for thy kind letter. I've only farm and fambly ter tell thee about. Work on the farm is bissy this toime ov year. But I love the spring, en all the flowers en young beasts a-birthen.

My liddle Boy is growen, en I've started larnen him ter read en rite, en to rackon with figgers. It beant easy, as I beant hem good at these things meself. I'm larnen un to ride, too. Tis Uncle Thomases pony. He's good with Boy. Us calls un Boy, insted of Thomas. He has a dog caad Dog. This dog follers Boy all over. He helped us find Boy wen he were lost.

I'll stop now en give this to Susan at church termorrer. God bless thee. William Lucke

He blotted his writing, read it over, and folded and sealed it. It was time for dinner.

Sunday mornings had turned into family gatherings. They regularly met after the church service and John and his wife would invite them to Court Lodge, next door to the church, for coger. This was when they caught up with each other's news, and had a good gossip. Edward didn't always join them. He felt a misfit in this grand house, and Peggy wouldn't go with him. Today, Stephen Porter, Maria's father, was talking about John Maynard, the vicar of Mayfield.

"My brother lives in Mayfield, and has told me that John Maynard married again. But his new wife died in childbirth, with her baby, leaving the poor man alone once more. It's said that Maynard spends a great deal of his time in London preaching to Parliament. His parishioners haven't seen him for months. He leaves a curate in charge."

John said, "I were talking to Cousin Richard, and he says that the Puritans in Parlyment are quarrelling with

King Charles. The King's trying to rally militia from Scotland."

His wife Maria asked, "What if it comes to Civil War, Father. Who will you support?"

Porter replied, "Our family have always been Royalists. But I'm not sure I agree with the King's methods of raising money for his army."

"Seems to me the trouble has always come from the Catholics. I be on the side of Parlyment and the Puritans," said William. "But d'ye think it will come to Civil War, Sir?"

"Let us hope not, William. I've no taste for warring and bloodshed. But we must be prepared."

"It'd be a good thing to get rid of all these foreigners and vagrants off the roads," remarked Michael. "if they was all called up to join the militia."

Boy was chasing Anne around the room, weaving in and out of the family's legs. The noise they were making was increasing, and William decided that it was time they left. The guests dispersed, thanking their hosts for their hospitality.

William asked Mary and Thomas Dyne if they would like to bring Anne over to the Slade to see the new born animals. Instead of going by road, they made their way home through the Brook. This was an area of meadow where the water from the surrounding slopes collected in wet weather. There were big yellow king cups, water irises and white daisies growing, mauve ladies smocks filled the air with their scent. The children knocked their feet against the buttercups as they walked, covering their shoes with yellow pollen.

Mary said to William, "'Tis good to see John so happy, en with a child on the way."

"Be Maria expecting? I didn't know," said William.

"Yus, he came and told us, t'other day. Didn't Boy..." she hesitated, looked at Boy, and called to Michael. "Did ye know Maria were quick with child, Michael?"

"Nay," he said. "I'll warrant John's main chuffed. 'Tis good for him to be wed into such a fine fambly. Did ye know that the Porter's elder darter is wed to Mr Hatley?"

The family walked on, digesting this imformation.

Mary said, "How be Tamsen, Michael? We ain't seen her for a while."

"Oh, we was at two again t'other day, and she bodged off in a hoe. She'll come round afore long." He laughed, and strode on ahead.

William saw Jone looking after Michael longingly. She had been looking pale and dreamy lately. He caught up with her and attempted to talk to her, but she carried on walking as if he wasn't there.

Chapter 43   1642
Civil War

After another lesson with Mary, Boy walked back with Dog into the yard at the Slade undetected. He wanted to keep his extra tuition a secret. He quickly took his books and left them in the hall. He slipped out again, heading in the direction of the copse. He hoped to find some pigeons to kill with the catapult Pieter had made for him. The day was fine but cloudy, with no wind. He came across the old charcoal burner's shelter, which had not been dismantled after last year's use. It was a little rickety now, but would make a good hide. Boy looked inside, and was shocked to see an old roader asleep on some dried leaves.

"This looks like one of them vagabonds they was talking about t'other day," he thought. He crept quietly away. The man might be dangerous. Out of earshot, Boy climbed a young oak tree and sat on a branch where he could still see the shelter. Dog sat the other side of the tree. They waited.

Boy's feet were wedged in the crook of a branch and after a long time they were beginning to hurt. He'd need to move soon. There was a stirring from the shelter. He saw the man come out and stretch himself, yawning. He wore a dirty black coat and his greying hair and beard almost covered his face. He lifted a big bag over his shoulder. After looking around him, he walked in the direction of the house, keeping to the trees. Boy dropped softly to the ground and followed. The man skirted the meadow in the shelter of the hedge and entered the garden. He must have been here before, for he went straight over to the low hedge surrounding the garden, where Martha had spread the laundry out to dry. Working quickly, the man took most of the men's clothes, breeches and round frocks, and stuffed them into the bag. Then he saw a long scarf, and whipped that away too.

Boy wondered how he could raise the alarm quietly. He hid in the hedge and waited. The man started towards the roosting house, where there would be eggs if he were lucky. Boy saw his opportunity. As soon as the man's back was turned he ran across to the door of the shed, gave him a push and shut him in. He leaned heavily on the door, found the whistle in his pocket, and blew it as hard as he could. But no-one responded. The door was being pushed from the inside. Boy turned round and pushed hard with both hands. The intruder must have thrown himself against the door, for Boy was nearly bowled over. He didn't think he could hold it. He shouted at the top of his voice, and Dog barked. Martha and Jone came running out of the house.

"There be a man in there stealing eggs. Keep the door shut while I gets help." Jone and Martha came and leant against the door. Boy ran to the hop garden where Michael and Pieter were busy tying bines to the poles.

"There be a man stealing things. I shut him in the roosting house. Come, dracly-minute." They put their tools down and followed Boy back to the roosting house. Martha and Jone released the door, and the man attempted to bolt. Michael and Pieter were too quick for him. They caught him by the arms, and pulled him down.

"Look in his bag!" shouted Boy, as he hopped from foot to foot, enjoying the drama.

Martha looked, and said, "The constable should see this."

Michael and Pieter marched the man towards the road. "We'll take him to the constable dracly," Michael said.

"Can I come?" asked Boy.

"Alright," said Michael. "You can tell the constable what ye saw."

At dinner that evening, Boy told his Father the story.

"I be considerable proud of thee, Son," said William, laughing at Boy's excitement. "We needs a guard dog or something to keep these vagrants off our land."

Pieter said, "I be avised that geese make considerable good guard dogs."

"They make a good dinner, too," said Michael.

"Yus, I be main partial to a good roast goose, meself," said Martha.

The next market day, Boy, Michael and Pieter drove a gander and five geese back from Wadhurst with some difficulty. None of them had dealt with geese before.

"Take it slow," the man said when he handed them over at the market. "They'll be frit if ye rush 'em." The geese had experience, and knew how to walk together in a group without scattering. But it took a while for them to relate to these strangers who were trying to drive them. Boy started by shouting at them. Then he realised that this only confused them and he kept quiet. Dog, who learned quickly that this was a herding operation, walked steadily behind. The drovers held their long sticks out to the sides, to make them seem wider than they were. They travelled slowly for a mile or so.

A horse rider came galloping towards them. The geese panicked and flew all over the road, hissing and honking, necks stretched forward. One tried to fly over the hedge, and became lodged in the top. Pieter reached up to lift it down, but was in danger of having his hand bitten off. Two other geese were running back towards Wadhurst. Boy ran after them with Dog, which made them go even faster.

He heard Michael calling him back. "We must take this slow, like the man said. Let the geese calm down, and watch what they do. I rackon they'll all get together again if we leave 'em be."

Boy came back to the others and stood in the ditch. Sure enough, the two on their way to Wadhurst slowed down and turned around. They came waddling back slowly, lowering their heads and snapping their beaks. Boy, Michael and Pieter stood still at the side of the road, and soon the four were together again. They allowed themselves to be herded to the side, muttering.

"How can we get that one down?" Pieter pointed to the goose perched on top of the hedge.

"We'll drive the others away, and you get your bat behind it and give it a shove," suggested Michael.

Dog had a different idea. He found a gap in the hedge and squeezed through. He came behind the goose, and ran around barking. Instead of jumping into the road, the goose turned round and hissed at Dog, flying off the hedge into the field. The goose chased Dog round the field. This upset the other geese, and they threatened to break away and scatter as before, but Michael and Boy were ready with their sticks, and contained them.

Meanwhile, Pieter walked back up the road, and found a gate in the hedge. He opened it wide and went into the field, circling round behind the goose. Boy called to Dog, who ran through the gate onto the road. Pieter drove the goose through, shutting the gate behind him. They joined the others, and continued down the road towards the Slade, the gander leading his flock.

A horse and cart came up behind them. Boy turned round to see his father returning from market, driving Gaffer. The others had heard it too, and they drove the geese into the side of the road. William slowed Gaffer down as he passed.

"You be taking your time with them geese! I'll tell Martha to keep your dinners hot." He drove on, chuckling. But the drovers had got the measure of their charges, and the last few miles did not take so long.

At last the gander proudly led his girls into the yard at the Slade, all heads held high, and tails wagging. Martha and Jone came out of the house, and went to open the gate into the close. But the geese took fright at the sight of strangers, and scattered, honking and flapping wings. Martha and Jone ran back into the house in fear and trembling, and Boy and the men laughed at the hullabaloo.

Michael said, "Go and put some grain down in the barn, Boy. We'll shut 'em in there for now."

Boy went into the close and left the gate open behind him. He opened the wide barn doors, scattered some grain inside, and waited by the entrance to guide the geese in. The gander pattered into the close, head down, not sure of himself in these strange surroundings. He hissed at Boy and Dog, but they stood their ground. The geese followed, and Michael and Pieter closed round behind them, ready to ward off any escapee. Warily, the geese walked into the barn and, seeing the food, started gobbling it up. Boy fetched a dish and filled it with water from the well. He put it in the barn by the door. Michael and Pieter pulled the doors shut.

"There'll be no visitors round here prensley. Even them as needs to see us'll be frightened away," said Michael at dinner that evening.

"We'll keep them in the close until they feels at home. Then they can wander where they will," said William. "Boy, mind you fother them when ye does the hens and pigs."

"Yus Farder," said Boy. He'd enjoyed the day, but was tired and glad to be home.

As he lay in his cot before going to sleep, goose voices came to him from the barn, quacking softly to each other.

Chapter 44

The family were all sitting round the table eating their coger the next day, when the geese set up a hissing and honking. There was a knock at the front door. William got up to see who it was. A stranger stood there with a letter in his hand. William took the letter and gave the man a coin.

"Thank thee," the man said, and went on his way.

William took the letter away to his chamber, and sat down to read it.

My dear William,

I would like you to address me as Susannah, if you would. You are my friend. I enjoyed reading your letter. You are a good father to your little Boy.

I had a visit from my son-in-law, John Maynard. He told me that King Charles is preparing to leave London with an army. The Puritans in Parliament are preparing an army of their own. The recruitment officers will be visiting all households, taking the unemployed away to be trained. Some members of Parliament are rallying their own supporters, and preparing them to fight. I fear Timothy may be impressed. But perhaps he'll think of a way to avoid it.

We need farmers like yourself, to continue to provide our food.

I send you my blessings.

Yours affectionately, Susannah Lucke

William folded the letter and put it in his pocket. His thoughts turned to his son. Their relationship was changing. Boy was becoming his own person and drifting away from William's shelter. Boy didn't share his own enthusiasm for husbandry, and found labouring a chore. What would become of his farm in Boy's hands, when he was old enough to take over? There were so many other things to deal with that he found himself spending less time working on the land. His workforce was capable and he trusted them. But he was losing track of the seasonal tasks, and relied on Adam to tell him what needed to be done. The vision of Susannah came to the surface, as it did constantly during his daily life. Her letter had unnerved him. Now it seemed that the country would soon be at war. Men would be marched away to fight, leaving women with families to manage on their own. Would William and his family be in danger if the battles came to the Wadhurst area?

The next Sunday after the church service the family gathered at Court Lodge as usual. William had persuaded Edward to join them for the last time before he went to live in his house in Wadhurst. John's wife Maria had not been in church, and William assumed that she was nearing her time. The room was buzzing with gossip, as they compared experiences over the Oath of Protestation they had all had to sign, and the imminence of Civil War.

The door opened slowly, and everyone fell silent as John appeared in the doorway holding a tiny baby in his arms, his face all smiles.

"May I present my darter, Dorothy," he said proudly. Loud exclamations of pleasure surrounded him and everyone murmured in appreciation, craning their necks to see the newcomer. John came into the room and sat on a bench, so that they could all have a look.

"How is Maria?" asked his sister, Mary.

"She be hem unwell yet. The birth weren't easy. Dorothy be already three days old," he said. William and Mary were watching Jone closely, but need not have feared. She was wrapped up in her own thoughts today, and looked sad and tired, with black rings round her eyes.

Boy thought the baby was too good to be true, and gloated over his cousin for a long time while John talked to other people. They all raised their glasses in congratulation.

A few days later, Boy and his father were in the hall, at the end of the afternoon lesson.

"Ye be larning well now, Boy," said William, as they were putting the books away.

"I be trying hard, Farder, but there be some things I don't understand."

"Ye must ask when ye don't understand, and I'll explain."

"When I do that ye gets short with us," Boy scowled.

"Maybe we needs to go more slow, like. Would that help?"

"Yus, Farder," said Boy. "I'll be doing me practise prensley. I'll need that book." He picked out the things he'd need to take to his Aunt Mary and sat down with the book open in front of him.

William left the room in the direction of the parlour. Boy heard him talking to Martha.

"I be worried about Jone…"

Boy picked up his slate and the books he needed, and quietly left by the front door. Dog was waiting for him outside. They slipped down the garden path before the geese started their racket, and made their way to Mary's house. He left Dog outside, and let himself in.

Mary poured them both a mug of cider, and sat down beside Boy.

"What be the lesson today, Boy?" she said.

Boy produced the book he'd brought, and read a passage to Mary, stumbling over the words.

"That be much better than last time, Boy. I be proud of thee. Now shall we play with some figures?"

Boy didn't like this part of the lesson, and dreaded making the usual mistakes.

"Farder said I be ready to do taking away, but I don't understand," he said, showing Mary his slate with some figures written on it. Mary got up and went to get the pot of dried beans they'd been using to help Boy. She was setting them out on the table according to the figures on the slate, when there was a knock on the door. Someone walked in, and quietly stayed behind Boy and Mary.

Mary glanced up, nodded, and away again. "See, how many beans have we here?"

Boy counted them. "Five," he said.

"Yus. And what does it tell us to do, on your slate?"

Boy looked at the slate. "Take away free."

"So do that, from the beans on the table." Mary was smiling. Boy took three beans away from those on the table, and realised what the answer was. "That leaves two," he said, laughing. Mary laughed too.

There was a movement behind them. Boy looked round to see his father, who stood there with a big smile on his face. "So that's where ye've been when I've been seeking thee," William said.

Boy grinned. "I did want thee to be proud of me, Farder."

"And so I be, young man," said William. Then he turned to his sister. "Thank thee for helping him, Mary."

Mary smiled and said, "He be doing main well, Will. And what brings thee here?"

William explained that Jone was looking unhappy lately. "I talked to Martha, and she said she couldn't make out what's troubling Jone. She suggested I come and talk to thee, as ye knows her better than all of us."

Mary opened her mouth to answer, but Boy spoke up, "Jone be partial to Pieter. She dreams about him all-on." The two adults looked at Boy in astonishment.

"Did she tell you this?" asked William.

Boy, who shared a chamber with Jone, knew more than any of them what was going on in her mind. "Nay, but she calls his name in her sleep, and looks at him all dreamy like."

Mary and William sat down to discuss the matter while Boy went to play with Anne. He took her outside to see Dog, who was nearly as tall as Anne. She patted him, and tried to ride on his back. Dog stubbornly protected his identity, and refused to be a horse. He walked away.

William came out and said, "I've done talking to Mary now, Boy. Be ye ready to bodge? Ye could ride with us on Damsel." Boy nodded and they took Anne back to her mother. Boy collected his lesson books and slate and put them in his satchel. He felt relieved that his father knew now and wasn't angry about his extra lessons with Mary. They said goodbye and went outside, where William lifted Boy onto Damsel, mounted and they trotted home. Dog trotted alongside.

Later that afternoon William found Jone sitting in the milk-house looking blankly into space. She'd gone to churn the milk into butter, but none of it was done. She jumped up when William appeared, and pretended to be busy with something.

William said, "Jone, will ye come with us to the hall. I be minded to talk with thee."

"Nay nay, I be churning, Will," said Jone. She started turning the handle of the great wooden barrel. The creamy milk inside sloshed about as it went round.

"Come, Jone, ye can get back to that 'forelong," said William gently. Jone put the handle in its resting position and followed him into the hall. They sat down on the settle, and William said, "D'ye miss muvvering Boy, Jone?"

"Yus but he be growed prensley."

"Would ye be agreeable to go and help Mary to muvver Anne?" asked William. Jone's eyes lit up.

She said, "Yus, I would surely like that, but can't I bide here?"

William thought for a while, then said, "T'would be best if ye bide along of Mary and Thomas, then there'd be no need for thee to travel to and fro'."

Jone nodded, "Alright then, I be agreeable." She sat awhile thinking about the proposition, and lifted her weary head to smile at William.

"We all loves thee, Jone. Ye knows that, don't ye?" he said.

She pursed her lips and muttered, "Yus." She swallowed, got up and walked out of the room, not looking back.

William felt easier about Jone's situation now. Mary knew how to manage her strange ways, and she would be happy looking after Anne. It was a shame he had not stopped Pieter from teasing her when they were at the table, winking and making her blush. Pieter didn't know about Jone's unfortunate history, so William could hardly blame him. He was only trying to cheer her up. Poor Jone, William knew how it felt when the object of one's affections was beyond reach. He would ask Michael if Tamsen would like to come and take Jone's place helping Martha. He could pay her a wage, and it would encourage her relationship with Michael. William was sure they were right for each other.

Chapter 45

Boy had been digging over the plot in the garden, ready for sowing the beans and peas. He cleaned the spade at the well before putting it away in the skillon. He kicked his muddy boots off at the door and walked into the house. Tamsen was in the buttery drawing off some ale for the next meal.

"Where be Martha?" asked Boy.

"She be upstairs changing the bed linen, I believe," answered Tamsen.

"Will ye tell her I be going into the village on Robin?"

"That I will, young Sir. Make sure ye be back for coger."

Boy went to find Robin in the croft, brought him back and saddled him up. He called Dog, and trotted out of the yard. They walked slowly down the hill towards the village, passing a group of people waiting to get water from the spring, across the road. He felt proud to be sitting on his pony, looking down on the neighbours. Some of them recognised him and waved, then went back to their gossiping. Further down the hill he had to slow down to allow a loaded hay wain to pass on its way up. The driver nodded his thanks, and Boy nodded. They came to the pump in the village where there were more people standing around talking. He waved at them, and some waved back. He thought he'd go and see if the blacksmith was busy. He liked to watch Mas Golding at work, shoeing a horse, or making tools.

He was passing the house where Uncle Edward lived before he moved to Wadhurst, and glanced over the hedge. Pieter lived there now, and was repairing the roof in his spare time. Boy noticed a movement in the garden. He stopped, surprised to see someone there at this time of day. A tall man dressed in black emerged through the gate and out onto the road.

"Good day to you, young Sir," said the stranger. "Does Mr Edward Lucke live here, do you know?" The voice was vaguely familiar. Dog growled and bared his teeth as the man came closer.

Boy felt uneasy. "Nay, he be gone to bide in Wad'rst." He clicked his tongue for Robin to walk on. They reached the forge, and Boy looked back to see if he was being followed. There was no sign of the dark stranger.

Nothing of interest was happening at the forge. There was a deal of hustle and bustle in the village, but the people were all too busy to stop and talk. Boy thought he'd call at Court Lodge to see if he'd be allowed to visit Baby Dorothy. His cousin could sit up now and look around her. He liked looking at her tiny fingers and toes and feeling her grip on his finger. So he trotted up the hill to the big white house next to the church. He felt small, as he approached the pillared portico round the front door, and wondered if he should try and find a back entrance. But at that moment the door opened, and a woman came out. Boy dismounted, and, not knowing what to do with Robin, he held onto the reins.

The woman looked at him. "You're William Lucke's son, are you not?"

"Yus, Mistus," replied Boy. "I be hoping to visit my Cousin Dorothy, Ma'am."

"Well I'm afraid that won't be convenient today. But I need to send a letter to your father. Will you take it for me? It's very urgent. You must not delay."

Boy nodded. "Yus, Ma'am. I'll take it dracly-minute."

"Bless you. I'll go and get it now. Wait there." The lady went back into the house, and Boy stood holding onto Robin, wondering what the letter was about. He felt important, being trusted with an urgent message.

The door opened again, and the same woman held out a letter, which he took and put safely in his pouch.

She handed him a coin, and said, "Take this for your trouble, young man. Now be off!" She watched Boy as he mounted Robin, and trotted down the hill with Dog following.

Boy urged his pony into the village, and up the hill towards the Slade. As he came into the yard, the geese came flying round the corner, screeching and hissing. He dismounted and tethered Robin, said "Shshsh!" to the geese and waved them away, then went into the house by the front door.

"Farder! Farder!" he called, and went through into the parlour.

His father was coming towards him. "Whoa! Whoa! What be the rush?" he said.

"I went to Court Lodge to visit Dorothy, and a woman asked us to take this to thee. 'Tis important, like." He handed the letter to his father.

William opened the letter, read it, and said to Martha, "I be going to see my brudder John. He be took bad." He went out to the close to collect his mare.

Boy stood, getting his breath back and slowly taking in the company in the parlour. There was Uncle Edward, sitting at the table with a mug of ale. Martha was putting the coger on the table, and Tamsen was bringing the plates. Michael came in from the close, and gave Tamsen a hug on the way past, and Pieter followed behind.

"Will said that John's took bad," said Michael.

The atmosphere was sombre as they ate their bread and cheese. They waited for news of John all afternoon. Boy hung around the house. His adventurous urges dispelled for the time being. He tried to practise his writing, but found it difficult to concentrate. At last he heard his father ride into the yard and he went out to meet him.

"Your Uncle John passed away this afternoon, Son," William said as he dismounted. "I happened by Mary's house and told her. Come, let's find the others. Be Edward here still?"

"Yus, Farder." Boy took hold of William's hand and they went into the parlour together, to tell the family the sad news.

Deeply shocked by the death of their brother, William and his family gathered in the hall at Court Lodge after John's funeral. There were a few mourners from the Porter family, John Hatley and his wife were there and Cousin Richard Lucke and his wife had come from Wadhurst, bringing Edward with them in their carriage.

William was pleased to see Richard. "You was a good friend to John after Farder died," he said.

"He were a lonesome man," said Richard. "We was so happy for him when he found Maria." They sipped their wine and stood in contemplation.

Edward limped over to join them. "I were telling Richard on the way here, Will, that housekeeper he found for us be a blessing. Thank thee for that."

William said, "I could see things were getting difficult, like, for Peggy, when I visited thee. I rackoned

Richard would be the best man to find thee a good woman in Wad'rst."

Richard said, "Her name's Hope. Her man were taken off to the military. She needed paid work, with a fambly to feed."

Edward added, "She do's whatever Peggy can't manage. And she be agreeable to tend the garden, if she can take some of the vegetables home."

"I'll give thee the money to pay her, Ed. I be main glad she turned out alright," said William. He turned to Richard. "I ain't heard naught of the Civil War hereabouts. Be there any fighting yet?"

"Not round these parts. There's been battles in the North. But they've been rioting in East Hoathley, where the militia be training. The sojers are upsetting the townspeople with their drunkeness and going with the maids. And there ain't enough food to go round."

"Thanks be they aren't round here!" said William.

"I must go and find me wife," said Richard. She be nearing her time with the child. She'll be tiring. I'll come and tell thee when we be ready to bodge, Edward." He walked away.

Edward said, "Cousin Timothy's been visiting us, Will. I can't make out why. And I don't know how he knows I've gone to Wad'rst. He be always polite and friendly, like. Asks how you be, and what's going on at the Slade. I be careful not to give anything away, mind."

Richard came back and called to Edward, who waved to William, "Goodbye!" William was left feeling dazed and apprehensive at the news he had heard. He went to pay his respects to John's widow.

Chapter 46

William sat on a log in his copse. He looked around him and breathed in the summer evening. The weariness after a day's haymaking slipped away, leaving him content. Late sunshine trickled through the leaves onto the ground before him, and a bumble bee droned past.

He took the letter out of his pocket and looked at it. He relished the regular correspondence he had with Susannah. Just to know that she was thinking of him was a great comfort, and it delighted him that his letters raised her spirits. It would be the third time he'd read this last one from her. He wanted to refresh his memory before he wrote a reply.

My dear William,

I am so glad that the farm work is running smoothly and productively. Your son may begin to take more interest when he's older. Growing boys can be rebellious sometimes, and perhaps he needs time to find out what life is all about.

The garden is so beautiful at this time. I've made friends with the man who tends it for me, and he has taught me the names of all the flowers. He restored the bower we had here years ago, when my dear husband was alive. I'm now sitting under it surrounded by sweetly smelling roses, a small table by my side for writing. Timothy has been spending more time away from home this summer, and never comes into the garden. We see each other at dinner, but he has little to say to me. There's a strange look in his eyes, which makes me feel uneasy.

God bless you and your family, William. I look forward to receiving your next letter.

Your affectionate friend, Susannah.

William folded the letter and put it back in his pocket. After resting for a little longer, thinking of Susannah in her garden, he got up, stretched and walked along the whapple way to the house.

Boy was at the well, rinsing off the dust of the day's haymaking. He saw his father passing.

"Farder," he called. "I be going to the Down with Robin." Will waved and nodded as he walked past and went into the house.

Boy went to fetch Robin from the croft. The pony came to him when he called, and Boy slipped a leading rein on, stroking him and giving him a pat. They walked back to the close, where Boy found a saddle and bridle, and made Robin ready for his evening exercise. Dog emerged from his siesta and followed them.

On leaving the yard, Boy nudged his pony into a trot along the slow hill up to the Down. They took the track to the top. Robin stumbled on the uneven ground. Soon a grassy expanse stretched before them, punctuated by gorse and hawthorn bushes.

Boy shouted, "Geewoot!" and they galloped across the grass, exhilarated by the speed and the wind in their hair. They came to the edge where, years ago, Boy had come to catch rabbits with the men and Dog. He dismounted to sit on the grass, leaving Robin to graze. Dog lay down beside him, panting. Boy breathed the fresh air and looked across the valley, unknowingly on the same spot where his parents sat when they were courting. He watched and listened to the same sounds drifting up to him from the valley, the clanging of the hammer on the anvil and the roar of the furnaces at the ironworks. He could hear the carters shouting, 'stan'fast', and 'holt', and saw dust rising in clouds as they rumbled along the road. After a few minutes, the animals around him crept out of their hiding places and bustled about their busyness: bees, butterflies, rabbits. A robin came and sat on a bush singing his luscious summer song. He flew down to catch an unsuspecting worm as it pushed its pointy nose out of the earth. A buzzard mewed in the distance, circling down in the valley, hunting for mice and baby rabbits.

Boy marvelled at the community of the natural world, going about its daily activities. He understood how each species relies on others to survive, and realised that humans, too, are part of this community. The trees are needed to fuel the fires, and for buildings, tools, and fences. The insects pollinate the flowers of the fruit and vegetables. The animals provide food and clothes. He'd watched the bugs and beetles break down the manure and mix it with the earth to feed the crops. The birds keep the pests down. He treasured this time among the wild creatures more than anything else. He never felt alone here.

Work on the farm was a chore to Boy. But it was part of life and survival. He loved his father above all others, and did his best so that William would be proud of his son. But it was hard work, which sometimes failed to be rewarding. The only ambition he had was to marry and have a large family, so that not one of them would ever be alone in the world, and that they could all share the burden of the work on the farm.

It was time to go. Boy got up and called to Robin, who had wandered away. They walked towards each other, and Boy knew how lucky he was to have faithful friends like Robin and Dog. He mounted, and they started cantering back the way they had come.

Boy caught sight of the shadow of a hole in the long grass ahead. Robin couldn't see it, as he was nearer the ground.

Boy pulled on the reins and shouted in warning, but it was too late, the pony cantered on.

Taking a deep breath, Boy shut his eyes, preparing himself for a fall.

Robin stumbled with one foot down the hole. There was a terrible cracking noise. The horse screamed with pain.

The sudden break in momentum flung Boy out of the saddle. He spun through the air, bracing himself for a hard landing.

William was sitting in the hall, writing his letter.

Dear Susannah,

Thank thee fer thy kind advice about Boy. Behopes you be right, en he'll be more intrested betimes e be growd. The weather's bin kind to us toyear. We had a good crop of hay, en twill be a bissy time fer us anon. Hop picken next week, then the carn ter arvest. En the froot en nuts will need gatheren. I shall get Ned en Boy ter do that...

He heard a shout from the parlour, and Martha came into the hall.

"Mas William, Dog be here by himself. He be fretful, and barking. D'ye know where Boy be?"

William stood up, leaving the letter unfinished on the table. He followed Martha through the parlour. Dog was at the door looking anxious. When he saw William, he barked and turned to go out of the close.

William took in all the implications of this turn of events. Boy was in trouble, on the Down. He may have had an accident, or been accosted by vagrants, or someone up to no good. Robin was with him, but one of them may be injured. William went to the drawer where he kept his pistol. He strapped it in its holster round his waist, took a bag of bullets and put them in his pocket.

"I be going to find Boy on the Down," he called to Martha on the way out. He fetched Damsel and saddled her. Dog waited, barking.

William followed Dog up the road to the Down, dreading what he might find there. They reached the top. William stopped Damsel and looked around. He could see nothing but empty space. Dog barked and went running on. William followed.

Presently he saw in front of him, lying on the grass, two bodies.

William dismounted and ran to Boy. His son was sprawled in an awkward position on his front, one arm underneath him. His face was turned to one side, and was the colour of calfskin. His eyes were closed. William crouched down and put a hand on Boy's head, stroking the pale yellow hair off his forehead.

"Boy, I be here. Wake up, Boy."

There was a flutter round Boy's eyelids and his limbs stirred. He opened his eyes and tried to lift his head. "Farder," he said, and relaxed onto his resting place, closing his eyes again.

William breathed a shuddering sigh. "Let's see where ye be hurt, Son. Where do it pain thee?"

Boy opened his eyes again. "Me head." He tried to lift it, then rolled over carefully onto his back, and lay there for a few moments, moving all his limbs. Then he half sat up, supporting himself on his elbows.

"Robin! Robin's hurt, Farder! Be he alright?" Boy tried to get up.

William noticed a graze on one side of the boy's head, where he'd hit the ground. "Stay there, Son. I'll have a look." He got up and went over to where Robin lay still. He struggled to get up when William approached. His eyes were wide open with pain. One foreleg was hideously misshapen. Nearby was the hole which had caused the accident.

"Whoa there, Robin!" William took hold of Robin's head and gently cradled it before laying it back on the ground. He knew now why he'd brought the pistol. Should he tell Boy first, or just do what was necessary?

He went back to Boy, who was sitting up, rubbing his neck. "Boy, Robin's broke his leg. He be in terrible pain. I'll have to shoot him."

"Nay! Nay!" screamed Boy. He got up and staggered over to his beloved pony, fell on the ground beside him and fondled his nose. Then he looked at his father.

"Do it, quick," he sobbed, and crawled round Robin's head to his shoulder. He sat there stroking and fondling his friend while William loaded his pistol, and came to hold it against Robin's head.

"Hold still," William said, and pressed the trigger. The gun fired. The pony shuddered, then relaxed into death.

William went round to Boy, and put his arms round him. He held him until the tears subsided.

The next day, the family were sitting round the table in the parlour at coger.

"You caught a wunnerful tumble, Boy," remarked Michael, regarding him across the table. The graze on Boy's face had turned bright scarlet. His black eye had a halo of yellow.

Boy nodded, and winced.

"I'll mix a special ointment to put on thy bruises," said Tamsen. "They'll be gone in no time."

Boy said to William, "We can't leave Robin up on the Down, Farder. How can we get him down?"

"I've been and collected the saddle and all after you went to your chamber, Son. We'll take Gaffer up there with the cart and bring him down 'forelong."

"I'll dig a pit to put 'im in, Boy," said Pieter. "We can do the job proper, like."

Boy pushed his plate away and had a last gulp at his ale. "Can I go en find a place to put him in, Farder?"

William nodded and watched Boy hobble out of the room.

"'Twill take 'im a while to get over that fall," said Martha. "Go easy on him, Mas William."

"That I will, Martha," said William.

"Tamsen and me's got some news," announced Michael. Everyone stopped eating and looked at him. "We be ringling come spring." He put his arm round Tamsen's waist and gave her a squeeze. Tamsen laughed, and her face turned bright red.

I be hem pleased," said William.

"About time too," remarked Martha into her plate. Then she looked up at them across the table, her face all smiles. Her eyes were wet.

Pieter clapped his hands and thumped Michael on the back. "Well done, my friend," he said.

They all raised their mugs to the happy couple.

Chapter 47

The harvesting was done, and there was a chill in the air. William had led the workforce in morning prayers, and given them their tasks for the day. He was settling down at the table in the hall to catch up with the accounts. There came a knock at the door. He went to open it, and Susan stood there looking distressed.

"William, I must speak with you," she said.

"Come in, Susan. Be ye riding?"

"No, my groom is out there with the trap. This won't take long."

William led Susan into the hall and showed her a seat. "Can I get you a drink of something?"

"No thank you. I'm very concerned about my Mother, William. She'll not be writing to you again, and you must stop all correspondence."

"How can that be? Has Timothy something to do with this?"

"I'm afraid so, William. She was in the garden, writing to you. Timothy came home unexpectedly and couldn't find her in the house. The maid was forced to tell him where Mother was. He went out and found her, snatched the letter and read it. He was angry, tore the letter up and took her into the house." Susan paused and dabbed her eyes with her handkerchief.

William was speechless.

Susan continued, "I called to see her yesterday as usual. She was shut in her chamber, and Timothy's at home, on guard. He ranted and raged at me for delivering your letters, and wasn't going to allow me to see her. But my husband was with me, and insisted that I be allowed into Mother's chamber. She's distressed,

William, and asked me to tell you how sorry she is. My husband and I were angry with Timothy, and demanded that he at least allow Mother the comfort of the parlour. I'll visit again when I can." She dabbed her eyes again and sighed.

"What kind of a man does that to his own muvver?" said William. "Can she not bide with thee for a while?"

"No, Timothy wouldn't allow that. I fear for her health, William. She's not a young woman." She looked at him with a worried frown. "If only she'd not been so soft with him when he was growing up."

"Thank thee for telling us, Susan. I'm mortal anxious too. But there be nothing I can do. Please give me news of her when ye sees her, and tell her how sorry I be."

"I will, William. Thank you for your friendship. It means a lot to her." Susan said goodbye, and left.

William stood in the hall, simmering with frustrated rage. He was trying to think of a way to help Susannah. He wanted to go and confront Timothy, but knew it would do no good. It may even make things worse for Susannah. He went through to the parlour. It was pointless to try and do the accounts now. He needed to go and vent his anger.

"Martha, I be going to dig turmuts," he announced as he went out into the close. He found Gaffer in the croft, and brought him into the court to hitch him up to the cart. He fetched his tools from the skillon, jumped up and drove Gaffer along the whapple way to the turnip field.

Boy and Ned had taken the sheep to new pasture. They gave them some chopped turnips to nibble, and checked that they were all in good health.

"They seem to be alright," said Ned "We should've gone round looking for breeches in the hedge afore we brought them in. Come, we'll do it now. We don't want them getting into that clover field." He nodded in the direction of the next field. They walked round. Boy saw a place where the hedge was getting thin and pointed it out.

"We'd best put a hurdle in there for now," said Ned. They went to get a hurdle from the close, carried it to the offending hole, and pushed it in as best they could.

"Mas William should know about this," said Ned. "Be sure to tell him when ye sees him."

"Yus, Ned," said Boy. "Be us finished prensley?"

"Yus, lad, go en get thy coger." said Ned. They parted company.

Boy went into the parlour, expecting to find the family gathered for coger. But there were only Martha and Tamsen.

He sat down and said, "Where be the others?"

"Michael en Pieter be drying the last of the hops for Mas Longley. They'll be in the oast for another day, I rackon." Martha looked at Tamsen, who nodded. "Thy farder said he were going to dig turmuts. I'll warrant he'll be here prensley."

But William didn't appear for coger. Boy went into the hall and got out his books and slates. He started reading one of the books while he waited, but his father didn't come. Boy wasn't worried. This happened frequently. He would see his father at dinner. He packed his books into his satchel, slung it over his shoulder, and, calling to Dog, he set off down the road to Mary's house. He knocked and let himself in. Mary was in the parlour.

"Hello, Boy! I didn't expect thee so soon. Anne be unwell. But Jone's with her."

"D'ye want us to go for the doctor?" asked Boy, worried about Anne.

"Nay, you can read awhile. It may be naught."

Boy got his book out, and started reading it. There was a loud knocking at the door. Mary went to open it, and a man stood there. He'd evidently been running, and looked distressed.

"Mistus Dyne, ye must come dracly-minute. Mas Dyne be taken bad. He be working by the forge on Master Tinker's stables. I'll fetch the doctor." He ran off down the road.

"I be going down the village," said Mary to Boy. "You go and tell Jone, and bide here till I gets back." She shut the door behind her.

Boy found Jone sitting by Anne's cot, singing to the child, who was flushed and fretful, and coughing frequently. They waited together for what seemed like hours, trying to sooth Anne with cool towels and drinks of milk. They were worried. Jone was near to tears, but Boy didn't want to leave her to get help, as Mary had been definite that he should stay there until she returned. A knock at the door sent Boy running to open it. There was Adam.

"I be bodgen home, and happened by on my way," he said. "Martha were wondering if you'd forgotten to milk the cows."

"Oh, I be hem glad to see thee," said Boy. "Aunt Mary be down the village. Mas Dyne's taken bad. Jone and me be muvvering Anne. She's ailing. Can ye fetch Tamsen? Maybe she can give her a potion."

"I'll fetch her dracly-minute," said Adam. He ran back up the road towards the Slade.

Boy waited with Jone who was crying.

"I've sent for Tamsen," said Boy. "She'll know what to be at."

Jone looked aghast. "I don't want her anywhere near Anne. She be a witch!" she shouted.

Boy wasn't sure how to deal with this new crisis. He was relieved when Mary returned. But she was looking anxious, and was closely followed by two men carrying Thomas Dyne home in a cart. The men lifted Thomas and helped him into the house. His face was blue and he was clutching his chest in pain. They carried him to his cot.

Mary said, "This was how his Farder died. Exactly the same. The doctor's given him a potion. He'll be coming back later."

Anne was crying, and Boy wondered if he should stay.

Tamsen appeared at the door. "Can I help?" she asked Mary. "I believe I may be able to do something for the child."

Mary nodded. "Do what ye can, Tamsen. Don't heed Jone." She took Tamsen to see Anne.

Boy could hear Jone shouting. He gathered his books together, and called to Mary, "I be bodgen now, Aunt Mary. I'll tell Farder ye be in trouble."

"Thank thee, Boy," she called back.

Chapter 48

William threw the last two turnips into the basket and took it to the cart. He heaved it up and added the contents to the load, with a rumble. He went back to collect his spade, threw it onto the pile of turnips and climbed onto the cart. He still felt angry about Timothy's treatment of Susannah, but the hard work had taken away the urgency. He drove the cart into the close, and unhitched Gaffer to take him to the croft. He'd leave the turnips in the cart and store them tomorrow. On the way to the croft, he passed the clover field. He glanced over the hedge, stopped and looked again. He didn't want to believe what he saw.

He hurried Gaffer into the croft and came back to look more closely. There were four sheep among the clover. Two were feeding greedily. Two were collapsed and lying on their sides, their stomachs distended, their breathing heavy and stertorous. There were four other sheep remaining in their pasture. William ran to find the breach in the hedge. There was a hurdle lying on the ground. He picked it up and pushed it hard back into the gap. He must get help quickly. He ran to the house and found Boy bringing the cows in for milking.

"You be late with that, Son," he shouted.

"I've been at Mary's house and Anne…"

But William interrupted, "The sheep's in the clover. They be hoving. Go dracly-minute and fetch the shepherd at Snellings farm."

Boy gasped, and put his hand to his mouth. He left the cows wandering around the close, and ran out into the yard and down the road.

William went into the parlour. "Martha, where be Tamsen?"

"She be gone to help Mary with liddle Anne. She be took bad," said Martha.

"Can ye milk these cows, Martha? The sheep's in the clover and Boy's gone for the shepherd."

Martha nodded. She added the remaining carrots and turnips to the stew pot, wiped her hands on her apron, and came out to the close. The cows had found their way into their stalls and were munching on the bags of hay Boy had left for them. William was going back across the close when he realised that he could do with some help with the sheep while he waited for the shepherd.

"Where be Adam?" he shouted to Martha.

"He be bodged off long ago," replied Martha, as she started to milk the first cow.

William threw up his hands in frustration, and ran back to his sheep. He took the hurdle away from the gap in the hedge, and went back into the clover field. He attempted to drive the two sheep that were still on their feet back through the hedge. They were dopey and unsteady. The remaining sheep in the pasture came to the breach on the other side and tried to get through. He turned them back and made a further attempt at saving the others, remembering some advice he'd been given. He put his arms round one of the dopey sheep and rubbed its stomach, and tried to stop it lying down. He did the same for the other. He was becoming impatient, knowing that he was to blame for this mess. He should have been keeping a closer eye on the hedges. He'd been distracted by his correspondence with Susannah. He should have been around at coger time, to see Ned before he went home. He heard a shout, and saw the

Snelling's young shepherd running towards him, followed by Boy.

Moses came and looked at the two recumbent sheep. "That one be dead," he said, checking its eyes. He looked at the other, and took a big pointed instrument from the bag he was carrying. He carefully felt the body of the sheep, his hands searching for the ribs. To puncture the wrong place could kill the animal. He placed the spike with precise care, lifted it in the air, and plunged it into the woolly mound. As he withdrew the spike, there was a whoosh of air, and the mound subsided.

"I ain't sure she'll live," he said. Then he went to the other two sheep, which had rolled onto their sides. He gave them the same treatment. "Ye'll need a hand to shift this lot," he said. Leave them be awhile. Hopefully they'll be able to walk prensley." He stood up and straightened his back.

Boy stood transfixed. William turned his attention to his son, and looked at his horrified face.

Boy said, "'Twere my fault, Farder. Ned told us to tell thee about the breach in the hedge."

"I believe we've both learnt a lesson today, Boy," said William. "Go and help Martha with the cows. Moses'll help us shift the sheep. I'll be there for dinner. Then ye can tell us all about Anne."

He watched Boy turn and walk with his head down in the direction of the house.

Boy didn't feel like eating anything after the events of the day. He sat at the table with a dish of stew in front of him, toying with his spoon.

Martha brought her plate and sat down with him. "Ain't ye hungry, Boy?"

William came in from the close. His face and hair were still wet after his wash at the well. He sat down at the table. "Now tell us what's going on with liddle Anne," he said to Boy.

Boy was about to tell his father the news, when they heard the geese raise the alarm. He jumped up and went out to meet Tamsen. She was coming in from the yard. "How be Anne? Be she alright?" he said anxiously. Tamsen didn't answer. She took Boy by the shoulders and propelled him back into the parlour. William watched Tamsen as she came to sit at the table. She brushed her hair out of her eyes, and sighed. Boy stood by Tamsen's side. William was slowly coming to realise that all was not well at Mary's house. Martha stopped eating.

"I did what I could," Tamsen said to Boy. "The child were quieter when I came away, but still feverish. The doctor came back to see Mas Dyne…"

William interrupted, "What be up with Thomas Dyne?"

Tamsen looked at William. "He be failing, Will. He were took bad at his work. They had to carry 'im home. I believe it's his heart. Mary says his farder died of it. The doctor said he could do no more for either of them. Only the morning will bring news, good or bad." She sighed deeply, and put her arm round Boy, giving him a hug.

"I must go and be with Mary. She'll be fretting, surely." William got up to leave.

Tamsen said to him, "Gregory Dyne be there, sitting with his brudder."

Martha pleaded, "Mas William, come and have some dinner afore ye go. You ain't ett all day. You'll be stronger for Mary with something inside thee."

William wavered on the threshold, then came back into the parlour and sat down again. Martha went to fill a dish from the pot, and put it in front of him.

"Will ye have some, Tamsen?" she asked.

"Nay, but I'll take some for them in the oast, and tell Michael what's been happening. Then I'll go and eat with Muvver and the children. I'll see thee all tomorrow." She dished up two bowls of stew, and took them out with her.

William was eating hurriedly.

Martha said, "Come, Boy, try and eat something. We all needs to be strong for Mary."

Boy went back to his place and stared at his plate.

William got up to go. "I may not be back afore morning," he said, and left the house.

Soon after dawn, Boy heard his father coming home and dashed downstairs to hear the news. He could see by William's face that all was not well.

"Anne passed away in the night, Son." William said, as he sat down at the table in the parlour.

Boy was shocked and frightened. How could a lively beautiful baby lose her life so easily? He'd seen animals die, but they were usually the runts of the litter that had been fragile from birth. He'd played with Anne and her dolls, making her laugh that tinkly laugh. She would throw her arms up in delight when he came to see her. How could she suddenly not be there? He felt he must see Anne for the last time.

Later that morning William and Boy walked over to Mary to offer condolences. Jone answered the door. She was angry, blaming the death of Anne on Tamsen.

"It were that witch's potion what killed 'er!" she shouted at Boy.

He flinched at the tirade and tears came to his eyes. He swallowed and walked through the open door with his father.

Thomas was still hanging on to life, but only by a thread. Mary sat by him, looking dazed. She got up and took Boy to see the dead child.

The room was draped in black, and there were candles burning all around. Anne was in her cot where she'd been last time he saw her. The fever and distress were over. She looked peaceful. Boy touched her face, imagining that she was asleep. It was cold, and there was no flicker of life. He took his hand away quickly. This wasn't Anne. It was only her dead body. She, the girl he knew, had gone to join Robin and Uncle John, wherever they may be.

He came out of the room to find his father comforting Mary, who was weeping. "Thomas's gone, Boy," said William. Mary howled with grief and William held her more tightly. Boy was horrified to see strong, dependable Aunt Mary collapse like that. William said, "Will ye go and ask the Headborough to come and confirm the deaths, Son? Then go home to Martha. I'll be here awhile."

Boy left the house and Dog followed him down to the village. They called at the Headborough's house and left a message, then walked back up the hill to the Slade. He came into the parlour, where Martha and Tamsen were baking bread.

"Mas Dyne passed away," he said. "Farder be staying with Mary and Jone."

He went out into the autumn sunshine and spent the rest of the day sitting by the pond throwing stones, wandering in the woods, taking pot shots at pigeons with his catapult and kicking a ball for Dog. Sometimes tears rolled down his cheeks and he punched the tree trunks with his fists until they hurt. He went back to the house when he was hungry, and Martha was waiting for him, ready to give him a hug. Then they set about bringing the cows in, milking, collecting eggs and feeding the geese, chickens, ducks and pigs. It was good to get back to routine work when feelings were raw.

The whole of Lamberhurst attended the funeral. Thomas Dyne was one of a long line of his family who had been builders in Lamberhurst for more years than anyone could remember. Boy helped to carry Anne's coffin. Mary looked frail and grey, and leaned on Jone. Thomas and Anne Dyne were buried under the yew tree near the church door next to Thomas' father.

For the next few months Mary and Jone held each other in their grief, and William went to visit frequently, giving as much support as Mary would accept.

A few weeks later, he said to Boy, "Aunt Mary's ready to larn thee again if ye be agreeable. I rackon 'twould make her feel better."

Chapter 49   1645

Life at the Slade took on a sombre atmosphere. William and Boy were shattered by the sudden death of Anne and her father. William was concerned for Mary and Jone, who were immersed in grief. He had never seen Mary so low, and Jone had a lost look about her, which reminded him of the way she was when she came home from Ticehurst.

His concern for Susannah's predicament also affected him deeply. He felt responsible, as it was he who initiated the correspondence between them. He felt angry and frustrated that he could do nothing to help. He was also aware that he was to blame for the loss of two sheep, so engrossed was he in his and Susannah's problems, and his burning hate of Timothy who ruled her life, and, consequently, his.

In order to counteract all of these thoughts and feelings which pervaded his mind, he stepped up the pressure on his workforce. He had Adam and Michael coppicing another cant of hazel, with Boy helping them. William and Pieter used some of the hazel rods to relay the hedges which were wearing thin. Then they all turned their shoulders to cleaning out the ditches before the wet weather. There was enough cordwood to make two pets of charcoal for next summer's oast. Martha and Tamsen used the twigs for making besoms, and taught Boy how to bind more of them into faggots for the bread oven. Gaffer and the cart wore ruts into the whapple way as they trundled up and down, taking wood to the store until it was overflowing.

The weather was kind to them this winter, and the men manured and ploughed the fields in good time for sowing when the ground warmed up. William involved Boy in all that they did, and made sure that they were both there for lessons after coger every day. In the evenings William, Michael, Pieter and Boy came home weary after a hard day's work, and took a wash at the well before dinner. There was a great deal of splashing and cavorting as they threw buckets of cold water over each other's naked bodies.

One evening William and Boy were towelling themselves dry when William said, "'Tis time ye had a horse, Boy. You've worked hard on the farm with us, and I rackons ye be missing your riding. Shall we go to the Horse Fair agin Frant tomorrow and ye can choose one thyself?"

"I'd be partial to that for certain sure, Farder." Boy punched the air and cried, "Geewoot!" Dog came to see what was so exciting, and they raced round the close together. Boy's lithe, naked body glowed in the setting winter sun.

Boy rode in front of William on Damsel the next day with Dog following. It seemed a long way to the Horse Fair. Boy wanted his father to urge Damsel into a trot, but he knew it may be dangerous.

At last they arrived. The field was a mass of men and horses. William lifted Boy to the ground. He felt small among the bustle and noise. They tethered Damsel and went to buy a bag of hay for her bait. Boy gazed around, taking in the scene. There were men leading handsome horses round the field at a brisk walk, and crowds of people watching the performance, nodding and shaking their heads as they shared their opinions with their neighbours. There were groups of horses tethered away from the circuit, being examined by wealthy farmers, and gentlemen and their grooms. In another part of the field there was an auctioneer standing on a stool, gabbling his rattle to a group of men gathered round bidding.

How would Boy ever find a horse among this throng?

His father led him into the milling crowds. All Boy could see now were round frocks and breeches, long boots and coloured hose, lacy cuffs and buckled shoes, bellies bursting their buttons, fat people and thin, all pushing and shoving. His nose experienced a variety of unsavoury smells mixed with heady perfumes. Dog followed, dodging between the many moving feet.

They came to a clearing where Boy was dazzled by the sun. He pulled the brim of his hat over his eyes, and saw some horses tethered. There were few people showing interest. Boy thought these horses looked friendlier than the smart pure breds he had seen being trotted round the field. Two men in rough dark jackets and long breeches were standing smoking pipes and talking. They looked up as William and Boy approached.

William raised his hat. "I be seeking a suitable young horse for the lad here."

"Can ye ride, boy?" enquired one of the men. He took his pipe from his mouth and knocked it on his shoe before putting it in his pocket.

"Yus, Sir," replied Boy.

The man went and picked two horses and brought them to William. "This one's a trifle spirited, but strong and brave. This be a gentle mare."

"Have they been ridden?" asked William.

"Nay, ye'll need to break 'em in."

William examined each horse. The other man, who had been watching Boy, went to find a third. This one was the colour of shiny conkers, with a black mane and tail. He led it to Boy and it reached out to nibble at his clothes. Boy patted its neck. Dog went to have a sniff, and the horse bent down calmly to say hello.

"That one be gantsy," said the first man.

"Can I ride him?" asked Boy.

William came over to have a look. "D'ye have a saddle?" he asked.

"Nay. And I rackon he'll buck the lad off."

"I want to try," urged Boy.

William lifted him up, while the horse's head was held firmly by the man with the pipe.

Boy talked to the horse, "Good boy. Will ye be friendly?" He reached forward and lay along its neck. The horse stood perfectly still, his ears twisting round to the sound of Boy's voice. Boy sat up and said, "Walk on, Hector," and nudged him with his feet. The horse started forward, led by the man with the pipe still between his teeth. They walked in a small circle and came back to William. Boy had made a friend, and there was no need for further discussion.

As he helped Boy to the ground his father asked, "Have ye come far?"

"Harting, West Sussex," the man said.

"I be avised there be fighting thereabouts," said William.

"Yus. The Royalists have garrisoned Petworth, and there's skirmishing in Arundel. They tried to cross the river Arun, but Roundheads beat them back."

"'Tis unaccountable quiet hereabouts, thanks be," said William. "Can I leave the horse with thee if I pay for him now?"

"Surely, Sir. Thank thee for thy custom."

As they walked away Boy asked, "Will we take Hector home today, Farder?"

"Yus, Son. We'll go and seek bait, and come back for 'im."

"Can I ride him home?"

"Nay, we must get to know him first. He may throw thee. And we need to fix him up with a saddle."

They found a stall selling food. William bought them a pie each, and some ale. They sat down at a table and watched men and horses going about their business. Boy's thoughts went back to the conversation with the horse dealers.

"Will there be fighting hereabouts, Farder?"

"Behopes not, Son. But 'tis getting close. If the Roundheads can hold this side of the river, we'll be all right."

A stout man wearing long wide boots and a tall hat approached them. "That's a hem cushti dog ye have there, young man. Be ye selling him?"

"Nay, he ain't for sale, Sir," said Boy.

"I'll give thee good money for him," persisted the man, and bent down to stroke Dog, who snarled at him.

"He be terrible crusty when he be picked upon," warned Boy. "I wouldn't touch him if I was thee." The man withdrew his hand and walked quickly away. Boy looked at his father and they laughed together.

As they walked back to collect Hector, they passed a saddler's booth and William stopped to have a look at the quality of the tackle.

"We'll come back and buy a saddle here," he said to Boy.

Boy's heart was full as he led his horse to be fitted with his saddle. Hector was calm and quite willing to be handled by Boy and William. Boy was shown how to find the right saddle, and he came away happily.

Michael and Tamsen were preparing for the wedding, and the mood of the family was lifted. They talked of nothing else when they were together having coger.

"How many brudders and sisters d'ye have, Tamsen?" asked Boy one day.

"Three brudders and three sisters," said Tamsen. "I be the oldest, then there's Jessica, two year younger."

"What do your brudders do for work?" asked William. They would soon be part of a larger family, and William knew hardly anything about them.

"Labouring, when they can get work. Me brudder Mart'n were called to the militia. He's been away these last three year. Tammy were too young, and now he works for the farrier, larning the trade, like."

"Be the house fixed up ready, Michael?" asked Pieter. "I can come and give ye a hand."

"That'd be fine. There be nobbut a few jobs needs doing prensley."

"Be Edward coming to the wedding?" William asked. "I believe Peggy be unwell."

"He'll come if he can," replied Michael.

"Did your fambly always bide in Lambr'rst, Tamsen?" asked William.

"Nay, we was travelling didicais afore. Muvver always wanted to bide in a house, and we happened in Lambr'rst when Farder died. So we stayed."

The wedding was a happy occasion. The two families went to Tamsen's mother's house for the celebrations. It was a small cottage, but, skilled as they were at finding space for everything, her family had cleared the parlour of furniture and there was room for all. There were fiddlers and dancing such as William had never experienced. Tamsen took William by the hand to join the company in a jig. He danced, tripping over his own feet, until he was breathless, and had to go and sit down.

Martha landed beside him, puffing and panting. "Struth!" she said, having been swept off her feet and frolicked around the room by Michael. "These folk do surely know how to enjoy themselves!"

William caught sight of Boy, and nudged Martha. Boy was being propelled round the room in an ungainly fashion by a very pretty sister of Tamsen's. Martha and William chuckled. William invited Martha to join him in a more sedate dance. Neither of them knew what to do, and they stumbled around trying to copy other people. Eventually they gave up, in fits of laughter at their incompetence.

Mary was sitting with Jone and Tamsen's mother. They were talking animatedly. But Mary didn't look well and Jone was glaring at Tamsen. It was a wonder they had come. William had hoped that the event would help to alleviate Mary's grief. He watched them get up and say goodbye to their hostess and leave. He was sad, too, that Edward and Peggy hadn't come, though neither of them would have been fit enough to join in the dancing. He got to his feet and went over to Jessica.

"Will ye larn us how to do this dance?" he asked.

Chapter 50

Christmas festivities were over, and William was checking his stores in the barns, calculating how much corn and hay they needed to last the winter. It had been a disastrous summer for corn harvests. There was plenty of fodder for the beasts, but he would need all the corn he had for sowing in the spring. He would have to buy more for the family's bread. He was grateful that he was getting an income from the hops and rent for his property in Wadhurst. Taxes had risen with the start of the Civil War, and there were more people needing help from the Parish Chest.

Martha came out of the house. "There be a visitor to see thee, Mas William."

He went through the parlour into the hall, where he found Susan waiting. This must be serious news.

"Susan, is there something amiss? How be your muvver?"

Susan looked pale and stressed. "William, Mother's dying. She's lost all her strength, and won't eat. She's now a great age, and life has finally taken its toll. I wanted you to know. It won't be long, and I intend to go and sit with her now until the end."

William felt weary and sad. He knew that Susannah must be getting old, but she had retained her good health, dignity and youthful outlook on life, in spite of adversities. He said, "Would ye be willing to take one last letter to her from me? 'Twill be short, and hopefully ye'll have a chance to read it to her without Timothy knowing."

"I'll try, William. It may be difficult, but I'll do my best."

William got his quill, ink and paper from the drawer, and sat down to write.

Dear Susannah, Susan tells us that ye be ailing. I want to thank thee fer all thy kindness en friendship en wish God's blessings on thee. I miss thee sorely. Your loving friend, William Lucke.

He folded the paper carefully, and handed it to Susan. "Thank thee for doing this, Susan." He briefly held her hand with the letter in it with both of his, then let go. "Behopes her suffering will be over soon."

"I've called for Thomas Maynard to come from London. Mother will want him to give her the last rights. I could have asked John Hatley, but I believe he's also ailing."

They said goodbye. Susan left and William closed the door after her. He sat in the hall with his memories before joining the family for coger, feeling deeply sad.

It was the following Sunday that William heard news of Susannah. Susan was outside the church waiting for him.

"We buried Mother on Wednesday," she said. "She slipped away quietly without pain. I found an opportunity to read your letter to her before she lost consciousness, and she nodded in appreciation. She was very frail, and I believe it's a blessing she doesn't have to suffer further."

"Thank thee for telling us, Susan. She's been in my thoughts often these last weeks. How has Timothy taken it?"

"He's shut himself away in that big house with one manservant to cook his meals. He wasn't at the funeral. My brothers and sisters all called on him afterwards, but he wouldn't see them. I think he's denying Mother's death, making believe that she's still there and he has to guard her."

It was time to go into church, and William shook Susan's hand before they parted company. He prayed for Susannah's soul and for his own release from Timothy's enmity.

Boy was helping his father move the pigs to the pasture one morning.

"Will ye be going to Mary for thy lesson this afternoon, Boy?" asked William.

"Yus , unless ye needs me for aught else. 'Tis time I gave Hector some exercise. I be minded to take him after I leave Aunt Mary."

"Nay, I don't need thee, so long as we can get the hog pound cleaned out this morning. I'll do the mannering after coger. Will ye take some provisions over to Mary when ye go? I don't rackon she be feeding herself enough."

"She ain't been larning us like she did. She just talks to us and we don't do work."

"Tell her I'll visit her after dinner."

"Yus, Farder."

They set about driving the sow and her litter to join the other pigs, and took some old apples to encourage them. After a great deal of grunting and squealing, they were safely through the gate. Boy and his father watched them running off across the clover stubble; eight pink bottoms, each decorated with a curly tail.

It was smelly work cleaning the hog pound, shovelling dirt and barrowing it to the cart. Boy thought of a hundred things he'd rather be doing. But at last they were collecting buckets of water to swill it all down. They would leave it to dry, and let the pigs enjoy some freedom for the summer.

"Where be Michael, Jessica?" asked Martha as the family sat down to coger.

"Tamsen were having some pains this morning. I happened by on my way here. Michael said he'd stay home in case she birthed."

William came in and took his place. He gave thanks for the food they were about to eat, and sat down.

"Martha, the goose be sitting on her eggs," said Boy. "D'ye want the eggs, or shall we let her hatch them?"

Martha looked at William. "After the fox had those two, we could do with some more geese. If there be too many they'll make a good meal for Christmas."

William smiled. "I can't see why not." He looked at Boy. "There'll be more to get into the barn at night," he warned.

"That's alright," said Boy. He would enjoy the goslings.

Boy's reading and writing skills were adequate now. He could read on his own, but was rarely inclined to study his father's books about husbandry. He'd proved to be good at figures, and had started helping his father keep the accounts once a week. His visits to Mary had become social. She would choose a book, and he'd read a passage to her. They spent time discussing the subjects: history, religious practises, social affairs and philosophical ideas. He enjoyed these times with his aunt. She treated him as an adult, and, although he didn't understand all they talked about, she was helping him to open his mind to things he would never otherwise have considered. Today, he saddled and mounted his beloved Hector, who had turned out to be a strong and faithful friend. Dog followed them out of the yard and down the road to Mary's cottage. Boy tethered Hector, and carried the bag of provisions into the house.

It was cool and dark indoors after the brightness of the day. It was also strangely quiet. There was no-one in the parlour. He put the bag on the table and was about to go through to see if there was anyone in the garden, when he heard it. A low moaning sound was coming from upstairs. Boy leapt up the stairs two at a time, stopped and listened. There it was again. He cautiously pushed open the door of Mary's chamber, and saw Jone sitting by the bed in semi-darkness. She was holding herself, and rocking in the chair. Tears ran down her face. She moaned again as Boy entered the room. She seemed unaware of his presence. He approached the bed. Mary lay on her back, pale, peaceful, with a small smile on her lips. Her eyes were closed.

Chapter 51

Boy came out of the room, ran down the stairs and out of the cottage to Hector. He unhitched the reins and mounted, called Dog and cantered up the road back to the Slade. They clattered into the cobbled yard and Boy leapt off his horse and tethered him. The geese hissed and flapped menacingly. Boy ran through the close and out to the field where his father was spreading manure.

"Farder! Farder!" Boy shouted, racing across the field, stumbling over the rough ground.

William halted Gaffer, and watched Boy coming towards him. "What be the trouble, Son? Ye looks like ye've seen a phantom."

Boy blurted out, "Aunt Mary! She be lying in her cot, peaceful like. Jone be sitting there, weeping and moaning."

His father was silent for a moment. He sucked in his breath. "I'll go dracly-minute. You go and find Pieter in the hop garden and ask him to finish spreading this manner for us. Then ye must go to the Headborough, and ask him to call at Mary's house."

"Be Aunt Mary dead, Farder?"

"Surely sounds like it," replied William.

Boy ran to the hop garden and explained to Pieter. Then he mounted Hector, told Dog to stay there and galloped off down to the village for the Headborough. On the way back he caught up with Michael who was running up the hill from his house. Boy reigned in and slowed Hector down.

Michael looked round and stopped. "Tamsen's birthing and her muvver's there, but she needs Jessica to give her a hand."

"I'll go and tell Jessica," said Boy. "I went to see Aunt Mary, and she looks to be dead. Farder's gone to see, and the Headborough's coming dracly."

Michael's mouth fell open. "Nay, not so sudden," he said, looking stunned. He quickly recovered and said, "I be going back to Tamsen. I'll see Will later. You fetch Jessica dracly-minute."

Boy nodded and galloped back to the Slade. He dashed round to the back door. Jessica was helping Martha in the milk-house.

"Tamsen's birthing and thy muvver's wanting thee to go en help," he announced.

Jessica stopped what she was doing and said, "Thanks be! I came on Tamsen's pony this morning." She washed her hands at the well and called goodbye as she ran out.

Martha looked at Boy. "You look all-in," she said. Come into the parlour and I'll get thee a drink. Then ye can tell us all about it."

Boy followed her into the parlour feeling dazed. He went and sat down, leaned forward to rest his elbows on the table, and cradled his head in his hands. He tried to collect his thoughts and to remember what had happened in the last hour since he'd set off to see Aunt Mary. Tears popped out of his eyes and rolled down his cheeks. Martha came and sat opposite, putting a mug of cider on the table in front of him.

She watched him for a few moments and said, "Get that drink down thee, Boy."

Boy slowly came out of his daze, looked at Martha and took a long, sobbing breath before lifting the mug to his lips and taking a few gulps of the cool drink. He put the mug down.

"Aunt Mary be gone," he said. The tears dropped onto the table.

Martha said, "What? Mary? Dead? Oh my! Oh my!" She put her hands to her face and rubbed her forehead.

"She be lying in her cot. She looked so... happy, like."

Boy looked at Martha, not able to understand how a dead person could look happy.

Martha said, "You be sure she be dead, not just sleeping?"

Boy shook his head. "Jone were weeping. They've been there all morning."

"Poor Jone. She'll need extra muvvering now," Martha said. She sighed, put her hands on the table and levered herself to standing. "Come, there be work to be done, and I'll need thee to help us. Let's do this butter and cheese then ye can get the cows in for milking while I collect the eggs."

Boy jerked himself into action and got up to follow Martha into the milk-house.

Chapter 52   1647

William sat in the hall after prayers, talking to Martha. They were remembering the months following Mary's death.

"How be Jone getting on, Martha?" he said.

"She be like she were years ago, when she first came back after her husband treated her so cruel. She seems like she's in a world of her own. She don't do no work without someone to watch over 'er, and she don't talk at all."

"We all be missing Mary. We be doing the best we can."

Jone's face brightened when Michael or Pieter joined them for coger. Today they were both there.

"How's me favourite sister today, Jone?" asked Michael, smiling at her across the table.

Jone smiled a pale smile, and looked down at her plate.

"Jone helped us feed the fowls this morning," said Martha. "We didn't find many eggs today, though, did we Jone?"

Jone took a mouthful of bread and shook her head.

"Pieter's courting," announced Michael. He turned to Pieter. "I saw ye down the village being hem friendly with a purty girl." Pieter blushed.

"When are we going to see this purty girl then, Pieter?" asked Martha. "Will ye bring her to meet us?"

"Yus, we'd be hem pleased to meet her, if she be agreeable," said William.

"What's her name?" asked Boy.

Peiter, who had not spoken yet, was looking embarrassed. "I...I'd like to bring her when she be ready. Her name's Rosy." He blushed and continued eating.

Jone had been listening to the conversation. William watched her looking at Pieter. She stopped eating and her brow wrinkled. Then she got up and left the room. Martha hurried after her.

The squawking of geese announced the arrival of a visitor, and William went out to see who it was. There was no-one in the yard. He chased the geese towards the orchard, and walked out into the road to investigate. Hiding behind the hedge was a small boy, no more than ten years old. He looked up at William.

"Be ye Mas Lucke?" he asked.

"I be Mas Lucke. Who may you be?"

The boy wore a round frock and breeches. He had almost grown out of them. His feet were bare and his hat was too large. "I... be come from my muvver at Mus Edward Lucke's house," he said. He took his hat off and screwed it between his hands.

"Come in and tell us the message," said William, ushering the boy through the yard into the house. If he had walked all the way from Wadhurst, he would be thirsty. He showed the boy to a seat and went to ask Martha for a mug of cider. He came back to find the boy sitting on the settle swinging his legs and looking all round him with interest. He took the cider and gulped it down.

"Now, what be thy message, young man?"

The boy wiped his mouth with his sleeve. "Me muvver said to tell thee that Mus Lucke's mistus passed away this morning."

While William was absorbing this news, the boy grabbed his hat and stood up. "Can I bodge prensley, Sir?" he said.

"Wait, lad," said William. "I have to go to Mus Edward. I'll take thee back on my horse. What be thy name?"

The boy's eyes widened, and he sat down again. "Jacob, Sir. I be obliged, Sir."

"You wait outside, Jacob. I'll go and get my horse," said William. He showed Jacob out into the yard. "The geese won't hurt thee if ye stands still."

William went and told the family the sad news and went to fetch Damsel. He took her round to find Jacob with his back pressed against the wall of the house, surrounded by hissing geese.

William said, "Shout *boo* and stamp thy foot at 'em." Jacob considered this, and did as instructed. The geese flew away shrieking. Jacob looked at William in amazement, and they laughed. William lifted Jacob onto Damsel, noticing how light and fragile he was. They set off on their journey to Wadhurst. Jacob sat rigidly in front of William, looking around him. His knuckles were white as he clung to Damsel's mane.

"Be ye comfortable, Jacob?" asked William.

Jacob nodded. "I've never been on a horse afore, Sir."

"D'ye like it up here?" William hoped that talking to the boy would help him to relax.

Jacob nodded again. "I can see over the hedges... But I might fall off." His fingers closed even more tightly.

"Damsel won't let thee fall off." William reassured him.

"Is the horse called Damsel?"

"Yus," said William.

Damsel walked on. William could not go faster, though he was anxious to get to Edward in his grief. Jacob's back remained rigid.

"D'ye have brothers and sisters, Jacob?"

"Yus, Sir. Me big brudder went to fight with the sojers. Farder went too." Jacob paused and looked down. "Muvver said they might not come back." He forgot he was sitting on the horse and turned his head to look up at William, anguish on his young face. He gasped as his body leaned to one side and turned quickly back to steady himself.

"D'ye have any sisters?" William said quickly to distract the boy from what was obviously a painful subject.

"Yus," Jacob nodded. "They be more years than me."

They rode on in silence. William thought about Jacob's mother, Hope, and how hard it must be with no men around her, and only the money from her work with Edward coming in. It would be harder now Peggy had gone. William would make sure he paid her more for her time, and tell her to take any spare milk or vegetables for her family. Jacob was certainly not getting enough to eat.

As they approached Edward's house, William saw the front door open and Timothy appeared. He walked down the path, opened the gate and went down the road into town. He didn't appear to see William.

Edward was sitting in his chair by the fire looking dazed. He glanced up as William and Jacob came in. "She's left us, Will. We'd promised each other we'd go together. Now I'm on me own again."

"Hope will be coming to do what she can, Ed. It's hard, I know." William sat in a chair opposite his brother. Hope came in and gave them both a mug of milk.

"Give Jacob a drink, Hope. He's a brave lad."

Hope's face lit up. "'E were main chuffed with 'is ride on thy horse, Mas Lucke."

William agreed to make arrangements for the funeral. Peggy had no other relatives.

Edward grieved for a while, and William wondered how long it would be before he started on the ale and whisky again. He could not expect Hope to control him as Peggy had, particularly as Timothy was visiting.

Chapter 53

Spring turned into summer, bringing with it warmer, wetter weather. It was time for a change in the working regime. Tamsen came most days with little John and helped Martha and Jessica with household tasks and the gardening. Jone seemed oblivious of the reappearance of Tamsen, with a baby. But the women all made sure that she was not left alone with little John. She had taken to sitting at the top of the stairs, rocking herself. Martha spent a lot of time coaxing her to help with the chores.

William took Boy to one side after prayers one morning. "Now that Tamsen's here 'tis time I started larning thee some husbandry. You'll continue bringing in the cows for milking, and taking them back to pasture. Adam's son James will help thee do this. Then, every day, you'll come with me and do whatever I'm doing, and larn ploughing, sowing, hedging, coppicing and all. When I goes into town you'll come along of us and be there when I sells and buys."

Boy's expression didn't change. He nodded and said, "Yus, Farder."

"Today we'll be mowing the hay meadow with Adam and James."

"Yus, Farder."

Boy prepared himself for learning to be a farmer. This wouldn't be easy, but he knew he must do what was expected of him as well as he could. As it happened, he got on well with James. Perhaps it would lighten the load having a friend to share the burden. A few days later, they brought the cows in through the drizzly rain, and were sitting down side by side on their milking stools.

"I'll fill my pail afore thee," challenged James, who was older than Boy, and had grown up competing with two elder brothers. This concept was new to Boy. He accepted the challenge, and set about pulling the teats as fast as he could. He soon realised that Dolly the cow could withhold her milk if she felt like it. James was milking steadily, filling his pail more quickly. Boy slowed down and tried to relax. He felt something on the back of his hand, and saw that James was aiming a teat in his direction. Another squirt landed on Boy's hand. Boy giggled, and attempted to return a squirt, but aimed wide and it landed on James' foot. They both hooted with laughter. Boy made another clumsy effort at squirting James.

Martha appeared in the doorway. Dolly objected to the treatment she was receiving and stamped her foot, kicking the pail over. Boy shouted, "Whoa!" and jumped up. He was standing in a pool of milk. James had his head down, milking as if nothing had happened. Martha came over and picked up the pail.

"No milk on thy porridge tomorrow. 'Twill be made with water. Ye'd best get that mess cleaned up, Mus Boy, and do the job with no more yoystering."

Boy managed to hold the giggles down until Martha had gone back indoors. He fetched a broom from the corner of the milk-house, filled the pail with water from the well and swilled and swept the spilt milk away. He sat down and started milking again.

"Filled my pail afore thee!" declared James, as he took his stool and a fresh pail to the next cow. Boy didn't respond. He lowered his head and endeavoured to concentrate on the task in hand.

William and Boy were returning with the cart after a day in Wadhurst. They'd been buying corn and visiting Edward. The geese ran to meet them as they clattered into the yard. Michael came out of the house and shooed the geese away.

"How's Edward?" he asked as Boy jumped off the cart and unhitched Gaffer.

"Fair to middling," said William. "Hope's muvvering 'im as best she can. But he be terrible aggy."

"I'll go over and call on him. He don't have many visitors, and I don't believe he goes out much," said Michael. He helped William unload the sacks of corn into the store.

"Don't take him any ale or spirit. I rackon he'll fall back to his old ways now Peggy ain't there to keep him off 'em, and I believe Timothy's visiting 'im again."

Michael nodded. "Were this corn costly?" he asked.

"'Twere costly enough. 'Tis coming from Holland. Behopes the harvest be better this year."

Boy came past to fetch the cows for milking.

"I'll be bodgen, Will," said Michael. "See thee tomorrow." They waved. William went into the house and poured himself a mug of ale. Martha was preparing the dinner.

"Mas William, Jone wandered off somewhere, a while ago. I be worried."

"I'll go and find her. Can't have gone far," William said. He knocked back his ale and went out into the close. He looked in the cow stalls where Boy was milking.

"Did ye see Jone?" he asked. "She's wandered off somewhere."

"Nay," said Boy. "I'll keep an eye open for her."

William looked around the garden, in the barn and stable, the hog pound and the fields behind. There was no sign of Jone. She may have gone down the road, thinking she was going to Mary's house. He went out of the yard and started walking towards the village. As he turned a corner, he saw three figures coming up the hill. They came nearer and William realised that it was Pieter leading Jone and a pretty girl on his other side.

William approached the three and called, "Thank thee Pieter. Jone, where did ye think ye was going?"

Jone looked up at him with a puzzled frown. She said nothing. William took her by the hand and they walked up the hill together.

"This be Rosy," said Pieter to William.

"I rackoned it were," said William. "Good day to thee, Rosy. I be main pleased to meet thee."

Rosy smiled and blushed. Her fair curls trembled round her face and her blue eyes sparkled. "Thank thee kindly, Mas Lucke, "she said.

"Call us Will. We all be fambly at the Slade."

Pieter and Rosy stayed to dinner. William looked at Rosy across the table. Her name suited her. She only spoke when spoken to. Pieter looked relaxed and happy. He stole a look at Rosy frequently.

Jone was sullen, and hardly touched her food. Halfway through the meal she left the table and went to sit at the top of the stairs. No amount of coaxing would bring her down, and Martha had to leave her there. William was at his wits' end to know what to do with her.

Chapter 54

A few days later, Boy and James had done the milking and James was taking the cows back to the pasture before going to join Adam. Boy took a route through the orchard on his way to help his father with the ploughing. It was a haitchy autumn morning. A swathe of mist hung over the pond. The air was still and damp clung to everything. The ducks were not dabbling as usual. They were huddled under the hedge, muttering to each other. The mist shifted and he caught sight of something floating on the pond. He went closer. The water was black and smooth. He peered into the gloom. Ripples surrounded a mass of floating hair, a hand near the surface, the edge of a dress. The body turned to reveal a familiar face. Her dress clung to her breasts, revealing prominent nipples, as if she were naked. Her mouth was open and her eyes stared at him.

He gasped. "Jone!" he shouted. He ran to the field where his father was about to start ploughing.

"Farder, Jone's in the pond. She be dead!"

William said, "What?" It took a moment for him to absorb the information. "You stay here and do your best to plough the field. Ye knows what I've larned thee. Take it slow, and stop when ye tire. I'll be back anon." He handed the reins to Boy and watched as he took hold of the plough handles, and nodded to his father.

Boy shouted, "Geewoot!" The two oxen moved off. Boy lifted the plough to bite into the clay, cutting a furrow as if it were cheese. He remembered how he must keep it straight by lining up the position of the plough with the back legs of the outer ox. Sometimes the plough hit resistance and attempted to go its own way, and he had to use all his strength to keep it on course. He heard a sharp clang and the plough stopped. He shouted, "Whoa!" and pulled on the reins, but the animals were experienced and had already halted. Boy went to see what he'd hit. A big lump of flint was buried in the earth, right in the path of the plough. He tried to shift it, but it was well embedded. He looked around. His father had left a pick leaning against the hedge. Boy took it to the offending flint and thrust the pick down beside it, into the ground, to wedge it underneath. He leaned all his weight on the handle, levering the stone out of its place. The clay released its prisoner with a sucking noise and Boy fell backwards to sit on the ground. He stayed there panting for a few moments before standing up and rolling the flint to the edge of the field. It was surprisingly light now it was free.

Boy returned to his driving position and lifted the plough handles, shouting "Geewoot!" The oxen plodded along the edge of the field until they reached the corner. Boy pulled on the reins and they turned. He came to the corner and struggled to hold the plough steady. He heard a shout, and turned his head to see James coming towards him. Boy halted.

"Mas Lucke told me to give thee a hand," said James as he arrived, out of breath. "Me farder's gone along of him to take the body out of the pond. Did ye see 'er? What did she look like?"

"She were sattered, and floating, and her eyes stared at me," replied Boy. It was an unpleasant memory. "Come on. Let's get moving," he said. He took hold of one handle of the plough and James took hold of the other. They lifted, and the oxen moved off, taking them round the turn and into the next furrow to complete the wint. It was lighter work after that, and Boy felt comforted to have a companion to help.

The family gathered in the hall that evening where Martha had laid the body in a coffin. Candles glowed and flickered, casting moving shadows over the walls and ceiling, and lighting up their sombre faces. William wondered if he'd failed Jone in some way. He wasn't able to care for her as Mary had. But could he have done more to alleviate her unhappiness?

Boy asked, "Why would she want to die like that?" This was a question they may all be asking themselves.

Michael said, "She were always the weak one of the fambly. But she cared for us bravely when I were a nipper."

"She were a good friend to me when I were a child," said Boy. She muvvered me unaccountable kind, like."

Pieter added, "She had a wonderful way with the animals. I believe she talked to them."

Martha said through her tears, "Poor love, she never had a chance in life."

William opened the Bible and read some passages.

"From the Book of James, verse 1. *Every good gift and every perfect gift is from above, and cometh down from the father of lights, with whom is no variableness, neither shadow of turning.*

"1 Corinthians, Chapter 15. *Moreover, brethren, I declare unto you the gospel which I preached unto you... By which also ye are saved, if ye keep in memory what I preached unto you, unless ye have believed in vain... how that Christ died for our sins according to the scriptures.*

"John, Chapter 5, verse 28. *Marvel not at this: for the hour is coming, in the which all that are in the graves shall hear his voice.*"

He shut the Bible. "Let us pray. O God our Heavenly Farder, we commit this, the body of our sister Jone to the earth, en we commend her spirit to thy care. May she rest in peace."

"Amen," they said in unison.

William looked at the family and said, "We all loved Jone and knew her failings. We muvvered her as best we could over the years, But all manner of things came to trouble her that she didn't understand. This morning she wandered out into the orchard, not knowing where she be going or what she be at. 'Twere smokey and she didn't see that she were walking straight into the pond. There were no-one there to stop her. She didn't know…" William stopped speaking as the tears welled up and his emotions got the better of him. It was a mortal sin to kill oneself, and he knew there would be questions asked before they would be allowed to give Jone a Christian burial. They must all be clear in their minds that she did not kill herself, nor was she pushed.

The Headborough, Abraham Shoesmith, was well known to the family by now. He came to the Slade the following morning to record the death of Jone.

He took his hat off as he entered the hall. "Good day to you, Mas Lucke. I be sorry for your loss. Ye've been bereaved so many times in the last few years. 'Tis hem ernful."

William replied, "There be nobbut three of us prensley, Sir, of a fambly of seven. We be in mortal grief."

Abraham approached the coffin and looked closely but respectfully at Jone's body. "How did she die?" came the dreaded question.

William held his breath. How could he explain without implying suicide? "'Twere early in the morning. She may have walked there in her sleep. She ain't been 'erself after Mary's death."

"What d'ye mean, *she ain't been 'erself?*"

"She were non-plush en distressed, not knowing where she were…" William paused. "'Twere haitchy and she must 'ave tripped, not seeing the pond. My son found 'er, but 'twere too late." he said. "She drownded."

Abraham was watching William's face as he spoke. William looked into the man's eyes and they both held their gaze for a few seconds.

Abraham looked down at the floor, then at William again. He cleared his throat. "You'll be wanting to give her a decent burial, I'll warrant. I'll report my findings to the vicar. Ye can make the arrangements. I wish thee all good health and fortune." He offered his hand and William took it. The handshake was warm and strong. "There be unrest and gossip in the village, and pesky people abroad. Let us know if I can be of any assistance at all. Good day to thee." He put his hat back on his head and went out of the hall. William watched Abraham mount his horse and ride out of the yard. He gave him a wave before going indoors. Relief flooded through him.

William rode over to Wadhurst with Boy to visit Edward. They left the horses by the jossing block in front of the cottage. Though it was a cold day, the front door was open. William knocked as they entered, and signalled to Boy to shut the door after him. It was dark in the parlour. The shutters were still closed and the fire had gone out. There was no sign of Edward, or Hope. William and Boy went through the house into the back garden. The cow was in her stall, and was evidently waiting to be milked. She lowed as she saw them approach.

"Milk that cow, will ye, Boy?" said William. "I'll go and find Edward." Boy found a milking stool and pail. William took a look in the small pasture before making his way round to the front of the house. He was setting off down the road wondering how far his brother had managed to walk, when he saw, coming towards him, Hope, with Edward leaning on her. Relief showed on Hope's face as William approached. He took Edward's other arm.

"Hello, brudder," Edward said. "I were minded to pay me friend a visit. 'Twere a middling stride more'n I rackoned."

"It seems ye've had a few to drink. Whatever would Peggy say?" remarked William. He and Hope assisted Edward to his chair in the parlour. Hope went to find something for Edward to eat.

Boy came in. "I've milked thy cow. D'ye want her out in pasture?"

"Oh, yus if ye please, Mas Boy. Thank thee," said Hope.

William drew up a chair next to Edward. "I've ernful news, Ed. Our sister Jone were drownded in the pond. We buried 'er yesterday."

Edward looked at William. "She were never a happy girl. D'ye think she did it a purpose?"

"Don't say such wicked things, Ed. She didn't know what she were doing since Mary died," scolded William.

Boy came into the parlour, carrying Edward's bread and cheese. Hope followed with a faggot and tinder.

They sat in silence while Edward ate his food and Hope got the fire going.

William asked, "Have ye had any visitors, Ed?"

"Nobbut one or two. Michael happened by." He paused. "Timothy, too. He didn't look well."

The fire burst into life. Hope brought drinks of fresh milk for them all, and they sat watching the flames. William got up to go, and Boy followed suit. They thanked Hope , and took their leave of Edward.

On the way home, Boy asked, "Farder, who be Timothy?"

"He be a cousin. Lives in Mayfild. I believe he be up to no good. 'Twas him that took ye away in the pony trap when ye were a child." William looked at his son.

"What do 'e want with Uncle Edward?"

"That's what I be wondering," said William.

Chapter 55

Michael had suggested that Boy join him and Pieter for a drink in the village one evening. William had agreed and James said he would come along. After dinner Boy fetched Hector from the pasture and saddled him up. Dog lay on a bed of straw in the cowstalls. He'd been sleeping a lot lately and never came away from the farm. He gave Boy a wag of the tail as he passed with Hector.

Boy rode down to Michael's house and left Hector there. They walked into the animated atmosphere of the tavern. It was hot and crowded. James and Pieter were already there, sitting at a table. Michael bought their drinks. The froth overflowed the tankard as Boy lifted it to his lips. He took several gulps before he followed Michael, pushing his way through the crowds to join Pieter and James. The cool brown liquid slid down his throat, leaving a tingle in his mouth and froth on his lips. It tasted so much better than the ale at home. Boy sat down and looked around him. He saw men he recognised from the village. The butcher with his red face and bare muscular arms was leaning on his elbow, chatting to the man behind the bar. The thatcher, still in his working frock and hat, stood with Greg Dyne, his father's friend. Another man was with them, wearing a black jacket and breeches, his hair an untidy mass of grey. James saw Boy look that way.

"That be the ripier. He brings fish from the coast and takes it to Lunnon to sell."

"Oh, yus. I've seen him in Wad'rst. Farder buys fish from him, and sometimes gets news of what's going on in Lunnon."

A tall, burly figure filled the doorway. The hubbub died down. The man's face was dark and weather-beaten. He had no hair. A band of red cloth covered his head, knotted at the back, and he wore a gold earring. His clothes were nothing like Boy had ever seen. A loose black shirt with voluminous sleeves covered his torso, and a wide length of red cloth was wrapped round his waist. Beneath this were baggy brown breeches gathered at the ankles. He wore no shoes on his dirty, calloused feet.

"I am Jack Barbary," boomed the newcomer. He surveyed the company. "I am come as a messenger from God. There be many sinners in these parts, and they will be punished. God has spoken to me. There be rich men who trample on the poor and maimed, who deny bread to the hungry and punish the destitute. I'll seek out these sinners, and with the help of good honest men like thyselves, I'll punish them in God's name." There was a deathly hush as Jack made his way to the bar. People moved aside to let him through. The barman's hand shook as he poured a tankard of ale and pushed it to Jack Barbary, whose huge figure appeared to fill the room. He took the tankard of ale and emptied it down his throat, then held it out for more. The company resumed conversations in hushed voices. People moved away from Jack's path. He went and sat at a table and started talking to the surrounding men. A degree of normality returned to the room.

"I wouldn't like to be on the wrong side of that man," said Michael.

"I'll warrant he be up to no good," said Pieter. "No man of God I know would knock back a tankard of ale in that manner."

A roar of laughter came from the other end of the room. Boy glanced up and saw a group of rough-looking men. One or two were in military uniform. One had lost an eye, another an arm.

Michael said, "They be sojers back home from fighting, some deserted. They be angry that there be no work for 'em. They blame all their troubles on Parlyment en the Puritan nobility."

"They be always drunk and disorderly," added Peiter. "T'wouldn't take much to stir them into trouble. You young uns wants to steer clear of 'em."

Jack Barbary lurched over to the rowdy group and drew up a stool to sit with them. They were quiet while he spoke to them, then nodded and shook their heads, speaking to him with anger in their eyes, and thumping the table with their fists.

"Drink up," said Pieter. "Let's be bodging." He drained his tankard. Boy and the others got up to go. Boy walked with Michael as far as his cottage.

"There be trouble brewing," said Michael. "Be sure ye always goes to the tavern with a friend. Don't go alone."

"I'll surely mind that, Uncle. Thank thee for letting us go along of thee." Boy said goodnight, mounted Hector and rode off up to the Slade. He would remember this evening for a long time.

At the end of January, William and Boy rode into Wadhurst. It was a cold bleak winter. They had to guide their horses carefully, to avoid the potholes and mud. The ditches ran with water.

"I be advised that Robert Longley were set upon along this road last week," said William.

"What happened?" asked Boy.

"Some robbers came up in the dark en knocked him off 'is horse, stole his money purse and chased the horse away. They left him in the dick."

"Be he alright?"

"More mad than hurt. He were bringing the money home from a good day at the market. I rackon they was lying in wait for 'im."

"Seems nowhere be safe these days," remarked Boy. "Michael said he saw that foreigner, Jack Barbary in the village. He were marching around with his followers as if he owned the place."

"Who follers him?" asked William.

"Mostly sojers come back from the war. Some foreigners looking for work. He were seen talking to that cousin, Timothy Lucke from Mayfild, in the tavern one night."

"Trust Timothy to find another troublemaker to befriend," remarked William. The news made him uncomfortable. They reached Wadhurst where there crowds of people in the streets, many of them with mugs of ale, singing and shouting, "The king be dead! We'll be poor no more!"

William and Boy rode on, hoping to find someone reliable to ask what was going on. There were little knots of people who were shouting, "They murdered the king! Regicide! Regicide!" Scuffles started between the opposing parties. William and Boy came into the square, where they dismounted.

"We'll walk up to Durgates. Richard'll know," said William. They made their way through the crowds and up the hill. It was quieter here. Richard's housekeeper opened the door to them.

"Come in Masters. 'Tis not a good day to be abroad. I'll go and fetch Mas Lucke." She bustled away, leaving

William and Boy standing in the hall, holding their hats. Children's voices reached them from the rooms above. There were footsteps on the stairs and Richard came in.

"Good day to thee, William, Boy. Come into the parlour. Have ye heard the news?"

"We heard people shouting *the king be dead*. There's a gurt start-up in the town. I rackoned you'd know the truth, Richard," said William, as they followed his cousin into the comfortable, warm room. It reminded him of Susannah's parlour. There was glass in the windows and carpet on the floor, padded armchairs and sofas to sit on. Boy looked around in awe. They sat down in front of a blazing fire. Richard stood facing them, resting his arm on the mantleshelf.

"The Puritans in Parlyment, led by Oliver Cromwell, tried the king and found him guilty of waging war against 'is people. They condemned him to death. He were beheaded this morning."

"Struth!" exclaimed William. He'd never imagined anything like this could happen. "That be grave news indeed." They were silent for some time.

Richard said, "Parlyment be in charge now. There be no royal court. The Royalists be angry that it came to this. There be great unrest in high places."

William said, "Some people in town were celebrating. They rackon this be the end of their troubles."

"Pray God there'll be no more fighting," said Richard.

William and Boy stayed and discussed the situation with Richard. They didn't want to leave the peace and security of the warm room and good company. But they had to visit Edward. William decided that he would not try to do business in town today. He would wait until things calmed down.

Edward was in a bad way when they called. It was a waste of time trying to talk to him.

"I can't stop him getting the drink," said Hope, wrinkling her forehead. "His visitors bring it when I ain't here." She twisted her apron in her hands and shook her head.

William tried to re-assure her. "We don't expect thee to control 'im like Peggy did. He's a grown man, and knows what he be doing to himself."

It was getting dark when they returned, to find Martha with a worried frown, waiting for them.

"I saw Dog get up from his bed in the cow stall this afternoon. He wandered off into the orchard. I believed he were going to relieve himself, and I thought no more about it. The men came and washed at the well and said goodnight. When I went to give Dog his dinner, he weren't no-where to be seen."

Boy said, "He knows what he be at. We can't look for him now it's dark. I rackon 'e wanted to find somewhere quiet." His voice stuck in his throat.

They went into the house, where Martha had prepared their dinner. As they ate their food they told her the news of the king's execution, and the trouble in the streets. Then they talked about Richard's house and how comfortable it was. But in the back of his mind Boy was thinking about Dog.

Everyone kept an eye open for Dog around the farm during the next two days. One evening before dinner, Boy took a walk round the copse. He came across Dog's body curled up in a pile of dried leaves. He went to find a spade to bury the body where he found it. He dug a deep hole, and sat down on the ground beside the cold, stiff corpse, tears coursing down his cheeks. Life wouldn't be the same without his old friend, his guardian and companion. Boy stroked Dog respectfully for the last time and thanked him for being so faithful. He put the body in the grave and filled it in. Then he sat for a while, remembering.

At dinner that evening, Boy announced, "I buried Dog just now. He were in the copse." William and Martha said nothing, knowing that Boy might find it difficult to say more, and they ate in silence for a while.

Boy paused in his eating. He took a deep breath, looked up and said, "I'd thank thee if ye would call us Thomas, as 'tis me rightful name. I ain't a boy no more."

They smiled and William said, "We'll gladly do that, Thomas, surely." Thomas looked at them each in turn, grinning broadly, and they shook hands all round, relaxing into their new relationships. From that moment, Thomas was one of the adults in the family.

Part 6

The Return of the Dragons

Chapter 56
The Commonwealth

An unusual noise outside roused William from a fitful sleep. Concerns about the corn harvest, Ed's drinking habits and the political situation drifted in and out of his consciousness. The noise came nearer; men shouting and the tramp of many feet. William lay listening until he could stay there no longer and he slipped out of bed to look out into the dark night. A flickering glow came from the road leading up from the village. Flames of torches appeared above the hedge. He could hear the shouting more clearly. Words reached him.

"Law breaker!" "King killer!" "Witch!"... A cold fear gripped him. This was an angry mob. The hue and cry. They were coming this way.

He dressed quickly and went down into the hall. He barricaded the door with the heavy table. He left the shutters closed, but wanted to see what was happening outside. He went back upstairs into his chamber and looked out. The noise became louder, and, as he watched, men holding torches and big sticks came round the corner into the yard. There were about twenty of them, led by a massive hulk of a man. William couldn't see his features.

The hulk came to the door and hammered on it with his fist, shouting, "William Lucke, I come from God to punish thee for thy wicked sins. Unlawful burial of thy sister!" The mob echoed, "Unlawful burial!" "Sheltering she who were a witch!" "Witch!" the crowd roared. "And being a Puritan, you be a king-killer." "King-killer!" they yelled. "Open the door and face thy punishment." Eight men detached themselves from the crowd and split into two teams, each running to surround the house.

This was Jack Barbary. William stood back from the window and wondered what to do.

The hammering came again. "Come out afore we torch thy dwelling house, sinner!" "Come out, come out!" the mob repeated.

William considered. He knew he must submit to this rabble if he went out. But if he stayed in the house, his son Thomas and Martha would suffer a painful death as well as himself. He went down into the hall and gathered all his courage for the ordeal that would inevitably follow. He moved the table away from the door and drew the bolt back. His hand was trembling as he placed his thumb on the latch and pulled the door open. A cheer rose from the crowd. He could see some of their red faces in the light of the torches, their eyes sparkling with excitement. He recognised Matt Jackson. William had looked after his wife and family while he was away soldiering.

William stepped out into the yard and closed the door behind him. "I deny the accusations. I ain't guilty of aught. You have no authority to bring these charges against me."

"William Lucke, we come in the name of God to punish thee for thy wickedness. We have witnesses." Jack Barbary signalled and two men stepped forward. Surely, one of them was the butcher's son from the village. They took hold of William's arms roughly and tied his hands behind his back. It was useless to resist.

Two men came from the close, with armfuls of faggots and firewood from the wood store. Another two went into the house. They came out with Uncle Thomas' armchair from the parlour, leaving the door open.

Jack Barbary came closer to William. The whites of his eyes flashed. His lips curled. He took hold of William's chin with iron fingers. "We be preparing a big fire for thee, William Lucke; a funeral pyre." William watched as two more men came forward with a rope, which they proceeded to tie to the rafters under the eaves over the front door. The other end of the rope was knotted into a noose.

Jack continued. "First, you'll stand on the chair over the fire with the noose around thy neck." He laughed. "When the fire burns the chair"-- he jerked William's head back, -- "you'll be hanged as ye falls into the fire, knowing that thy house will burn after thee." There was a shout. Jack stepped back and looked round. "And who have we here?" Two men came from the close with Thomas, who was struggling to be free. "Thy son will have the pleasure of watching ye die, afore we decide what his fate will be." Jack grimaced and raised his fist to his rabble. They cheered. William's heart sank as he watched his son stare helplessly in his direction, and make another attempt at breaking free.

The fire had been laid, the chair perched on top, and William's captors led him towards it. "Climb up," they ordered. It was useless to struggle. William's legs trembled and they had to help him up onto the chair. They placed the noose around his neck.

"Now, William Lucke, pray to God to have mercy on thy soul," shouted Jack Barbary, signalling for the torches.

Thomas screamed, "Nay! Farder! Nay!"

The mob called, "Fire! Fire!"

The men put two torches to the faggots, which caught fire immediately. William's heart thumped against his chest. Flames shot up all round him. He felt their heat through his clothes. Then the flames died down as the faggots burnt out. But the firewood was alight.

"There be dragons," whispered William. He hoped that his hanging would be quick and clean, so that he wouldn't have to bear the pain of the fire. Smoke surrounded him, and his eyes were smarting. He remembered Shadrack, Meshak and Abednego in the fiery furnace, and prayed to God to give him faith. He started to recite the Lord's Prayer to himself.

"*Our Father, which art in Heaven...*" Flames licked around the legs of Uncle Thomas' chair. William's feet stood on the seat that had been made shiny by so much sitting. He had held Baby Thomas in his arms, sitting on this seat.

"*Hallowed be Thy Name...*" His mind began to wander. It must be the smoke. He couldn't see clearly and he felt dizzy. He must not collapse.

"*Thy Kingdom come on earth...*" He saw Jane's smiling face above him. She was holding out her hands. He tried to hold his hands out, but his wrists were tied. "Jane!" he called, but only a croak came from his mouth.

"*As it is in Heaven...*" The chair shifted. William flinched and adjusted his position. The rope around his neck tightened. His clothes had caught fire. The mob was shouting again, "Burn! Burn!"

"*Give us this day...*" His feet were getting hot. The chair shifted again. The noose tightened.

Thomas watched in helpless agony. His father was already engulfed in flames, but he could still see his head with the noose round it. His lips were moving.

There were horses coming up the road. Could that be help on its way? The shouts of the mob died down.

Four riders came round the corner into the yard, and surrounded them. Thomas struggled again and one of his captors let go and ran towards the whapple way.

There was Michael coming towards him out of the gloom, and Pieter. Pieter captured the fugitive. Thomas continued to struggle. The man held him firmly. Michael ran towards the fire and William. Another figure appeared from the road, Greg Dyne. He ran to William. Greg and Michael reached through the fire and lifted William just as the chair burst into flames. They removed the noose and carried William away in the direction of the orchard and the pond.

The mob was scattering, but the horsemen were blocking their escape into the road. Young Thomas was free. He must put the fire out to save the house, but his hands were still tied. He ran to the skillon, and lifted the latch with his chin. The door swung open. He went inside, and groped around for a sharp tool. He could feel the familiar shape of a fagging hook. He took hold of it and wedged it in the door frame to keep it steady, and lifted his hands behind him to the level of the blade. It was awkward. He couldn't see what he was doing. At last the rope met the blade and was severed. With his free hands he picked up an armful of sacks and ran with them to the well. He soaked them in water from the bucket and took them round to the fire in the doorway. He threw them onto the flames to smother them, and left them covering the fire. There was hissing and smoke, but the fire was doused. He shut the front door to protect the hall from escaping sparks.

He stepped back and looked around the yard. The Headborough, Abraham Shoesmith, and three constables had captured Jack Barbary and a number of his followers. They were standing in a group shuffling their feet. Barbary was arguing with Abraham. Rob Longley and Pieter came from the garden with another two fugitives and handed them over to the constables. They saw Thomas and came over to him.

"Where be Michael and Greg? They took Farder away. Be he still alive?"

Rob and Pieter were not sure. They were all about to go and search, but Abraham came over to them.

"Thomas Lucke?"

"Yus," said Thomas. "D'ye know where they took Farder?"

"Nay," said Abraham. "He were taken down from the noose by his brudder. But I ain't seen 'em since. I wanted to ask thee if I can borrow thy cart to take this lot away to the Town Cage in Wad'rst?"

"Surely," said Thomas. "But…"

Pieter said, "I'll get Gaffer and the cart en take them away, Boy, er…Thomas. Go and find thy farder."

"Thank thee Pieter," said Thomas. He picked up a discarded torch, which was still alight, and went off with Rob in the direction of the orchard. There was no sign of anyone there. They retraced their steps and went to the back door of the house. Thomas doused the torch in the well bucket and they made their way into the parlour.

They found Michael sitting on the floor cradling William's head and shoulders, while Martha knelt bathing his feet. William's eyes were closed. His body was limp.

"Farder! Be he alive?" said Thomas, crossing the room to kneel by William's side.

"He be alive, but not conscious," said Michael. "I believe 'tis the shock. 'Tis like he's asleep."

Thomas took his father's hand in his. "Farder, 'tis Thomas. 'Tis all over now. Ye be safe at home." He picked up the limp hand and put it to his face. The skin around the wrists was raw. "Have ye tried putting water to his lips?" he asked. Michael shook his head, and Thomas got up to get some water.

Chapter 57

William was floating. He didn't have a body. That had been burnt in the flames. He wondered if it would always be like this now; floating in nothingness. He thought he could see the parlour at the Slade, but it was a long way off. So they didn't burn the house down, after all. He seemed to be getting closer. There were some people gathered round a corpse, which was lying on the floor. One of the people was Martha. Thank God she was safe. She was bathing the feet of the corpse. Michael was there too, sitting on the floor. The picture was becoming clearer. He watched as young Thomas came into the parlour. William's heart leapt for joy. His son was safe too. Greg Dyne and Rob Longley followed him.

He heard Thomas' voice. "Farder, 'tis all over now…" He felt someone touch his hand. But he didn't have a body. The picture faded.

Water was trickling into his mouth, lovely, cool water, soothing his dry throat. He couldn't see anything now. He tried to open his eyes, but the lids were glued together. He tried to turn his head and felt hands on his brow, and a warm cloth bathing his face.

"Farder, you be alive!" William's eyes opened and he saw faces bending over him. Martha, Michael, Thomas. There were tears in their eyes. He coughed violently and tried to get up, but his body wasn't working properly. He lifted his arm and pulled Thomas towards him. They embraced. Tears welled up in his eyes and his body started shaking. He was cold. He tried to speak, but could only croak. Michael helped him to sit up.

Martha launched into action. "We must keep him warm and make him comfortable," she said. "Light the fire. Get the spare cot in my chamber, and blankets from his bed. I'll warm some milk."

William relaxed back into his son's arms while the others ran round to Martha's bidding. They made a bed for him and lifted him gently onto it, wrapping him in blankets. Soon a fire was lit. William couldn't look at it. The flames brought back the fear. He closed his eyes and sipped the warm milk.

Thomas left his father sleeping peacefully and went outside with Michael, Greg and Rob. Dawn was breaking and they saw the aftermath of the night's ordeal. Spent torches littered the yard and the remnants of the fire in the doorway lay under the sacks. Little plumes of smoke puffed out round the edges. The empty noose hung above it. Michael helped Thomas untie the noose, and the others collected the torches. The sound of a horse and cart approached from the direction of Wadhurst, and Pieter drove Gaffer into the yard. He leapt down from the cart.

"How be William?" he called.

They all went to tell him the good news, and embraced each other. Tears of relief flowed once more.

Weary as they were, they worked to tidy the yard and clear the ashes away from the doorway. Just as they were finishing, Adam and James arrived. Michael and the others left to go to their families and rest before they came back to work. Thomas related the night's events as briefly as he could to Adam, and asked him to start the day on the farm. As he trudged back into the house, he realised that, for the moment, until his father had recovered, he would be Master.

Later that day, William lay on his cot in the parlour eating a bowl of porridge. Martha was quietly getting on with her work, and Jessica was singing loudly in the milk-house. William heard footsteps on the stairs and Thomas appeared, yawning and stretching his arms, his hair tousled.

He looked at his father and asked, "Farder, be ye feeling better?"

William was glad to see his son. "Fair to middling, Thomas but I'll be on my feet afore long. He handed the empty porridge bowl to him. "Will ye help us out to the close, Son? I be wanting to relieve myself."

Thomas put the bowl on the table and went to support his father while he swivelled round to sit on the edge of the cot. He put his feet to the floor and winced with pain. He looked down and saw that they were covered in bandages. He looked up at Thomas. "This ain't going to be easy." Slowly and tentatively they walked across the parlour. William had his arm over Thomas' shoulders.

Martha watched, concerned, then said, "Go back and stay on thy cot, betimes thy feet be well, Mas William. I'll get a bucket." William and Thomas stopped, turned round and returned to the cot. William would have to allow his feet to heal before he walked. He shook with anger, embarrassment and frustration. Martha brought the bucket and put it by the cot.

Thomas went out to wash at the well. Martha left the room. William relieved himself in the bucket. He heard voices out in the close. Tamsen and Michael came in with little John. Tamsen was beginning to show her pregnancy. Martha followed them in and whisked the bucket away before John had a chance to investigate. William was still sitting on the edge of the cot.

During the greetings that followed, Pieter came and joined in making a fuss of William. William's anger died down. There was knocking on the front door, and he started nervously. Thomas went to answer, and came back into the parlour with Abraham Shoesmith.

"Heaven be praised! 'Tis hem good to see thee alive, Mas Lucke. Be ye recovered?"

"'Tis my feet. They be burned, Sir. Otherwise I be middling, thank thee, Headborough. Will ye take a seat? Ye'll be come to hear the full account, I rackon."

"That I be, Mas Lucke." Abraham went to sit at the table. Martha and Tamsen left the room, taking little John with them. Michael and Pieter sat at the table with Abraham. Thomas remained standing by his father. Martha came back with mugs of ale for them all then disappeared again. There was silence as they supped their ale, except for the crackling of the fire. William averted his eyes.

Pieter spoke up, "I believe I were the first to see what were brewing. I were in the tavern with Greg Dyne. Jack Barbary were rallying his ruffians in a corner, and I couldn't hear what was said. Then one of them shouted *Witch*! Jack shushed him up, and they all goes out, excited, like.

"Later, we was bodging down the road, and sees them all marching up the hill towards the church, with torches and digging tools. They was up to no good, we rackoned, and we agreed to follow them. We got to the church, and they went straight to Jone's grave. Jack Barbary stood over it. We heard them shout, *unlawful* and other words we couldn't hear. Jack said, *Dig*. They started digging..."

William sucked in his breath though his teeth.

Pieter continued, "They lifted the coffin out of the grave, and carried it out of the litten and down to the village pump. We followed.

"There were other men there, digging a hole in the road. Greg went to fetch the constable. I hid by the well. They was all too occupied to see us. It didn't take them long to fill her in, and they druv a stake into the ground over where the body would be. Jack says to them all, *To the Slade! William Lucke will be punished!*

"The constable comes, but he couldn't do much with that mob. He and Greg goes to collect more men, and I goes to get Michael. We came through the field and the copse, to stop any escaping that way." Pieter stopped talking and took a long drink of ale. His hands were shaking.

William was speechless with horror. He felt nauseous when he heard what they had done to Jone's body.

Abraham nodded and said, "Thank thee, Mas Pieter. Hopefully ye'll be agreeable to appear in court. Did ye see any faces enough to know 'em again?"

"Some of them I recognised from the village, but most were travellers and foreigners," said Pieter. "Yus, I'll be in court to see they gets their just punishment."

William had never seen Pieter so aroused in anger. He said, "But how did they know about the manner of Jone's death?"

Abraham turned to Michael. "Now, I believe Mas Michael Lucke has something to say about that."

"Yus, I rackons I knows. I were in the tavern last week, en sees Cousin Timothy Lucke talking to Jack Barbary, close like. Another man who were with them says, *They say she were a witch.*

393

"I were on me own, mind."

"Hm," said Abraham. "Be that Timothy Lucke of Mayfild? He be a trouble-maker, I be well avised. But we can't prove aught. Never can with that sly one."

Pieter said, "When I were in the litten I believed I saw a figure slipping behind some bushes. And again, at the Slade, when we was all in the yard, there could have been someone lurking by the oast barn. But we was all trying to save Will and catch the mob..."

William felt it was his turn to speak. He cleared his throat, and took a sip of ale. "I heard 'em coming up the road, chanting, they was. When they came to the door, Jack Barbary shouted accusations like *unlawful burial! shielding a witch!* and, being a Puritan, he rackoned I were a king-killer. I believe ye can figure out what happened next." He sat holding onto the edge of the cot, shaking with renewed fear.

Abraham said, "D'ye have brandy in the house?"

Thomas said, "Yus, Sir," and went into the hall. He came back and handed his father the glass. William took it and sipped the brown liquid, allowing it to warm his frail body.

Thomas said, "I were sleeping in my chamber, and didn't hear aught until the mob was in the yard. I heard 'em come into the house, and came down to see them carrying Farder's chair out. They caught hold of us and marched me out into the yard. I were mortally afeared to see what they were about. They was chanting, *King-killer! Unlawful burial! Burn! Burn!* and other such things. I couldn't do aught to stop them." He broke down in tears at the memory.

Abraham said to William, "You'll be wanting to put your sister back in where she belongs. I'll speak to the vicar." He nodded to them all. Thomas showed him out and brought the brandy bottle and some glasses back with him.

"I rackons we could all do with a drop of this," he said. He poured them all a glassful and topped up his father's. Everyone was in a daze. They sipped their brandy and were unable to speak for several minutes. Thomas thought of all that he had heard and his heart warmed at the attentiveness of his friends. He would not be alive now if they had not rallied round as they had.

Chapter 58

Tamsen came and attended to William's feet and other burns every day, anointing them with herbal salve. When William could stand and walk a little way without pain, he said to Thomas one morning, "Go and saddle up Damsel and Hector, Son. We'll ride to Wadhurst and talk to Edward." It was impossible to get his boots on. Martha had made him some soft woollen slippers with soles of sheepskin.

It was good to get out of the house into the fresh air. As they strolled to Wadhurst the spring sunshine was casting a golden glow on the world around them, shimmering through the trees. Young, bright green leaves were pushing their way out of the falling bud cases, which were littering the ground. A soft wind ruffled their hair.

"You've managed well these last weeks, Thomas," William said.

"'Twas Adam telling us what to do. We did it together, Farder."

"I'll be able to get back to work afore long," said William.

They reached Woodcroft and tethered the horses. Hope heard them coming and opened the door.

"My, 'tis good to see thee on thy feet, Mas Lucke. They said ye nearly died."

William hobbled into the parlour, and sat on the nearest chair.

Edward was sitting in his usual place in front of the fire. He looked up. "Hm. It'll take more'n Jack Barbary to break thee, brudder."

"'Twas my rescuers we need to thank," said William. "I believed I'd met me end. If Pieter hadn't seen what the mob were about in the churchyard, I'd be dead."

"There's talk all over town," said Edward. "I don't know what to believe. Did they really dig Jone up?"

William determined to stay calm, but he was beginning to tremble. He held on to the arms of the chair.

Hope asked, "Shall I get thee a mug of milk?" William thought he could do with something stronger, but accepted Hope's offer.

He said to Edward, "Yus, and they buried her in the road at the pump with a stake through 'er. What I want to know is who gave Jack Barbary the idea that Jone's burial were unlawful?"

"There's gossip all over," replied Edward, and shrugged his shoulders. He looked away into the fire.

"Michael saw Timothy talking to Jack Barbary," continued William. "Have ye said aught to Timothy about Jone's death?" William raised his voice. Hope brought mugs of milk and handed them round.

"May have done." Edward was looking at the floor. He said, "He tricks us into saying things," and looked at William, his forehead knotted.

"I rackon he gets ye cranky afore, to get ye to talk. They dragons have got the better of thee again." He paused, looking at his brother. It was pitiful. "I'd best be bodging, afore I gets real mad. Come Thomas." They got up to go.

Hope showed them out. She looked sad and worried.

"'Tis not your fault, Hope. Ye be muvvering him well. We all knows he can be hem cantankerous," said

William as they left the house. He'd had enough for one day. He had his answer. Thomas heard it. Timothy had resumed his attacks on William, with more cunning. There seemed to be nothing William could do about it.

During the next few months, Thomas noticed that his father had slowed down. The shock of the attack had taken its toll. He was giving more responsibility to his son. Thomas felt more capable now, but he was not as ambitious as William had been. His interests were being aroused in a different quarter.

Whenever he went into the village, or into town, groups of girls looked at him with their big eyes and whispered and giggled among themselves. He watched them flirting with other men and felt attracted to their company.

One day he'd taken a cartload of hops to the brewery in Lamberhurst, and was starting to unload them when he saw a young girl carrying two pails of water across the yard. He smiled at her as she went past. She tripped and dropped one of the buckets. Thomas ran over and picked up the empty bucket. She was overcome with embarrassment.

He said, "I'll fill this again for thee, if ye like."

"Much obliged, Sir." She dropped a curtsey and continued on her way with one bucket.

Thomas took the other bucket to the well in the far corner of the yard, filled it and carried it back to the girl, who was on her way to collect it from him. Her eyes were deep blue, and wisps of her dark brown hair draped from under her cap to rest on her shoulders. They came closer, and he saw the deep valley plunging down between her breasts. He gave her the bucket and their hands touched in passing.

She blushed and said "Much obliged, Sir" again, before turning to go.

Thomas went back to the hops. One of the brewer's men was unloading them, lifting each sack onto his back and carrying it into the warehouse. Thomas said, "Purty wench, that one. Do she work here?"

"Nay, she be dairymaid at the farm next door," the man said.

Thomas unloaded the rest of the hops and went into the building to settle up. He wouldn't mind seeing that girl again.

He was going into the tavern to meet James for a drink. A group of girls were standing on the corner by the butcher's shop, his dairymaid among them. It was a fine evening and he took his ale outside to sit at a table in view of the girls. The dairymaid was pointing to him and simpering with her friends. He raised his tankard and they all giggled. At last the dairymaid took the arm of another girl and they walked across the road together. They came to sit at his table.

"I be Susy, and this be Meg," the dairymaid announced.

"I be Thomas," he said. "Pleased to meet thee. Can I get you girls a pot of ale?"

They looked surprised and doubtful. Then Meg, the bolder of the two, said, "Thank thee kindly, Thomas."

Thomas went into the tavern, bought their drinks, and brought them out to the girls. They both took sips, and grinned at Thomas.

"Be ye both dairymaids?" he asked.

"Nay," said Meg. "I be parlour maid for Mas Shoesmith. You be son of Mas Lucke at the Slade, ain't ye?"

James came to join them and they made their acquaintance. Thomas and sometimes James met the girls regularly outside the tavern that summer. One or two of the other girls came too. One evening, Susy was there on her own. Thomas bought her a drink and sat down next to her.

"Where be thy friends today, Susie?" he asked.

"They be playing stoolball down by the Brook with some other people."

"Didn't ye want to go with 'em?"

"Nay, stoolball don't interest me. I'd rather be 'ere with thee." Susie turned and smiled at him.

Thomas couldn't keep his eyes away from the bulge of her breasts squeezed up by her tight bodice. The conversation became hesitant. Thomas' feelings were aroused. Susy was sitting closer. Their hands and legs touched.

He said, "Shall we take a walk, Susy?"

"I be agreeable to that, Thomas." She stood up and smoothed her dress. Thomas stood up and drained his tankard. He took her arm and they walked down the road together. They pointed out the houses of friends to each other as they passed, by way of conversation, neither of them listening.

Then Thomas said, almost before he thought about it, "Have ye ever been with a man, Susy?" Then he thought he may have said the wrong thing.

Susy looked at him and giggled. "You be hem forward Thomas Lucke." She swivelled round and kissed him on the mouth. When she'd finished, she said, with her head on one side, "Have ye ever been with a girl?"

Thomas was speechless. She took him by the hand and said, "There's a quiet meadow I know," and led him on.

By the time they reached the meadow, Thomas was acutely conscious of his rising excitement.

Susy knew what to do. She found a place on the grass, shielded from prying eyes by trees and bushes. As she undid the fastening on his breeches, she said, "Ye be unaccountable handsome, Thomas. I do want thee dracly-minute." She lay back and lifted her skirts.

Thomas was having misgivings. This felt all wrong. This wasn't how James had described it. He wanted to see her breasts and hold them in his hands. He wanted to see her hips and the mound of hairs hiding her cunt. He was on his knees. She was pulling him towards her by his shirt. He didn't want her to see his penis just yet.

"Wait," he said, and sat back on his heels. He pulled his shirt off over his head, revealing his strong, muscular torso. If he was going to do this, and she was evidently ready, he had to do it properly. With shaking fingers he loosened the laces of her bodice to see those luscious, full breasts. He lifted her skirts, and she sat up, and ran her fingers through the fine hairs on his chest. He took the dress together with her shift, pulled it carefully over her head and saw her naked, lithe body, the rounded curve of her hips. His penis recovered its libido. They fondled each other. Thomas kissed her breasts and her shoulders. He felt her guiding his penis until it was in its place. He pulled her to him. His chest met the warmth of her breasts. He was overwhelmed with desire, and they met in mutual ecstasy.

Later, as he walked Susy home, Thomas felt like a man. He kissed her mouth when they said goodbye, and said, "Thank thee, Susy."

She looked at him with her blue eyes and said, "I never had it like that afore." She squeezed his hand and reached up to kiss him again before she went indoors.

Chapter 59

They had finished the harvesting. There was a better yield this year, and William felt satisfied. He wanted to celebrate, but the Puritans had banned all celebrations. The family wouldn't even have a proper Christmas. They gave a harvest supper to the workers, but there was no music or dancing afterwards and they had to reduce the amount of ale they served. There were government spies everywhere and William would be fined if he were suspected of encouraging drunkenness and debauchery.

He settled down in the hall with Thomas to plan the next week's work.

"We could get another crop of hay afore the grass stops growing," he said. "Will you and James start that tomorrow?"

"Yus, Farder, and Michael and Pieter be going to have another hop-picking afore the fall."

William thought he heard Michael's voice in the parlour. Surely, Michael and Pieter had the afternoon off before the next period of work started in earnest. The accounts were done, and he and Thomas collected the books and put them away in the drawer. They went through to the parlour to see what was going on.

The room was full of people. Michael and Tamsen were there with Johnny and baby Michael. Martha and Jessica were serving mugs of ale for everyone. Pieter had brought Rosy, and Adam and James had come in from work early. There was a large object in the middle of the room covered in a sheet. Everyone cheered when William entered the room, followed by Thomas.

Thomas approached the mystery object. "Farder," he said, "This be a gift from all the fambly, to celebrate your rising from the dead like a Phoenix." He pulled the sheet off to reveal a beautiful new chair with a back and arms. "Ye can sit now in comfort and rest your back in your old age!" He grinned. The family clapped and raised their mugs.

William was overcome with pleasure and affection for his family. "I ain't old yet, young man. But I'll surely enjoy sitting on this. She be main purty." He stroked the seat and examined the carving on the back of the chair.

Thomas said, "Uncle Michael did the carving. He and Pieter's been working on it a few months. They made a fine job."

"They surely did. Thank thee kindly." William took a mug of ale from the table and went to sit in his chair. He raised his mug. "To the fambly and the next generation."

Martha put food on the table; pies and bread, fruit and puddings.

Tamsen brought baby Michael and sat him on William's knee so that she could help. William enjoyed the warmth of the child's body next to his. He held the baby's hands and bounced him on his knee. Michael giggled and dribbled over William's breeches.

Thomas sat on a bench and Johnny went to show him his latest toy, a horse on wheels that he could pull across the floor.

Pieter and Rosy sat together and Tamsen went to talk to them.

Michael Senior stood in a corner gossiping with Adam and James.

When the meal was over, they gathered round in a circle and sang songs of harvesting, of spring, of roses round the door and young lovers.

After the family had gone home, William and Thomas sat together and supped a last mug of ale.

William said, "I be avised that ye be flirting with the maids down in the village, Thomas. Be ye minded to find a wife one day soon?"

Thomas looked at his father. "There be plenty of time, Farder. I be enjoying meself. Betimes I be ready, I'll pick a good one, don't worry."

"Be careful ye don't get any of 'em with child, lad. Ye may not have a choice."

Thomas smiled, and looked at the floor.

It was market day in Wadhurst, and William went with Thomas and Martha, who still, at the age of sixty, insisted on coming with them. She was remarkably healthy, though she had to have a stool handy in case her legs gave way. William rode behind the horse and cart. He helped to set up the standing, and went off to collect the rent and visit Edward.

Edward was sitting in his chair looking seriously inebriated. His head was hanging over his knees. He stirred when he heard William enter. "What've ye come for? Come scrounging have ye? I ain't got nothing, ye knows that."

"Edward, 'tis William, thy brudder. Ye've got thyself unaccountable cranky."

Ed looked up. "'Tis the pain, I have to do something on account of the pain, Will. Don't take on so," he whined.

"I dunno what to do with thee, Ed. Ye're killing thyself!"

Ed's face changed. He looked at his brother directly and said soberly, "I knows that. I can't fight they dragons no more. They've beaten us. Best if I die, then there'll be no more trouble."

William put the provisions he'd brought with him on the table.

Edward sank back into his chair. A brown trickle came from underneath him and made a pool on the floor around his feet. William watched in disbelief. He went to find a clean pair of breeches. Edward co-operated while William struggled to peel off the wet ones. William wondered how often Hope found him in this state, and how she coped with it. He must remember to speak to her about it.

Ed winced as William removed his boots. His foot was swollen, bright red and oozing with pus at the nails. So that was the origin of the smell. Poor Ed. William now understood how his brother must have been suffering. He'd heard that gout was more painful than anything else. He'd have been better without that leg. William dumped the wet breeches into a bucket and cleaned up the puddle on the floor. He built up the fire, and sat beside his brother.

William's attentions seemed to have sobered Edward. He sat in his clean breeches with tears in his eyes, gazing into the fire.

William said, "Who gave thee the spirit, Ed?"

"'Twere Timothy. He can be remarkable persuasive, like. I takes a few sups, and forgets meself."

"What do he talk about?"

Edward turned to look at William, his eyes wide. "I told him I knows his guilty secret, Will! He were mortaceous mad. He asked us if ye knows it too. But he didn't wait for an answer. He ran out of the house and galloped away." Ed chuckled to himself.

"What d'ye think is 'is guilty secret?" asked William, wondering how Ed could know.

"D'ye mind when thy haystacks were fired, years ago, after harvest supper?"

William nodded. "I believed that were thee."

Ed laughed. "I rackoned ye did. But that were Timothy! I saw 'im do it! I were with Jack Paine, watching the fambly having a good time. We'd had a mug or two of ale, mind. Then we saw Timothy ride up the road and set fire to your haystack with a tinder. He watched to make sure it'd taken afore bodging. I laughed about it at the time, like." He looked at William ruefully.

William said, "But that ain't 'is guilty secret. There were something happened when he were a child. The fambly's always kept quiet about it. He's said he'll kill anybody that finds out! You mustn't let him in this house again, Ed, if he thinks you knows it. He be a dangerous man."

Ed shrugged and said, "Oh well, 'twould be a quick way to go." He turned back to watch the fire again, and, to William's surprise, started nodding off to sleep, apparently oblivious to the danger he was in.

William got up and went out of the house, shutting the door carefully. He rode back to the market to find Martha gossiping and the produce nearly all sold.

"'Twere a good day, Mas William," she said proudly.

Thomas was chatting to an elderly farmer, but looked up when William approached. "Shall us go and see what's happening at the beast market, Son?" he said.

That evening over dinner, young Thomas announced, "I be minded to marry afore long Farder. I've been courting Mas Golding's darter, Dorcas. She be a fine, pountle wench, and I believe she be fit to be my Mistus. "Well, that be wonderful good news, Thomas. Be ye going to fetch her to visit us?" asked his father.

"I'll ask her to come to dinner tomorrow, if that be agreeable." Thomas seemed calm about his future wife. William thought it sounded like a business arrangement, rather than a betrothal. Were the couple genuinely in love? He remembered how excited he was when he was courting Jane.

Chapter 60

That night William woke from a bad dream, of fire and screaming. He dressed quickly, and, riding bareback, galloped to Wadhurst as fast as the rough road would allow. It was pitch dark, but Damsel knew where the potholes were.

As he approached Ed's house, smoke and the smell of burning were in the air. Turning the corner, he saw that he was too late. The house was in flames. There was nothing anyone could do except watch. The dragons had won the battle. William saw figures through the smoke, huddled in groups in the dark. Hoping to find Edward there, he went to see who they were, and met Richard among the neighbours, their faces lit up by the flames.

"I sent a messenger to fetch thee just now, Will. Did ye see him on thy way?"

"Nay, I woke sudden like, and rackoned I must come."

"The flames was well lit afore the neighbours woke. They come to fetch us, but there were nothing I could do," said Richard.

There was an ominous creaking noise. The roof collapsed with a roar. Sparks flew into the night sky. William saw dragon's tails and tongues flicking in the flames. A lump came to his throat and he turned away. He couldn't watch. Richard put his hand on William's shoulder in sympathy.

Two horses galloped round the corner and the riders dismounted. The messenger had seen William on the road, so didn't call at the Slade. He'd gone to fetch

Michael before coming back to Wadhurst. William was grateful to have his brother with him.

He said to Michael, "I saw him this afternoon. He were cranky. I built up the fire afore I left. I rackon a log fell out onto the floor and he never realised."

"Don't blame thyself, brudder. T'were an accident," Michael said.

They stayed to see the fire die down. William was devastated at the loss of his childhood soul-mate. He wished he had been kinder to Ed when he was in trouble. If only he had realised that it was not his brother who fired the haystacks all those years ago... He said a prayer for Edward's poor soul.

A hand was touching his elbow. It was Hope, with tears in her eyes.

"Mas Lucke, I be sorry for your loss. He were a cantankerous old man, but he did have a spark of fun in him now-en-again. I'll miss him, surely."

"Thank thee kindly, Hope. Ye've muvvered him well. It can't have been easy. I'll come and rackon up with thee 'forelong." She nodded, and walked away back to her house.

Thomas was woken by the noise of a door slamming. He looked out of the window onto the close, to see his father mounting Damsel's bare back. He watched them gallop away, and wondered what could suddenly be so urgent in the middle of the night. He lay awake worrying, and finally got out of bed to wait for his father's return. He went into the milk-house and poured himself a mug of milk. He thought he heard talking, and went to listen at the back door.

"...known about my secret, farmer's boy? ...let you live...will die with you." There was a chuckle. There

412

must be more than one of them out there. But then there was silence.

There were no windows in the milk-house. Thomas cautiously opened the back door and peered into the darkness. There was no one there. He closed the door again, thinking he must have imagined it. The geese in the barn were muttering. He went back into the parlour and sat in his father's chair to drink his milk. He started to doze.

He woke again with a start. Hector was nuckering. He sounded agitated. The geese were making more noise, too. Thomas went to the window and could see nothing. He went to check the back door again. He pulled on his boots, and gently opened the door, hoping not to disturb the intruders. Light flickered from the cow stalls.

He went outside and saw that the rack in every cow stall was filled with burning hay. A dark figure was capering at the far end with a lighted torch in his hand. Thomas could hear laughter above the roar and crackle of the fires. He had to catch the culprit before he did any further damage. He hoped there were not two of them. He crept out quietly and took a circuit round the close, passing the barn and then the stables on his left. He was opposite the cow stalls now, and saw the full extent of the fires. The racks were wooden, and would soon catch light to increase the blaze. The intruder was lighting the last rack of hay, cackling to himself.

Thomas ran up behind the man and held him tightly by the elbows. They struggled. The torch fell to the ground against a wooden post. Thomas held on tight, but this man was like a slippery snake. Thomas hooked his foot round the man's leg. They fell to the ground. He was determined not to let go. He could hear the fires blazing. The cow stalls were being destroyed. The next thing to catch light would be the roof, then the eaves of the house. He rolled over, clutching the intruder to him until he lay face down, with his arms held behind his back.

Thomas hauled his captive to his feet, still holding his arms firmly. There was no time to find a rope to tie him up. The safest place to put him was the barn. He marched the man across the close, unlatched the door of the barn and stood back. The geese came out flapping and screeching, and ran towards the yard. Thomas pushed the intruder into the barn and closed the door. He secured the door with the wooden bolt.

Now he had to deal with the fires. He doubted whether he would be able to put them out on his own. Martha may be some help. He went to the back door and shouted for her, then went to the well to fill a bucket. Martha appeared in her nightgown and cap, and saw the fires with horror on her face. She grabbed the full bucket from Thomas. He realised that the racks would do less damage on the ground. The first to be lit, nearest the house, had already fallen. Martha flung her bucketful onto the flames, and they went out. She went to refill the bucket. Thomas found a broom against the wall and worked his way along the line of fires, using the handle to knock them off the wall. But the roof had caught fire. They couldn't reach that with buckets. He took another bucket to fill and they carried on, quenching the fire in each stall.

Martha was tiring. She stopped and wiped her flushed face with her sleeve. Thomas heard the man in the barn screaming. He couldn't make out whether it was laughter or fear. Another sound met their ears. Horses were approaching.

Chapter 61

William and Michael rode home from Wadhurst together. William was too upset to talk. Michael was coughing frequently, and William thought he must have been affected by the smoke.

When they reached the Slade, he said to Michael, "Will ye come in for a mug of ale afore ye bodge?" hoping that the answer would be yes. He didn't feel like going back to bed now. Michael nodded.

They rode into the yard. The geese came to greet them. William was surprised that they were running loose, but hadn't the energy to investigate. He thought he could smell smoke, but it was probably on his clothes. They dismounted. Michael tethered his horse by the jossing block. William led Damsel into the close and found mayhem.

Screams were coming from the barn. Martha was standing by the well in her night clothes. Smoke was pouring from the cow stalls.

Thomas turned and came towards him. "The roof! We must save the roof afore it sets the house afire!" he shouted.

Michael was behind William. He took Damsel to tether her in the yard. William's exhaustion melted away. He went and got a ladder from the skillon, and two lengths of rope.

"Climb up onto the roof, Son. Be careful, it may not be safe. Take one end of this rope with thee. I'll tie the other end onto a bucket." Michael came back, and William gave him the other rope. "Two of thee up there should do it." He turned to Martha. "Ye be all-in,

Martha. Go back indoors and warm us some toddies, for when we've done." Martha hobbled away.

William tied the buckets to the ropes and filled them from the well, handing them up to Thomas and Michael who doused the roof with water. William refilled them as they came down empty.

There was a creaking sound. The end post, which held up the corner of the building, had been burnt through by the discarded torch. It was all collapsing.

"Look out!" called William.

Michael and Thomas were at the other end, where the roof was supported by the house. William took a bucket to the collapsing framework and threw it on the flames. They worked on, until only smouldering wood remained. Michael and Thomas jumped down and they stood back to look at the damage. Most of the roof was saved. The house was saved. The cow stalls would need to be rebuilt.

William asked, "Did ye catch him what did this?"

The screams in the barn had subsided. Thomas said, "I caught him at it, and shut 'im in the barn." There was smoke puffing out through the gaps round the doors. Thomas pulled the bolt back and William cautiously opened one door. Thomas and Michael stood by to catch the man if he attempted to escape. Billows of smoke poured out into the close. William coughed and choked. He couldn't see a thing.

"Fetch water!" he shouted.

Thomas and Michael ran to the well and back with full buckets. They threw the water onto the source of the smoke. The smouldering straw was set alight by the air from outside. More water doused the flames. Through the smoke, William saw a figure curled up on the wet ashes. He called to the others, "Give us a hand."

They dragged the body out into the cold light of dawn. His wet clothes were singed. He had tried to set himself alight. The tinder box was still in his hand. But he must have been overcome by the smoke. His mouth was open as if gasping for air.

"He must have been insane to do that to 'imself," said William.

He and Michael took a leg each, and hauled the body back into the barn and shut the door. They followed Thomas into the house. They were all wet, smelling of smoke, and covered in dust.

Martha was in the parlour. She was dressed in her clean grey dress, with a white apron. The wide white collar covered her shoulders. She wore her white bonnet over her grey hair. Only the red-rimmed eyes told of the rough night she had been through. The fire was lit in the hearth, and there were three mugs of ale warming. The men sat down with their ale, wrapping their hands round for comfort. William's mind was in a whirl.

Thomas was the first to speak. "Where were ye Farder?"

William was slow to reply. "I had a dream...I were worried that thy Uncle Edward were in danger..." He looked at Thomas. "I got to Wad'rst and his cottage were afire...He's dead, Thomas." William stopped speaking and had a sup of ale. "I rackoned a log fell out of the fire and set the house alight. He were sozzled when I saw 'im yesterday." William looked at Michael. "I've believed wrong of Edward all these years, ever since the haystack fire after the harvest supper. I rackoned it were Ed. He told us yesterday 'twere Timothy. Ed saw 'im do it." William leaned forward, his elbows on his knees. He looked at the floor and shook his head. "I've never trusted Ed since."

Michael said, "D'ye rackon t'were Timothy set fire to Edward's cottage, afore coming here?"

William nodded. "Timothy believed we knowed his guilty secret. He intended to kill us both. Now his secret's died with him."

They sat in silence. They were too stunned to talk any more.

Martha said, "Ye should all rest afore the day begins."

William roused himself out of his reverie. "Yus... Michael, d'ye wish to stay and rest here? We must go back to Wad'rst dracly and seek Ed's remains."

Michael shook his head. "I'll go and tell Tamsen what's happened. I'll be back 'forelong."

William looked at Thomas. "We must shift the corpse in the barn. Best go and tell Headborough Shoesmith, Son. He'll know what to do. Get some rest first."

Later that morning, William and Michael took Gaffer and the cart to Wadhurst. William went first to buy a coffin, then to the vicar, to arrange a funeral.

Smoke still hung over the burnt embers of Edward and his house. Now his suffering was over. William had come to realise that people behave badly when they're unhappy or deprived of love. Edward had been a victim of his circumstances and upbringing, and hadn't had sufficient inner strength and courage to overcome this. William believed that God would know, and would have mercy on his soul. But he felt sad and ashamed that he had misjudged his brother so cruelly. He remembered seeing the figure in the church litten at family gatherings. Ed, believing himself to be an outcast, had been hiding there, watching over his family from a safe distance.

William and Michael took their shovels and searched for Edward's remains in the mass of charcoal and ashes. They heaved charred timbers to one side and choked on the disturbed dust. They found the shattered and moulten remains of his possessions, and finally dug out his charred body, its mouth gaping, its arms and legs stretched out in the death spasm. They laid it gently in the coffin and covered it with the lid. Richard agreed to keep it at Durgates until the funeral. The Headborough and Coroner would need to see it in the meantime.

It was a drizzly day. William, Richard, Michael, Thomas and Hope were there. As they carried the coffin out of the church, to put it into the prepared hole in the litten, William was sure he caught sight of a figure creeping out from behind a bush, and disappearing into the mist. He said "goodbye, Ed" softly as he threw the dark brown clay soil, soggy with rain, onto the coffin in the grave.

Chapter 62

The events of the last few days had shocked the family to the core. William was glad to see the corpse removed from his barn. The constant threat of Timothy was finally over. And in spite of his anger and grief at the way things had turned out for Ed, William felt that a burden had been lifted from his shoulders. He settled his brother's affairs as quickly as he could, and turned his attention back to his son's future.

"Be ye going to fetch thy lady to meet us somewhen, Thomas?" he said one day.

"Yus, would tomorrow be agreeable, Farder?"

"Surely, Son. Fetch her to dine with us."

Dorcas came with Thomas, and they sat down together at the table. She was a quiet, rather plump girl with friendly brown eyes, and brown hair tied back from her face. She looked directly into William's eyes, and smiled at him. He'd expected someone more attractive, and was surprised at his son's choice, having seen him with some very pretty, saucy girls.

"'Tis a pleasure to meet thee, Dorcas. Ye be Mas Golding's darter, I believe. D'ye have any brudders and sisters at home?"

"I be the only girl, Mas Lucke, but there be four brudders that's older than me."

"Do they help thy Farder with his work, or be they otherwise employed?"

"The oldest, Nathan, he be smithying with Farder. The others, they be labourers, working for yeomen hereabouts."

Thomas chipped in, "One of them be at cousin Longley's farm, Farder." They began to relax, discussing the people they knew in Lamberhurst, and in the process learned that Dorcas was a solitary person, having little opportunity to socialise. But she would make a good wife, as she was experienced in cooking for a large family and caring for the animals and the garden. She looked at Thomas with adoring eyes, but William wasn't sure that her feelings were returned.

Afterwards, he asked Thomas, "Did ye ask her Farder for her hand in marriage?"

"Yus, and he were main pleased to give us his blessing."

"D'ye love this girl, Thomas? Ye knows ye'll be obliged to bide with her for the rest of thy days, don't ye?"

"She don't stir me heart like some of the other wenches, I'll allow. But they be flighty and stocky, and I needs a Mistus that'll raise my children and keep me house. Dorcas be a good girl, knowledgeable, and faithful to God. And she likes us." Thomas smiled, and blushed.

Dorcas was accepted into the household. The wedding was quiet and serene, in true Puritan style. Goody and Goodman Golding and their family, of which there were large numbers, were there in force, including Dorcas' four brothers with wives and girls on their arms. Dorcas' parents were homely people, and sociable. They were considered pillars of the church and of the local community. William was satisfied that his son had married into a respectable family.

He allowed the newly-weds to have the hall chamber, and he moved into the parlour chamber. Thomas was now Master Thomas and Dorcas his

Mistus. William remained head of the family and employer of the labourers, as Mas Lucke.

Martha came to William one morning after the workforce had gone their separate ways.

"Now ye've a Mistus in the house, ye have little need of me. I be getting in years, and can't do what I did. Maybe its best I leave thee, Mas William."

William was astonished. "I believed ye were getting on with Dorcas well, Martha. Has she said aught to bother thee?"

"Nay,'tis not that. We be geeing well enough. But there'll be more mouths to feed afore long. I won't be able to earn my keep."

"Martha, this be thy home. Ye be part of the fambly. Ye'll not be leaving us." William smiled. "Besides, they wouldn't allow thee to be in charge in the poor house. That wouldn't suit thee!" He took her hand. "I promised Uncle Thomas you'd always bide here, and ye will till thy dying day.

Martha's face wrinkled with tearful happiness. "Thank thee, Mas William. I be obliged. I'll try not to be a burden to thee."

"We'll always need thy wise counsel and thy comfort when things get rough."

They sat together in the hall, and William thought of all the times Martha had pulled them through.

She said, "There be so many chattels from the wedding guests, I be flummoxed trying to find space for them. Linen, towels, bowls and dishes. They be minded to have a gurt fambly, I'll warrant!"

The geese raised the alarm, and there was a knock on the front door. Martha went into the parlour, and William answered the door.

Susan stood there. Her groom was waiting with the trap in the yard.

"I've come to give you an explanation, William. I think we owe it to you as a family, and it's what Mother would have wished."

"Come in, Susan. Can I offer thee some refreshment?" William said.

"A glass of wine, if you have it. Thank you."

William showed Susan to a seat and went to find Martha.

Martha found two glasses and the wine in a decanter. William took them into the hall. This visit could only be about Timothy, and he wasn't sure he wanted to talk about him just yet. He gave Susan her glass and sat down.

Susan looked at him. Dark shadows were round her eyes. "This is a long story, William. I hope when I've finished we can both forget the past and look into the future. Now that poor Timothy is dead, I can reveal what I believe was the cause of his abnormal behaviour."

The dark secret was at last to be released from the long silence. William sat calmly and waited for Susan to continue.

"When Timothy was the youngest child, he doted on Mother, who always let him have his own way. There were already five older children. I was the second. We didn't get on with Timothy, who was moody and spoilt. When he was five years old, and I was nine, our brother William was born. Timothy was jealous. He pinched and hurt William when he was a baby, and took his toys away when he began to crawl.

"My brother John and I were in the parlour one day, watching over the two of them. William got to his feet and walked across the room for the first time. We were delighted. It's always exciting when a baby gets to his feet. John went to find Mother to tell her the good news."

Susan stopped and took a sip of wine. Her face crumpled in distress.

"I'm sorry, I haven't talked about this to anyone before. I didn't realise how painful the memory would be after all these years." She took another sip of wine and a deep breath, and continued.

"Timothy looked up from what he was doing. He got to his feet and marched across the floor to where the baby was still standing, rocking perilously on his little legs, looking into the fire. I watched to see what Timothy was going to do. He must have thought I was out of the room... I watched him push his little brother into the fire." Susan looked up into William's face, horrified. "...I could have saved him, William," she said.

Her mouth set. "I got up and dragged Timothy out of the way, and tried to save the screaming baby. Timothy stood by, laughing. Mother and John came into the room... I have little recollection of what happened next. I had burns on my hands and forearms, and must have passed out." Susan looked at William with tears streaming down her face.

"I'm sorry," she said, taking a square of linen from her sleeve, and dabbing her eyes.

"The baby died, of course." She sobbed.

William, aghast at this horror story, went over to comfort her. He put his arm round her shaking shoulders, and held her hand. When the tears subsided, Susan started talking again.

"Our father, as you know, was the vicar of Mayfield, and a strict Puritan. He loved his children, and adored Mother. But if the parishioners found out about this, Father believed that his reputation and the respect they had for him would be destroyed. For a six year-old child to murder his brother was a criminal offence. It was a stigma that Father was determined to avoid.

"Timothy, from that day, throughout his childhood, was kept a virtual prisoner. He was not allowed out without an escort, and, when the other siblings were born, he was shut in his chamber unless closely supervised by one of our parents. The servants were never told. The family were sworn to silence.

"Timothy was exceptionally intelligent. His older brothers and sisters were given the task of going to amuse him in his chamber. We read books and played board games. We took him riding when he was older. Always there had to be someone with him. He grew up angry and frustrated, and, terrified that if his secret were discovered, he would be severely punished. He read many books and became extremely knowledgeable. He always beat us at our games. He doted on Mother, and after Father died it became more difficult to keep him under supervision." Susan looked up and sighed. "I think you know the rest, William."

William nodded. Susan added," To this day I have never known if he was aware of what he was doing when he pushed William. But he did know when he set fire to your brother's house, and I am so sorry."

Part 7

Epilogue

Chapter 63   1666
Sixth year in the reign of Charles 11
The year of the Great Fire of London

William sat in his armchair by the fire. The smoke from his pipe curled up to the ceiling and dispersed, leaving a spicy aroma. His eyes were failing and his spectacles did not help. They lay rejected on the dresser. He had no need to see his surroundings clearly. He knew the room well enough and heard the family coming and going, and recognised their step, their voices, their presence. His mind habitually wandered into the past through the laughter, joy, fear, anger and love he had experienced over the years.

Sounds came to him from outside. He could hear Moses whistling to his sheepdog. They were rounding up, to move the sheep to new pasture. Moses had been a godsend. After Snelling's farm sold up all those years ago, Moses joined them at the Slade. They bought more land and increased the size of the flock. He earned them the reputation for fine wool and tasty mutton.

Thomas' footsteps approached from the close.

"Farder, be ye ready for a beer? 'Tis hard work out there today. They're mannering, and the land's cledgy after all the rain."

"Yus, I'll have a jug. Be ye having one?" William asked.

Thomas came and sat with his father while they supped their beer.

"What have ye done with the liddle ones, Son? 'Tis main quiet round here today," said William.

"Junior's with the coppicing team. 'E be shaping up nicely now 'e's put 'is mind to it. Mary's with Dorcas

429

and Jessica. They've taken the two babes to see Tamsen. They'll be here anon for coger. I'll go en do the accounts while it's quiet." Thomas got up and went into the hall.

William topped up his pipe. It had been hard work persuading Thomas Junior to co-operate and start helping on the farm. Dorcas had spoiled her first-born. When Mary was born, two years later, Junior was fiercely jealous. Their screams and arguments reverberated in William's ears to this day. Thomas kept out of the way and chaos had reigned for years, it seemed. The loss of the next two babies, one at a year old, hadn't helped. Thomas was devastated and Junior and Mary continued to get under Dorcas' feet. William remembered the day she took charge, telling Thomas to take Junior out on the farm with him. William had breathed a sigh of relief. Mary was given domestic tasks, and peace reigned at last. Now there were two more little ones. William could hear their voices as they came through to the parlour.

"Gaffer! Gaffer!" shouted Elizabeth. She climbed up on his knee. "See what I've got!" She opened her fist to reveal two wriggling worms. One dropped onto the floor. "Oh! Oh! Don't run away!" Little Elizabeth jumped down and retrieved the escapee.

William said, "They won't be happy indoors, Beth. Ye'll have to let them loose in the garden. They'll dig the dirt for us."

Elizabeth looked at William with disbelief, and trotted outside. Baby Richard was scrabbling to get up.

William lifted him. "Struth, you be a gurt lump, Richard! 'Tis all that fodder they keeps giving thee, I rackon!" He grasped the boy's stomach in his big hands, making him squirm and giggle.

"Come for coger, children, afore the men gets here," Dorcas called. "You can come en get yours, too, Gaffer."

Jessica brought food to the table and they all gathered round.

"How be Tamsen?" asked William.

"Middling. Tammy's muvvering 'er. She should be away to work for the Squire at her age. But Tamsen's hanging onto 'er. The boys call in now en again with money and gifts. Mary don't get time off very often and it's a long way to foot it from Rotherfild."

It seemed only yesterday that William was at Tamsen's house, teaching Johnny to grow vegetables and help his mother when Michael was on his death bed. With five children to bring up, Tamsen had been at the end of her tether. One day Michael was drying hops with Pieter, the next he was on his sick bed coughing his heart out. William remembered hearing Michael coughing after the fire that killed Edward. That had been the start of it. All those years in the oast, breathing the pollen, had taken their toll. William felt the pain of Michael's death even now. He and Tamsen were arguing about getting the older children baptised properly in Wadhurst, which was traditionally where the Luckes were baptised and buried. William told Tamsen to leave it be. But she knew there was not much time to resolve the problem. She had them baptised in Wadhurst years later.

It took a long time for Michael to give up gasping for breath. William and Tamsen sat each side of the cot, holding his hands. Tamsen helped him to sit up to make his breathing easier.

She said, "There, there, my love. Rest in peace now, and God bless thee."

Michael relaxed, his eyes clouded over and a long sigh passed his lips...

"'E's gone into one of 'is dreams." Jessica's voice burst through William's remembering. "Come, Gaffer. Let's help thee back to thy chair. Then ye can nod off if ye feels like it." She put her arm under his and he stood up shakily to go and sit in his chair. His face felt wet and he wondered why he had been weeping.

"Why don't ye go and rest awhile, Dorcas?" Jessica said. "Thy time be hem nigh. I can take the liddle ones out to the garden. There be beans and peas to sow. Elizabeth can help us and Richard can play..."

William felt himself drifting off. Jane was sowing beans, or was it peas? She was heavily pregnant, but the baby wasn't expected yet. That was his last memory of her. He'd forgotten what happened next, but it was something he didn't want to remember.

Thomas and the men were at the table having coger. He heard the rumble of their voices though the memories. Thomas had turned out to be a capable manager of the work force. But he rarely joined them in their work. He kept the books and was good at buying and selling. There had been a time when William couldn't imagine his son taking any interest in the farm at all. Dorcas was a good wife to him, and she was fulfilling his wishes for a large family.

"Yus, Jessica, I believe it be time I laid me head down." That was Dorcas' voice. Or was it Martha's? A baby was being born and Jessica was upstairs with Dorcas. Martha went to her chamber. They found her later. The old lady was lying peacefully on her back. Her face was parchment white, her mouth slightly open, her eyes closed. They hadn't had a chance to say goodbye, to thank her for her mothering and faithful friendship.

She had slipped away quietly without bothering anyone.

There was bustle in the kitchen. Tamsen had come over with Tammy and they were helping Jessica and Mary tidy up, milk the cows and collect the eggs before dinner. William was wide awake now, and felt the need of some fresh air. He'd been sitting all day and his limbs were stiff.

"I be minded to take a turn up the whapple way afore dark," said William, pushing himself out of his chair by the fire with some difficulty.

"Be sure and not to go too far, Gaffer William," called Tamsen. "I'll get young Mary to come with thee." But William had already left the house. He wanted to be on his own, to sit in his copse for what may be the last time.

He met Thomas and Junior on the way, bringing the tools back to the skillon. William gave up any hope of being alone. Junior was told to accompany his Gaffer, and Mary and Tammy caught up with him. They reached the copse and found a tree trunk to sit on, fallen by last winter's storms, and the youngsters heard the old man begin to talk.

"I helped to plant all these trees when I were a nipper. My Uncle Thomas larned us to coppice them when they was grown enough." He told them the story of the storm when the cows breached the hedge, and how they mended it with layering. He talked about Jane, and the birth of their son, and Jane's death. He told them about the bluebells in the spring, and how precious this place was to him, and that it must be cared for, for ever. They listened, enjoying the sound of his voice in the quiet of the copse, among the chirping of birds as they found their sleeping perches. They would remember this for the rest of their lives.

Later that evening Dorcas' labour pains started, and the women went with her to her chamber. William and his son sat quietly by the fire, with their hot toddies and their own thoughts, until the lusty cries of the newborn reached their ears. Thomas ran upstairs, and William was left gazing into the flames, thinking of Edward and how his life had gone so horribly wrong. He grieved still over the way he had so misjudged his brother. How could he have thought that Ed had set fire to the hay? He was his bre'ncheese friend.

Presently, Thomas came down the stairs carrying a bundle and showed his son to his father. William took the child and cradled him in his arms. He was a fine, sturdy baby, with eyes dark as pools. He looked straight into William's eyes, and sighed deeply.

"Ye shall call him Edward," said William.

Edward was baptised in Lamberhurst Church on 17th March 1666.

William Lucke died peacefully in his sleep at the Slade, a few months later.

Historical Notes

This story is based on my researches into the history of the Lucke family from whom my paternal grandmother was descended. The tree at the front of the book gives details of births (b) or baptisms (bp), deaths (d) or burials (bd), and marriages wherever known. Where a date is not known, I have invented it to fit in with the story.

I have renamed the central character of the story William, as the number of Thomases in the family is confusing, and I have altered the spelling of others for purposes of identification. All names in brackets are the originals.

By the 17th century the Luckes in East Sussex were well established in Wadhurst, Lamberhurst and the surrounding area as yeoman farmers. There were more branches related to our family, some members of which are mentioned briefly in the story.

Many of the places and people were taken from historical records, and some I have created, using local names. Slade farm has survived to this day, though the house has changed. The original Durgates and Marlinge have long gone. Newer houses with the same names are on the same sites.

For those who are familiar with the area, I have taken some liberties with the geography to fit in with the story. The situations of the ironworks and the down are approximate. According to Richard Budgen's map of 1724, the road from Lamberhurst to Frant did not exist, but there were probably footpaths and drove roads. The location of Scotney Castle is further east than depicted.

The village pump is an invention, though there could have been one in the centre of Lamberhurst at that time.

The personalities of the characters and their experiences are entirely fictitious. I have been led by what I know of their lifestyles through wills, and manorial and parish records. The results of my researches can be found in the book *Luckes of Sussex, a family history*, a copy of which is deposited in East Sussex Record Office in Lewes.

The Civil War had very little impact on this quiet backwater except to deprive families of their working men. The religious restrictions imposed by the Puritans were often ignored by the local clergy if they could get away with it. John Maynard, vicar of Mayfield, was well known in Parliament and greatly respected until the Act of Uniformity, which he refused to comply with. He was deprived of his living and ended his life in Cranesden under the protection of the Baker family, one of whom was his patron.

Sussex dialect has all but disappeared now. The words I have used and their meaning can be found in the glossary on the following pages.

Joan Angus alias Clemens Lucke, my spiritual cousin.

Glossary

abed	in bed
abide	live, put up with
abode, bidance	place to live
abroad	away, outside
afeared	fearful
afoot	walking
afore	before
aggy	peevish, out of sorts
agin	against, near to
agreeable	would like to
ague	plague, high fever
ailing	unwell
all manner of things	all sorts
all-in	tired out
all of	as much as
all-on	all the time, incessantly
allow	admit, give an opinion
along of	together with
anon	at once
appleterre	apple orchard
applety	loft for storing apples
at two	quarrelsome
avised	to know for a certainty
bait	refreshment on a journey, or in the harvest field
backturned	turned away
backwent	went away, went back
bat	stick
be	am, is
beant	am not, is not
be at	to do

beazled	tired out
be bound	be sure
befit	to be suitable
behopes	hopefully
besom	broom made of hazel twigs
betimes	by the time
bidance, abode	dwelling place
bide	live, stay
bine	stem of hop plant which binds round the pole
bly	resemblance
bodge	go away, home
boffle	confusion, mistake
brave, bravely	in good health, well
breech	break through (animals through a hedge)
bre'ncheese friend	true friend
brudder	brother
bunt	push, shove
buttery	place where beer barrels are stored
call	cause, reason
call cousins	on intimate terms, usually used in the negative.
cant	upset, let fall
cantankerous	bad tempered
catch hot	take a fever
catched hurt	had an accident
check	taunt, tease
chipper	lively, cheerful
cledgy	sticky (Wadhurst clay)
close	farmyard, any walled enclosure

clung	cold and damp, musty, rotten
coger (pron. cojer)	lunch
cole	charcoal
come	when such time arrives
cone	flower of hop plant
cord, cordwood	wood cut up for burning
costrel	leather or wooden bottle
coulter	plough share
course	rough, as in weather
cranky	drunk
creckett	the original form of cricket
croft	pasture for horses
cushti	nice
Dan'l	Daniel
dang	bother, damn
darter	daughter
dearly	extremely
dick	ditch
didicais	true gypsies
doddle	walk infirmly
dozzle	small amount
dracly-minute	immediately, at once
druv	drove, driven
dunnow long	don't know how long
dunnow the time when	don't know when
Earl	corruption of Harold
egg on	encourage, urge
en	and
ernful	sad, lamentable
ett	eaten

fagging hook	blade used for hedge trimming
faggot	bundle of twigs to start a fire
fail	fall ill, catch a disease
fairing	getting on
fair to middling	not too bad
fall	autumn
fambly	family
Farder	Father
fet'n anon	fetch him quickly, at once
fitting	appropriate
footing it	walking
foreigner	a person from outside the county
forelong	as soon as possible
fother	fodder
founding	mould into which is poured moulten iron for casting
frit	frightened
frith	new hazel cutting, planted to grow into a stool
frock, round frock	loose over garment worn by country people
furze	gorse
Gaffer	Grandfather
gantsey	lively, frolicksome horse
gee	to get on well
geewoot	call to the horse to move on
getting in years	becoming elderly
gimme	give me
git	go on/ away
Gowd'rst	Goudhurst
Grammer	Grandmother

gratten	stubble field
	hens and pigs forage in the gratten for left over grain
groat	small coin of unknown value
gummut	lout, stupid fellow
gurt	great
haitchy	misty
happened along	called in when passing
hem	very, a lot
hike	a mess
hoe	fuss, temper
hog-pound	pig stye
hop bin	sack into which the hops are collected
House of Correction	local goal
housel	household belongings (when moving house)
husbandry	farming
hoving	sheep bursting with eating over rich plants
jack-up	give up, give in, retire
jigger me	a mild oath
just now	recently, at this present moment
justabout	certainly, extremely
justly	really, exactly, rightly
kine	cows
knowledgeable	well educated
Lamb'rst	Lamberhurst
lamentable	very

lapsy	lazy, slow, indifferent
larn	teach
larruping	beating
lash and swear	get into a passion
latchety	not working properly
lay up	hide away
let be how 'twill	let the consequences be how they may
liddle	little
litten	churchyard
like	adds to force of meaning
likely	probably
lonesome	lonely, far from friends and neighbours
lope- off	go away in a secretive manner
Lunnon	London
maid	young girl
main	very
manner	manure
Mas	title of married master of the house
Massypanme	exclamation of surprise
masterful	self-willed
Mayfild	Mayfield
me	my
Medston	Maidstone
middling	can mean anything from all right to very bad
mind, minded	remember, have a mind or intend to
Mistus	Mrs, mistress, wife

moithered	bothered, perplexed
mortacious	very, mortally
mortal	very, mortally
mucked-up	in confusion
Mus	title of master of a workforce
Muvver	Mother
muvver	take care of
nay	no
nigh	near to
nipper	youngest in the family
no'but	nothing but
non-plush	completely bewildered
no-ways	in no way
now-en-again	sometimes
on account of	because, the reason being
order	temper, state of mind
Papists	Roman Catholics
Parlyment	Parliament
partial	to like very much
ped	willow box or crate for taking live chickens to market
Pens'rst	Penshurst
personable	comely
pet	a stack of wood covered with turf to make a clamp for charcoal burning
pervension	inconvenience
pesky	troublesome
poke	long sack
praper	proper, unusually good
prensley	presently, now

purty	pretty
put by	prevent
put out	upset
put in	bury
Quality	gentlefolk and nobility
quern	small hand mill
quick with child	pregnant
rackon	reckon, suspect, count
Ratherfild	Rotherfield
Rigging	clothes
Ringle	wed/ put a ring in a hog's or bull's nose
ripier	man carrying fish in baskets from the coast to towns
rod	straight stems cut from a hazel stool
sattered	saturated
scratch along	pull through hard times
screel	scream
sidy	surly, moody
skillon	shed or outhouse
skits	plenty, a great many
sogers	soldiers
smoky	foggy
spry	vivacious
standing	market stall
stan' fast	hold on, to riders on the waggon before moving off
start /start-up	a fuss, excitement
steddle	temporary table made with trestles

stocky	strong, well-grown
stotter	stagger
summat	something
swallocky	the appearance of clouds before a thunder storm
tallyman	busheler, who measures hops from the bin
Teec'rst	Ticehurst
tight	drunk
to be at	attend to
toddy	warmed up ale
tott	hazel stool
turmuts	turnips
tuzzy-mussy	a bouquet of herbs, for good luck and health
twit	taunt, tease
twitten	narrow path between two walls or hedges
unaccountable	unusual, unexplainable (used often)
upstanding	upright, honourable
varmint	vermin, rascal
vittels	food
Wad'rst	Wadhurst
wain	cart for carrying hay
whapple way	a bridle way through fields or woods
willocky	wild, mad
worritted	worried
wunnerful	wonderful

yanger	yonder
yar	aghast, frightened
yet	still
yoystering	playing around roughly
yus	yes

Acknowledgements

A big thank you to friends and family who have given me much help and encouragement in the course of writing this book. Special thanks go to Chris Sparkes, my tutor, and my fellow writers at his class in Petersfield.

In the course of researching for this book, I have made use of many publications, some of which are listed here:

Wadhurst, Town of the High Weald by Savidge and Mason

Mayfield, An Old Wealden Village by Bell Irving

Rotherfield, The Story of some Wealden Manors, by C. Pullien.

Lamberhurst Essays by John H. Moon

The Kent and Sussex Weald by Peter Brandon

A History of Sussex by J. R. Armstrong

A County Community in Peace and War. Sussex 1600-1660 by Anthony Fletcher

A dictionary of the Sussex Dialect by W. D. Parish, augmented by Helena Hall

I have also spent many hours studying records at the Record Offices of West and East Sussex, and Kent, and visited the Weald and Downland Open Air Museum at Singleton a number of times. Thanks to the staff at these places for their valuable help.